The Stronghold

Other books by Lisa Carter
Aloha Rose (Quilts of Love series)

Carolina Reckoning
Beneath a Navajo Moon
Under a Turquoise Sky
Vines of Entanglement
Beyond the Cherokee Trail

LISA CARTER

THE
STRONGHOLD

Abingdon Press
Nashville

The Stronghold

Copyright © 2016 by Lisa Carter

All rights reserved.

The persons and events portrayed in this work of fiction are the creations of the author, and any resemblance to persons living or dead is purely coincidental.

Macro Editor: Teri Wilhelms

Published in association with the Steve Laube Agency

All scripture quotations are taken from the Common English Bible. Copyright © 2011 by the Common English Bible. All rights reserved. Used by permission. www.CommonEnglishBible.com.

Library of Congress Cataloging-in-Publication Data

Carter, Lisa, 1964-
 The stronghold / Lisa Carter.
  pages ; cm
  ISBN 978-1-4267-9548-0 (binding: soft back)
  I. Title.
  PS3603.A77757S77 2016
  813'.6—dc23

                                                                   2015030776

16 17 18 19 20 21 22 23 24 25—10 9 8 7 6 5 4 3 2 1

Manufactured in the United States of America

To my Aunt Grace—Thank you for your encouragement over the years. For your gracious hospitality in opening your home and heart to me. For living as a true example of your name, a grace note in my life and in our family. For being there when I've needed you the most. I love you.

To my friend who somehow found the courage one night when we were in college to share for the first time—with me—a terrible secret of what happened while on a date. I've never forgotten your story nor the undeserved pain you carried. This is for you and for all the others in a sisterhood to which no one ever wants to belong.

Acknowledgments

Ramona Richards—What an adventure this has been! Thanks for allowing me to tell these stories. And being the best editor in the world. I am so grateful for your friendship.

Tamela Hancock Murray—Thanks for your prayers and constant support. You've made this writing journey fun.

Thanks to the **Abingdon team**: Cat Hoort, Teri, Russ, Susan Cornell, and Sarah—Thanks for all you do to make the books and me the best we can be.

Thank you, **Jacqueline Gonzalez**, for your English-to-Spanish and vice versa expertise. Some of the law enforcement and cartel terminology aren't exactly standard classroom fare. Thanks for not thinking I'm crazy when I needed to know how to tell someone to put their hands in the air and get down on their knees.

Jesus—Thank you for always being with me—when I walk through the fire and when I pass through the waters. Thank you for calling me by name. For I am Yours. And You are mine.

But now, says the LORD—
the one who created you, Jacob,
the one who formed you, Israel:
Don't fear, for I have redeemed you;
I have called you by name; you are mine.
When you pass through the waters, I will be with you;
when through the rivers, they won't sweep over you.
When you walk through the fire, you won't be scorched
and flame won't burn you.
I am the LORD your God,
the holy one of Israel, your savior.
I have given Egypt as your ransom,
Cush and Seba in your place.
Because you are precious in my eyes,
you are honored, and I love you.
I give people in your place,
and nations in exchange for your life.

—Isaiah 43:1-4

1

In the Sierra Madre a long time before

WHEN THE MEXICANS—THE NAKAYÉ—CAME, SHE RAN.

The Old One grabbed the rifle. "Do not let them take you, Ih-tedda."

She did not wait to be told twice. She darted toward the brush. Only then did the other children run, too.

Behind them, pounding hooves. Guttural cries of defiance from the old woman. Gunfire. Curses from the riders in their hateful tongue. Bullets dinged the earth.

She flew swift as the wind and called under her breath to the name Nana had taught her. The children dogged her heels. The little one whimpered. The Other panted for breath. Their legs were not as long as hers. They'd not trained as she had.

If they could make the tree line...find the cave. Hide until the men grew tired of searching, of making sport...

Almost...

"Help me!" the Other cried. "We can't keep up."

Cursing her and the Nakayé, she slowed and scooped the little boy into her arms. The Other pointed to a clump of scrub brush. "There."

Dragging them both, she hunkered under the scant cover. The boy wailed as a thorn bush pricked his bare legs. The Other laid her hand over his mouth. Beads of sweat and fear dribbled the length of her nose. They stared wide-eyed at each other.

The boy tried to squirm free of their tight hold. Angry, Ih-tedda placed her hands around his throat.

"No." The Other tugged at her hands.

"We must not be taken. Last time, the Old One…"

The Other shook her head. Sadness filled her eyes. She trembled.

Ih-tedda, too, quivered at the memory of the last time the men found their camp. How the last protector had sacrificed his life to give the women time to escape. How a girl child had been too frightened to be quiet. The old woman had taken the child's face between her hands and snapped her neck to stop the noise. And thus they'd escaped detection.

Her grip tightened on the boy.

"No," hissed the Other.

Voices shouted. She and the Other ducked their heads. They covered the boy with their bodies and prayed to the name for invisibility. She wished the earth would swallow them whole to protect them from discovery.

Her breath caught at the sight of the scowling, scar-faced rancher leading the posse. He hated her people, Nana said, with a fierce, scorching hatred that would only be extinguished when their blood soaked the ground and he'd exterminated them from the earth.

Blood vengeance she understood. She vaguely recalled the woman of his they'd taken after leaving him for dead on the road. The woman had not lasted long in their camp. Carrion or traded, Ih-tedda didn't remember which.

The boy twitched. Something in his hand rattled. The Other grabbed for him. But too late—

Scarface jerked his reins toward their hiding place. *"Mira! Aquí!"*

They'd been discovered.

Abandoning them to their fate, she dashed into the open and headed for the deer path. She scrambled from boulder to boulder. The Other heaved the boy from rock to rock.

Gunfire scored the cliff face. Dodging the flying chips, Ih-tedda climbed higher and higher.

Must not be taken, Nana's words pounded in her brain. *Must not be taken.*

With a cry, the boy latched onto her long skirt, hampering her forward progress. Cursing him, she pried his tiny fingers free as he sobbed.

"Help us," whispered the Other. "Do not leave us behind."

Ih-tedda reached for the boy. His small body, shaking in terror, slumped against her chest. "Be brave," she whispered in his ear.

And then jerking him away, she flung him over the rocks toward the mountain ponies who did not give up. Toward those who'd never give up until her kind were gone from the earth.

The Other screamed as his body bounced onto the hard-packed ground. The horses reared but stopped at the broken obstacle in their path. The Other grew as quiet as the boy lying in the pool of blood below. With a final glare, the Other descended from the precipice and lay beside the child. The men and their horses surrounded them, blocking them from Ih-tedda's view.

Not waiting to learn their fate, she resumed her climb. Hand over hand, she pulled herself upward. Her bare feet scrabbled for placement. Rocks skittering, she turned to find Scarface, knife clutched between his teeth, climbing after her. Panic laced her heart. Her breath constricted, she hauled herself the last ten feet.

Wobbling, flailing, she edged as far as she dared until only nothingness yawned. And still he came, relentless as death. He removed the knife from his mouth and brandished it.

"Come," he beckoned. "Come to me," he crooned.

She'd heard the women talk. She understood what awaited her if taken alive. She'd heard of the slave markets.

Do not be taken, Nana had drilled over and over.

She swallowed and peered at the gorge beneath her feet. She swayed. Fear of the chasm assaulted her senses, numbed her heart, froze her reasoning.

He inched closer. She shrank until she could retreat no further.

One step and all would be over. Only darkness. Where was the name the old woman called upon now? Where had the name been when the men died, when the children were hungry and cold, when the *soldados* came?

She teetered. Her arms flailed. She righted herself.

And moved away from the edge.

2

Arizona

Pilar To-Clanny had been murdered when she was about the same age as the dead girl lying face down in the shallow grave.

Only difference?

Pilar's body hadn't died.

Just everything else.

The wind whistled off the escarpment behind Pilar. She shivered and wrapped her arms in her uniform jacket. The sun had yet to make its way above the rim of the rugged mountains. Shadows engulfed Pilar and the makeshift burial site.

An inexplicable foreboding teased at the edges of her consciousness. She'd learned the hard way to always trust her gut. Tensing, she scanned the unspoiled wilderness of her people. Her eyes darted in the remote canyon for movement or any sign she wasn't alone.

Nothing.

And yet...she couldn't shake the feeling of eyes. Of lingering malevolence. An eerie stillness hung suspended.

Her eyes flicked to the partially unearthed grave. To the bundle of skin and bones. A lonely, helpless place to die.

She wondered sometimes if the ground—blood-soaked since the Ancient Ones—somehow retained the essence of the violence perpetrated upon it. If the evil committed between the dark cliffs continued on—past the barbarism of the Conquistadors or the wickedness on both sides of the Indian Wars. If an unholy force yet preyed upon those unlucky enough to lose themselves in the forbidding ramparts of this mountain fortress.

Where were Special Agent Edwards and his team from Phoenix? Why was her heart pounding? Why was it so difficult to breathe?

Her hand flexed above her duty belt. She wasn't defenseless. Not anymore. Or as ultimately helpless against her fate as the girl rotting in the desert tomb.

Pilar had fought—and would continue to fight—to survive.

Never allow yourself to be taken was the mantra she taught the women at the tribal center self-defense class. The mantra by which she lived. Yet she also told them that, if taken, they must adapt quickly or die.

Buffeted by a gust of wind, Pilar huddled inside her jacket. An unearthly howl pierced the air. She flinched. Coyotes? A cougar?

Flipping off the safety catch, she drew her gun and whirled. The air pulsated with palpable menace. The harbinger of death, an owl hooted somewhere in the pine-topped ridge above.

And a memory too terrible for words forced itself to the forefront of her mind. Of another time and place. Of utter desolation.

Sucking in a breath, she squeezed her eyes shut.

Flashes. The smells. The terror.

This wasn't real. This wasn't happening again. She was better, stronger than this.

But sometimes retreat was the better part of valor. Her eyes flew open. Maybe best to wait for the feds at the road in the safety of her cruiser.

Adapt or die. Adapt or die.

Canvassing her escape route with her gun extended, she back-pedaled across the scrub grass. Clambering across an arroyo, she struggled to regain control of the distorted images filling her mind. She hurried around a massive butte, desperate to push the horror once again into the black pit of nothingness. But unable to deflect the inexplicable panic, finally she just ran.

Out of the canyon. Toward the road. Toward sanity.

And the farther she traveled from the canyon, the farther the darkness receded.

Reaching the sanctuary of the tribal cruiser, she reholstered her Glock and gathered the carefully constructed shards of her numbness once more. Her breathing rapid, she willed herself to think of Manny. To remember her life now.

She scrambled inside the car and concentrated on taking even breaths to slow her heart rate. Slamming and locking the door, she cranked the engine. Pilar threw the car into drive and gunned the vehicle. Ten minutes later, on the cusp of the San Carlos rez, she parked off the graveled shoulder of the road.

As the sun rose over the dusky pink horizon, so too did the September temps. Loosening the collar of her uniform, she got out of the car to wait for the feds. Here in the sunlight, where you could see friend and foe coming for twenty miles, she felt foolish over her sudden terror in the canyon. Maybe not so over the PTSD as she'd hoped.

Sound, too, traveled far over the desert floor. Her breath whooshed out in relief at the red haze preceding the feds' arrival. She shaded her eyes with her hand and watched the dust cloud kicked up by the tires as the black SUV drew closer. Typical fed vehicle.

Took them long enough. Always a federal case when a major crime occurred on the rez. Special Agent Edwards wouldn't be pleased to find "his" crime scene already tampered with.

And as first responder for the tribal police, she'd be blamed for the trampled evidence. She blew out a breath. As if anyone, much less the tribal archaeologist from the college, had expected to find a fresh corpse amid a nineteenth-century Apache campsite.

The SUV braked and shuddered to a stop. She closed her eyes as the dust cloud billowed. Voices emerged from the vehicle. Male and female. Car doors banged shut.

Out of habit, she kept her elbow against her ribcage. Her hand hovered within easy reach of her Glock. She coughed to clear her throat. She opened her eyes.

And when the dust particles dissipated, he—not Edwards—stood not six feet away from her. Plus two blond women, one on each side.

Pilar blinked to clear the grit from her eyes.

It couldn't be—her stomach muscles tightened. A mirage. The dust and sun playing tricks on her mind. Conjured by her subconscious, as happened so often in the years since she'd seen him.

But then he tilted his head in that way of his.

And her heart raced.

His eyes lit as the air cleared between them.

Alex was supposed to be on assignment out of the country. Not here. Not close enough to—She ground her teeth.

Where was Edwards? Why was Alex here? How—?

Her mouth tightened. Abuela.

Abuela knew everything. And Pilar recognized an ambush when she saw one. She'd deal with Alex's grandmother later.

Pilar took a step back. "Still a blonde on each arm, eh, Alex?"

The warmth in his eyes seeped away.

Alex—Special Agent Alex Torres—lifted his chin a fraction. "Is that, too, a crime on the rez these days, Officer To-Clanny?"

She met his glare with an unfriendly glower of her own. "If it isn't, maybe it ought to be."

An uncomfortable silence ticked between the members of Alex's team. Five, including Alex. The two blondes, an Asian man, and a real Indian—the ones Columbus had been looking for when he stumbled upon her people's continent.

"Where's Edwards?" Pilar widened her stance. "Why are you here?"

A muscle pulsed in Alex's jaw. "We're working a serial. The description your tribal archaeologist gave of the body matched another case we caught. So they sent me. Deal with it."

One of the blondes disengaged from the pack. "I'm Dr. Emily Waters, a forensic anthropologist." She extended her hand to Pilar.

"Don't," Alex barked. "She—they—Apaches don't like to be touched."

Emily Waters stopped mid-stride and dropped her hand.

The look Alex threw Pilar seared her flesh. "Isn't that right, Officer To-Clanny?"

She quivered as the memory dangled between them, taut as a bowstring. Across time and distance. The caress of his hand against her cheek as real as if yesterday.

Emily Waters's gaze ping-ponged between them. "I take it you two already know each other?"

The connection between Pilar and Alex snapped.

Adapt or die. Adapt or die.

Folding his arms across his blazer, Alex leaned against the hood of the SUV.

Pilar's lips twisted. "You could say that."

She gave them a nice view of her back as she pivoted toward the trail where the corpse waited. "A lifetime ago, when we used to be married."

Alex jerked and straightened.

His forensic specialist, Emily, threw him an uncertain glance.

Alex fought to remind himself of his purpose here.

Pilar nudged her chin toward the butte. "You'll need to follow me in the rest of the way." She gave him a look. "If you think you can keep up."

"I'll keep up." He broadened his shoulders. "I'm not as easy to get rid of as you think."

Uncertainty passed over her face before the aloof Pilar regained control. "You can try."

His hands gripping the steering wheel, he ate the dust of Pilar's tribal car as they hurtled toward the crime scene. She veered off the main highway and onto a gravel road, which led nowhere as far as he could tell.

Emily, a brown-eyed blonde, fanned her face. "This red dust." She coughed. "It's everywhere."

"Yeah." He angled. "Welcome to Arizona." His teeth rattled as they bounced over a cattle guard.

Pilar swerved south onto what amounted to little more than a washed-out arroyo. The hard-packed trail jolted the occupants of the SUV. Emily grabbed hold of the dashboard to steady herself as the car lurched forward. The rest of his team—Charles Yao, Sidd Patel, and Darlene White—muttered imprecations in a varied mixture of their mother tongues—Mandarin, Hindi, and Texan.

Typical Pilar. She never slackened her speed over the rough places, just charged ahead. Alex set his jaw and accelerated, determined not to allow her to lose him.

He pulled in alongside Pilar's vehicle behind a clump of junipers at the mouth of a box canyon. He and the team exited the SUV.

Impassive and remote as the jagged mountains surrounding them, Pilar leaned against the clicking, cooling engine of the tribal car. She pursed and jutted her lips, Apache-style, toward the blue tarp-covered grave in the distance. "Have at it, Torres."

His jaw tightened. Time to assert his jurisdiction and exert control over this crime scene. Over Pilar? Fat chance of that.

Since the day they met as children, to the best of his knowledge, no one had ever managed to rein in Pilar from doing exactly what Pilar wanted to do. Not her brother, Byron. Certainly not Alex.

"I'm going to do an initial walk-through first." He motioned toward the shade of a cottonwood. "Let's establish a command post over there, Em."

He felt rather than saw Pilar stiffen. In for a *peso*, might as well go in for a pound as Abuela would say. "Walk with me, To-Clanny."

Pilar clenched and unclenched her hand.

She wanted to smack him. Even after all these years, he could still feel the sting of her hand across his cheek. Best to keep things professional.

For now.

She stalked alongside him, struggling to match his long strides.

He assessed the canyon surrounding the crude grave. Desolate. Forsaken.

Alex repressed a shudder. Squatting, he peered beneath the tarp someone had rigged to keep out the elements until his team arrived on site.

"You'll find out who did this to her?"

He rested his hands on his thighs. "How do you know the vic is female?"

"It's usually a her, isn't it?"

He lowered his eyes to the grave. "How long since the body was unearthed?"

At his deliberate tone, she uncoiled a notch. "Late afternoon yesterday. Dr. Chestuan didn't realize the remains were fresh"—she searched for a more palatable word—"from a more recent homicide until he uncovered a cell phone tossed in the grave underneath the shoveled dirt."

Her mouth twisted. "Thrown in and thrown away like somebody's old garbage."

"Where's the cell now?"

"He and I left everything we found as is for your agents to bag and tag. But it'd been crushed. A job for the geek squad to decipher." She brushed her hands against her pants. "I'll get out of your way and let you do your job."

"Don't leave." His tone came out harsher than he'd intended.

"I-I won't." A frown creased her forehead. "I'm the tribe's liaison until the tribal detective returns from a case in Peridot."

"Lucky you."

Her look speared Alex. "Yeah. Lucky me."

Over the next few hours, the early morning sunshine topped the ridge and blazed high in the turquoise sky. As team leader, he directed the exhumation and designated crime scene responsibilities. Photographer. Evidence Recovery. Evidence Recorder.

Surveying the scene, he prepared a narrative description of the crime scene and instructed others on the crew to cordon off the perimeter. He set Charles to sweeping the immediate area—just in case—with ground-penetrating radar. Sidd sketched and photologged the canyon.

With painstaking precision, Emily dug out one body part at a time, freeing the cadaver from the confines of the grave. Shifting the soil to a ground cloth and sifting the particles through a wire screen, she documented her findings in a running commentary on her digital recorder.

As more of the victim surfaced, Darlene took photographs to document the body *in situ*. Using her pick and shovel, Emily found the outer edges of the body. Only scraps of denim encircled the victim's legs. The remnant of a tattered blouse covered the torso.

Finally at her signal, Alex, Charles, and Sidd hunched over the pit and helped Emily remove the body to an adjacent body bag. With the corpse flipped onto its spine, Emily did a cursory check of the remains.

"Hypodontia."

"English, Em."

"Missing teeth." Emily feathered sand off the jawbone with her brush. "Shoveled enamel on the incisors. Ridge on the edge of the teeth. Native American ancestry probably. But physiology in a melting pot nation can be deceptive and unreliable."

"Makes sense." Alex glanced around. "Considering where we are. But for the record, they prefer *American Indian*. Better yet, their own tribal affiliation."

Strawberry-blonde Darlene looked at him sharply. "What makes you such an expert?"

Alex nudged his chin in the direction of the evidence tent. "Her."

Her elbows clamped to her side, Pilar lingered out of the way, yet close enough to answer the team's questions. Although Pilar had never been a traditional Apache with their deep-seated aversion to the dead, she didn't get any closer than necessary. Probably not taking any chances.

Emily gestured to the long forearm bone. "Growth caps fusing to the end of the ulna."

Alex growled at his Midwestern forensic specialist.

Her lips curved. "Means she's young. Late teens?" She pointed the end of her pick at the exposed white bones of the pelvis. "Large sciatic notch. Definitely female."

No scraps of fabric there.

"Sexually assaulted?"

"Like the others. Probably her, too." Emily's mouth thinned. "When I get to the lab, I can determine more fully."

"Cause of death?"

She sighed. "There's a slash that cut to the bone. I'm guessing her throat was cut from ear to ear. And from the marks, a knife blade. Long. Serrated. Like a hunting knife."

He caught her eye. "Did you find the mark on her? His calling card?"

With the tip of her gloved finger, Emily brushed aside a portion of the mauve blouse. "Like the other girls. Carved so deep he hit bone."

He fought the bile rising in his throat at the savagery and cruelty. "Premortem?"

Emily nodded and bent over the desecrated body.

Alex's eyes strayed to Pilar, the most perplexing, confounding woman he'd ever known. Her eyes, the blackest he'd ever seen, searched the terrain. For what he didn't know. Looking everywhere, anywhere but at him.

He couldn't keep his gaze off her, however. With a strange mixture of joy and pain, he beheld Pilar once more, the flowing black hair bound in a tight bun per police regulations.

But instead of the vivacity he remembered, this Pilar wore a brooding expression. Something—grief, bitterness, rage—had worn grooves around her mouth. Put there by *someone*. His stomach clenched. Someone like him.

19

Underneath the bulk of her patrol jacket, she was as fit as ever. Slim and petite in stature. He'd towered over her then and now.

But from the set of her jaw, probably as tough as ever. The toughest girl in school. Who ran, played, fought as hard as any boy—himself included.

And because he couldn't help himself, Alex gradually drifted closer to the tent until he found himself next to Pilar. She bristled at his proximity but kept her eyes trained on the desert horizon.

"Pilar…I need to talk to you later…" His Adam's apple bobbed. "I want to apologize for what happened…to explain…to—"

"No apology's going to change what happened, Torres. What's done is done. You and I got nothing to say to each other."

Guilt surged anew. No surprise she hated him. He hated himself for what had happened.

"We've got nothing to talk about except the case. Let's try to do our jobs and keep this professional." She cleared her throat. "How long has the victim been dead? Any ID on the body?"

The contralto huskiness of her voice did funny things to his nerve endings.

His heart hammered. He wasn't sure he could be this close to her and live with that. He'd hoped maybe—

Alex swallowed. He was a fool. "Em—"

Pilar shot him a look out of the corner of her eye.

"Dr. Waters says at least a year." Alex strove to match her detachment. "No ID. We'll need to look through the tribe's Missing Person register. But you were right. The vic is female."

"Apache?"

He shrugged. "The teeth indicate Indian. Apache, Navajo. Puebloan, or Tohono O'odham. This is, after all, Arizona. Prelim will require DNA confirmation."

"But she was found on San Carlos land."

"The probability is strong she's Apache," he conceded. "And a teenager. You got any missing San Carlos girls?"

Pilar stiffened. "Too many, Torres." The radio on her shoulder crackled. She stepped away to answer the call.

She moved toward her parked cruiser. "Gotta go."

"Wait."

He caught her arm and she reared.

Stupid.

He withdrew his hand. He knew better. Pilar of all people didn't like to be touched, especially after... "Where're you going? My team may have questions."

She squared her shoulders. "Much as I enjoy watching you and your Anglo women do hard labor, there's a domestic dispute in Bylas. I'm closest."

He grimaced. "I'm not Anglo."

"No, you just act like one."

He ignored the jibe. "Domestic dispute? Those can be dangerous."

She gave him a look that could've singed the wings off a butterfly. "No duh, Torres."

But at her caustic tone, he relaxed. This Pilar he knew. The give-as-good-as-she-got Pilar.

"Need backup? Cause I can spare—"

"Don't need federal help, much less yours, with a rez issue. You grew up here. You know the drill. Not enough manpower for the vastness of the territory. We make do." Her lips flattened. "Like always."

She'd been gone only a few minutes when Charles shouted and waved him over.

Alex came at a run.

Charles paused in his radar sweeping and pointed to a narrow depression in the sand. "I think we've found another one."

3

Before

ABUELA'S GRANDSON WAS THE HANDSOMEST BOY—ANGLO, LATINO, or Apache—twelve-year-old Pilar To-Clanny had ever met.

Okay—she'd actually not met him. Yet.

She peered between the blinds in the darkened interior of the ranch foreman's house she called home. She watched her brother put Abuela's grandson through his paces. Never one to trust much, Byron wouldn't be satisfied until he determined what this skinny kid with the too-new boots from L.A. was made of.

A cowboy wannabe. Byron hated wannabes. He'd soon show the big-city Latino teenager how things were done in Indian country. Show him how Apaches did things.

Her fifteen-year-old brother demonstrated once more how to lasso a fence post. This Alex Torres person made a joke about fence-post bovine. Pilar's stocky brother stared at the taller, also fifteen-year-old, boy. Letting the rope fall into the red dust of the Arizona ranchland, Byron's brow wrinkled.

"Bovine," she whispered into the windowpane. "A cow, Byron. He's talking about cows." She clutched the library book to her chest.

School wasn't Byron's strong suit. Helping out the real cowboys on Abuela's off-rez ranch was—roping steers, riding the range, fixing wire-strung fences. Byron, unlike this big-mouth grandson, was the real deal. That and he was training for a spot on the high school football team come August.

Abuela—as she'd encouraged Pilar and Byron to call her—was this big-mouthed kid's grandmother. Big Mouth had gotten into trouble with the law in California. So his parents shipped him to Abuela's ranch for safekeeping and straightening out.

The aristocratic old woman with her iron silver hair made everything work out and everyone—including Pilar and Byron—feel safe. Her goal to learn a new vocabulary word each day, Pilar mouthed *imperious*. Imperiousness was Abuela's superpower. Pilar and Byron had spent the spring between chores watching Marvel comic movies.

"Bovine?" Perhaps fearing his intelligence was being mocked, Byron clenched his hands into fists on his hips. "What did you call me?"

The Torres boy's eyebrows rose. "Bovine. You know, cows. I was making a joke about cows, man, not you."

Not sure he should believe him, Byron's eyes squinted in the bright noonday sun. "You joke too much, dude."

Ain't that the truth.

Everything was a joke to Abuela's grandson. He called his grandmother his "get out of jail free card." To her face...

And his charm was such, the mighty Abuela—who could cow (not the bovine kind) hardened cowboys with a look—melted at the twinkle in her grandson's black-brown eyes.

Pilar sighed. Her breath billowed the curtain. Those eyes...

Torres was the real deal when it came to gorgeous. Confidence oozed out of every lanky pore. He might not be a real cowboy yet, but something about him made her heart flutter like butterfly wings.

An unsettling feeling.

She vaguely resented him for the sensations he stirred inside her. For making Pilar, who liked to be in control of her emotions if not her circumstances, anxious. On edge.

Prince Charming jerked his thumb at the window where she hid. "Who's that inside your house?"

Her breath hitching, she shrank into the shadows.

"Nobody." Byron regathered his rope. "Just my baby sister."

Pilar narrowed her eyes. She wasn't a baby.

"What's she waiting for? She going to come out or what?" Prince Charming took a step toward the porch.

She backpedaled further.

"Too shy?"

Byron snorted. "Hardly. She's probably trying to decide if you're worth the effort. Come on." Her brother headed for the barn. "Let's see if your biceps are as big as your mouth. We've got stalls to clean."

Prince Charming made a face. "This is so not L.A." But he followed Byron.

Abandoning her book, she crept out of the house and headed toward the hayloft. She spent the afternoon observing the prince pitch hay and scoop poop. Lying prone, she discovered a knothole in the planks above the boys' heads perfect from which to spy upon this too-handsome-to-be-real cowboy wannabe.

She shifted her weight, and the floorboards creaked. The prince's head shot up. She held her breath.

A smile quivered at the edges of those full, beautiful lips of his.

Pilar bit off another sigh—beautiful in every soon-to-be manly bit of him. Problem was, she suspected he knew it.

God's Gift to Women put his back into scooping another shovelful of horse dung and spoke to the rafters. "That sister of yours. What's wrong with her, Byron?"

She went still.

Byron dumped a shovelful into the wheelbarrow. "Ain't nothing wrong with her."

God's Gift snickered and darted a significant look toward the ceiling. "How come she's hiding?"

Byron shrugged. "She's funny that way. Only people she talks to are me and your abuela."

"So ugly she scares small children or something, huh?" God's Gift hitched his thumb through a belt loop on his jeans. "Makes dogs howl?"

Pilar gnashed her teeth. She ought to go down there and make him howl.

God's Gift cut his eyes skyward. "Looks like the hunchback of Notre Dame?"

That cocky wannabe...

Byron's brow scrunched. "Hunchback of who?"

She scrambled down the ladder.

God's Gift leaned his weight against the shovel handle with an amused glint in his melt-in-your-mouth chocolate eyes.

Byron smirked. "She could beat your butt with one hand tied around her Apache back, I'll bet."

As Pilar strode forward, her hand-me-down boots from Goodwill clanked across the barn floor. She extended her hand, businesslike. "I'm Maria Caterina Pilar To-Clanny."

"What kind of name is To-Clanny?"

She raised her lip. "It means 'lots of water.' But I think, Brother," she flung a look at Byron. "This one's all gas, no beans."

Mr. Gorgeous stroked his chin. "That Arizona-speak for all talk, no action? Plenty of action here, Sister." He broadened his chest.

She jutted her hip. "I ain't your sister."

"No, you're not." He gazed at her from the top of her long black hair to the ragged hem of her cut-off jeans. "But you are short."

She cocked her head. "I'm tall enough to beat you in a race any day of the week." Running was her superpower.

Handsome stuck out his hand. "Pleased to meet you, Maria Caterina Pilar To-Clanny. I'm Alejandro Roberto Torres y Gonzalez. But my friends call me Alex."

She crinkled her nose. "Who says we're going to be friends?"

He threw back his head and laughed.

Tingles went up and down her arms. Alejandro Roberto Torres y Gonzalez even laughed handsome. She fought the inexplicable urge to fall into a puddle at his too-new cowboy boots.

"I think we're going to be friends, good friends." His eyes flickered to Byron. "Maybe the best of friends. Like the Three Musketeers."

Byron blinked. "The who?"

"Never mind." She crossed her arms over her yet-to-develop chest. "You want to race or what, Torres?"

Alex threw down the shovel. "Any time. Any place."

"There." She pointed with her lips to the mesa towering behind the Torres hacienda. "To the top. Whoever gets there first, wins."

Alex swaggered alongside to peer at the gigantic outcropping.

Her nerve endings zinged as his shirtsleeve brushed against the bare skin of her arm. He smelled like leather and sandalwood.

"Wins what, Cater-Pilar?"

Byron frowned. "Why did you call her Cater-Pilar?"

Alex grinned. "Like a caterpillar. 'Cause when I leave her to eat my dust, she's going to look a whole lot like her name."

She tossed her head. "When I win, I get to knock you down a peg or two."

Alex passed his hand over his dark, short-cropped curls. "And what happens if I win?"

She pursed her lips. "Trust me, you won't."

He didn't.

Feet pounding, she soon pulled ahead on the trail fit only for mountain goats. Jumping over rocky boulders, zigzagging along the switchbacks, she quickly outdistanced this sea-level grandson unused to the altitude.

Groaning, Alex bent over, hands on his knees in a vain attempt to breathe. His pace more sedate, Byron caught up to them.

Pilar let out a whoop and gyrated. "I win. I win. I win. Alex Torres runs like a boy." She reached her hands over her head and did something Abuela once described as the Watusi.

"Seriously?" Alex glared. "An Apache war dance?"

Byron laughed. "Not tribal. Her version of a victory dance." He flicked a glance at the struggling-to-inhale Latino. "Not bad for a first-timer. You interested in playing football this year at high school?"

Alex nodded. "Love to, though I'm more into basketball. And next time, I'll beat her."

Byron's barrel chest rumbled. "Next time, I bet you still won't. Not Sister. She's like the wind."

She smiled. Byron's superpower was loyalty.

"Who's the caterpillar now?" She sauntered over to the drop-your-jaw-handsome—but winded—young man. "I'm a butterfly, and I flew right past you, Alejandro Roberto Torres. I win. Time to pay up."

He straightened. "Pay wha—?"

She socked him in the gut. He doubled over.

"All gas, no beans." She moved toward the trail. "Like I said, Byron. You've got training to do with this one if you want him on the team. I didn't even hit him hard. He's soft."

"I'll show you soft, Mia Pia."

She skidded to a halt. "What did you call me?"

"Maria Pilar. And *mia* in Spanish means mine." He gave her a crooked smile that set Pilar's sturdy knees aquiver. "Because some-day soon, I'll demand a rematch and victory will be mine."

She stretched on her tiptoes into his face. "Any time. Any place."

But before that, as Alex Torres predicted, he and Byron became best friends.

She tagged along everywhere to Byron's disgust and Alex's quiet tolerance. Alex, in fact, often urged Byron to just let her come along to save them the hassle of sending her home to Abuela.

Then Pilar's cat went missing.

It was Alex who helped her search the sprawling ranch. Alex who spotted the tabby in an arroyo, killed by a wild desert creature. Alex who dug a hole and held a funeral for Calico. Alex who brought another stray kitten from Saguaro Gulch for Pilar.

Alex who became her hero and champion. Until he and Byron started high school at summer's end. Until she and Byron uncovered Alex's other not-so-hidden talent—a way with the female gender.

'Cause Alex's superpower was his charm.

4

By the time Pilar arrived at the public housing complex, the perpetrator was long gone, and the woman whose face would resemble a checkerboard of bruises tomorrow refused to name her abuser or bring charges.

Pilar returned to the cruiser and radioed her location before heading to the station. She only hoped the next call to this address didn't involve a homicide.

After clocking out at the end of her shift, she changed out of her uniform into well-washed jeans and flats. Pilar retrieved her personal vehicle from the back lot, stowed her weapon in the glove compartment, and headed for the tribal youth center.

Two decisions she'd never regretted—becoming the custodial parent to her deployed brother's son. And becoming a tribal cop.

But after all these years, to come face to face with Alex in the line of duty... she'd not seen that coming when dispatch sent her to investigate a reported homicide in the desert barrens at the edge of the rez.

With any forewarning, she would have... would've what?

She frowned at her reflection in the glass-fronted door of the tribal teen center. She'd have taken time to neaten her cop bun. Maybe not enough time to lose those last five irritating pounds, but she certainly wouldn't have inhaled the diet-destroying fry bread omelet this morning.

Her mouth flattened. Like any of that mattered. Or changed what happened between them so long ago.

Stop being stupid, Pilar.

Taking a deep breath, she seized the handle and threw the door of the teen center wide. The phone call informing her that Manny had been expelled from school merely put the cap on what was shaping up to be a total in-the-toilet day.

And when she got through giving Manny a piece of her mind—grounding him in his foreseeable future—he'd be wishing he was back to solving algebraic equations.

While Manny wouldn't grieve over missing freshman algebra, she'd bet burritos he'd not be so willing to skip out on his current favorite pastime—the after-school cultural activities.

Manny had always been fascinated with Apache customs and lore. Until this year, he'd been an energetic if bookish child. And then, the hormones hit and being smart was suddenly geeky for the teen whose only aspirations revolved around making the high school basketball team.

He spoke better Apache than she, thanks to the linguistics electives the school offered. Kids were taught to be proud of their heritage. To embrace their identity.

Unlike the stigma she and Byron endured. When her brother and Alex Torres were best buddies. And she and Alex—

Her heart beat a furious clip at the thought of the filled-out, grown-up version of Alex Torres. Always tall, the gangly young man she'd known—and loved—had fulfilled his physical potential. A goofball back then, his charm and quirky sense of fun had also hidden a sharp intelligence.

A lot of things had changed since last they laid eyes on each other. But fundamental things had not. Including the effect Alejandro Torres had on her heart rate.

"Manny's not here, Miz To-Clanny."

Pilar's eyes adjusted from the desert glare to the florescent-lit teen center. Thirteen-year-old Reyna Bui sat atop a white laminate table. Her jean-clad legs dangled.

The child's sneakers were ragged, and with dusk approaching, Reyna's threadbare gray sweater would soon prove inadequate. "You waiting on your mom?"

"Yes, ma'am." Reyna's dark eyes slid away. "She'll be here soon as she finishes her shift at the Wild Bill."

Make that soon as Reyna's mother finished hustling customers at the off-rez bar in Globe. Or, failed to find other sleeping accommodations.

"Let me take you home."

Reyna shook her head. "I can walk home if it gets too late."

Pilar's mind shifted to the unidentified body in the canyon grave. Nobody bothered to monitor Reyna's comings and goings. Another throwaway rez kid.

Like her and Byron once upon a time.

"Not tonight." Pilar yanked the door open. "Come on. No arguments. I get enough of that from Manny."

Her brow puckering, Reyna paratrooped off the table and landed, agile as a deer, on the balls of her feet. "You don't have to do that, Miz To-Clanny."

"It'll be fun." Pilar held the door. "I get tired of nothing but guy talk from Manny. We'll get enchiladas and bring some to Manny before I take you home."

"You don't need to do that." But Reyna's stomach rumbled as she crawled into the Jeep Cherokee.

What Pilar didn't need to do was to look at her watch to know it'd been hours since Reyna's free and reduced lunch at school. Too well Pilar remembered the hunger of an empty belly and an equally empty trailer refrigerator. Too well she remembered the shame of her and Byron always being the poorest kids in school.

Until Abuela came into their lives.

"I don't have any money for dinner, Miz To-Clanny." Reyna squared her shoulders. "Mama says Buis don't take handouts."

Pilar fought hard to keep what she thought of Reyna's mother from showing on her face. She averted her gaze and inserted the key into the ignition. "Don't worry about that, honey. Pay me with one of those pretty rocks you find."

"You've already got a lot of those from me."

Pilar cranked the engine. "Actually, you'd be doing Manny a favor by putting off the mammoth-size punishment he's due. And," she cut her eyes at Reyna. "I figured since you and Manny were such good friends, you could give me a clue to what's going on in that boy's head these days. One female to the other."

"Used to be good friends." Reyna's gaze dropped to the floor-board. "Females is what he's got on his mind, I imagine. The high school ones, anyway."

Pilar wanted to bop Manny upside the head for hurting the too-skinny girl who'd not yet bloomed. Been there, been her.

Over a decade ago while playing ball in the yard with four-year-old Manny, she'd looked up to find the little girl with big brown eyes gazing at Manny as if he hung the moon. Pilar couldn't believe the child had walked all the way from next door.

'Cause next door in the middle of nowhere was a good two miles down the road. And thereafter, she'd made it her business to keep an eye out for the neglected child.

Reyna had never met a rock she didn't love. And she and best-bud Manny spent hours scrambling around the mountain vistas under Pilar's watchful eye. On a visit to Abuela's, it was Manny who taught Reyna to ride a pony. Manny who kicked butt at school when one of the other kids made fun of Reyna's less-than-stellar wardrobe. Or mocked her brains.

Manny used to be proud of his own braininess, too, until this year at high school when he discovered it wasn't quite the social commodity Pilar had led him to believe. Especially around the guys and adolescent girls he was so eager to impress these days. Middle-schooler Reyna—like Pilar—was still trying to adjust to Manny's new reality.

Adapt or die.

Pilar gritted her teeth. "Boys—men—take it from me—the whole lot of them are jerks, Reyna."

"He's going through a tough time." Reyna—ever the Manny champion whether he deserved it or not, mostly not—lifted her chin. "Manny's got a good heart. He'll be okay, you'll see."

Giving Pilar a tough time more like it. Skipping school, getting into fights, hanging out with those Indian gangster lowlifes—at this rate Manny would either end up in jail or dead. Policing the rez by day, policing Manny was proving the hardest job of all.

"Where'd Manny go this afternoon, Reyna?"

Facing forward, Reyna put her knees together, prim as a schoolmarm.

"You're not doing him any favors by protecting him."

Reyna laced her fingers in her lap.

Pilar blew out a disgusted breath as she turned into the drive-through lane. "Come on, Reyna. You've got to give me something. I'm at my wit's end with the boy."

What troubled Pilar more than anything was how the sweet, even-tempered boy had become so angry and secretive.

Reyna folded her arms over her flat chest. "It's Bui, Reyna. Don't have a rank or serial number. But I'm prepared to give you my tribal enrollment number if required."

"There'd be a chocolate milkshake in it for you, Reyna, if you come clean."

Reyna gave Pilar a haughty look. "I'm no snitch."

Pilar swallowed past the lump in her throat. "Is Manny using, Reyna?" As a police officer, she didn't kid herself about the avail-ability of drugs, especially to rez kids.

Reyna's eyes enlarged. "No. He'd never...not after what hap-pened with his mother."

Pilar strangled the wheel. She'd failed Manny. As his auntie, she'd tried so hard to give him normal—or what passed for normal in their broken family tree. To give him the safe and secure child-hood she and Byron missed.

But sometimes—Pilar bit her lip so hard she tasted blood—you couldn't fight genetics.

That thought—and Alex Torres—kept her awake a lot of nights.

A car behind them beeped. Glancing in the rearview mirror, Pilar inched to the intercom and ordered three chocolate milkshakes, two enchiladas *grande*-style, two fries, and one taco salad. Time—Pilar took stock of herself in the side mirror—past time to work on those five extra pounds.

She crept to the cashier's window and paid. Pilar passed the bulging bag across the console for Reyna to leverage at her feet. She handed the shake caddy for Reyna to balance in her arms.

Reyna counted the number of shakes. "But I didn't give you any dirt on Manny."

Pilar eased onto the highway. "I always get you a chocolate shake, Reyna, you know that."

Reyna's lips quivered. "Don't have any real pretty rocks in my col-lection right now, Miz To-Clanny, but I'm going to find you some-thing special this time."

Pilar smiled over at her. "I know you will, honey."

Reyna seemed to come to a decision. "Ole Miz Clum asked Manny to chop firewood for her this afternoon. Going to be a bad winter the old lady said. Offered to pay Manny. Which he refused." The girl tossed her head with an I-told-you-so look in her eyes. "As was only proper her being an elder and all."

"Clum? Talitha Clum?"

Whose property abutted the box canyon.

Pilar shivered at the thought of Manny so close to that horrible place.

Reyna nodded. "She volunteers at the center. Manny likes her stories of the old days. When Apaches weren't afraid, Manny says, to raise—"

"I get the picture, Reyna."

Reyna rummaged in the bag and chomped on a shoestring fry. "I overheard her tell Manny she'd bring him home."

Yet when Pilar reached the trailer, Talitha Clum was nowhere in sight. And Manny wasn't the only one making himself at home.

With Emily busy with multiple autopsies, Charles coordinated by phone with a tribal detective to identify the missing teenagers. Darlene updated the suspected serial's profile. And Sidd's record search revealed one homestead closest to the crime scene.

The home belonged to an old lady Alex planned to interview with Pilar's help. Something Sidd and the detective could've handled, but Alex's brief conversation with Pilar in the canyon hadn't been enough.

Not by a long shot.

He headed out of their temporary office at the tribal police department toward the mountains halfway between the rez and Saguaro Gulch, the closest town to Abuela. Alex exited off Highway 70 onto 191 heading south. He turned off the highway onto a secondary road.

A few twists and turns further, he sighted a run-down trailer and checked the GPS. The isolated trailer abutted the looming mountains. But it wasn't Pilar's house.

Following a tertiary road, he found her trim mobile home set amidst sagebrush against the backdrop of the wilderness area. Next to the trailer stood a freestanding basketball goal. He pulled into the driveway and switched off the engine. As neat and tidy as the other trailer had been ramshackle, he waited in the vehicle as per Apache courtesy to be invited inside.

He'd made it his business to inquire what time she went off shift. He'd made a lot of things his business over the years in regard to Pilar. But from a distance.

Alex watched as the front door swung open. He pushed his aviator sunglasses onto the crown of his head as a long-limbed teenage boy emerged from the depths of the mobile home.

Thirteen or fourteen maybe? Alex wasn't good with kids' ages. Hadn't much experience with kids of any age.

Light-skinned and tall for an Apache, the boy's eyes narrowed at the sight of the parked SUV. His dark, plaited braid hung over his shoulder. The boy hugged a basketball to his stomach.

Alex flung open the door accompanied by much dinging and stepped out of the vehicle.

Clad in jeans and a tank top, the boy didn't respond.

Alex flashed his badge. "Special Agent Alex Torres. Are you Manny, Byron's son?" He handed the boy his business card.

Manny examined the card and tucked it into his jeans. "Yeah. That's me." Something akin to recognition flickered in the boy's eyes. "You're Abuela's grandson. She lets me call her Abuela, too. I've seen pictures of you at her house."

Alex smiled. "Guilty as charged. And Abuela is everyone's grandmother. I caught a case on the rez with your auntie. Came by to ask for her help in an interview tomorrow."

The boy straightened. "So you've seen my auntie today already? Uh," his eyes searched left and right. "She in a good mood or what? Do you know when she'll be home?"

Pilar didn't do "good mood." Not around Alex.

He shrugged. "She seemed like she always is."

"I hear you." The boy slumped against the doorframe. "I also hear you and my dad were best friends a long time ago. Played football."

"A long, long time ago."

"You played basketball in your day, too."

In his day?

He fought the grin threatening to break free. "Back in the day, I was known to pick up a game or two."

Actually, he'd gotten a scholarship once upon a time based on his basketball prowess.

Manny nudged his chin toward Alex's white-collared professional attire. "Think you could handle a little one-on-one while you're waiting for Auntie, old man?"

Alex rolled his tongue in his cheek. "I think I could manage that. Maybe teach you a few moves in the process."

Manny came off the stoop. "Or maybe I'll teach the old dog a few new tricks."

Alex laughed. "You can try." An echo of Pilar's words to him.

In a sudden lunge, he stole the ball out of Manny's hands, took a flying leap, and dunked the ball with a swish. "Nothing but net, my man. Nothing but net."

Manny caught the rebound. A smile teased at the corners of the boy's mouth. "Not bad for an old guy." He dribbled the ball out of Alex's long-armed reach. Hustling the ball past Alex's defensive posture, Manny pivoted and did a quick layup.

Alex got the rebound. "Pretty good for a rookie. But I'm afraid experience wins over inexperience every time." He bounced the ball between his legs.

"Fancy move, old man. But despite what the Anglos claim, beauty *will* win out over age." Darting, he captured the ball, dribbled, and made the shot.

Alex grinned and struggled to catch his breath. The boy might be right. Manny didn't appear winded. Mid-thirties didn't play with the same gusto as a teenager.

"Mercy." Alex planted his hands on his knees. "The joints and the legs aren't what they used to be."

The boy snorted. "That's what Auntie says right after I beat the tar out of her score."

Alex's mouth curved. "You and Pilar scrimmage?"

The fourteen—maybe?—year-old boy nodded. "She's helping me get ready for basketball tryouts next month. She's got game for an old lady."

Old lady? Pilar was early thirties. Her birth date forever seared into his mind.

Alex made an effort to breathe. "Bet you don't beat her in a race, though. She's like the wind. Beat me a few times back in the day."

"She doesn't quit either. Outlasts and outruns the guys on the force at the yearly marathon."

Manny held the ball to his chest. "She's going to be furious when she gets home." He avoided Alex's eyes. "I got into trouble today."

Alex wiped the sweat from his brow with his hand. "What kind of trouble? How bad?"

Manny bit his lip. "Bad. Expelled for two weeks. A fight."

"Been in a few of those I was unable to walk away from. Didn't solve anything. Usually made things worse."

Manny grimaced. "I've been walking away. Got tired of walking away. Got tired of hearing them say I'm—" His eyes scudded toward the darkening sky over the mesa.

Alex frowned. "Are you being bullied? I'd be glad to listen if you want to talk."

"Talking isn't going to help." Manny glanced at him. "Besides, it's an Apache thing between the guys and me. You wouldn't understand."

"Maybe not. Maybe if you tell Pilar what's going on—"

"No." Manny concentrated on bouncing the ball. "She's full like my dad. And I'm not. Not like the other guys, either." He stuck out one skinny arm in the fading light as if to prove his point.

"Full? I don't under—oh." Alex stiffened. "Are the guys at school giving you a hard time because—?"

"Because my mother was a no-good Anglo junkie who dumped me on Auntie Pilar the first chance she got." Manny threw Alex the ball. "They say I got to prove I'm a real Apache or I don't belong." He twisted the red bandana around his neck.

Gang colors? Alex's heart constricted. This would kill Pilar if true. From what Abuela told him, Pilar had poured her life into Byron's boy.

"I don't belong anywhere." Manny shuffled his feet, unable to look Alex in the eye. "And now my dad..." He raised his head at the sound on tires on the gravel.

Alex angled as a burgundy Jeep with Pilar at the wheel rolled to a shuddering stop. He chucked the basketball to Manny as a white-lipped Pilar jerked the gear into park and shot out of the car.

"What're you doing here, Alex?"

His pulse leaped at the sight of Pilar in the ribbed sandstone Henley. "Figured you'd want to be kept in the loop. Thought I'd stop by and finally meet Byron's son."

A teenage girl climbed out of the passenger side. Her long black hair blowing in the autumn breeze, she clutched a white bag and drink caddy in her arms. "Hey, Manny."

Manny rolled his eyes before tossing Alex the ball again.

Pilar slammed the door so hard the Jeep rocked. "How do you know where I live, Alex?" Her eyes flickered between him and Manny.

Alex passed the ball from hand to hand. "I'm FBI, Pia. I got skills."

"Don't call me Pia." She curled her lip. "And you've got nothing but Abuela. She told you, didn't she?"

He tried one of his lazy grins on her for old times' sake.

She glared at him, hands on her hips. "You can save the charm for the blondes, Torres. Thank God, I'm immune."

He cocked his head, his fingers spread wide on the ball between his hands. "Oh, really? 'Cause that's not how I'm remembering things."

"Remember?" Her nostrils flared. "I've made it my life's mission to try not to remember anything concerning you, Alex Torres."

Alex tightened his jaw and let the ball roll away.

"We're trying to have a game here, Auntie."

Her gaze focused on the strip of red cloth wound around Manny's neck. "You better not have gotten that bandana from those lowlife Conquistadores, Manuel To-Clanny. Are they the reason you've been expelled from school?" She shook her head. "Expelled, Manny? You're too smart to get mixed up with them."

The young girl extended the bag to Pilar's nephew. "Sunday we're still going rock hunting, right, Manny?"

He hunched his shoulders. "Are you stupid or something, Reyna? Got no time for baby stuff."

The girl flinched.

Manny made a face. "Why'd you have to go and bring Tagalong, Auntie?"

Pilar grabbed his arm. "What's gotten into you, Manny? You never used to be this mean. You're the stupid one if you think hanging out with those juvenile delinquents makes you a bigger man."

Manny wrenched free. "Just leave me alone. You're not my mother."

He snatched the bag from Reyna. She stumbled and would've fallen if Alex hadn't steadied her. The girl quivered, her shoulder bones as fragile as a bird's beneath Alex's hand.

Manny's gaze flitted between Alex's hand and Reyna. Something flashed in his eyes before Manny's face hardened. "And stop following me around, Tagalong. It's embarrassing."

Tears hovered like dewdrops on the edges of the girl's lashes. "I'm sorry, Manny…I didn't mean…"

Manny scowled. "You don't mean anything to me, Reyna. Why can't you get that through your thick skull?"

Reyna's face crumpled.

Alex stepped between the teens. "Manny, that's enough."

Pilar gave him a look.

Alex wasn't sure if she was irritated or grateful for his interference.

Pilar tilted her head. "What were you fighting about?"

Manny pushed out his lips. "My business. Not yours, Auntie. Get off my case."

"What's with the secrets these days, Manny? If you'd talk to me, let me—"

"I'm done with you people. I repeat, leave me alone." Manny whirled and pounded up the steps into the trailer.

"We're not done with this discussion, Manuel," Pilar shouted through the screened door. "And you can consider yourself grounded for the next month."

Alex stuffed his hands into his trouser pockets. "He's being bullied at school, Pilar. Manny doesn't feel like he belongs."

Her eyes widened. "Bullied?" Her hand fumbled for the nonexistent Glock at her side. "Who? I'll—"

Alex watched with amusement as she switched to Mama Bear mode. Loaded for bear. "You gonna shoot 'em, Pilar?"

"I might." She dropped her hand. "And Reyna, I apologize on behalf—" Swiveling, Pilar bit her lip.

Alex turned to find the drink caddy placed on the ground and the young girl nowhere in sight.

Pilar sighed. "Poor Reyna. It's hard to see your idol with feet of clay. She's walking home by herself. Again."

"Reminds me of another young girl I once knew. She tagged along everywhere her brother and I went. Hard to shake as a sandbur. As prickly as a saguaro."

"Like I said, Torres, it's hard to see your idols with feet of clay." Pilar's fingers flexed as if she wanted to shoot him. "But I've had time to get over it."

He caught her gaze. "Well, if so, then once again, you're ahead of me. 'Cause that's something I've never been able to do."

5

Disconcerted, Pilar started for the Jeep.

Alex moved to intercept her. "Where're you going?"

"I'm going to make sure Reyna gets home." She glanced beyond him to the shadow-draped mountains. "Too many dangers out there for a girl her age. I should know."

A fleeting expression too quick for her to decipher crossed Alex's face. "Let me drive. I'll update you on the case."

"I'll drive myself. I don't need—"

"Please, Pilar." He reached for her arm, checked himself, and dropped his hand. "That way you'll get rid of me quicker." He opened the passenger door of the SUV for her.

She edged past him. "The quicker the better."

A muscle leaped in his jaw. "If that's what you want."

That *was* what she wanted? Wasn't it? But the scent of him filled her nostrils as he leaned over to shuffle papers out of her way. Her fingers fumbled with the seat belt. He helped her click the belt in place.

His cologne sent her pulse into overdrive. Sandalwood and Alex—a combination she'd never been able to banish from her heart. Her mouth went dry.

She trembled from the effort not to touch his hand. Because what she'd wanted was a life with him. To keep him close. Always.

He stepped back a pace. "I'm so sorry for everything, Pilar."

Everything?

Proving he'd never wanted her the way she'd wanted him. The skin on her arms underneath her sleeves itched, aching with an insatiable need to release the pain. She bit her lip.

"If I could change what—"

"Are we going to check on Reyna or not?" She yanked the car door shut.

Rounding the hood, he slid into the driver's seat. "Still collecting strays, Pilar?"

"What are you talking about?"

"Like Calico. And me."

She curled her lip. "You've never been anyone's stray."

"We need to talk about why I—"

"Doesn't matter what happened." She couldn't bear for him to know how he'd hurt her then or now. "Ancient history. Some things can't be fixed."

She pointed her lips at the keychain dangling in his hand. "Wouldn't want to keep God's Gift to Women from a date with the blonde. Or," she threw him a nasty look. "Are you into both of the blondes these days?"

He cranked the engine and revved the motor. "Pushing buttons must run in the family, eh, Pia? I could help you with Manny. Offer my take on the folly of getting involved with gangs. I'm here for you and him."

"Like you were here for me then?" She laughed. "Thanks, but no thanks."

Jerking, he faced forward and navigated the rough stretch of road per her directions.

She allowed herself a longer look at the boy—become man—she'd once loved so impossibly. The white Oxford shirt he wore contrasted nicely with his Latino skin tone. The shirt cuffs rolled to his elbows, his forearms were rock-hard muscle. But Alex had always looked good in clothes.

And without them, too.

She blushed at the memory.

The SUV jolted over a pothole, and she lurched into Alex. He caught her. His hand electrified the skin on her arm.

She inched away and steadied herself against the armrest. "Sorry."

"Don't be."

He removed his hand, and as if unsure what to do with it, he raked his hand over his short-cropped hair.

She tracked the movement of his hand as he gripped the steering wheel. His hands large enough to palm a basketball, the fingers were lean and well-formed. His face was more serious than she recalled. Not the same happy-go-lucky boy she'd so lov—

"I've called a team meeting for tomorrow morning to pool our notes on the case."

She shrugged. "I'll be on patrol. Haven't made detective yet. Not my case."

"I've requested you be temporarily reassigned. There's enough work for my team, the tribal detective, and you."

She frowned. "I don't think you and me on the same team is a good idea." She sniffed. "'Cause that worked out so well with us before."

A muscle ticked in his jaw. "Based on what we already know about this perp, he targets Apache girls and he's not done killing by a long shot." He didn't bother looking at her. "You saying you won't be a team player for the good of the tribe?"

"You'd be the expert on being a player, wouldn't you, Alex?"

Tight-lipped, he pulled to a stop on the road beside Reyna's home. Pilar watched a silhouette of Reyna move from room to room switching on table lamps.

"You want to go inside?"

Pilar shook her head. "She'll want to lick her wounds in private. I'll touch base with her tomorrow."

"Kind of what you do when someone hurts you, Pilar."

She stared at his hands, where he white-knuckled the wheel. "Is that a question?"

"More like a memory."

His voice was deeper than she remembered. And he topped six feet now. His shoulders were broad.

"We found two more bodies."

This time, her gaze found his. He'd been a boy the last time he looked into her eyes. No—he'd been unable to look her in the eyes that last, terrible day—

He switched off the engine. "Thought you'd be up for the challenge, Cater-Pilar."

She bristled. "Don't call me that. In case you haven't noticed, I'm no longer thirteen."

He cut his eyes at her. "I noticed. A long time ago. I married you, didn't I?"

Pilar's chest constricted. She fought for a nonchalance she didn't feel. "And divorced me, too."

He shuffled his feet on the floorboards. "About that, Pia—"

She growled. "If we're going to catch this killer before he strikes again, then I suggest you stick to the case. What do you already know about the killer?"

"We know he operates on both sides of the border. At first, we suspected a sex trafficking ring. But when bodies emerged in New Mexico's bootheel, close to the border, we realized we were dealing with a serial killer. Maybe affiliated with Franco Salazar's cartel because once on the other side, he seems to disappear out of law enforcement's reach."

"Franco Salazar, the drug lord?"

Alex's lips thinned. "It's been a war zone since the Flores patriarch was captured by Mexican Special Forces. Rival gangs and cartels are locked in a bloodbath to see who will emerge as the new king of the hill. Intel says Salazar appears to be the winner."

He made a face. "At least until someone stronger knocks him off the heap."

"And this serial killer is Mexican?"

"We think so. Although the girl kept repeating '*Oos dah.*'"

Pilar leaned forward. "The Enemy. What the other tribes called the Apache."

"Exactly."

"What girl?"

He shifted. "There's been a flood of illegals this year. From as far away as Guatemala. Mostly children. Border Patrol picked up a bunch of them last month. Took them into temporary custody at the Nogales Detention Center."

"But this girl?"

"Got a file." He jutted his chin toward the backseat. "To get you up to speed." Engaging the ignition, Alex did a three-point turn and headed back to Pilar's house.

She reached over the seat and retrieved the file. She extracted the photo of a dark-skinned girl in her mid-teens. "What's her name?"

"Don't know. Seemed to understand Spanish and English. Refused to speak either." His mouth tightened. "And you note how she's dressed?"

Pilar studied the overblouse and traditional three-tiered skirt. The dirty, matted hair was chopped off shoulder-length. Resembling photos she'd seen of nineteenth-century Apache women. Except this photo was in color.

"You think the girl's Apache? News flash, Torres. I promise you every girl in San Carlos speaks better English than Apache. And nobody wears this getup anymore unless they're one of the Old Ones or for a ceremonial purpose."

She lay the photograph between them. "How'd the FBI get involved in a border issue? This have something to do with your undercover work in Mexico?" She reddened at what she'd let slip.

He grinned. "Glad to hear you were keeping track of me."

She scowled. "Keeping track so I'd be sure to steer clear."

He veered into her driveway and parked. "I'd already been compromised when—"

She inhaled. "Your cover was blown?"

Before she could stop herself, her finger brushed the small scar at the edge of his brow. "Is that how you got this? Did they hurt you?"

He caught her hand and ran her palm across the five o'clock stubble of his jawline and across his mouth. His breath warmed her skin.

She snatched her hand away. What on earth possessed her to touch him? Except for Manny, she didn't touch people.

Pilar buried her hands in her lap. Just because they'd loved each other once—correction, hindsight always 20/20—she'd loved *him*. A long time ago. A lifetime ago.

But her fingertips tingled.

Alex swallowed. "Though I never met him, I guess I'm the Salazar expert after I managed to infiltrate the cartel. Only just escaped, too."

He shrugged. "Lots of scars, most not so visible." He put a finger to the scar on his brow. "Afghanistan, not Mexico."

She'd spent a half-dozen years not watching the news when she learned Alex was over there. "What makes you think this girl is connected to the bodies here on the rez?"

"Emily says—"

"Your Emily seems to be an authority on everything."

He settled against the seat. "First off, she's not my Emily."

Pilar grabbed the door handle. "Why don't the both of you take a long walk across the desert and interview this girl?"

He shook his head. "She was like a caged animal. Pacing, the guards said. Howling. Frightened the other children. Wouldn't eat. Starving herself. She was scared out of her mind. By us. By everything."

Pilar placed the folder on the seat. "Take her back to wherever she came from. She sounds mental. This isn't some story about a feral child raised by Mexican wolves in the desert, is it?"

"Look, I'm as patriotic as the next. Maybe more than most. But I've more than a little sympathy for those desperate enough to sell their soul to the coyotes promising them the American dream across a river. I've seen the poverty. The violence. The fear that keeps them heading north toward hope."

She pursed her lips. "Where they end up, often as not, on our land. Rez land. No love has ever been lost between a Mexican and an Apache."

"Don't know as I'd agree with that last statement." The look he gave her scorched Pilar. "Would you?"

Pilar's heart hammered. "We were talking about the girl."

His eyebrow quirked. "Were we?"

She fidgeted under his scrutiny.

He blew out a breath. "Before we could interview her, the girl escaped and climbed onto the roof of the detention center. When one of the agents followed, she jumped."

Pilar released the catch on the seatbelt. "She must've been Apache then. Death before captivity. Never surrender is kind of our thing."

Alex flicked her a glance. "Tell me about it."

He shoved the folder at her. "She'd been marked. Like another dead Jane Doe we found on the New Mexico side. Not far from the Mescalero rez. Marked like the body Dr. Chestuan found on San Carlos land."

Marked...nausea churned Pilar's stomach.

"We think maybe she got away and the others weren't so fortunate. I'm here to do a job and then I promise to be out of your—" He flushed, biting off his words as a palpable memory surged between them.

Of his fingers entwined in her hair. Those five glorious days when she loved him so completely. Reckless of her heart. In total disregard for the future.

With an abandon perhaps only possible when one is as young as she'd been then.

She blinked back tears. Apaches didn't cry. Her eyes strayed to the panic and hopelessness etched on the young girl's face in the photograph. What had been her story? Where had she come from? Was it fear that drove her north?

Or something else?

Perhaps you only learned self-preservation as you grew older. When you no longer believed in immortality, much less invincibility.

The silence lengthened.

He moistened his lips. "Another disturbing fact has come out of the autopsies. Each can be traced to the perigee."

At her upraised brow, he continued. "The supermoon. When the moon's larger on the horizon due to its closest orbital proximity to earth. Including according to Em the latest vic, dead only a month sometime during August's perigee."

"The killer stalks his victims by the light of the moon?"

"And I back-checked the night you disappeared, Pilar. All those years ago, when a supermoon filled the night sky."

She sucked in a breath.

He gestured toward the darkening horizon. "He targets Apache girls. We've got two days to stop him before the second of this year's tetrad, another Apache Moon, comes round again."

Could the serial be the monster who destroyed her life? Pilar fought to steady herself. Was this a chance to, once and for all, end the nightmare she'd been living? To make sure he never hurt anyone else the way he'd hurt her?

She schooled her features. "Okay. I'm in."

"Good." His brow creased, Alex examined her a moment before glancing away. "Team meeting at the tribal station at eight a.m. sharp. Then I need to interview the canyonland neighbor."

He leaned across her and threw open the door. "Tell Manny we'll finish the game we started soon as I get a chance."

The door dinging, she inched past him. His overwhelming physical presence as usual weakened whatever resolve she ever drummed up concerning him.

"And Pilar?"

One foot on the running board, she paused, clutching the folder to her chest.

"I've always believed you and I make a great team."

Alex drove a further twenty-odd miles southeast toward his grandmother's ranch. Passing under the crossbars of the bull and the T for Torres, he reckoned his abuela counted him first and foremost among the bullheaded.

The headlights swept the sprawling adobe ranch.

He'd spent time in a multitude of countries, yet here's where he considered home.

Because here he first met Pilar.

Parking in the circle drive, Alex laid his forehead on the steering wheel.

God, how he loved her. How he'd always loved her. And seeing her again after all these years?

She reduced him to feeling like the same gawky teenager he'd been when he dared to reach for barely understood dreams and failed so miserably. His stomach knotted—when he'd failed her so miserably.

He'd lived the last decade and a half in a sort of sensory deprivation. Only today had the colors of the sky and desert sprung to life once more for him. And with his nerve endings no longer numb, he felt a raw, searing hurt every time he looked at her.

Every time she glared at him with such icy hatred, his gut clenched at what his irreparable mistakes cost them. Cost her.

The front door opened, spilling light onto the wooden planks of the veranda. And the diminutive form of his grandmother stepped into the night air.

She motioned. "Come, *mi nieto.* Tell me about this long-awaited reunion between you and your Pilar."

If only she were still his…in every way that mattered.

His grandmother sat down in a rocker at the corner of the porch. She patted the rocker's twin and he sank down.

"Knowing Pilar, I'm going to hazard a guess she's livid with me for not warning her you were taking this case."

He scrubbed his face. "Livid's not the half of it. Although, most of her rage is rightly aimed at me."

Isabel Torres sighed. "Despite my best efforts over the years, I'm afraid our Pilar doesn't do forgiveness. Only revenge."

"Don't know why we'd expect anything different." He dropped his chin. "Vengeance, after all, is the Apache Way, isn't it?"

"It is the human way." Abuela wrapped the fringed shawl closer around her shoulders. "It will be good for Pilar to have you here. But her anger's far better than the state she was in when she first returned. After…"

He gripped the rocker. "I pursued this case because it's a chance to put things right, Abuela." He grimaced. "As right as they can ever be between Pilar and me."

She rested her blue-veined hand on his. "It is good this thing you do. You will bring justice and healing to Pilar. It is long past time for the both of you to move forward with your lives."

And what if moving forward involved someone with Pilar other than him?

His heart squeezed.

Alex had blown his chance with her. Pilar deserved closure and so much more. A chance at happiness.

His grandmother stilled. "I was so worried about Pilar then. She'd gone inside herself somewhere, and no one could reach her. Not Byron, nor I. We were so afraid…" Abuela's voice trembled. "I'm fairly certain she was hurting herself. To release the inner pain."

Shrinking inside himself, he closed his eyes.

"Having Manny in her life has been her salvation. He kept her from the brink of the abyss. And I don't think she's…" Again, his grandmother faltered. "I don't think she's done those things to herself in a long while. Manny gave her a reason to live, to get up in the morning. A purpose greater than herself."

Alex set the rocker in motion. "When Byron called me, he said Manny was in trouble."

"She and Manny need your help. Manny may be the only way to get through to Pilar. Though our rather-take-a-fist-in-the-mouth Pilar is never going to admit to that."

"I think fist-in-my-face is the way Pilar's leaning right now, Abuela."

Isabel laughed and sounded younger than her years. "That's the Pilar we know and love, isn't it, *Nieto*."

"She's determined to keep me at arm's length for the duration of this investigation."

"After losing both parents early, she's spent a lifetime erecting barricades." Abuela rose, her joints creaking. "You'll find a way to breach her defenses. You always do."

She smiled. Her teeth flashed white in the darkness of the night. "You've always been the chink in her armor."

"Her downfall, too."

"You must stop punishing yourself. Not everything was your fault."

She planted a quick kiss on his forehead. "Your parents and I were equally afraid we'd lost you, too, back then. Afraid your self-flagellating penance would bring you home in a body bag."

Alex would never tell Abuela or his parents how close he'd come to dying on a dusty battlefield in the Helmand Province. Later after his Quantico training, he'd poured himself into his undercover work in Mexico, battling not only the insidious evil of the cartels but also his own despair and self-loathing.

But he'd not understood why he'd survived when so many good men hadn't, until Byron called him a month ago with an opportunity for absolution.

Absolution was all Alex dared to imagine.

"God has a plan for you and Pilar, Alex." His grandmother placed her cool, dry hand against his cheek. "Plans for a future and a hope. He's not done with either of you yet. Hang on to your faith. Don't let go of it or her."

Faith—hard won and wrested from the brink of his personal abyss.

An owl hooted.

His grandmother straightened. Venturing to the edge of the porch, she gazed into the inky blackness of the desert night. She lifted her face and sniffed the air. A strange look crossed her lined, broad-planed face.

"What is it, Abuela? Can you smell the rain coming?"

Isabel was legendary for reading the natural signs of her desert homeland. Drought or thunderstorm. Tornado or blue skies. She had married the only son of the powerful Don Torres and, after her husband's early death, had been the driving force behind the success of the Torres family brand.

"Not rain. But something is a-coming." She tucked her hands into her elbows. "Something not good."

He darted a glance at the foreboding tone of her voice.

She shooed him toward the door. "Get some rest. You've got a busy day ahead of you tomorrow."

"Aren't you coming, Abuela?"

"Not right this minute. Going to commune with nature a bit longer. But I'll be in soon, I promise."

Over the years, he'd seen her do her "communing" countless times. As if she put out her antennae to things only she could see.

She stood where he'd left her, poised and alert on the top step. Her stance guarded. Her head with its elegant silver chignon tilted as if she listened.

Listened to what? Alex wondered as he closed the door softly.

To sounds only she could hear.

6

Before

Fɪꜰᴛᴇᴇɴ-ʏᴇᴀʀ-ᴏʟᴅ Aʟᴇx ᴅɪᴅɴ'ᴛ ᴍɪss L.A.

Truth be told, he was relieved when the judge and his parents removed him from an environment increasingly out of his control. The gang pressured him to do things with which he wasn't comfortable. Once in, forever in, and he'd escaped just in time.

Being that this was Alex's first offense, the judge ordered probation. And at their wit's end, Alex's parents arranged with his probation officer to send Alex as far from the gang's reach as possible: to his grandmother, where the Torreses had ranched longer than the Anglos had been in Arizona.

On the ranch, there was open space, towering mountains, and blue sky. Room to breathe. Room to dream. Room to be.

Here he met the two best friends, Alex suspected, he'd ever have. Byron—quiet to the point of invisibility, but a force to be reckoned with on the football field. Coiled energy with something to prove, Byron loved only two people: his sister, Pilar, and Alex's abuela.

As for Pilar?

He smiled at the thought of the defiant, Apache girl who almost matched him for competitiveness.

She'd punch him in the gut for even thinking that. Just like she did every time she beat him to the top of the mesa. And he didn't let her win. Cater-Pilar was, as Byron warned, swift as the wind.

Little in stature, mighty in mouth. Feisty, tough as the spikes on a saguaro, and smart. She made him laugh. And unlike the other females he'd twisted around his finger with a smile since birth, Pilar didn't seem overly impressed with Alejandro Roberto Torres.

She was halfway between being a child and—he swallowed—halfway to being whatever Pilar was yet to be.

Pilar and Byron were also the angriest people the laid-back Alex Torres had ever met. They didn't erupt or rage. But anger seethed beneath the surface of their broad, high-cheekboned faces.

Because their Chiricahua mother from the Mescalero rez in New Mexico was dead? Or because of their stepfather, a Western Apache from the White Mountain rez farther north? He was a strange, morose man.

Morose. One of Pilar's new words. And like the To-Clanny kids, Alex steered clear of the man whenever possible.

Byron and Pilar had called the ranch home for the last two years. The longest, Byron told him, they'd ever lived anywhere after their mother drank herself to death when Pilar was only eight.

Pilar—Tagalong as he liked to tease her—followed them everywhere that summer. Always dogging their heels. Never backing down from any challenge.

He didn't mind her hanging around. Surprisingly—because she was still such a little girl with her books, stray cats, and flyaway hair—Pilar was a lot of fun. She upped the ante on whatever scheme Alex devised. Brought a charge of electricity to every adventure he concocted for himself and his best pal, Byron.

But when school began in Saguaro Gulch, Alex turned his attention to the future. He used his considerable charm on his teachers and the plethora of females who flocked around the football squad. Thanks to him, he and shy Byron never lacked for female attention.

The first game of the season Alex scored a touchdown toward the final victory. The rest of the team engulfed him in a frenzy of triumph. And for the first time, he belonged.

He emerged from the locker room to find Pilar waiting. "You gonna do one of those victory dances for me?" Alex grinned.

Pilar looked down and then up at him out of the corner of her eye. "Maybe." She tossed her long, glossy braid over her shoulder. "Once we get home."

Unease nettled him. Byron should've explained their plans to Pilar. "Where's Abuela?"

Pilar shrugged. "I told her I'd ride home with you and Byron."

Byron stepped into the hallway. "Not happening, Sister. We've got places to go." He clapped a meaty hand across Alex's shoulder blades. "Thanks to my man, the night is young."

The exit door squeaked open and the two blondes Alex had courted for Friday night dates waved.

Pilar went rigid. Her eyes alternated between cold fury and a strange vulnerability.

He and Pilar had been best buddies, too, all summer. But now? Summer was over.

"Ladies," Byron gestured to the freshmen girls. "Ready to go?"

Alex's so-called date clamped a possessive arm around his waist. His arm went reluctantly around hers in response. The strawberry blonde nuzzled his neck with her cheek. And she gave a throaty laugh that had intoxicated Alex in algebra.

Pilar glared. If looks could've killed, he'd have been spit-roasted, Apache-style.

"Go home, Sister." Byron dug the keys to Abuela's ranch Jeep out of his pocket. "Shall we, ladies?"

The blondes giggled. Pilar rolled her eyes. Alex broke out into a cold sweat.

Byron and his date ambled away. Alex's date surged forward, putting his feet into motion. Chewing his lower lip, he glanced over his shoulder.

Pilar remained where they left her.

Motionless. Abandoned.

And on her face, a desolation that plucked Alex's heart.

7

THE LANDLINE RANG AS PILAR CROSSED THE THRESHOLD INTO HER home. Tossing the folder onto the coffee table, she caught the call on the last ring before it routed to voice mail.

"Hello?"

She placed one hand over her ear to drown out the blaring noise of the television. Manny sprawled on the couch, his long legs extended. His big, socked feet propped on the coffee table.

"Byron? I can barely—" She scowled at Manny who kept his face turned toward the television screen. "Hang on. Let me get to the kitchen where I can hear..." She nudged Manny's legs.

Manny didn't budge.

She stepped over his legs and, with a not-so-gentle back-kick, shoved Manny's legs off the table. Unbalanced, Manny rolled off the couch and landed with a thud onto the carpet.

"Hey!"

She positioned her hand over the receiver. "Hey yourself, Manny. Get off your butt and turn the television down. Byron's calling from overseas."

Manny muttered something under his breath, but he got up and switched the television off.

"You need to tell him, Pilar," Byron urged.

She turned her attention to her brother over seven thousand miles away on a peacekeeping mission.

Pilar swiveled toward the living room. "Go to bed, Manny."

"Dad's got nothing to say to me?" Manny's dark eyes glittered. "Good. 'Cause I got nothing to say to him, either." He stomped down the hall to his room.

She heaved a breath. "I guess you heard that."

Byron gave a mirthless laugh. "Sister, half of Arizona heard that."

"I'm doing the best I can, Byron."

"That's why you need to tell him."

She shook her head as if Byron could see her. "That's why now isn't a good time to tell him. He's already hurting and confused."

Byron snorted. "He's a teenager. When's he not going to be hurting and confused? When he hits middle age? You're not doing him any favors by shielding him from the truth. Fee and I have set the date. Time to move on, Pilar."

She leaned against the refrigerator. Its low hum mimicked the thrumming in her head. "Easy for you to say now you've found religion and the love of your life."

"You're wrong on both counts, Sister. It's not a religion. It's a relationship. What Abuela tried to teach us. As usual, she's right about everything. But don't tell her I said that. And this relationship with my Creator *is* the love of my life. The always and only constant love. Fee's the icing on the cake."

Pilar stiffened. "Some love after what you and I both endured at the hands of a monster."

"I've made my own mistakes since." Byron's voice softened. "It's a cop-out to blame the failures of my life on him. I made my own bad choices after that. Including what happened with Alex."

She scrubbed her forehead as the headache mounted. "I don't want to talk about that."

"You never want to talk about that. And, God help me, I let you suffer in silence. Instead of confronting what happened and lancing the wound."

She laughed at the irony. "Trust me, lancing the wound doesn't help. Not much anyway."

"Healing for me came when I forgave our stepfather and Alex, Sister. When I finally found the courage to tell what happened to the platoon chaplain. I experienced a peace and a lightness I'd never known before."

"It's the forgiveness part where you lose me, Byron."

"How's the bitterness and revenge working for you, Sister?"

Pilar's lips twisted. "Keeps me on my feet and swinging, Brother."

He let out an exasperated breath. "It keeps you chained in a prison of your own making, Pilar. A stronghold forged in the fires of hate. I learned the hard way that secrets only feed the stronghold. One day you'll decide you want to be free, but by then, I fear it'll be too late. The bars will be too strong to bend, and you'll be captive forever."

"Stop..." She shouted at the receiver. "Just stop."

Byron sucked in a breath. "Pilar...Please...I'm sorry. I promised I'd never speak of that and I won't. But Manny needs to know. His entire future is at stake."

"He got expelled today, Byron. For fighting."

Byron sighed. "The To-Clanny gene doesn't fall far from the tree, does it?"

"I told you about this new gang on the rez last time you called. I'm afraid they're recruiting our Manny." Her voice quavered. "I'm scared. I'm not sure how to save him."

"There's only One who can save him, Pilar."

She growled. "Don't start with that again, Byron. You and I know there's no rescue there. Just a bunch of hymn-singing, pew-pounding, red on the outside, white on the inside apples."

"Then you better start packing his bags and send him east to Bragg and Fee. 'Cause that's the only way you're going to get him away from the gang."

Her breath hitched.

"Once they pressure him into going through with whatever wicked initiation scheme they've got planned for him, Pilar, there'll be no going back."

She gulped past the boulder lodged in her throat. "I know, Byron."

"You either get him the help he needs there, or send him here. If the darkness gets a foothold, our boy as we know and love him will be swallowed whole."

She ground her fist against her eye.

Apaches don't cry. Apaches don't cry.

"I know, Byron," she whispered.

"Please, Pilar. I'm begging you. Do what's right for the boy. Before it's too late."

"I've always tried to do what's right for Manny."

Someone on his end called Byron's name.

"I've got to go." Byron's voice changed. "I'll call next chance I get. There's more I need to talk to you about. But you need to have made your decision about Manny by then, Pilar. Do you hear me?"

Alex's offer drifted past her mind.

With her brother so far away, perhaps another male influence wouldn't be such a bad idea. Even if that influence meant Alex Torres. Wasn't like she had that many options.

She'd never had many options. And that stark reality only fueled the anger she kept stashed deep inside herself.

"I hear you, Byron. Be safe."

"Tell Manny goodnight for me. Fee sends her love. I'll—"

Static filled the airwaves between them as the connection ended.

Pilar scrounged around the kitchen, cleaning the mess Manny left of dinner. She took one look at the taco salad she'd ordered and hurled it into the trash.

She drifted through the rooms and turned off the lights as she went. Double-checking the locks. She hesitated outside Manny's door. No light shone underneath its frame.

Pilar rested her forehead against the wood. It hadn't been that long ago Manny wouldn't go to bed without her goodnight kiss and a bedtime story.

How she missed those days. Now Manny preferred to follow his own interests. He couldn't be bothered to turn his homework in on time, but he made sure those dry, scholarly tomes on Apache history returned to interlibrary loan.

"Good night, Manny," she whispered through the door.

For a moment, she imagined Manny whispering back to her. Byron wasn't wrong about the fortress she'd built around herself. She'd tear down those walls and more if it meant keeping Manny from making irreparable choices. Even if it meant making Alex a temporary fixture in their lives.

She secured her firearm in the safety box on the top shelf of her closet. Her skull pounded. Sleep or the other thing she shamefully did were the only things that ever helped.

It'd been a long, long time since she'd endured one of these migraines. Probably brought on by the stress of seeing the girl in the shallow grave. Triggered by the shock of finding Alex on the rez.

Flicking off the light, she changed into her pajamas. Releasing the pins that bound her hair in the tight bun at the nape of her neck, she shook her hair free. Giving in to the urge to lie down, she slid underneath the comforter. Laying her head on the pillow, she massaged her temples.

What she wanted to do was scream every obscenity at Alex she'd rehearsed in her mind over a dozen years in the off chance they ever met again.

She wanted to rail and beat her fists into his too-handsome-to-live face. She wanted to hurt him as deeply and as irreversibly as he'd hurt her. A hurt far deeper than anything done before or since Alex came into her life.

And that—she closed her eyes, wishing for oblivion—was saying a lot.

Instead, she dreamed of his fingers tangled in her hair and his breath on her cheek. Of the distant strains of a mariachi band. Of the fiesta revelry. And of the fluttery anticipation in her stomach as his mouth moved closer.

But just as suddenly her dream switched to the first time Alex Torres told her he loved her. At the top of the mesa behind the ranch. With the wind blowing the tresses of her hair, he'd taken her face between the palms of his hands. She basked in the sensation of his lips touching hers. Then, it was no longer Alex.

An implacable shadow took control of her mouth. Recoiling, she ran. If It caught her, she'd be lost forever. But no matter how hard she strained, she couldn't outrun the suffocating, oppressive darkness.

She screamed for Alex. For God. But the Wicked One gained. Arms held her down. Hurting her. Dragging her against her will to the pit, to the hole in the earth from which she'd never emerge—

"Auntie! Wake up, Auntie!"

Choking off a sob, she jerked upright.

The sheets entwined around her limbs, she forced the terror into the dark place where she held it at bay during her waking hours. Her eyes darted around the familiar confines of her bedroom as the night gave way to molten streaks of light. A cool breeze from the open window blew against her face. Had she left a window—?

"Auntie?" At Manny's frightened voice, her gaze flitted to where he stood beside her bed.

"It's me, Auntie. Manny. It was only a dream. Like the others."

Barefoot in his pajamas, he displayed his hands before smoothing a hunk of hair from her face. Careful because last time, she'd not recognized him at first and lashed out in her confusion.

"M-Manny?"

"It's okay, Auntie. You want to tell me about your dream?"

She inched farther onto the pillows. "No."

Manny shouldn't have to play the adult. And she had no intention of ever befouling his life with the horror of her nightmares.

"I-I'm okay. I'm sorry I woke you, honey."

Manny frowned. "It'd been so long I hoped the dream wouldn't return."

She swung her legs off the bed. "You and me both. Thank you for—for..."

Apaches don't cry. Apaches don't cry.

She swallowed. "For being here."

"How about I fix pancakes?"

She eyed him. "I meant what I said about grounding you."

A smile played at the corners of his lips. "Yeah, I know. But a guy's got to eat, right? And I won't forget to put chocolate chips on yours."

Their special Saturday breakfast ritual. Hers and the old Manny's. She almost sent out a prayer of thanksgiving before she remembered she didn't believe any of the stuff Abuela peddled.

Promising to be out of the shower in five minutes, Pilar grabbed the water glass on her bedside table. She probably looked like a wreck. Stretching, she plodded into the adjoining bathroom and yawned. Reaching for the faucet, she shot a glance at her reflection in the mirror.

Her hand spasmed. The glass struck the porcelain sink. Shards of broken fragments ricocheted everywhere.

She covered her mouth with both hands and fought the primal scream rising in her throat.

He'd been here. He'd found her. Despite her efforts to fly under the radar.

Yesterday at the canyon somehow she'd known. She'd felt him there. Staring. Waiting to devour her again.

This couldn't be happening.

Pilar moaned, her knees buckling.

She wouldn't let this happen again. She wasn't the same girl he'd taken. She'd never allow herself to be taken again.

Pilar squeezed her eyes shut and opened them. Hoping against hope her eyes deceived her. But in vain. He was back.

He'd written one word in soap on the mirror. The word forever carved into her soul.

Mia. Mia. Mia.

The loathsome word he'd whispered over and over into her ear. Mine.

8

Before

PILAR LIKED LIVING AT ABUELA'S RANCH—BETTER THAN ANY place she and Byron ever lived. They'd moved around a lot after her mama died. She couldn't remember her real father. Byron said sometimes he thought he remembered—though more shadowy figure than the substance of an actual human being.

Abuela made sure they had three meals every day, warm clothes in the winter, and shoes for school. She and Byron liked it so well, they made a pact not to tell Abuela about their stepfather. Afraid if they told, their stepfather would make them move again.

She and Byron were used to keeping secrets. The first time her stepfather hurt Byron, she walked all the way by herself to the church and told the priest. The priest's Anglo face had whitened, and he'd turned away. He told her to go home and stop speaking lies about her father.

Byron fussed when she returned to the trailer on the rez. Scared the priest would tell their stepfather and next time it'd be worse. Though she wasn't sure it could get worse.

Mainly, though, Byron was ashamed. He didn't want anyone to know what happened when their stepfather started drinking. During the workweek, their stepfather was a model employee. Organized, efficient, hardworking.

On the weekends, he drank. Not enough to get drunk. Just enough to let loose the mean, Byron said. To forget, Pilar realized as she grew older, what had been done to him as a boy, shipped off in another day and age to the Indian boarding school. A threat he hung over her and Byron's heads. A taunt at how lucky they were to have him instead of being sent away to the mercy of Anglo strangers.

By the age of ten, she also understood something else. There was no mercy. No grace like the priest talked about on Sunday mornings. No goodness. Only secrets.

And survival.

"We're going to get out of here," Byron whispered as she bandaged the cuts their stepfather had made with his fists. "We're going to leave this godforsaken rez and make something of ourselves. You and me."

He bit off a groan.

Pilar's tears fell onto his bruised cheek.

"Stop that, Sister." He wiped her tears away with the pad of his thumb. "Apaches don't cry. We get even."

And because it was Byron's secret to tell, she kept silent. How could she not when every night Byron stood between her and the sickness that drove their stepfather?

Her mama had been dead a month the first time their stepfather came for her.

"Run." Byron shoved Pilar toward her bedroom. "Lock the door. No matter what you hear, don't open it until I tell you."

And then Byron offered himself in her place.

Making a bargain with the devil.

"I won't let him hurt you, Sister. I'll keep you safe. I'm not going to let him take away your chance."

But the second summer after Alex came, when she was fourteen, her time finally came. Her stepfather watched her when he believed no one was looking. And Byron became increasingly desperate to protect her.

They never told a soul as the tension grew thick. Not Abuela. Not any of the Anglo, Latino, or Apache cowboys Abuela employed on the Torres spread. Certainly not Byron's best friend, Alex.

Byron would rather die than have Alex know what happened at the foreman's house after the sun went down. Die before Alex learned what Byron endured to protect Pilar.

And one June night while Alex visited cousins in Texas, time ran out for Pilar.

"Run, Sister." Byron's voice choked with fear. "Go. Now."

He pushed her inside her bedroom and slammed the door shut. "Lock it, Sister. Push the dresser in front," he called from the other side.

She grabbed the iron skillet she'd hidden underneath her bed. Reining in the sobs as Byron taught her, she held the heavy frying pan aloft with both hands. She listened at the sounds coming from the living room.

Byron's low-voiced responses to their stepfather's enraged shouts. But Byron was unable this time to divert their stepfather. Unable to quench the fire in their stepfather's gullet.

When he finished with Byron, she heard his heavy tread coming down the hall. She tensed. Somehow, Byron got between their stepfather and her door.

This time Byron fought. This time he stood his ground.

But the burly Apache was stronger than the sixteen-year-old boy. And Pilar couldn't stand it any longer. She couldn't stand being afraid. She was tired of running and cowering.

Grunting with each blow to Byron's midsection, her stepfather didn't hear her unlock the door.

He didn't hear the door squeak as she flung it wide.

The man never looked up from beating Byron until she swung the skillet against the back of his head with a strength she hadn't known she possessed.

Staggering, her stepfather collapsed against the wall.

His eyes widened at the sight of the skillet she gripped, traces of his blood and hair matted to the black surface. Maddened, his face transformed with pure rage. Snarling, he lunged.

She swung again.

With one last blow, in a sickening crunch of bone, the metal made contact with his face.

He landed not far from where Byron lay in a pool of blood. Wheezing noises came from what had once been her stepfather's nose. Blood gurgled between his lips.

She slumped against the wall. The skillet slipped from her hand and clanged against the floor. Her chest heaving, she sucked in a breath of oxygen.

Byron moaned.

Her eyes flicked from him to their stepfather.

Pilar surged over their prostrate forms and toward the phone in the kitchen. Abuela would know what to do, how to help Byron. Pilar would go to jail for what she'd done, but she'd saved Byron.

She wasn't sure what she said after Abuela answered on the first ring. But Isabel Torres, her long, silver hair unbound and streaming down her back, arrived not five minutes later. Backed against the wall between Byron and her stepfather, Pilar squatted in the narrow hallway, her chin propped on her knees.

Isabel's breath hitched. In a glance, Abuela took in the situation. Comprehension dawned in Abuela's dark eyes. She spoke to someone over her shoulder.

For the first time, Pilar noticed the Apache cowboy at Isabel's side. He was dark, darker than her or Byron. And despite the spectacle she and Byron presented, his face reflected neither surprise nor anything else. She'd seen him around the ranch before.

Mostly evenings on the veranda with Abuela. Or riding far, far away toward the horizon. He came and went according to whim. Returning to work when he ran out of money. Leaving for his own pursuits when flush with cash.

Abuela gestured toward Pilar's stepfather, coughing blood. "These children are under my protection, Segundo."

Segundo? Her second?

At the sight of the Apache's fearsome face—mapped like the canyonlands, full of scars and chasms—Pilar squeezed her arms around her drawn knees.

The Apache surveyed the battered form of her stepfather. "Understood, Doña." His slightly skewed right eye went dull as a winter's day. "It will be taken care of."

Pilar shivered as if something cold and dreadful had walked over her grave.

"We must all adapt or die." Abuela extended her hand to Pilar. "Come, child. Let me help you."

Her gaze ping-ponging between the sinister-looking cowboy and her dear abuela, Pilar inched up the wall.

The Apache reached for the skillet at her feet.

Hissing, Pilar snatched it from the floor and cradled it against her chest.

One corner of the Apache's mouth lifted into what may have passed for a smile.

To Pilar, it more likely resembled a grimace.

But with great deliberation, the Apache offered his hand.

"Pilar?" Isabel coaxed.

And at Abuela's urging, Pilar surrendered her weapon to the Apache.

Isabel placed an arm around Pilar and led her out toward the brightly lit hacienda. Hefting Byron into his arms, the Apache deposited her brother inside and departed.

Pilar never saw the Apache cowboy again.

She also never saw her stepfather again.

Tending Byron, Isabel hastened to assure Pilar she hadn't killed the wicked man.

Leaving Pilar unsure if she was glad or sad about this fact.

She returned to the foreman's house the next day to find all traces of blood and tissue wiped clean.

And when Alex returned to the ranch, he found Byron and Pilar ensconced at the big house in rooms of their own. To the best of her knowledge, Alex never knew what happened that night—or before—to her and Byron.

"We will not speak of this again," Isabel told her.

Apaches weren't the only ones, Pilar discovered, who could keep secrets.

Isabel telephoned the San Carlos Tribal Child Protective Services and explained how the children's stepfather simply walked away without a word.

Although Pilar was fairly sure her stepfather hadn't walked anywhere. Carried, maybe. Disappeared, for certain.

The highly respected Doña Isabel Torres was taken at *her* word. Child Protective Services left Pilar and Byron in Abuela's loving foster embrace for good.

And life, as Pilar entered high school, became good, too.

Because indeed, Abuela's superpower was her ability to make everything right.

9

THE SHRILL RINGING OF HIS CELL WOKE Alex BEFORE SIX A.M. Praying another girl hadn't been taken last night, he half-fell out of bed in his haste to answer the call. But it wasn't Charles or Sidd or the tribal detective he'd yet to meet.

It was Manny To-Clanny.

"You gave me your card yesterday and said if I ever needed you..." The boy's voice sounded muffled. "I need you now. Actually, it's Auntie who needs you now."

"What's wrong, Manny?" Alex's tone sharpened. "Are you alright? Is Pilar—?"

"She's not alright. I can't get her to unlock the bathroom door. When she screamed, I found her on the bathroom floor, surrounded by broken glass. She..." Manny took a deep breath. "She's cutting herself. I-I don't know what to do." The boy's voice rose and ended with a whispered sob. "She yelled at me to get out. Then she slammed the door and locked it."

Alex squeezed his eyes shut. *Oh, God.*

"Please, Mr. Torres."

"Call me Alex."

"I never told anybody about what she does after one of her nightmares. I never told Abuela, though I think she knows. I shouldn't have left Auntie alone when she woke up. But she's been better for so long, I didn't think—"

"This isn't your fault, Manny."

66

"Something bad—really bad—happened to my auntie before, didn't it, Alex?"

"Yeah," Alex whispered into the phone.

He, Alejandro Roberto Torres, happened to Pilar.

"I think maybe only you can fix her, Alex."

Alex sank onto the bed, his head in his hand. "I'll come right away. But it's God, not me, who'll help her, Manny."

Help me to help her, God.

"You plus God, I'm sure of it." Manny sighed. "'Cause it's your name, Alex, she calls for in the dark."

A fist pounded the door. The wood rattled against the frame. "Open the door, Pilar. It's Alex."

Curled into a ball on the bathroom floor, her eyes widened.

Not him. Anybody but him.

How had—? Manny must've called him. The look on Manny's face when he spotted the jagged shard of glass in her hand...

Oh, God. Pilar shuddered. She was so broken.

Lines of blood flowed down her arm.

More fist pounding. "Pilar? Answer me."

She had no business raising Manny. No wonder he was getting into fights and about to join a gang. She was so messed up. Too messed up to be playing mother.

And now for Alex to see her like this?

She pressed a towel against the cut to staunch the bleeding.

"Pilar, if you don't open this door right now, I'm going to break it down."

"Leave me alone," she shouted, her heart thundering.

"Good," he yelled. "Glad to see you're still in the land of the living. You've got until the count of three and then—"

"Just go away, Torres."

"One..."

A soft thud against the door panel as if his shoulder tested its strength.

She scowled. "Manny shouldn't have called you. There's no reason for you to be all up in my business."

"Two...Might be a good idea to climb into the bathtub so the door doesn't land on your head."

"I hate-hate-hate you, Alex Torres!" she screamed.

"So you've said before," his voice thickened. "Three...I warned you, Pia."

"And I told you," she scrambled to her feet, unlocked and jerked open the door. "To stop calling me—"

Caught off-guard in the middle of ramming the door, Alex's momentum carried him over the threshold. He barreled into her. She shrieked.

The both of them reeled backward in the grip of gravity.

Wrapping his arms around her, Alex pivoted, and turned. He—they—landed. His back took the brunt of their fall.

The breath knocked from her lungs, her head collided with his. Alex's lips brushed across her cheek. Her nerve endings jolted from more than the force of the impact.

She pushed at his shoulder. "Get off me, Alex."

Manny poked his head inside. "You two okay?"

"He's got a hard head," she grunted. "He'll be fine."

Alex massaged his forehead. "I'm not the only one."

"You can let go of me now, Alex," she huffed.

His gaze flitted from her eyes to her mouth and back again. "I could..." He tightened his one-armed hold around her waist. "Letting go works both ways, Pia."

Both arms locked around his neck, she reddened.

She planted a hand on his stomach to leverage herself and shoved. He let out a whoosh of air, groaning. Rolling off him, she stumbled to her feet.

Using the tub for support, Alex hoisted himself upright. His eyes flicked to the bloody towel, and then his gaze fastened onto the mirror. He went rigid.

Manny frowned. "*Mia.* Did you write that, Auntie?"

Her attention fixed on Alex's reflection. "No," she whispered. "I didn't."

Alex's face underwent a kaleidoscope of transformation. From thin-lipped shock to lip-curled rage.

Manny's eyes enlarged. "Somebody broke in?" His head rotated as if an intruder lurked in the corners of the bathroom. "Who, Auntie? What does 'Mia' mean?"

"It means..." Her eyes dropped to the floor. She couldn't bear to see Alex's expression. "That the Wicked One has found me. Again."

This couldn't be happening.

She sounded so resigned. Beyond fear. As if somehow she'd known all along, the beast from whom she'd barely escaped would find her again. As if deep inside she'd always known she'd never truly outrun him.

Alex scrubbed his hand over his face as he made the call for the team to do a forensic sweep of the break-in at Pilar's. Perhaps the serial killer had for once left traces of his identity. Justice was long overdue in this case. He'd been hunting this particular monster for three years.

He checked the rest of the house. "Let me know if you think anything appears missing."

With careful instructions to disturb as little as possible, he herded Manny to his bedroom while Pilar got dressed. She emerged, head down, eyes on the tips of her regulation shoes and headed for the kitchen. "Okay, if I make coffee?"

It gutted Alex to see how she wouldn't—couldn't—meet his gaze. As if her admission of what happened so long ago shamed her so completely.

"The team would appreciate it, I'm sure. But Pilar, this invasion wasn't your fault. Nothing that happened was your fault."

He stuffed his hands inside his trouser pockets. What he wanted was to take her into his arms and soothe every hurt she'd ever suffered.

But he knew better. Comfort wasn't something she'd accept from him. Least of all from him. She hated him and rightly so. What happened to her—the reason she fell into this devil's hands—had been his fault entirely.

The long sleeves of her uniform shirt hid the telltale scars on her arms. From his brief glance in the bathroom, old scars except for the recent cut.

She removed the coffee grounds from the refrigerator and scooped several tablespoons into the coffeemaker. "Excuse me..." She edged past him in the tiny galley kitchen to fill the carafe with water.

He backed against the countertop. His hand went to the silver chain he always wore underneath his shirt. His fingers rubbed the black volcanic rock against his flesh.

"You already knew it was the same perpetrator, didn't you, Alex."

Not a question, a statement.

She shut off the water. "How did you know?"

Alex folded his arms. "By the marks he leaves."

She sagged against the sink. "You knew about—?" Her shoulders slumped. "I thought—I hoped—no one else knew what he did to me."

"We believe you were his first victim, Pilar."

"I'm nobody's victim."

She poured the water into the coffeemaker. "You think he was still perfecting his MO and that's why I managed to escape." She started the coffeemaker.

"Manny told me about the nightmares. Probably your mind's attempt to deal with the trauma."

Pilar's mouth hardened. "I believe psychiatrists call it 'delayed onset post-traumatic stress.'" Her lip curled. "Not that I've spent much time with them. Talking about what happened is the last thing I want to do."

"I thank God every day you escaped."

"God?" She whirled, the familiar defiance in her eyes. "What's God ever done for me?"

The chip-on-her-shoulder Pilar Alex knew and loved. The broken Pilar undid him.

She jutted her hip. "That's why you came home, isn't it? You think if I remember everything you'll catch this monster."

"He's left a trail of bodies from New Mexico to Arizona. And the ones he didn't kill outright..." Alex swallowed. "Once he gets them over the border, they simply disappear."

She glared at him. "You banked on the fact he'd come looking for me."

Alex blew out a breath. "Fact is, Pilar, we suspect he's never stopped looking for you. The others—his sick attempts to replicate you. Finding you, I fear, has been his obsession."

Her mouth twisted. "The one who got away?"

"The *only* one who ever got away until this wild girl stumbled north across the border last month."

"So you bided your time." She balled her fist. "Allowing his web to tighten around Manny and me. Using me as bait."

Alex shook his head. "It wasn't like that. I'd never—"

"Well, news flash." She got in his face. "I don't remember anything more than what I told the detective in the ER all those years ago."

Alex jabbed his finger in the air. "You shut down. You don't want to remember anything more."

"I went catatonic, you mean." She threw him a hard look. "Surely you got enough semen from the evidence kit for a match."

Alex flushed. "He's somehow managed to fly under the radar. With nothing in the system to match it to, we haven't been able to link the-the..." He'd never been able to actually verbalize what had been done to Pilar. "...the DNA to anyone."

The aroma of strong coffee wafted through the kitchen. She opened a cabinet and removed several mugs. "I can't believe even you would want me to relive those four days of hell."

Her words flayed him. "*Even* me?" Alex crushed the stone against his heart.

At the movement of his hand, her brow knotted.

"Healing may only come in the remembering and in the catharsis of telling, Pilar."

She banged the cabinet door shut. "Thanks, but no thanks, *Dr. Torres.* I'm doing okay."

"Are you?" He gestured at her arm. "Doesn't look like you're doing okay, Pia. Not from where I stand."

She hugged her arm to her chest. "Then maybe you should stand away from me."

"They're here," Manny bellowed at the sound of tires on the gravel.

"Shouldn't be too hard, Alex, to stay away." She headed toward the living room. "An art form you've perfected in the dozen years since I last saw you."

Not by choice. If only she knew what forcing himself to stay away had cost him....He followed her out of the kitchen.

"What're you doing with the file?" She snatched the folder from Manny's hand. "This is official police business."

LISA CARTER

Manny gulped. "Is that what the Wicked One did to you, Auntie? Like the dead girls in the photos? I'm not a little kid anymore. I need to know these things. I will protect you."

The boy pounded his chest. "On my life. My word of honor."

"Oh, honey." Pilar placed her palm on his cheek. "I don't want you anywhere near this monster."

She bit her lip. "Maybe you should stay with Fiona in North Carolina until Byron returns from his deployment."

"No, Auntie, please." Manny wilted into the little boy Alex supposed he'd been not so long ago. "We take care of each other."

Her mouth trembled. "I should've realized he'd come back for me. I should've never kept you—"

"Don't send me away, Auntie." Manny's arms engulfed Pilar. "I don't want to live with Fiona and Dad after they get married." He buried his head into her shoulder. "I want to stay with you."

"You know about their upcoming wedding?" She lifted his face with her hands. "You never said anything. You'd have two parents to love you. Normalcy. Security."

"But I wouldn't have you."

Outside, car doors slammed.

She sighed, but a smile licked at the corners of her full lips. "I love you, Manny."

The boy brought out a tenderness in Pilar Alex hadn't seen since they were teenagers.

Manny tilted his head. "I love you, too, Auntie." He also possessed considerable charm when he put his mind to it. "Can I stay?"

Her hand stroked his hair. "For now. But I can't let anything happen to you, Manny." Her voice went ragged. "I-I wouldn't survive that."

Alex cleared his throat and opened the door to his team. "Neither of you will be staying here. I'm relocating you both to Abuela's where you'll be safe."

"Good idea for Manny. But me?" She straightened. "No way I'm letting you track this psycho without me. You need me, Torres. You won't catch him without me and you know it."

Of all the stubborn, hardheaded...

But with a sinking feeling, Alex feared she might be right.

72

10

LATER, THE TEAM REASSEMBLED AT ABUELA'S WOOD-BEAMED hacienda for a strategy meeting.

The willowy blonde settled beside Pilar on the chili-red sofa. "So you're the one."

Pilar's eyebrows arched in her best imitation of the indomitable Doña Isabel. "The one who?"

Emily Waters laughed. "The one who ruined the elusive, hunky Alex Torres for women for all time."

Pilar sniffed. "Elusive? Alex Torres and women?"

"Oh, it's true. And true that women adore Alex." Emily gave her a wry smile. "Maybe because he *is* so elusive."

Pilar rolled her eyes. "Women have always adored Alex Torres."

"I can see why."

Pilar went rigid.

Emily smiled. "Just a scientific observation. No need to go territorial."

"I'm not territorial." She lifted her chin. "Alex Torres is not my... We—"

"Whatever you say, Officer To-Clanny." Emily held out her hand. A diamond ring caught the light. "I've got my own cowboy. Not interested in your"—at Pilar's motion of protest—"*vaquero*. He's all yours."

Pilar pursed her lips. "Hardly."

"I suspect—since whatever went down between the two of you— he's always been yours."

"You're wrong."

Oh, how Pilar wished she wasn't.

"He's the one who walked away from me, Dr. Waters. Not the other way around. And it's been well over a decade."

"Don't see a ring on your finger. Married? Engaged? Boyfriend?"

Pilar chewed her lip. "I steer clear, thanks to Alex Torres, of relationships. Not worth it."

"Not worth it or you've never found anyone to replace Alex?"

Pilar shifted, the forensic anthropologist hitting too close to the mark. "Trying to psychobabble me, Dr. Waters?"

"I've known Alex a long time. Though not as long or as well, I'm sure, as you."

Pilar dropped her eyes. "I have a hard time believing a ladies' man like Alex has ever denied himself. He's not the monk type."

"The Alex I know is an insightful leader and team player. He fraternizes off-duty with the other agents but when the party's over, he goes home alone."

Definitely not the wild Alex Pilar remembered. She wondered what else about Alex had changed. And wondered why she couldn't seem to stop caring.

At the sound of the doorbell, Abuela ushered in San Carlos Tribal Detective Woodrow Kenoi. Pilar patted the seat cushion beside her. Woodrow eased his bandy-legged frame onto the sofa.

Returning from the kitchen, Alex stopped mid-stride. "Kenoi," he hissed.

"Tribal Detective Kenoi, Torres," Woodrow grunted.

Woodrow's broad face creased. "You okay, Pilar?"

She nodded. Woodrow's shoulder brushed her sleeve.

Alex stormed over to the stone fireplace. "Team report."

Draping himself over "his" chair at Abuela's, Manny's eyes dared Pilar to make him leave. Abuela sank into the leather wingback beside the giant hearth.

Alex's eyes widened. "Seriously, Abuela?"

Isabel gathered her knitting needles from the table at her elbow and raised one eyebrow at her grandson.

Alex swiveled to Manny. "The subject matter isn't kid-friendly, either."

Manny scowled.

Alex fisted his hands on his hips. "Pilar?"

She sighed. "Manny, he's right—"

"No more secrets." Manny hunkered into the recliner. "I'm tired of secrets, Auntie."

Ouch...

Swallowing, she gave Alex an apologetic shrug. "If you think you can eject him, be my guest. Otherwise..."

Alex muttered something under his breath about pigheaded so and so's she figured wasn't complimentary to her or Manny's lineage. Then, "Charles, what do we have thus far?"

"Detective Kenoi helped us ID the most recent victim." The Asian-American glanced at a paper in his hand. "Violet Robertson. Sixteen. Disappeared about six weeks ago." Charles passed the photo around the room.

Pilar studied the pretty features of the girl found in the shallow canyon grave whose remains rested in the tribe's morgue. This could've been her once upon a time. Her chest tightened as she handed the photo to Emily.

Alex raked his hand through his dark hair. "And the other vic, Sidd?"

Pilar's fingernails clawed her palms at the remembered feel of his curls. She cut her eyes toward the wall of windows overlooking the rugged Peloncillo range.

"Ramón Aqnitso. The second body turned out to be Violet's boyfriend. Autopsy results, Em?"

Emily grimaced. "It's bad. Worse than what he does to the females."

Pilar's stomach cramped. She couldn't imagine worse—didn't want to imagine worse—than what he'd done to her.

She felt Alex's gaze on her, and she bit her lip so hard she tasted the metallic taste of her own blood.

Alex angled to Manny and Abuela. "Last chance before the gory details come out."

Neither responded.

Emily moistened her lips. "Staked to the desert floor over an ant hill, Ramon was cut multiple times. Cuts usually associated with a cartel reprisal." She hesitated. "Including his eyelids."

Isabel gasped. Manny turned a greenish shade.

Alex straightened. "Cause of death?"

"He baked to death in the hot Arizona sun as best I can determine."

"We think," Woodrow added in his quiet, steady voice. "When this sadist grabbed his girlfriend, Ramón—a high school junior—went after Violet and her assailant."

Pilar's heart lurched. Ramón could've been Manny.

Alex's jaw tightened. "Nobody deserves to die like that."

Isabel clutched one of the knitting needles as if a knife. "Why weren't they found until now if they went missing almost six weeks ago, Woody?"

Woodrow blew out a breath. "Sources indicated they might've run away together as they'd been threatening. And where to look? The rez is so vast, so..." He lifted and dropped his shoulders.

"No one found them," Pilar gritted her teeth. "Because Anglo law enforcement and their resources don't get motivated unless a white kid gets snatched and murdered."

Her eyes shot to Alex. "You know what I'm saying is true."

"What do we know about this son of a—?" Alex clamped his lips together. "What profile have you worked up for the perpetrator, Darlene?"

Darlene's limpid blue eyes hardened. "He's a cruel one. Narcissistic. He gets off on control and humiliation. Probably has a coercive disorder. He targets Apache women for whatever inexplicable reason."

"Because violence here is multigenerational." Pilar fisted her hands. "Because with so many dysfunctional families, they're easy pickings. One in three Indian women will be sexually violated at some point in their lives."

And what she didn't say—often violated by a husband, a father, an uncle, cousin, or brother.

"With this creep, those who fight, die." Darlene's eyes flitted to Pilar. "Unless they escape."

She met Darlene's gaze. "And I'm the only one who's ever escaped him and lived."

"As for what he does with the ones he manages to take over the border?" Darlene shrugged.

"The fun and games continue I imagine."

Alex stiffened at Pilar's forcibly dry tone.

Darlene locked eyes with her. "He despises women and as a sociopath most likely—"

"Try psychopath," she corrected Darlene.

"Not in the true definition of the term. Psychopaths are social oddities. They stand out in the general population. Sociopaths like this perp have managed their entire lives to blend seamlessly into society without anyone ever noticing their aberrations. They're often intelligent and successful in their chosen careers."

Alex gripped Manny's chair. "And somehow this nut job manages to infiltrate the United States, abduct, murder, and / or transport women across the border."

Woodrow stirred. "Makes you wonder what he does for a living enabling him to travel so freely back and forth, doesn't it?"

"I'm working that angle, Detective." Sidd looked up from his laptop. "We've also never been able to pinpoint his route over the border. Nothing jumps out from the official border crossing footage."

Sidd distributed a sheaf of papers. "And then there's the third body we found."

Pilar's breath hitched at the skeletal remains of yet another mutilated corpse.

Sidd assumed a professorial tone. "Dead, Em estimates, at least a year. Probably around the perigee last year. Several other bodies, New Mexico side, indicate he's roamed at will across both states and multiple Apache reservations for the last decade. The kills skip years. He seems to hunt only during the years and months that contain the supermoon."

"His trigger for whatever dark reason." Alex pursed his lips. "We're dealing with a ruthless man without conscience or boundaries—either geographically, physically, or psychologically speaking."

Isabel crossed herself. "*Malvado*, wicked."

"He probably suffered abuse as a child. Or was exposed early to someone else's suffering," Darlene expounded. "Physical and emotional, for sure. Sexual, probable. He's operating out of an overwhelming urge to expunge the hurt he endured or witnessed by acting out the wounding on others. He's attempting to master control over a situation he likely was unable to control as a child."

The new cut burned on Pilar's arm underneath her sleeve. Her attempt to expunge the wound on her soul. Her attempt to exert control over the uncontrollable.

Sidd clicked a key on the laptop. "Except for the boy, the two females were killed elsewhere and their bodies dumped in the canyon. We ID'd the third body. Desiree Mendoza."

Pilar cut her eyes at Woodrow. "Her name we know."

"I worked that case." Woodrow frowned. "Her pimp reported her missing fourteen months ago. Witnesses say she was last seen leaving an off-rez bar with a potential john. Of course, the witnesses were either too drunk or high or afraid to give an accurate description."

"A hooker?" Alex rubbed his jaw. "That fits the profile of the New Mexico victims. This guy's about opportunity and easy access. He prowls the local bars, although so far he's been too smart to get caught on videotape. The women are mid- to late-teens."

"Throwaways." Pilar lifted her chin. "The neglected or prostitutes he figures nobody cares about."

She'd been two out of the three.

Pilar reached an inescapable decision. "And we've got less than forty-eight hours before his next killing spree with tomorrow night's full moon. Time for a game changer. Time to let him feel what it's like to be hunted."

Alex tensed. "What are you proposing?"

She took a breath. "Let me go undercover. Let's nab this animal for good."

"Absolutely not." A sick panic welled in Alex's gut. "No way."

"It's the only way," Pilar countered. "I've done this before on a joint task force with the Sheriff's Vice Unit and the tribal police. We need to lure this monster out of the shadows."

His heart stuttered. "I told you I won't use you as bait. I won't allow—" he bit off his words. "I can't allow—"

"She may be right, Alex." Charles held up both hands. "Hear her out."

Alex clenched his jaw. "Another agent maybe."

"He's got a thing," Pilar's mouth seemed to turn inside out. "An unholy attraction to Apache women. Anglo agents won't draw him."

"Uh, guys?" Manny raised his hand.

Alex willed himself to take it down a notch. "What is it, son?"

Pilar's brow creased.

Manny shuffled through the photos. "I'm not sure this dirtbag's Mexican." He glanced up. "No offense, Alex."

Alex's lips twitched and he uncoiled another notch. "No offense taken, Manny. I'm not Mexican. I'm from L.A."

Pilar rolled her eyes. "Why don't you think he's Mexican, Manuel?"

"He may live in Mexico, but are you sure he's Mexican?"

Alex peered at the photo Manny clutched. "What makes you think he's not Mexican? You think he's Anglo?"

"Not Anglo. This dude's MO"—Manny's eyes darted around the room—"*Modus operandi*, right?"

Manny pointed at the faint circles in the dust Sidd photographed at the canyon crime scene. About five inches in diameter. "These track marks remind me of how the Apaches used to sew buckskin over the hooves of their horses before a raid."

Woodrow inched to the edge of the couch. "You think this guy's an Apache, preying on Apache women?"

Manny shrugged. "Maybe Mexican. But a Mexican obsessed with the Apache old ways."

Alex cocked his head. "You think this guy travels across the border on horseback?"

Manny flushed. "I know it sounds crazy, but the eyelid business . . ."

Pilar grimaced. "True. Never been real interested in the old ways unlike Manny, but that's what they did to some captives. That and worse. Especially the soldiers they caught. We're a bloodthirsty lot, I guess."

"Miz Clum's the real expert." Manny pushed the photo at Alex. "She'd know. Heck, she's so old she was probably around the last time the Apaches raided Arizona."

Alex scrutinized the photo. "Talitha Clum, whose property borders the canyon?"

"The one and the same." Pilar tilted her head. "And she can't be that old, Manny."

"Last recorded raid was Douglas, Arizona, 1924. In Mexico, the raids lasted much longer. Into the 1940s."

Everyone turned at Abuela's soft-spoken rejoinder.

Darlene's eyes widened. "Like World War II 1940s?"

The crinkles in Abuela's face lifted. "My father had just returned from the Pacific when a distant cousin's ranch in Mexico was raided."

Sidd removed his hands from the keyboard. "I thought the Apache Wars were over by the turn of the twentieth century."

Pilar smirked. "Yeah, most like Geronimo and Naiche already captured and placed in Florida concentration camps for the next twenty-plus years. Or at least that's what happened to my army scout ancestor so I'm told. So much for government employee loyalty, eh Torres?"

Manny leaned forward. "After the last bands surrendered to the army, some managed to escape off the train headed for the Florida swamps. They joined groups who never surrendered but remained out of the American government's reach on the Mexico side."

Woodrow studied the photo. "Where they harassed Mexican farmers and American cattle ranchers for years well into the twentieth century until the Mexican and American armies joined forces to wage war on them from both sides of the border."

"Twenty dollars for a male scalp. Ten for a woman or child's."

Again, everyone stared at Alex's grandmother.

"Not so much a war, as an annihilation." Abuela's eyes flickered. "My father's father took part in the 1930s revenge expedition that searched for the lost Fimbres boy taken by The Wild Ones."

Charles frowned. "Wild Ones?"

Pilar sighed. "They're rez legends, Abuela. Not real."

His grandmother folded her arms. "Also called the Bronco Apaches, those who remained in the mountain strongholds of the Sierra Madre."

Pilar angled. "Boogeymen the Old Ones use to get children to obey."

She imitated the singsong guttural tone of an Old One, whose first language had been anything but English. "Better not hang around after dark in the mountains or the Broncos will carry you away."

Manny nodded. "Rumor has it these renegade Apaches crossed the border many times over the decades in which they'd supposedly been tamed. To acquire Apache brides and reinforce their dwindling blood line."

Abuela positioned her feet flat on the hardwood floor. "It's said they took brides—willing or not—back to the Sierra Azul where they were never heard from again. Mexican girls, too."

"The Blue Mountain?" Alex squinted. "You think wild Apaches still roam the Sierra Madre? In this day and age?"

Abuela's eyes slid toward the window. "One of the ancient trading routes crossed these mountains from Arizona through the New Mexico bootheel and into Mexico." Her eyelids fell to half-mast. "My father showed me once. A long time ago."

"Interesting." Alex turned his attention to the case. "But only relevant if this monster's acting out some weird Apache Bronco fantasy."

"We need to interview Talitha Clum." Pilar rose. "Do you know the old woman, Abuela?"

His grandmother shook her head. "No."

Alex itched to catch this killer before he harmed anyone else. "We'll inter—"

"She doesn't like Mexicans." Manny gave Alex a sheepish look. "She won't care you were born in L.A."

"Woodrow and I can handle this." Pilar planted her hands on her hips. "Leave the *really* important jobs to you feds." Smiling, she nudged Detective Kenoi's shoulder.

Alex bristled. Apparently, the only person Pilar had trouble touching was him.

"Better take me, too." Manny bounced up. "She's old and cranky, but she likes me."

"He might be an asset." Pilar looked at Woodrow. "If he promises to do exactly as we tell him."

"I have a colleague," Emily stood. "A jaguar guardian who works with Arizona conservationists to protect the endangered species whose migratory patterns are threatened by the proposed border walls."

"A jaguar guardian?" Manny whistled. "Cool."

Emily smiled at the teenage boy. "Dr. Velarde also has a degree in cultural anthropology. He's an Apache expert, and his family owns a ranch at the foot of the Sierra Madre."

That piqued Alex's interest. This Velarde might prove useful in developing Alex's theory that the serial had ties to Salazar, the drug lord.

"I could arrange a meeting at his office at the community college. He could provide intel on whether our killer is indeed mimicking the customs of the Apache. Maybe allow us to get ahead of this perp and his next victim instead of always playing catch-up."

"Sounds like a good idea." Alex massaged his forehead. "See if you can set up a meet."

Emily began texting.

He pivoted to Pilar. "You and I will interview the old woman. But our discussion about this little undercover op you've suggested isn't over, Pia. Not by a long shot."

11

Before

SOMETHING PINGED IN ALEX'S CHEST WHEN PILAR APPEARED on the broad, curving staircase at the hacienda one night during his senior year. Without realizing it, he rose from the sofa.

His grandmother's black bean eyes glistened. "So lovely."

Pilar fingered the soft, spaghetti straps of her new party dress. Her expression alternated between an endearing mixture of uncertainty and a desperate desire for approval.

Byron crossed the foyer. "You clean up nice, Sister." He grinned.

Pilar's smoky black eyes shot to Alex.

He'd wondered over the years if tough, tomboy Pilar could do girl.

Question answered.

Yes.

She could.

He swallowed.

The thick, straight black hair—usually contained like a horse's mane in one long braid—hung free. Cascading around her almost bare shoulders. The orchid-colored dress teased her kneecaps and reflected well on the smooth, mocha color of her arms and face.

Pilar arched those perfect brows of hers like the wings of a butterfly. No longer his Cater-Pilar. A butterfly, which continued to beat Alex to the top of the mesa.

His heart did a curious thump.

The silence had lengthened too long, Alex realized, as Byron turned toward him.

Abuela nudged her chin at him. "Alex?"

"Nice, Pia." His voice cracked. Alex cleared his throat. "What's the occasion?"

The doorbell rang. Abuela motioned to Byron.

Pilar descended the staircase. Her manicured hand trailed the length of the banister. Alex's eyes remained locked on Pilar. Her gaze latched onto his.

"Come in, Woodrow."

Alex pivoted.

His hitherto beloved abuela ushered Woodrow Kenoi inside. The Kenoi boy from the track team clutched a corsage. He also stared full bore at Pilar.

Alex's stomach tightened.

Byron extended his hand. "Woodrow."

With an uncertain look, Woodrow grasped Byron's hand. When Byron's hand closed over Kenoi's, the track star winced.

Smirking, Alex crossed his arms over his chest. Message received. Good.

Pilar's brother would handle this... this intruder. Send this wannabe packing.

Alex flicked a glance toward Pilar. And was disconcerted to find her attention fixed not on Kenoi, but on him. As silent and impassive as only an Apache could be.

Byron clapped a hand on Kenoi's shoulder. "I want you two to have a great time tonight at the dance."

Alex growled.

Her plum-tinted lips curving upward, Pilar floated toward Kenoi. As did the scent of desert wildflowers.

Alex clenched his fists as Kenoi towered over Pilar. Her face upturned as Kenoi's stupid, thick paws attempted to pin the corsage to her dress. She giggled.

Giggled? Pilar? At this Neanderthal Apache?

Her eyes danced with laughter. "Can you help, Abuela?"

Alex wanted to puke.

His grandmother smiled. "Let me fix it."

At Kenoi's frank admiration for Pilar, Alex thought his head would explode. Alex moved toward Pilar.

Byron stopped him with a look. Unsmiling, Byron pushed him into the family room. "You need to back off, Alex."

He shook free of his best friend. "If you're not going to protect your sister's honor, somebody's got to."

Something dark engorged Byron's face.

Alex stepped back a pace.

"What do you know about my sister's honor?" Byron's lip curled. "I've seen your version of honor every Friday night in the backseat of Abuela's car. What was the girl's name last weekend, Alex? Do you even remember?"

"We're not talking about me, Byron."

Byron broadened his stance. "Oh, aren't we?"

Alex raked a hand across his close-cropped hair. "I'm talking about that Kenoi dude. You really want to trust Pia to that . . . that . . . ?"

The shorter, stockier Byron got in his face. "That guy who's going to be valedictorian of his class? From a nice family who attends Abuela's church? Who's going to get off this rez and make something of himself?"

"I don't trust Kenoi," Alex spat.

"Your problem is you think everyone treats women same as you." Byron stabbed a finger into Alex's chest. "But Pilar? She's. Not. For. You." A jab punctuated each word.

Alex backpedaled further.

"I won't let you ruin her chance for a good life. A happy life," Byron snarled. "You mess with her, Torres, and you're no friend of mine. I'll see you dead first."

Unnerved by the soft-spoken Byron's vehemence, Alex watched helpless as Pilar walked out the door on Kenoi's arm.

He spent a long, terrible night in his bedroom. Angry.

At Byron. At Pilar. At Abuela for not giving him a heads-up. Most of all at himself for the nonsensical way the sight of the almost-grownup version of Pilar affected him.

Him, Alejandro Roberto Torres.

King of the love 'em and leave 'em. The romantic embodiment of a rolling stone. The prince of "let's just have a good time."

Tossing and turning. Waiting for the jerk's truck to rattle across the cattle guard. Watching for the roof of the truck cab to roll through the Torres crossbars.

Panicked. Certain Pilar was in a situation over her head. Desperate but unable to do anything about it. Wanting to vomit every time he envisioned that sophomoric moron touching Pilar. His arms around her in a slow dance...

Alex tortured himself with futile thoughts of what usually came after high school dances. That son of a frybread-eater putting his hands on Pilar's skin. His mouth claiming hers.

He wanted to smash Kenoi's face. Alex's gut burned. He wanted... Alex buried his head in the pillow.

Mine.

Pilar was his.

Alex lifted his head. Why hadn't he understood before? Why didn't the rest of them see?

He punched his fist into the pillow.

Mine. Mine. Mine.

He fell back onto the headboard, his fury and fear exhausted.

And picturing the implacable resolve on Byron's face, Alex realized it might not matter what he wanted. Alex's well-deserved reputation with the ladies and his charm might actually work against him this time.

Because this time, Pilar might not want him.

12

ALEX AND MANNY TOSSED BASKETBALL STATS OVER THE SEAT of the SUV like bosom buddies.

Pilar remained quiet during the drive to Talitha Clum's remote dwelling on the edge of the rez. It was hard to adjust to Alex's renewed presence in her life. Harder still to adjust to the funny things his proximity did to her heart.

After a bone-jarring ride, Alex pulled to a stop under the lone shade of a juniper on a ridge high above the slotted canyonlands. Dust continued to swirl as he switched off the engine. "Kind of desolate for an old woman. She lives alone?"

Pilar's gaze swept the dilapidated adobe home and the old-fashioned wickiup a few yards away. "A real recluse. One of the most traditional of the Old Ones."

Manny gestured to the rusted, paint-peeling truck circa 1964. "She drives to town to buy groceries at the trading post and volunteers at the teen center. She says if those like her don't pass on our heritage, what makes us Apache will die out."

Pilar eyed the conical-shaped wickiup. "She lives in that thing or is it for show?"

Manny shook his head. "Miz Clum uses it in the summer. She's going to show us the proper way to build one next spring at the teen center so we won't forget our ways."

Pilar made a face. "Give me central heat and air any day. I'm all for keeping our heritage, but progress is progress."

Manny scowled. "Miz Clum says that's what's wrong with Apaches like you today. Gone soft."

Alex laughed.

Pilar stiffened. "I ain't soft."

"...Sold out to the Anglos for cable and lattes."

Pilar pivoted in the seat. "Cable and lattes? For your information, I drink my joe black and strong. I'm no apple."

Alex's eyebrow rose. "A what?"

"Red on the outside, white on the inside." Manny hunched his shoulders. "And some of us aren't even red on the outside."

Where had that come from?

She leaned against the gray upholstery. "Progress includes education, smallpox vaccinations, and interlibrary loan, Manny."

Manny huffed. "Miz Clum says real Apache men—"

"Real Apache men get a good education and a good job so they can take care of their families." Pilar flung out her hands. "Real Apache men don't disrespect girls like Reyna, and they certainly don't get kicked out of school."

Manny kicked the seat.

Alex reached for the door handle.

She laid a hand on his arm. "Wait."

Alex's eyes dropped to her hand.

Pilar tucked her hand into the pockets of her cargo pants. "We'll get nothing out of a traditional like her unless we follow Apache protocol."

"Sorry. In the Anglo world too long." Alex stared out the windshield. "You think she knows we're out here?"

Pilar smiled. "She's letting us cool our heels and asserting her right to talk or not talk to us. This SUV screams *fed*. No love lost between Apaches and the feds."

"Or Mexicans," Manny reminded. "She may've spotted Alex and decided not to talk to anyone."

Pilar cut a glance at Alex. "I know the feeling."

"I'm not Mexican." Alex clenched his teeth. "I'm from L.A."

"Close enough." She glanced at the clock on the dashboard. "Step out of the vehicle, Manny. She likes you."

Manny hopped out. And an old woman emerged—perhaps one of the oldest Pilar had seen in a people noted for their longevity.

Her face was a myriad of wrinkles, her clothing the three-tiered traditional skirt and Mexican overblouse favored by more traditional Apaches. Plus the one long, white braid, also typical Apache.

Talitha Clum shuffled to the porch railing and motioned. A double-gauge shotgun rested casually across her folded arms.

Alex shot Pilar a look before easing out of the SUV. "How old did you say she was? And she still drives?"

"You gonna be the one to try to take her license and trigger another Indian war?"

Manny threw out a hand in greeting. "*Dagot'ee*, Miz Clum."

The old woman's beady black eyes softened. "*Dagot'ee*, So-kus-n."

Pilar frowned. What was with the *So-kus-n* business?

Alex moved forward. "I'm Special Agent Alex Torres, Ms. Clum. I'd like to ask you some questions regarding a homicide."

The old woman's gaze hardened. "Why'd you bring that Mexican here?"

Pilar fought amusement at Alex's exasperated breath. She stepped around the Mexican-American federal agent. "I represent the tribal police, and we're investigating the murder of three teenagers in the box canyon not far from here. My name is—"

"I've heard of you." Talitha Clum gestured to the slatted wooden chairs. "You and the boy sit." Her eyes, with the pronounced epicanthic fold common to Apaches, blazed at Alex. "He can stay right where he is—in the dirt."

Pilar sashayed past Alex toward the porch. At last, another female who didn't swoon in Alex Torres's exalted presence. Give the old lady points for putting Mr. Charm in his place.

Talitha Clum settled into the rocker. With a significant look at Alex, she lay the gun across the armrests within easy reach.

"Auntie," Pilar used the Apache term of respect for a female elder. "Three bodies were found not far from your home. At the entrance to the box canyon. Three young people."

Talitha's gaze swept upward at the cry of a red-tailed hawk.

"We wondered if you might have any information that could lead to their killer."

Talitha's eyes followed the swirling loops of the bird's flight above the canyon.

Manny leaned forward. "Violet Robertson. Ramón Aqnitso. Desiree Mendoza."

The old woman's eyes dropped to Manny. "I shared our ways with them at the Teen Center. But they weren't as interested in their heritage as you, So-kus-n."

Pilar's mouth tightened. "His name's not—"

"It means 'one who thinks.' My secret Apache name." Manny gave Pilar an irritated glance. "Something my parents should've given me at birth."

Talitha's twin chins wobbled. "He's of the age to embark upon his vision quest and tap into the source of his true power."

Alex broadened his shoulders. "True power doesn't come that way."

The old woman speared Alex with her eyes. "What would a Mexican know of Power? So-kus-n is Apache, not Mexican."

Pilar tensed.

"You follow the god of the whites." Talitha rested a gnarled claw upon Manny's arm. "We follow the old ways, don't we, So-kus-n?"

Alex edged closer. "I follow the One True God. He's my strength. My source of power."

Since when?

Pilar didn't recall Alex liking those hard church pews any better than she or Byron back in the day. Byron's views had radically changed over the last few years. Alex's, too?

So where did that leave her?

Dark memories surged. What had God ever done for her?

Saved your life . . . More than once . . .

But maybe after what happened, she'd no soul left to save.

The old woman patted Manny's hand and rattled off something in one of the tonal Apache dialects.

Alex narrowed his eyes. "What did she say, Pilar?"

She shook her head.

Manny answered the old woman in the Apache tongue.

The deliberate exclusivity of their shared language made Pilar's skin prickle. "Manny!"

He jumped.

Manny poked out his lips. "She says to run to the mountain and back makes a warrior strong."

Pilar gave Talitha Clum a measured look. "Abuela told me to put a feather in my shoe, Old One, and I ran faster than the boys."

Alex's forehead creased.

Talitha's snaggle-toothed grin reminded Pilar of a carved jack o'lantern. Past its prime and rotting. "I, too, was fast as a girl. *Nah-Goy-Yah-Kizn*, a tomboy. Sos-kus-n didn't tell me you were so traditional. Nor about your Power."

"I'm not traditional." Pilar tucked a tendril of hair behind her ear that escaped her bun. "Manny's power lies in his own strength and education. Besides, Manny's grounded. And he's not going anywhere, much less a four-day desert pilgrimage."

Perhaps she'd been wrong to allow Manny to hang out with strange, old Talitha Clum.

"You knew the victims," Alex pressed.

Talitha's liver-spotted hand caressed the wooden stock of the shotgun. "I knew them when they were much younger. They abandoned the Apache Way for Anglo ways. As do too many of our young people these days."

Alex scanned the old woman's face. "Two were killed about six weeks ago. In August."

"During the Apache moon." Talitha shrugged. "The predators come out during a good hunting moon." Her gaze flitted to Manny. "Also when warriors timed their raids for maximum impact."

"This isn't ancient history, Ms. Clum." Alex set his jaw. "This predator tortures, rapes, and murders his prey. Mostly teenage girls."

Clum's hooded gaze lifted. "A savagery learned from our Mexican foes." She cocked her head. "Perhaps not so ancient a history as you think."

Manny's breath hitched. "Do you think it's the Wild Ones, Miz Clum?"

Alex kicked a small pebble. "We're looking for a sexual predator. A serial murderer. Not some nineteenth-century Apache warrior."

"One day, Sos-kus-n, I will earn my place in their band and follow the Apache Way home." The old woman's eyes glittered. "In the meantime, there's much to be learned from the old ways."

Not from you. Pilar gritted her teeth. *Not from you.* Manny didn't need Clum's brand of mystic weirdness in his already troubled young life.

"Another girl was killed over a year ago. Also the month of an Apache moon." A muscle jumped in Alex's jaw. "Have you heard or seen anything out of the ordinary, Ms. Clum?"

"Only the Ghost Ponies." Clum's mouth flattened. "Every Apache moon, I hear the horses."

Manny jutted his chin. "I told you."

"Horses?" Alex shoved away from the railing as the phone clipped to his belt beeped. "I'd appreciate any help you could give us, Ms. Clum."

Alex scrounged a business card out of his jacket pocket. "Next moon's tomorrow night. If you hear the 'horses' again," he made a face. "Would you call me ASAP?"

Talitha Clum's face scrunched into a fair imitation of a dried prune and turned away.

Interview over.

His cell beeped again. Alex glanced at the caller ID.

Thanking the old woman, Pilar took her cue and waved Manny toward the SUV.

Clum cackled. "It'll take an Apache to catch an Apache, Agent Torres."

Pilar halted mid-step and repressed a shiver.

The old woman hefted the gun to her shoulder. "Come back, Sos-kus-n, when you're ready to begin your vision quest."

So not happening.

"Get in the car, Manny. Now."

Manny slung himself into the backseat and slammed the door. She resumed her place in the front, and Alex wheeled away from the old woman's house.

Pilar blew out a breath. "A waste of time."

Manny muttered something under his breath.

Alex's eyes went to the rearview mirror. "We have to track down every lead." He gunned the motor once free of the narrow canyon road paralleling the ridge.

"Not a total waste of time." He laid his cell on the console between them. "Emily texted me. The anthropologist has agreed to meet with us this afternoon. And I know a great lunch spot near campus."

"An anthropologist?" Pilar groaned. "You're going to pursue this ridiculous angle about the Broncos?"

"It's not ridiculous." Manny leaned over the seat. "You heard Alex. We have to track down every lead."

"*We?*" She and Alex chorused in unison.

Manny crossed his arms around his skinny chest. "Besides, I'm a growing boy and I need a snack."

"A man after my own heart, *muchacho.*" Alex grinned at him in the mirror. "I'm always up for food."

13

Can I get a sweatshirt while we're here, Auntie?"

Strolling through the main campus, Alex's lips twitched as he waited for Pilar's reaction.

"Grounded people don't get special favors."

Manny stuffed his hands in his pockets. "You never let me do anything..." He kicked a pebble down the sidewalk.

Alex relaxed his pace, allowing more time to talk with Pilar. "You've done a good job with Byron's boy."

She cut her eyes at Alex. Gauging his sincerity. As if she didn't trust him.

He'd given Pilar little reason to trust him thus far. But her distrust hurt. More than he'd believed possible.

"Manny's a good boy. He's devoted to you. Like Byron."

Her lips thinned. "You can tell that from this one visit home after all these years?"

Alex had stayed away because he thought that's what she wanted. She'd wanted him to stay away... right?

His throat tightened. "I-I—"

"Abuela missed you."

But not Pilar?

Pilar wrinkled her nose. "Too busy cavorting with blondes to check on your elderly grandmother?"

Anger churned in his gut at the unfairness. Yet not far off the mark from the old Alex, he reminded himself. He fought to keep his temper in check.

Pilar surged up the steps of the social science building and yanked the door. She held it wide, waiting for them. Seemed like most of Alex's life he'd been playing catch up to this woman. And it made him mad. Furious.

He took hold of the door. For a moment, they struggled for control.

"Must you make everything so hard, Pia?"

She leaned close enough he smelled the wildflower scent of her shampoo. "Must you always behave like the backend of a mule?"

He let go and raked his hand over his hair. "You make me crazy."

Manny passed between them with a snarky grin.

Giving Alex a black look, she followed Manny. The door swinging shut, Alex stutter-stepped over the threshold before it closed in his face.

She moved toward the elevator. "Goes both ways, Torres. Third floor?" She punched the up button.

Torn between a deep-seated desire to throttle Pilar for her stubbornness and an equally deep-seated desire to—

He clenched his jaw so tight, his teeth hurt.

Inside the elevator, the three of them watched the floor numbers rise as the elevator ascended. Fuming, he struggled to regain his professionalism. Five years with the Bureau and an exemplary service record.

Twenty-four hours with Pilar To-Clanny and every ounce of training out the window.

When the elevator doors slid open, she was first out.

Some things never changed. Like her total disregard for caution. Charging at life instead a more measured reconnaissance.

"Dr. Umberto Velarde," Manny read the nameplate on the office door. "We're here."

Alex fisted his hand and knocked. Harder than he meant to. Not as hard as Pilar's head, apparently.

"Come in, *por favor.*" A Spanish-accented voice echoed through the door.

She seized the door handle and turned the knob. Alex crossed in front of her. She sidestepped him and jockeyed for position.

Bookshelves lined the room, overwhelmed with thick academic volumes. Seated behind a large desk, the anthropologist's eyes flickered. But Velarde's face smoothed, and surprise gave way to something else. He rose and came around the desk, hand extended. Toward Pilar.

"*Bienvenido.* Welcome, my American friends. A most unexpected pleasure."

Alex didn't like the look in the forty-something anthropologist's black-brown eyes. He assessed the blazer-clad professor. Not what he'd expected.

Pilar went all funny at Velarde's touch. Which lingered way too long in Alex's expert opinion. Her eyes huge, she tilted her head at the not quite six-foot anthropologist.

But Alex conceded—judging from the bemused look on her face—some women might find Velarde's chiseled, aesthete appearance compelling.

The hooded eyes and cheekbones sharp enough to slice bread. The black hair swept back from his broad forehead. The longish, hipster sideburns.

She allowed the man to lead her to an overstuffed leather chair catty-corner to the desk where Umberto Velarde perched, the knife-sharp creases of his trousers millimeters from her knees. And the open-collared dress shirt revealed the professor didn't spend time enhancing just his intellectual capacities.

Irritated, Alex cut between them on his way to an adjacent chair. Causing Velarde to shift and straighten. "I'm Special Agent Alex Torres." He offered his hand.

The professor's eyes flared as they shook hands. Alex didn't relax his grip until Velarde winced.

Withdrawing his hand, Velarde resumed his seat behind the desk. His gaze flitted to Pilar. "And you are . . . ?"

She took a deep breath. "Pilar . . ."

Alex didn't like the husky note in her voice. "She's San Carlos Officer To-Clanny, and this is Manny." Feeling the need to stay on his feet, he drew Manny forward to take the empty chair.

Velarde's eyes narrowed at the boy.

Manny pointed his lips in the Apache Way at the large, glossy photo of a tawny jaguar on the wall behind the professor. "Cool."

Et tu, Manny?

"The biggest cat in the Americas. A stalk-and-ambush, opportunistic creature at the top of the food chain." Velarde smiled. "The *Panthera onca arizonensis* is an apex predator."

Manny's eyes widened. "The Arizona jaguar?"

"*Excelente.*" Velarde chuckled. "You know your Latin."

Manny ducked his head. "Don't tell my friends."

Alex folded his arms. "What is it you do with these apex predators?"

Velarde contemplated the photograph. "Once this magnificent species roamed from Arizona to Sonora. But only a few have been spotted north of the border in recent years. I work with wildlife reserves in both countries to increase their chances of survival."

He fingered his chin. "I fear the American border fence will hamper gene flow from our Mexican populations and prevent the northward expansion of the species. To truly thrive, the jaguar must be established in an area with an adequate prey base."

Manny leaned forward. "That's so cool, man."

Alex's lips twisted. "Unless you're one of the prey."

"But after what you've seen in the line of duty on the streets of America," Velarde gave Alex a calculated look. "You'd agree, Special Agent Torres, that humans by far are the ultimate apex predator?"

Alex didn't like this guy. "Certainly the cruelest."

Velarde handed him a brochure. "More information about the work we do and about this most fascinating of animals." His eyes glinted. "You should read it sometime."

Alex stuffed it into his jacket pocket. He'd by necessity developed his own survival instincts when it came to killers of the human species. And Velarde raised the hair on the back of his neck.

Manny got out of his chair to peruse the artifacts displayed on the shelf. Alex flicked a glance at Pilar. She'd been quiet. Too quiet. She'd never been quiet in her life. It rankled him that her gaze remained locked on Velarde.

Like a mouse hypnotized by a serpent and about to be devoured. Willingly devoured.

Velarde moved with a sleek, muscular gait, not unlike a jaguar, toward Manny. "My life's work. The study of the Apache people."

The anthropologist placed his hand on Manny's shoulder. "You're an admirer of our culture, Manuel?"

Alex resisted the urge to knock Velarde's hand off the boy. Instead, he raised his brow into a question mark. "Our?"

"Not yours perhaps." Velarde shot him a look that set Alex's teeth on edge. "A lot of us have a mixture of ethnicities in our blood."

The conservationist's gaze swung to Manny and then lingered on Pilar. Alex's blood pressure rose several notches. "Many Apaches intermarried with Mexicans."

Alex curled his lip. "By choice or force?"

Dr. Velarde crossed his arms. "The Apaches themselves were once the apex predator of this land. The good old days."

Alex stiffened. "If you regard kidnapping and gang rape as the good ole days."

Manny frowned. "That's not what he said, Alex."

"It's what he implied."

The anthropologist-*cum*-conservationist raised his hands shoulder-width and let them drop. "My English...often doesn't translate."

In Alex's opinion, Velarde's accent thickened at will.

Velarde's mouth curved as if Alex amused him. "I only meant in light of my expertise on the old days. I assumed after Dr. Waters called that's what you came to question me about. A case."

He directed a visceral masculinity Pilar's way. And she—Alex thought disgustedly—practically coiled over the armrest. He'd have believed Pilar too intelligent to fall for such in-your-face *machismo*.

A bad taste in his mouth, Alex cleared his throat.

Pilar jolted. She flushed and glanced at her interlocked fingers.

"Dr. Velarde?" Manny's eyes shone. "Is this an Apache *mano*, a grinding stone?"

"Intelligent and curious." Velarde uncrossed his arms. "He is the future of his people."

Manny broadened his shoulders, soaking in the man's praise like desert rain. "I never saw anything like this in real life before."

Velarde squeezed Manny's arm. "Examine it for yourself."

The boy hefted the rock in his hand. "How did you learn about this stuff?"

"My family's *rancho* is on the Sonoran side." Velarde ran the tip of his finger across a beaded deerskin bag on the shelf. "The property borders the Sierra Madre. Abandoned Apache campsites litter the mountains."

Velarde stared out the window. "Most of the Sierra is now private property. But much of the Sierra Madre remains to be explored. And much still remains to be discovered."

Manny's face glowed. "I'd love to see those camp ruins."

"Some are still in remarkably good shape. Undisturbed. Waiting as the mist rises over the ridges and engulfs the valleys." Velarde smiled.

Reminding Alex of the crouching cat in the photo.

"As if any moment the Broncos may yet return in time for the evening meal."

"Wow," Manny breathed.

"No wonder you're such a good teacher, Dr. Velarde." Pilar cupped her elbows with her hands. "You paint a romantic image."

Finally, she'd found her voice.

Alex withdrew the crime scene photograph of the strange markings from his jacket. "Fiction, considering how those romantic warriors of yours terrorized the countryside."

Velarde turned his languid stare onto Alex. "Fair game in war."

Alex widened his stance. "A war waged on women and children?"

"Let's not forget the slave markets and mining camps your Spanish dons inflicted upon captured Apaches, either."

The two men bored holes into each other with their eyes, a war of wills.

With a small, secret smile, Velarde was the first to turn his gaze. To Pilar.

Resentment burned in Alex's gut.

He shoved the photo at Velarde. "We found these strange markings at one of our crime scenes. What do you make of it?"

The strutting peacock examined the photo. A frown puckered his brow. "Ghost pony."

"I told you," Manny crowed.

"One theory is our perpetrator may believe himself to be the reincarnation of an Apache warrior. What can you tell us about old-time Apache strategies?"

Velarde removed a book from the shelf and thrust it at Manny. "My doctoral dissertation. You might find it interesting reading."

He pivoted toward Alex. "The Apache warrior favored early autumn for raids. Revenge parties painted stripes across the bridge of their nose and under their eyes."

Alex felt Pilar tense.

"They painted their body red and placed white dots around their lips to resemble foam. They waited for the full moon to cross the mountains and canyons. They traveled at night and could go without sleep for five days."

Velarde squared his shoulders. "Every Apache moon was a time of great fear for farms and ranches. They stalked their prey until dawn and then struck." He pounded his fist on the desk.

All of them jumped.

Velarde swiveled toward Manny. "An Apache boy went on his first raid at the age of fifteen. After four raids, he'd be a warrior. He had to be able to endure hardship. To be strong. To kill." Velarde clapped Manny on the back. "Then, he was ready to take a wife."

"You make killing sound noble and glorious." Alex rose. "It's not. It's something a man should be forced to do only as a last resort."

Velarde inclined his head. "As you say, of course." He offered his hand to Pilar.

Alex drew a sharp breath. Something uncomfortable roiled in his gut. She stared at Velarde and then took his hand, rising from the chair.

Velarde's attention settled upon Manny once more. "I'd love to invite you to explore other Apache artifacts at my *rancho*, Manny."

Manny angled toward Pilar. "Could we go down there?"

The roiling moved from uncomfortable to acute pain. Alex didn't like the proprietary way Velarde watched the boy. Much less the predatory masculine gleam in his eyes for Pilar.

She moistened her lips and touched her throat. "Perhaps…"

Velarde broadened his chest. "Such treasures I could show you."

Alex wanted to show this guy the treasure of his fist.

"Perhaps in the meantime, you'd do me the honor of accompanying me to dinner tomorrow night?"

"Dinner?" Alex barked.

Velarde ran his lips across Pilar's knuckles. "Domingo's has the best tapas this side of Argentina."

Quivering like an aspen in a stiff breeze, she blinked and nodded.

"We've got a case," Alex growled.

Velarde raised his eyes above her hand. "With your permission, I'll pick you up at seven?"

Alex snatched her hand free. "No."

She glared at Alex. "Yes."

Alex grasped her elbow. "She'll meet you there."

Pilar jerked her arm out of his hold.

No way this slimeball needed to know where she lived. If he didn't already, judging from the serial's calling card last night.

"There could be a development, Pia. You'd need your own car."

She pursed her lips, but nodded.

Velarde gave a slight bow. "Until then, *mi hermosa*. Until then."

His beautiful one? Alex grimaced as he ushered Manny and Pilar into the hallway.

Not if he had anything to say about it. Not while he, Alejandro Roberto Torres, had breath in his body.

Manny elbowed him. "Zorro one. Don Quixote zip." He snickered. "Kind of lost that legendary touch with the women I've heard so much about from Abuela. Better up your game, Alex, and quick."

Don Quixote...? The boy compared him to a figure who tilted at windmills? Alex gritted his teeth.

Though on second thought, when it came to Pilar perhaps that's exactly what he'd been doing all these years. Chasing an impossible dream. Reduced to a comedic tragedy.

On the sidewalk outside, he reached in his wallet and thrust a wad of cash at the boy. "Didn't you say you wanted a T-shirt or something?"

Pilar wheeled. "I told him no."

"Get some ice cream then, son."

The book tucked under his arm, Manny jammed the cash in his jean pocket. "Time to let the grownups fight." He grinned and headed toward the Student Union.

"You have no business going off with that crazy anthropologist."

She planted her hands on her hips. "You've got no business telling me what to do."

"That guy's certifiable." Alex snorted. "Apex predators. Apache bloodlusts."

"He's passionate about his area of interest."

Alex tossed a look her way. "So am I."

Her eyes slitted. "Seems like, though, I remember you being passionate about *lots* of areas of interest."

"Wrong." Unable to restrain himself any longer, he touched his finger to her cheek. "Only one I was ever truly passionate about. Still am."

To his surprise, she didn't move away. A vein throbbed at the hollow of her throat. "You had a funny way of showing it."

Stung at the truth of her remark, he dropped his hand. "The virile anthropologist probably drives the coeds wild."

Pilar cocked her head. "Looks like my dismal taste in men hasn't changed much over the years, eh, Alejandro?"

"I'm nothing like that puffed-up pretender."

"Same hot Latin charm. Same smooth Mexican—"

"I'm from L.A.!"

Students underneath a shade tree stopped chattering and stared at them.

Pilar laughed.

Only Pilar could wind him up like that.

"Something's off with that guy."

"Only thing off was he appeared to appreciate my Apache self. Not blondes."

"I appreciate your Apache self." Alex bristled. "Anyway, that's our guy."

"Our what?"

"A real lady killer." He scowled. "And I mean that in every sense of the word. Velarde fits the profile. His profession gives him access to both sides of the border."

"That's ridiculous. He's a renowned scholar. Besides, I would've recognized him if..." Her eyes dropped to the pavement.

"You were drugged out of your mind, Pia. You wouldn't have recognized your own mother after what happened. He's the serial, I'm sure of it."

"Alleged perpetrator. And you're just mad because someone else might actually find me attractive."

"You think this is about jealousy? This guy lives in Salazar's self-proclaimed kingdom. You can't be naïve enough to believe there's not a connection between Velarde and the drug lord."

"I think Alejandro Torres is nothing if not territorial. You didn't want me, but you can't stand anyone else wanting me, either."

"I did want—I still…" He raked his hand over his head. "You have no business going to dinner with someone we suspect may have kidnapped, raped, and tortured multiple victims. It's crazy."

She glowered at him. "It's a date. Let's call it what it is." She lifted her chin. "This time, I'll watch my drink. And come armed."

"There's something's off with that guy. I feel it in my gut. He's holding something back."

"Sure it's not an organ a little lower in your anatomy?" She gave him a look out of the corner of her eye. "And all the more reason for me to find out what I can."

He beat his fist against his thigh. "No way I'm letting—"

"Letting me?" Her eyes flashed.

Wrong choice of words.

"Like you think you're the boss of me? Like you think you've got any right to tell me what to do? Like you think you're my husband or something?"

"About that, Pia…"

She turned away. "And another reason for me to go to dinner with him? Tomorrow night's another full moon. He's our only lead."

"Is this really about our investigation or just a good excuse to push my buttons?"

She patted his cheek. "When have I ever needed an excuse to push your buttons, Alejandro?"

His heartbeat accelerated at the touch of her fingers.

When indeed?

14

Before

PILAR'S SNEAKERS POUNDED UP THE MESA. PUSHING HERSELF farther and faster. As free and light as a butterfly. Maybe not a butterfly, remembering the feather Abuela told her to insert into her shoe. Maybe a bird.

Alex raced behind her, determined to beat her to the top. She smiled. So not happening.

She was the happiest she'd been since Byron reported to Basic and Alex went to college. Just her and Abuela at the ranch. Just her books, her latest stray cat, and high school. Boring without the guys there.

But earlier today she'd opened the nail-studded oak door to find Alex grinning at her on the other side.

He leaned against the doorframe and cocked his head. "Surprise, Pia."

She thought she might liquefy on the spot. How could she have forgotten in only two months what the sight of him did to a person? A female person.

Alex looked bigger, broader. The muscles starting to fill his once gangly form. Still lanky but now...

"Basketball training." He curled his bicep, correctly reading her admiring gaze.

Pilar scowled. It maddened her how this cowboy wannabe read her so well.

Several hours and several of Abuela's enchiladas later, he challenged Pilar to a race. She gladly accepted. Some people were gluttons for punishment and humiliation.

Then she made a rookie mistake, glancing over her shoulder to empty air. He passed her as if she stood still. She dug into her reserve as Alex's long strides ate the ground and left her to eat his dust.

He reached the big boulder seconds ahead and collapsed against its solid sandstone surface. His black bean eyes danced. "I win, Pia. I win."

She grimaced and put a steadying hand on the boulder. Her sides ached. Her lungs craved air. Her legs felt like jelly.

"Haven't had anyone to race these last few months," she huffed. "I'm off my game. Won't happen next time."

Alex folded his arms across his T-shirt. "Doesn't matter about next time. I'm talking about this time."

She blew out a breath. "I demand a rematch."

The muscles in his chest flexed as he laughed. "You lost, Pia. Fair and square. Accept your defeat."

She lifted her chin. "Apaches don't surrender."

He rolled his eyes. "You get even. I remember." He unwound. "But this time, I won. And I'm here to claim my prize."

She straightened and prepared her stomach muscles to take his punch. "Go ahead."

He tilted his head. "I don't hit girls, Pia. That's not what I want from you."

"What do you want then?" She widened her stance. "Do your worst."

He gave her a lazy, one-sided smile. "How about I do my best?"

Pilar's nerve endings jumped. She hugged her arms over her flannel shirt. "And what exactly does your best involve?"

He broadened his shoulders. "A kiss, Pia. I won, and I claim as my prize a kiss."

Pilar's mouth went dry. Her heart thudded, harder than in any race she'd ever run.

"Stray cat got your tongue, Pia?"

When she didn't answer, an unfamiliar uncertainty passed over his handsome face.

He stuffed his hands into his pockets. "You said if I won I could claim my prize."

She tucked a tendril of hair behind her ear. His eyes went opaque. Something fluttered in her chest. She dropped her hand.

"Why do you want a kiss?" She cleared her throat. "From me?"

His eyes flitted toward the mountain range where a lone red-tailed hawk borne aloft on the desert breeze swirled in graceful figure eights.

"Because you were always the prize, Pia." His gaze returned to hers. "The only prize I ever wanted."

She pressed her back against the rock, her legs unsteady. "Okay..." she whispered.

A muscle jumped in Alex's cheek.

For a second, they stared at each other.

Silence roared between them.

His Adam's apple bobbed. "Okay..." he whispered back.

Moistening his lips, he moved closer. Until only inches separated their bodies. He lifted his hands. Dropped them. As if he didn't know what to do with them.

"Alex."

He jerked.

She leaned forward. Her bare kneecaps brushed against his jeans. He placed his palms flat against the rock on either side of her head. Holding her in place. Keeping her in the circle of his arms.

Her arms drifted around his waist to explore the contours of his muscled back. He cupped her face in the cradle of his hands. Her lips parted.

She closed her eyes at the warmth of his palms upon her skin. She held her breath. Waiting. Anticipating. Yearning.

His lips grazed hers, featherlight. She inhaled and opened her eyes. His dark eyes blazed. Yet his body trembled beneath her hands.

Alex let go of her. "I—we shouldn't...Byron and Abuela wouldn't—"

"Byron and Abuela aren't here, Alex." On tiptoe, Pilar knotted her hands around his neck and tugged him closer. "Just you and me."

"You and me." His voice went husky. *"Mia..."*

She took a deep breath. "Yours." She threaded her fingers through the short hair at the nape of his neck.

He closed his eyes, and his mouth found hers again. This time, hungry. Demanding. Probing. Exploring.

A latent wildness sparked Pilar into like-minded response.

His heart thrummed beneath her hands in a drumbeat similar to her own. He gripped her forearms.

Pilar's hands kneaded his shoulder blades. Came round to rest on his chest. Her fingers slipped beneath the neckline of his shirt and found the tender flesh at the base of his throat.

His knees buckled. "Pia, don't..."

But she didn't care. Didn't want to stop. She wanted to own him, every inch of him. Claim him as hers. Fire scorched her veins. And she knew she'd do anything he asked of her, anything to never lose him. She pressed her body into his.

"Pia." He wrenched her shoulders back. "Stop."

She wrested free of his restraining hands. "Alex...please."

"I won't do that to you." He shook his head, his breath ragged. "Not this way. Not with you." He edged away.

Pilar took a step toward him. "I'm offering."

"Stop it, Pia. You scare me sometimes."

He ran a hand over the top of his head. "When I'm around you, I scare myself."

She glared. "But the others..."

His sienna skin flushed. "No more others, Pia. I promise you, not since I realized. We're meant for more than that, don't you see?"

She stamped her foot, sending a small puff of dust airborne. "What've you been waiting for then?"

He laughed. Some of the tension left his face. "Waiting for you to grow up. What else?"

"Arrogant much, Torres?"

He chuckled. "Missed me a lot, did you?"

She gave him a nice view of her shoulder as she turned. "Like you'd miss scurvy maybe."

He caught hold of her shirttail. "Don't go away mad, Pia. I missed you, too. More than a lot."

And the ever present, tangible awareness quivered between them.

She gave him a slow smile. "Want to race down the mountain and see who's the fastest this time?"

He arched his brow. "You gonna kiss me when I win again?"

"You assume you're going to win."

"I'm going to win from now on when it comes to you, Pilar." His eyes crinkled. "Just for the sake of curiosity, though. If you manage to win next time, what prize would you claim?"

His mouth curved. Revealing the twin set of dimples that brack-eted his face. As if already sure of her answer.

Time to take this cowboy wannabe down a peg or two.

"A kiss? Or a punch to the gut?" She lifted her shoulder and let it drop. "I haven't decided yet which you deserve."

His laughter followed her to the base of the mesa.

15

Alex crossed his arms over his chest. "For the record, I don't think this is a good idea."

"You don't think anything I do is a good idea, Alex."

Pilar tucked the wire farther into the cleavage of the skintight red dress. A dress that only just barely concealed more than it revealed.

"That's not true." He gestured at her getup. "But this?"

She propped her stiletto-clad heel on top of Abuela's coffee table and hiked the hem of the skimpy dress a few inches. "You don't like?"

His mouth went dry.

She checked the knife inserted in the black band cinched around her muscled thigh.

That was the problem. He did like. Very much.

"I've learned a lot since the old days, Alex. I know how to take care of myself."

She tugged her hemline—what there was of it—into place. "Besides, I'm wired and you guys will be in the van on the street."

The front door opened. Catching sight of Pilar, Woodrow Kenoi's eyes lit. Alex stiffened.

Kenoi let out a wolf whistle. "Whoo-whee!" He hip-bumped Pilar.

She grinned. Alex wanted to bump Kenoi's face with his fist.

"Look at you." Kenoi touched his fingertip to Pilar's arm and made a sizzling sound. "Hot to trot. A real hoochie-coochie mama—"

Alex threw a punch.

Eyes enlarging, she deflected his hand, inches from Kenoi's nose. Kenoi jogged back a pace, his brow furrowing.

She glared. "What is wrong with you, Alex?"

"I don't like him talking to you like that."

Kenoi clenched his fists.

She got between the men, her hand on Alex's chest. "He's joking, Alex. He didn't mean anything by it."

Alex pushed against her hand. "I won't allow anyone to treat you like that."

"Is that what this is about?" Kenoi burst out laughing. "Better call off your Mexican pit bull, Pia, before he ruins our undercover op. I'll be in the van." He headed for the door.

Alex started after Kenoi. She caught his arm.

"I'm not Mexican," he yelled.

Kenoi underscored his laughter by shutting the door in Alex's face.

"We've done an undercover prostitution sting on the rez before, Alex." She tapped her foot against the tile. "Unlike you, he sees me as a law-enforcement professional. And he's also a friend."

Alex jabbed his finger. "That man's not your friend. He's been trying to get his grubby paws beneath your clothes since high school."

Her face hardened. "Other than the attacker, only man ever managed to do that was you, Alex."

Alex's nostrils engorged. "Are you comparing me to the man who hurt you, Pia? Who—"

"There's all kinds of hurt, Alex." She adjusted her dress. "Woodrow meant no disrespect."

Alex seized her hand. "And I married you, let me remind you, before I ever…ever…"

"Married me so you could." She scowled. "That's what you said, right?"

He felt the anger boiling, rising. Perhaps seeing something in his face, she took a step back. He placed both hands on either side of her body, locking her into place against the door.

"Despite what I said that last day, it wasn't that way between us and you know it."

"I believed I knew a lot of things then." Her breath came in rapid spurts, brushing his cheek. "Turns out I was wrong." But her eyes fixated on his mouth.

His pulse jackhammered.

"Wrong about everything."

"Not everything, Pia." His voice sounded hoarse. "Not about—"

Someone hammered the door. They jerked.

Kenoi pounded the door again. "Let's roll."

Alex closed his eyes. "I hate that guy. I don't like the way he looks at you."

"You don't like the way anyone looks at me." She ducked her head and moved out from under his arms. "And for the record, Woodrow *is* a friend. Who also happens to be a happily married man with two children and another on the way."

Alex sagged. "Oh."

"News flash, Alex." She gripped the doorknob and wrenched it open. "I don't belong to you. And despite your empty charm and ego, I never really did."

Maybe Pia was right. With a mounting sense of despair, he watched as she stomped to the porch and climbed into the van. Maybe the truth was that it was Alex who'd always belonged to her.

"Tell me about what makes the lovely Apache policewoman tick." Umberto Velarde propped his muscular arms upon the snowy white tablecloth.

With her hidden earpiece, she detected the faint sounds of Alex gnashing his teeth. This promised to be a fun evening, yanking Alex Torres's chain. 'Cause, man, did he have it coming.

Of course, the last time she'd done that...

Not wanting to go there, she gave Umberto a bright smile. "As a noted scholar, you probably know more about my culture than I do."

"You didn't have a changing woman ceremony when you reached puberty?"

She rolled her eyes. "Are you kidding? I'm the least Apache Apache you'll ever meet."

Ain't that the truth... The Alex peanut gallery in her ear laughed out loud.

She thumped her earring with its secret receiver.

Owwwww...

Velarde smiled. "Thoroughly modern Pia. May I call you Pia?"

No…You may not.

"Yes." She gave the professor a languid look. "Yes, you may."

In her ear, words that shouldn't be repeated. She worked to keep her lips from twitching.

Velarde's dark eyes narrowed. "Not religious?"

"If by religious, you mean praying to the Apache deity, no I'm not. Nor the Christian one, either."

Despite Abuela's best intentions. Despite Byron's urgings. Despite—her throat clogged—the change in Alex. Disturbing. Contrary to every previous notion she'd held about him or his new God.

Never say never… Alex murmured in her ear.

Pilar squirmed. She'd never been able to extricate Alex from her head. But it was weird having him in her ear.

"And your son?" Velarde leaned forward. "He seems well-versed in the old ways."

She lowered her eyes and fingered the stem of the water glass. "I'm raising him, but Manny's my nephew."

"Tribal cop. A surrogate mother. A modern woman." Velarde raised his eyebrows. "Facets enough for a lifetime."

Alex breathed—angrily—through her earpiece.

She took a tiny sip before giving Velarde an abbreviated—and highly Alex-redacted—version of her life story.

"What about you?" She practiced a smile. "Before you earned multiple degrees from both sides of the border."

His sensuous lips curved. "I'm flattered. You checked out my curriculum vitae."

Tufts of dark hair peeked from the open collar of his white silk shirt as he broadened his chest. "Growing up on the cattle ranch at the foothills of the Sierra Madre, I spent enormous amounts of time roaming the spread, creating my own adventures." A heavy gold chain rested against his clavicle and gleamed in the candlelight.

"Fighting Apaches?" Her lips quirked. "In their ancestral stronghold."

"*Sí.*" He threw back his head and laughed. "But never the pretty ones, *querida.*"

Querida. Darling? She blushed.

There was something about this man. Something electric that scrambled her senses. Unsettled, she turned the cubic zirconia stud on her ear without thinking.

Owwwwww...What are you doing? hissed Alex.

She dropped her hand.

"I'm on sabbatical from the anthropology department in Mexico City. I'm taking time to fully explore my interests in the apex predator. Studying their habitat." Velarde steepled his hands on the table. "Learning how they stalk their prey."

Alex growled in her earpiece. She ignored him.

"What kind of prey?"

"Deer. Cattle. Occasionally, the human." Velarde's eyes glowed. "They do not hunt, you understand. Rather, they lie in wait and allow the prey to come to them."

Her stomach tightened. "Ambush the defenseless, you mean."

"Not all are defenseless. Some prove more of a challenge than others." Velarde stroked his chin. "A strategy perfected by your own Apaches, I think."

"A philosophy practiced by the drug cartels, too?"

Velarde went still. "Are you asking me, Pilar, if I'm a member of the Salazar organization?"

Her eyes skittered. "No..." Not exactly.

Yes... Alex breathed in her ear.

Shut up, Alex.

"Is this what you wish to know or is this what that special agent wannabe wanted you to ask me?"

Sputtering erupted in her ear.

"I'd hoped you, being Apache, would know better than to make assumptions based on anyone's ethnic background."

She fidgeted. "Assumptions? What are you talking about?"

"You've surely heard it said Apaches are vermin. Apaches are thieves. Apaches are drunks. Sadistic and cruel."

She tilted her head. "Is this what you think of my people? Of me, *Señor?*"

Velarde's eyes flashed. "On the contrary, I've spent my life studying your people. Fiercest fighters on the planet."

His lips curled upward. "The American military even named an attack helicopter after your people. I have nothing but the highest admiration for their ability to survive despite the harshest of environments."

"Survive? Maybe." She shrugged. "Thrive? The jury's still out on that one for the majority of my people."

"And all Mexicans aren't drug dealers, Pilar."

She made the mistake of placing one hand beside her plate.

With one smooth motion, he took her hand in his. Velarde's admiring gaze raked Pilar from the top of her elaborately coiled updo to her décolletage. She fought the urge to shiver.

Thank you very much, Alex Torres.

Pilar told herself it was Alex's dark insinuations, not the handsome anthropologist, that made her skittish. For the first time, she regretted wearing the dress. Though it definitely served its purpose—to attract Velarde's interest. In the hope of disconcerting him into a slipup.

Sending Alex into orbit?

An added bonus.

Velarde's touch rattled Pilar. She'd made herself go out over the years to test herself. But every time?

The overwhelming fear and claustrophobia returned in waves. The shrinking recoil from men she felt was more about her issues than them. But the familiar despair washed over her.

Of never loving and being loved again.

Pilar resisted the urge to yank her hand free. When the waiter returned to remove her half-eaten entree, she took advantage of the interruption to ease free. A tiny frown marred the perfect bridge of Velarde's nose.

Swiping her hand against the fabric of her dress, she resolved to keep her hands folded in her lap underneath the table unless engaged in eating. And then, closer to her knife.

Pilar settled her shoulders against the chair, putting distance between them.

The hot-blooded Latino's gaze lingered on her cleavage. "In the mood for dessert?" His eyes undressed her.

Goosebumps rose on her skin. Other men had found her attractive in the years since Alex. She ought to be flattered. In the modern dating world, it wasn't unusual for a man to want—expect—more. Alex had moved on and so should she.

Not every man wanted to hurt her. She had to get over the fear and sense of betraying Alex every time a man desired her. Alex betrayed *her*, not the other way around. And yet...

"Perhaps another time, Dr. Velarde." She pushed back her chair. "Thank you for dinner and the conversation."

He reached across the table for her arm. "It's Umberto. Perhaps we could skip dessert and continue the conversation elsewhere."

She dodged his hand. "Not tonight."

Her heartbeat accelerated. She beat a hasty retreat. Her temples throbbed.

Slipping around her, Umberto blocked the exit. "I cannot allow our evening to end so soon."

Pilar clutched her purse to her chest.

In a crowded downtown restaurant, she wasn't isolated like before. But the beginnings of a migraine blurred the edges of her vision.

And no always meant no.

Her eyes flickered at a whoosh of air. Alex filled the entrance. And the look on his face...

"The lady said she needed to leave."

Umberto pivoted. The two men stared at each other. She would've declared it a Mexican standoff, except Alex would've protested he was from L.A.

"Leave with you?" Umberto's voice took on a silken, dangerous quality. "All work and no play will make for a dull girl."

"I don't play, Velarde." Hands on his hips, Alex brushed open his coat. Gunmetal glinted. "Pia?"

She sidestepped Velarde and edged to Alex's elbow. "A-another time."

Pilar swallowed, angry for feeling shaken. The cop in her even angrier that she felt relieved to have Alex at her back.

Velarde widened his stance, mirroring Alex. "Alas, the duties I've inherited from my late father on the *rancho* require my return."

"Your responsibilities at the college have come to an end?" Alex's gaze didn't waver. "Heading across the border tomorrow?"

"Perhaps I'll return tonight." Velarde cocked his head. "With the full moon, I may change my plans."

Alex's brows rose.

Umberto angled toward her. "When you find yourself in my country, I hope you will pay the *rancho* a visit." He opened his hands. "*Mi casa es su casa.*"

Alex stiffened. "Don't you mean 'if'?"

"I find all roads eventually lead to my villa." Velarde gave him a cool look. "The señorita would greatly enjoy the views."

Velarde signaled a waiter. "Check, please?" He reached for Pilar's hand.

Alex sucked in a breath.

She stepped between the men and permitted Umberto to bring her hand to his lips.

"A most enjoyable evening, Señorita. The first of many I dare hope."

She extricated her hand and retreated until her shoulders grazed Alex's chest. "Th-thank you for an illuminating evening."

Alex wrestled open the door and nudged her onto the sidewalk.

Out in the fresh air, she took a deep breath. "That was a bust."

Alex steered her toward a side street where the van sat parked out of the range of the streetlights. "He's our guy. I feel it in my gut."

"I overreacted. I didn't need you to rescue me. He said nothing to indicate—"

"You were breathing too quickly. I didn't like where the conversation drifted. I pulled the plug on the operation."

"I'm not sure why I got so spooked."

She bit her lip. Actually, she understood exactly why she'd gotten spooked. One of the legacies of her assault—distaste for being touched by a man.

But she couldn't speak of that. Not with Alex.

"If I'd played it smarter, left with him—"

"No way." Alex's nostrils flared. "No way I'd ever allow you to leave with that man. Your instincts were screaming a truth your brain might not have realized until too late."

"What truth?"

"That man may not be our serial. But he knows something. He toyed with you—with us."

Alex yanked open the side door of the van. Woodrow and Sidd looked up from their monitors. Alex ushered her inside.

She hitched her skirt to climb aboard. Alex glared as the men's gaze darted to her legs. Dropping their eyes, the men returned to their perusal of the monitors.

Alex slammed the door shut. "Contact Charles," he instructed Sidd. "I want that piece of trash tailed until he leaves American jurisdiction."

Sidd nodded and spoke into the handheld radio. Woodrow crawled behind the wheel and started the engine.

Alex fell into a seat. "He was taunting us with his superior knowledge. Made me want to smack his overweening pride where the sun don't shine."

"Overweening. Good word." She settled beside him. "And I love it when you go all professional on me, Special Agent Torres."

He laughed and some of the tightness in his shoulders eased.

"Think he'll prowl the local bars?"

"If he does, we'll be there and intercede before another woman becomes his next victim."

"Right."

"When I said 'we', I meant me." Alex motioned. "And the team."

"Thought I was part of the team." She bristled. "I'm perfectly capable—"

"You've done your part for tonight."

"So you're shutting me out?" She squared her shoulders. "Leave it to the boys, is that it?"

"Abuela and Manny will be anxious until you return to the house. Kenoi will be on guard duty tonight until we catch and stop that Mexican scumbag."

"I don't need a babysitter, Alex."

"Sure you do. And if you want any role whatsoever in the investigation, you'll learn to follow orders. Or else."

Pilar narrowed her eyes. "Or else what?"

A tiny smile quirked his mouth. "Or you'll miss all the action."

16

AT ABUELA'S, PILAR'S DREAMS WERE ONCE AGAIN FULL OF VAGUE, drifting shadows. Of firelight flickering off tomblike walls. And chains.

Holding her fast. Tearing at her wrists. And she beheld white dots around a cruel mouth, resembling foam.

Jerking awake, she bit off a sharp cry. Downstairs, she found Alex trying to calm an agitated Manny.

"What's wrong? Did another girl disappear?" She tucked her uniform into her pants. "What happened when you tailed Velarde?"

Manny stiffened. "Since when did Dr. Velarde become a suspect?"

Alex pursed his lips. "Something's not right about that dude, Manny." His shoulders slumped. "And somehow, Velarde ditched our tail."

"You lost him? How does that happen?" She glanced around. "Where's Woodrow?"

"It happens." Alex stuffed his hands in his pockets. "I sent him home already."

Manny slammed his fist against a wall.

She and Alex jolted.

"I'm talking about Reyna. Why won't you listen, Alex?"

Pilar pointed to the dent. "And while you're grounded, you can add fixing the damage to Abuela's wall to your punishment, Manuel To-Clanny."

He swiveled to Alex. "Please..."

"I'm listening, Manny. What's wrong, son?"

"They've taken Reyna. You have to do something." The boy paced the length of the living room. "Before they hurt her."

She exchanged glances with Alex. "What're you talking about?" She caught Manny's arm.

He yanked free and extracted his phone from his jeans—the cell she'd confiscated when she grounded him.

She scowled.

"Reyna's not answering." His voice choked. "She always answers when it's me."

Manny turned to Alex. "They wanted me to—" He shuffled his feet. "They saw how much she meant to me. Please…"

"Who threatened Reyna, Manny?"

Manny rattled off names she recognized from rez juvie records.

"Conquistadores?" Her eyes widened. "Manny, what've you done?"

"Nothing." He hung his head. "That's why they took Reyna. To teach me a lesson."

Alex speed-dialed his cell and barked instructions.

When Alex clicked off, Manny pulled him toward the door. "We need to help her."

"I've got Charles and Sidd checking her house. They're closer. I've also put in a call to Detective Kenoi with his local contacts. We're handling it, Manny. Best thing for us to do is to wait before we rush off half-cocked."

Manny clenched his fists. "I can't just wait and do nothing. This is my fault."

He strained forward on the balls of his feet. "I tried to act like she wasn't important. Just a stupid, little girl. But they—" He squeezed his eyes shut.

"That's why you were fighting at school?" Pilar's voice sharpened. "Because they threatened Reyna?"

"I wouldn't go through with the initiation, and I told them so." Manny looked ready to cry. "I thought if I let them pound me, they'd leave Reyna alone."

She draped her arm around his shoulders. "Why didn't you tell me, honey?" Her tone hardened. "I'd have locked their sorry—"

Alex's phone beeped. "Torres. What you got?" His eyes flicked to her.

Manny chewed his lip.

Alex closed his eyes and let loose a gusty sigh. "You're sure? No mistake?"

"Where's Reyna?" Manny whispered. "What's happened to her?"

Alex ended the call. "The Conquistadores don't have her. The trailer was empty when Charles arrived, but he got a call from Kenoi. Big bust-up last night between rez gang rivals over turf at the high school. Those boys couldn't have taken her. They've been in the lockup since midnight."

"Rocks…" Pilar's eyes shot to Alex. "Reyna said she was going rock collecting on Sunday. Today"

Manny tensed. "I didn't think she'd go without me."

"Go where, Manny?"

"The canyons beyond Miz Clum's place."

Pilar fought against panic.

"She wanted to explore the caverns Miz Clum told us about. An old Apache trail. Miz Clum said there was good rock hunting there."

Pilar's heart hammered. "The moon last night—" She placed a hand over her mouth.

"You think the Wicked One took her?" Desperation tinged Manny's voice. "Maybe it was the Broncos."

"There aren't any Broncos anymore, Manny."

"You're wrong, Auntie. They're out there. Watching, Miz Clum says."

Pilar gritted her teeth. "Miz Clum's a crazy old woman, Manny. Living in the past."

"'Cause the present is so much better?" Manny's voice cracked. "Like what the Wicked One did to those girls? And you?"

Manny pivoted between them. "The Wicked One, he'll hurt Reyna. He'll—" Manny flung himself at Abuela.

Pilar jumped.

She'd not seen the old woman enter. Much less heard her. As always, the woman moved like a sure-footed mountain goat. Silent as a panther. Abuela gathered Manny close.

Alex removed the phone from his ear. "I'm afraid it is the monster, Manny. When his attempt to retake Pilar failed last night," his lips thinned. "Maybe he moved on to easier prey."

She caught his eye. "You have no proof it was Umberto."

"I have no proof it wasn't since he eluded our surveillance."

Manny's mouth drooped. "I was supposed to be with her today. But I believed if I stayed away, she'd be safer from the Conquistadores." He jutted his jaw. "It's got to be the Broncos."

Pilar sighed. "You think the Broncos would be better? You've got to stop with this romanticized version of history, Manny. Despite whatever Talitha Clum and Umberto Velarde said, those women who were taken a hundred years ago didn't go willingly. They were taken from their families against their will. Hurt as surely as what that animal did to me."

Alex flinched and averted his eyes.

Her spirit sank. She'd been right. Alex couldn't bear to look at her. She was defiled in his sight forever.

"We've got to find her, Auntie. We've got to get her back."

Alex grabbed his jacket. "The San Carlos police are searching the rez."

Pilar swallowed. "But if he gets her over the border..." She started forward. As did Manny.

Alex blocked Manny. "Uh, no."

"It's my fault," Manny shouted. "I have to do something."

The strangest look flashed across Alex's face. "I know how you feel, son. But I can't allow—"

"You don't understand. She's my..." Manny's lips trembled. "F-friend."

Pilar laid her palm against Manny's heaving chest. "Let law enforcement handle this. Think about what happened to Ramón when he tried to stop this serial."

Alex checked his gun. "Plus, you're only fourteen years old."

Manny shoved away and slouched against the wall. "I'm fifteen."

She cut her eyes at Alex. His forehead furrowed.

"How did Reyna plan to get out there, Manny? It's too far to walk from her house." She threw the boy a look over her shoulder. "Or ours."

Manny shrugged. "Miz Clum said any time we wanted to go, to give her a call. She'd pick us up."

"I knew the old woman was lying." Pilar fumed. "She's up to her gnarly neck in these abductions."

"And the canyon where the serial seems to bring his kills isn't far from Clum's. As the crow flies, the ranch is closer to the canyon."

Alex scrubbed his neck with his hand. "Maybe we can intercept Clum if she's involved before it's too late."

"I'm getting my weapon." Pilar moved to the stairs. "Stay here, Manny."

Manny kicked the wall this time.

But moments later, she and Alex sped across the cattle guard, under the capital T of the crossbars and hit the open road.

Forty minutes later, leaving the highway, she directed him across the alkalai flats. The SUV bounced as he gunned it across the rolling grasslands and parked at the gaping mouth of the box canyon.

Pilar exited the vehicle. "I'm not waiting for the backup you called." She avoided looking at the empty graves on the edge of the desolate, wind-swept chaparral.

He hopped out. "For better or worse, I am your backup."

Venturing inside the looming red buttes, her eyes raked the sandstone fortress.

He pointed to indentations in the dust.

She raised her eyebrows. "More Ghost Ponies?"

"Or one of his calling cards every time another girl's taken." Hunching, he scanned the boulder-strewn slopes.

Both of them thinking what neither wanted to voice. About the monster's other calling card.

"Reyna!" Pilar's voice echoed off the jagged, sunbaked slopes.

Alex veered left. "Reyna Bui!"

Heading right, Pilar searched for signs—anything—to indicate the child's presence. Where had he taken her? Where did he take any of them?

The special place...

Her skin crawled.

She pushed away a dark memory and stumbled over a rock. Blinking, she focused on the fist-size chunk of quartz. Streaks of pink glimmered in the morning sun.

Reyna.

"Got something," she yelled.

He rushed over through the buffalo grass. "What?"

She shaded her eyes as she scrutinized the ground ahead. "And there."

Dodging a spiny yucca, she hustled toward a chunk of turquoise. Beyond a giant century plant, she pounced on the dirt-encrusted sliver of topaz stuck upright in the ground.

He followed close on her heels. "How can you be sure it's Reyna?"

"Reyna's pockets usually bulge with rocks." Hope burgeoning, Pilar studied the path ahead. "Anything bright. Anything shiny."

The desert light bronzing his face, he took up the hunt. "She's laying a trail like breadcrumbs. Here, too."

Pilar surged higher. "Smart girl. She's not drugged, apparently. She's kept her wits, and she's trying to show us where she's been taken. There, look."

His breath hitched. "A cave." They scrambled upward.

With his greater height, Alex climbed hand over hand with ease. Pilar's shorter legs? Not so much.

Breathing heavy, he offered his hand over a particularly enormous obstacle. Panting, she frowned, but with time of the essence, she surrendered her pride and grasped hold.

She could tell from the flicker in his eyes she'd surprised him. As if he hadn't really expected her to accept his help. As if all he expected from her was rejection.

He tightened his grip and lugged her sunward. Dangling momentarily, her boots scrabbled for a foothold.

She slipped. "Alex!"

He grabbed her other hand and hoisted. "Hang on. I'm not letting go. I won't let you fall." He leveraged his stance. "Not this time." He gritted his teeth.

With her elbows resting above the top of the rock, he transferred his grip to a more secure one underneath her shoulders. Hauling her away from the edge, he collapsed against the cliff.

His arms wrapped around her torso, she rested against him and drank in great gulps of oxygen. His heart thumped beneath his FBI windbreaker. His chin brushed against the crown of her head.

And he stilled.

For a moment, despite everything that had gone down between them in the past, she wanted to relish the feel of his arms around her one more time.

She closed her eyes. For just this minute, she could forget. Maybe he could forget, too. It could be as it was between them before. The hardest part was never knowing what could've been.

He stirred. "Are you okay?" His arms dropped away.

Bracing against the stone surface, he inched up the wall to a standing position. "Pilar?"

Shaking, she nodded.

"Are you sure?" An awareness of her glimmered in his eyes.

He brushed a wisp of hair off her forehead.

Alex's face clouded. "I shouldn't have..." He dropped his hand. "I promised myself I wouldn't touch you."

Touch me, her body cried.

Kiss me, her heart shouted.

Don't be a fool, her brain warned.

She wrapped her arms around herself. "I'm Apache tough, remember?"

"Toughest I ever knew." He threw her his trademark smile. "For a girl, anyway."

Pilar shoulder-butted him. Like the old days when Alejandro Roberto Torres got too big for his boots.

She'd surprised him again, but a pleased smile lit his face.

He gestured to a glint of mica near the cave entrance. "Come on."

Friends? Could they do friends again? After such a long time without him in her life, friends was more than she dared hope for. She gulped as she scrambled after Alex. Was Abuela right?

That true healing would only come when she faced the truth? That only then, the damage done to her would lose its power to control her life. Was Alex essential to making that happen?

She blinked, the sun dazzling her eyes, at the blank entrance to the limestone cave. Where'd Alex—?

"Pilar!" His voice barked from the interior.

She hurried inside.

And straight into her nightmare.

Alex noted with concern she'd gone completely rigid. Barely breathing, so it seemed to him. A shaft of light penetrated the opening of the cave. The smell of decay permeated the air.

Her eyes flitted across the chamber. A kerosene lantern perched on a stone niche. The ashes of the fire pit in the center of the room.

"The special place," she whispered.

"Pilar."

Her chest rose and fell as if she'd run a great distance.

She whirled and fled the cave.

Dashing after her, he found her scrubbing her eyes.

He took hold of her wrists—once again breaking this vow he couldn't seem to keep. "You're hurting yourself."

Alex pried her hands off her face. "Stop gouging your eyes."

She went limp. "That's what I did. I took off my ring and went for his eyes."

He caught her before she fell.

"I took off my wedding ring." She hid her face in his shirt. "Every night, he carved a letter into my flesh."

Alex closed his eyes. Since working the case the last three years and reading the reports, the similar nightmare Pilar endured had played over and over in his head. And he struggled to seek justice for the victims rather than *venganza*, vengeance for Pilar.

Because if Alex were honest, he'd eradicate this beast from the planet.

Alex schooled his features. She didn't need this from him. She needed him to be strong.

"M-I-A. Mine. I somehow knew when he finished the word, he'd kill me. So I pretended. To drink the water he laced. To be compliant. To regain my strength."

She shuddered. "That last day I stopped trying to fight and started planning how I could fight to live. I let him think he'd broken me." Her voice wavered.

Alex's throat tightened. He hadn't wanted to face this. The pictures she painted made him physically ill, sick to his soul.

But healing might come only in the telling for Pilar. And through him, in the hearing. *Lord... Help me.*

"I let him...I did things...I gave myself so he'd lower his guard."

Her eyes flew to Alex. "I gave him my soul. I became his, as he'd boasted. And he became mine."

"No," he gripped her arms. "You were never his. He forced himself on you."

"I betrayed our love, Alex."

He shook his head. "You did what you had to do to survive."

"I allowed him to foul me. To use and corrupt me in a way no water can ever cleanse. I willingly conjoined with the evil inside him."

"You're wrong about that. There is a water that can cleanse."

"No man would ever want me." She dropped her eyes. "You could never want me. Not you, nor your God. Not after knowing what he—what I—did."

Alex clenched his teeth. "That's not true."

"I don't remember much until those people found me on the highway. I have no real memory of how I got from here to there. Only vague fragments of sound, smell, and movement."

"All that matters to me is you're alive."

"I don't blame you for staying away. I can barely stand to look at myself. I loathe myself."

"That isn't why—"

Sirens pierced the unnatural stillness of the canyon. Far below, the tribal cruisers and federal SUVs braked to a stop. Men and women, guns drawn, poured into the barren wasteland.

He windmilled his arms. "Up here!"

Alex guided her toward the rock wall. "There's a tunnel that fans out from the entrance. I'm going to see where it leads. See if Reyna—"

Pilar grabbed his sleeve. "No way I'm letting you go by yourself."

Alex drew his weapon. "He could have her back there."

"Exactly why I'm going with you." She lifted her chin. "I'm not going to let this Mexican moron control the rest of my life. I'm going through that room to the other side."

His face gentled. "Never-say-die Pia."

She rolled her eyes. "It ain't over till the fat armadillo sings."

He laughed as she'd meant him to. "Always so eloquent, Pia."

She removed a flashlight from her duty belt. "Either take the lead or get out of my way, Alex."

He made sure he didn't linger in the room of horrors. Traversing its length, he whipped around the next corner. He paused to make sure she followed and hadn't gotten clotheslined by memory.

She scuttled around the curve and bumped into him. "What're you waiting for, Torres?" she huffed. "Stop slowing me down."

"Pil—"

His heart skipped a beat as the thick, oppressive darkness swallowed her. He set off at a run, catching her where the passage narrowed.

Inserted in a crevice, she held the light below her chin, jack-o'lantern style. She edged sideways. "Suck in those killer abs of yours and let's go."

Alex grinned in the nearly impervious darkness. "You think I have killer abs?"

He sidled through shoulder-to-shoulder with her. "Glad you noticed."

"Slip of the tongue." She continued to slide her feet. "If I wasn't afraid of losing the light, I'd whack you and that ego of yours."

"Freudian slip?"

"You wish."

He sucked in his gut the last few feet. Not that he'd ever let her know it or he'd never hear the end of it.

Pilar weaseled through and popped like a cork into a larger passageway. "Light ahead." She bounded forward and stopped dead in her tracks. He plowed into her back.

Sunlight spilled inside from another opening. For a long moment, she teetered. Her boot tips hanging out into the nothingness above the canyonland. She gasped and her arms flailed.

He reared, dug in his heels, and wrapped his fist in her shirttail.

"I wish," his heart thundered in his ears, "one day you'd look before you leap."

She craned her neck out the opening. "There's a trail."

Alex snagged her sleeve. "We can't."

He took a good, hard look over the desert floor. Upside-down hoodoo rock formations stretched across the horizon. "Over there's out of our jurisdiction."

Alex grimaced. "Over there is Mexico."

17

Before

ALEX HAD HOPED TO TALK HIMSELF OUT OF HIS FEELINGS FOR Pilar. Flashing the smile that never failed to secure his objectives, he dated a bevy—another Pilar word—of coeds.

To no avail. Because right when he had said female, breathless and willing, he was the one to call it off. He—Alejandro Roberto Torres—was actually starting to acquire the reputation of a tease.

When he could stand the separation no longer, he went home. To quench the aching thirst of his heart for Pilar. But he decided to play it cool. Until she swung open the door of the hacienda. And smiled at him.

Okay. She smirked at him. One hand propped on her hip. The Pilar he knew. And loved.

Not that he'd tell her that. Not yet. She was only a junior in high school. Talk about robbing the cradle. He ought to stay away.

But he didn't.

He came home every weekend that autumn. Determined to outrun him, Pilar suggested a training ritual practiced by the old time Apaches, she learned about from Abuela.

Each of them, she explained, must hold a mouthful of water to the top of the mesa. Without swallowing. Without losing a drop.

Would teach them how to breathe better. Improve his performance for the upcoming basketball season. Strengthen their will.

Putty in her slim hands, he complied. His lungs burning each and every time. But he'd have run uphill with a mouthful of sand if that's what she wanted.

His grandmother's black eyes missed nothing.

"You need to slow down, *mi nieto*." Abuela held up her palm. "Pilar's seventeen. She's smart and deserves to explore the possibilities for which God created her."

"I'd never—"

Abuela arched those aristocratic brows. "I will not allow you to ruin her life on a whim, Alex. She's not like the bimbos you—"

"I'd never hurt her."

Abuela tightened her full lips. "I don't think you would. Not intentionally. But you can be rash. The both of you, impetuous. You wait and do the right thing. Or one call to Byron and he will end it for you. For good."

"I want to protect her."

"And who," Abuela's eyes narrowed. "Will protect her from you?"

He clenched his teeth. Inexplicably, Byron had become Abuela's favorite of the Three Musketeers. And they all knew it.

Including Byron.

Alex didn't doubt Abuela would side with Byron over his and Pilar's wishes. It'd been agreed Pilar would remain with Abuela to finish high school before heading off to college. Now wasn't the time to push his grandmother. Later, when Alex was in a stronger bargaining position, he'd win Abuela over with a hefty dose of charm.

Byron came home at Christmas after finishing Basic before reporting to his first duty station in the South. Fort Bragg. Where the women promised to be as sweet as the tea, Byron joked.

For fear of betraying her feelings, Pilar took to leaving on a pretext every time Alex entered the same room. Yet a palpable cord tethered them each to the other. Byron watched them, too.

And before he left for Bragg, Byron filed to have Abuela's guardianship transferred to him. He made arrangements for a senior year transfer to a school on the base. Sending Alex into an absolute panic.

If Pilar went to North Carolina, Byron would do everything—anything—in his power to keep her away from Alex for good.

Abuela forbade Alex to come home for the summer. So Alex got a summer job in Tucson. He got three jobs. Anything not immoral or illegal to make extra bucks. He didn't sleep. Much.

Whereupon Abuela had a change of heart. Or, at least a small, temporary measure of mercy. She invited him home for the Fourth of July weekend.

Pilar flung open the door before he even exited the Jeep. She hovered on the top step of the porch. With Abuela, arms crossed, just behind. The skin underneath Pilar's eyes was purple and smudged.

He scowled at his grandmother. "You made her cry?"

Pilar touched his arm. "You know better." Her mouth drooped. "Apaches don't cry."

Abuela tilted her head. "Apparently over you, Alex, they do."

His heart thudded. His hand covered Pilar's. Abuela's birdlike eyes followed his motion.

And then the old woman shrank before them. "I can't fight you both."

Isabel Torres leaned against the adobe wall of the hacienda. "One last time before she goes east next month. Don't make me regret trusting you, Alex."

The panic knotted his stomach, threatening to implode in his belly. Time was running out. Abuela vanished within the interior of the house.

Pilar rubbed her cheek against his sleeve. He felt the warmth of her mouth through the fabric.

"One more race, Alex?" Her breath caught on a sob. "One more."

He ran without heart, Pilar easily besting him. She frowned as she took heaving breaths of air as if she suspected he'd not given it his all. He bent over, hands on his knees.

"I wanted to give you something."

He straightened at the wobbly tone of her voice.

"So you won't forget about me."

His gut lurched. "I'm not going to forget you. Never, Mia Pia."

She foraged for something in her jean pocket. She removed a pebble-size black rock. "This is for you."

Like many stones littering the ground in Arizona. This one polished, though. A rounded, volcanic nodule with a hole chiseled near the top.

She held it to the sun. "It's translucent. See?"

He wrapped his arms around her and pressed her shoulder blades against his chest. He nuzzled her neck with his cheek.

"They're called Apache Tears."

She inched out of the shelter of his arms. Reluctantly, he released his hold. She extracted a silver chain from her other pocket.

"Legend says long ago a band of Apaches were chased by an enemy to the edge of a cliff. Rather than surrender, they chose death for themselves and their horses."

"I'm not giving up, Pia."

After threading the chain through the stone, she reached around his neck and fumbled for the catch.

"I won't let you go, Pia. I'm working on a plan. Trust me."

The necklace secured, her fingers feathered the short hair above his ear. "It's said when their loved ones heard of the tragedy, the Apache women cried. And as their tears hit the ground, the teardrops turned into these stones. A memorial to their true love."

He lifted her chin. "I don't want a memorial. I want you. For all time. Forever. I love you, Pia." He choked on a laugh. "Always have. Always will."

The words so long contained could no longer be denied.

Her obsidian eyes searched his face. Not quite believing this Alejandro Torres was for real? He couldn't quite believe this Alejandro Torres was real, either.

Except for the rightness swelling in his chest.

Why didn't she say something?

These stoic Apaches would be the death of him.

"I love you, too, Alex. Forever. For all time."

Something long tight in his belly uncoiled a notch.

His beautiful, ever serious Pilar. He traced her delicate jawline with the pad of his thumb. He brushed his lips against the jutting apple of her cheekbone.

Melting at his touch, she nestled her mouth against his palm. "I trust you, Alex."

He buried his nose in her hair. *"Mia?"*

Mine.

Her breath fanned his cheek. "Yours."

"Will you marry me, Pilar?" He took a deep breath. "Today?"

18

Reyna is a departure from his previous MO." On the sofa in Isabel's living room, Emily Waters consulted her notes. "Reyna's mother said she watched her daughter get into Ms. Clum's truck this morning. Our serial usually takes the girls at night."

Pilar knotted her hands.

Emily bit her lip. "It couldn't have been Dr. Velarde."

"Border footage confirms Velarde crossed at Douglas last night." Sidd glanced up from his laptop. "Alone."

"So we're back to zero with suspects?" Alex exhaled. "And what about Talitha Clum's part in this?"

Emily frowned. "Maybe the serial spotted them at the canyon and took advantage of the opportunity."

Alex pursed his lips. "That's assuming he took Clum and that she wasn't part of his operation. For all we know, she's been luring those girls into the canyon."

"But why would she do that, Alex?" Pilar cocked her head. "Have you found a connection between her and this animal?"

He massaged the back of his neck. "Maybe if we'd ever catch a break and ID this guy we could. If only Reyna wasn't across the border."

"Why can't you go get her?" Clomping across the terracotta floor, Manny threw himself onto the sofa. "The Broncos have taken Reyna, and we need to get her back."

The Stronghold

Pilar blew a breath between her lips. "The Broncos haven't taken anybody, Manny. And even if they had, they've gotten her across the border where we can't follow."

Manny pivoted toward Woodrow. "She's one of ours."

Woodrow dropped his eyes. "I'm sorry but one inch off the rez, if she were in Tucson, we'd have no jurisdiction. Much less in Mexico."

Manny swung around. "You're federal, Alex. You go after her. Please..."

At the catch in Manny's voice, she watched Alex's eyes glaze. Reliving that bad time when she'd been taken?

The thought of the monster hurting a little girl like Reyna... Pilar's heart quaked. Nothing had changed. They were still helpless against this wickedness.

Alex scrubbed his face. "Mexico is a sovereign nation. It's not like in the movies. We can't steamroll across the border with guns blazing. Charles is working diplomatic channels now with our boss at Quantico. Requesting entry and law enforcement privileges."

"Which are highly unlikely to be bestowed." Abuela bunched her arms over her denim shirt. "They'll not want armed Americans on their turf. Same as before."

"Maybe, maybe not," Emily soothed. "But we've requested the *federales* look into the case and investigate on their side. Maybe they'll find her."

Pilar's mouth flattened. "Maybe chuckwallas will fly."

She couldn't sit here doing nothing. Not while she—of all people—knew what was probably happening to Reyna.

Alex gave her a look. "Stop pacing, Pia. You're not helping."

"I watch television." Manny scowled. "Those Mexican dudes are on the take. Bribed by the drug lords. They won't help us."

"Not all of them, Manny." Alex kept his voice low. "I've done undercover ops with their version of DEA. Most want their country free of the brutality the drug trade brings."

Manny bolted to his feet. "I just want Reyna to come home."

Alex rested his hand on Manny's shoulder. "We all want that, son."

Pilar's gaze locked on Alex's strong, brown fingers.

"I promise you," Alex scanned Manny's face. "We won't stop looking. We won't stop trying. I'll do everything I can to bring her back."

Isabel herded Manny toward the kitchen. "I cannot stand by and allow this to happen to another child under my protection without doing something."

Leaving the federal agents to strategize, Pilar drifted to the porch and leaned against the railing. Alex joined her, close but not quite touching.

"Reyna's gone," she whispered. "I didn't have the heart to tell Manny we'll likely never find her alive."

Alex gripped the railing. His knuckles whitened. "If I'd been smarter, quicker on the uptake, this would've never happened. If we'd been able to stop him at the last perigee, last year's perigee..." He shoved away.

"This isn't your fault. What happened to me wasn't your fault, Alex."

"Yes, it was."

She touched his arm. A muscle jumped in his jaw. "It wasn't your fault. We both made mistakes—"

"Mistakes I've spent a lifetime repenting." He raked his hand through his hair. "Mistakes for which you were the one to pay the price."

"If anyone is to blame, it's that so-called loving God of yours. By creating that kind of evil."

Alex's eyes snapped. "God is neither evil nor does evil. God gave men and women the right to choose goodness or wickedness."

She shrugged. "At best, He allows it to exist. Which is bad enough. Like He's allowed this animal to roam for over a decade destroying lives."

"The only thing I've managed to cling to, Pia, is the great love of God for his children. A love that desires a real relationship. The kind of relationship that offers a choice. To love or not to love."

Alex's chest heaved. "And not to love Him, I realized, was the first step on the path toward evil. Because real love, like His, loves enough to let us choose Him or the darkness. To make our own mistakes. But He's also there to pick up the pieces of our brokenness when we cry out to Him."

Her eyes traveled over his face, familiar as the back of her own hand. Beloved and always longed for. "You *have* changed. You've become a theologian."

Alex laughed. Genuine amusement lifted the corners of his mouth. "Hardly."

His shoulders relaxed a notch. "Out of necessity maybe. Because to continue the way I started led only to destruction. God's mercy was something I didn't deserve. His grace, an offer I couldn't refuse."

The pure, holy God Abuela implored—now Byron and Alex, too—would want nothing to do with her. Someone desecrated and ruined.

Alex's phone beeped on his belt. He pressed the cell to his ear. "Torres speaking."

She shifted. "What?"

He was already moving toward the Suburban in the driveway. "Darlene and Sidd at Clum's. They say there's something I need to see."

"Reyna?" Pilar hustled down the steps. "What did they find?"

Alex threw open the car door. "Mice."

His mouth curled in on itself. "They found what's left of Clum's pets."

Alex fought the bile rising in his throat. Ever the animal lover, Pilar covered her mouth and scrambled outside Talitha Clum's wickiup.

"What kind of person does something like this, Darlene?"

Squatting beside the ring of stones, his behavioral analyst poked at the ashes of the fire. The blonde Texan's face looked as green as he felt.

Darlene flicked a glance at the row of mice suspended upside down from an iron rod. "Torturing animals is classic psychopath. Practice before graduating to humans."

"Clum did this? Or the serial who took her and Reyna?"

Darlene chewed her lower lip. "From the putrefying bodies, I'm gonna guess the kills are a week old."

He backed farther from the buzzing flies and the smell. "It's looking less likely Clum was taken and more like she's a willing participant in whatever sick games the serial is playing."

"Birds of a feather." The tribal detective, who had also been called out to Clum's rez-located home, grimaced. "She's reenacting stuff straight out of the Apache past."

"What do you mean?"

Kenoi crossed his arms over his barrel chest. "Unlike Pilar, I've always been interested in the old ways."

At the mention of her name, Alex narrowed his eyes. "I find it kind of interesting you—valedictorian of your class—chose to stay on the rez as a low-paying tribal detective."

Kenoi widened his stance. "I'm a stay-at-home Apache. Like Pilar."

Alex mirrored Kenoi's stance, his feet spread even with his hips.

"Went off-rez for college. Being an in-and-out Apache didn't suit me. Wanted to be with family and friends. Missed the sense of tribal belonging. Some of us, like Pilar, feel a call to serve our community."

Darlene cleared her throat. "You were saying about Apache old ways?"

Kenoi gestured to the rodents. "Different time. As brutal as what I've heard the cartels do to informants. Rats..."

Alex nodded. "Interesting theory. We've speculated this serial had cartel connections. Maybe putting an Apache spin on the usual cartel violence."

"What happened here?"

Alex turned at the sound of Pilar's voice.

Facing her fears, she'd crept back inside. His heart beat faster having her this close. His protective side kicked in and he edged nearer, but she gave him an annoyed glance.

In her I'd-rather-die-than-admit-I'm-scared mode. But anything was better than the Pilar he'd witnessed in her bathroom. With the self-inflicted wounds.

That Pilar undid him.

Kenoi sighed. "Captured soldiers—Mexican or American—were suspended from a tree branch over a bonfire."

"You cross an Apache?" She gave Alex a look. "We don't play."

No surprise that tough, little Pilar grew up to become law enforcement.

Kenoi poked out his lips. "The soldiers were roasted alive like these mice." Darlene bent for a closer look.

Alex reared. "Seriously? I've seen a lot of things in war and on the job, but...?"

Kenoi's face hardened. "Like I said, another time, another place."

Pilar tossed her head. "How could someone like this fly under the tribal radar for so long?"

Darlene straightened. "Sidd and I found a 'pet' cemetery beyond the house. She's been doing this awhile. Way out here in the middle of nowhere, she was able to get away with this without anyone suspecting. She 'played' normal when she went into town, I'm guessing."

"So we've got two freakazoids to track." Alex set his jaw. "Why did she take Reyna? What's Clum's connection to this? What's her motivation?"

Darlene frowned. "There are documented cases of murderers with separate killing sprees joining forces. Partnering to heighten the scope and intensity of the pleasure they derive from the camaraderie of joint murder."

He glanced at his watch. "Let's reconvene at the San Carlos PD after you and Sidd finish here. We need to see if there's something in her background that'll give us a clue as to why she's doing this and, more importantly, where she's headed."

Kenoi hunched his shoulders. "Probably not much in the records to find. Talitha Clum's been around as long as most people remember. And the Old One's electronic footprint is slim to none, I'm thinking."

Pilar skimmed a loose tendril of hair behind her ear. "Woodrow and I will canvas the elders and see what they know."

Alex's stomach clenched.

Not what he'd prefer, Pilar spending the day with her old boyfriend. But she was right. The most efficient use of manpower while they waited for instructions from Quantico.

That afternoon, Alex swiveled from the computer monitor. "It's like Talitha Clum simply materialized one day on the rez. No records of any kind."

Pilar sank into an office chair beside Emily. "Talitha Clum predates the grid. Calvin Cojo, the oldest of the Old Ones, thinks she's from another rez, not originally a San Carlos Apache. Taken in by the Clums. Maybe from the Mescalero rez in New Mexico. He couldn't be sure."

Kenoi poured himself a cup of coffee. He sipped and made a face. "A female Old One would've been better. Women always remember stuff about a person's background better." He dropped into the empty seat on the other side of Pilar.

She play-slapped his arm. "Did you just call women nosy busybodies?"

The playful banter between these two old "friends" made Alex want to shoot something. Or somebody. Starting with Detective Kenoi.

Kenoi grinned over the rim of his cup. "If the nose fits."

Shooting the tribal detective a nasty look, Alex practiced taking a steady breath. "So when the Clums died, she stayed on?"

"Looks that way. Never married. Scratched out a living from gathering herbs and selling them at the trading post."

Alex exhaled. "We need to go deeper. Find out more about the Clums."

Sidd clicked a button on his keyboard. "On it."

Charles, lines of weariness carved on his face, replaced the landline phone on its receiver. "Bad news, Alex."

He braced himself.

"Quantico won't give approval, nor will Mexico City. No go ahead to cross the border to pursue."

Alex slammed his hand on the desk. "Don't they understand a child's life is at stake? An American child's life is at stake?"

Pilar curled her lip. "Like I said earlier, less care for non-Anglos like me. Only good Apache is a dead Apache. Some things never change."

Charles loosened his tie. "Mexican-American relations are at an all-time low right now—"

"Which is saying a mouthful," Alex interjected.

"—owing to that business between DEA and the dispute about who took down the Juarez cartel leader, Flores, a few years back."

"My buddy, Aaron Yazzie, was involved with that." Alex's lips twisted. "Flores specialized in human trafficking, murder, and cocaine. Think they'd be glad anybody took him down. Another case of politics at its finest."

Sidd beckoned. "Got a hit on the Clums."

The team—federal, Pilar, and Kenoi—gathered around his chair.

Sidd pointed at the screen. "Interesting little factoid. Ealdon Clum was a well-known tracker and scout. He's listed as one of the members of the famous expedition that set out from Douglas to find a missing woman taken by the Bronco Apaches in Mexico in the 1940s."

Alex exchanged a significant look with Pilar. "Didn't Abuela mention a Torres took part in that, too?"

Her lips thinned. "We keep coming back to Mexico."

"And the Broncos."

He turned to his team. "Keep digging, Sidd. Follow the few leads we have at this point. Charles and Emily, see what you can unearth at the university's wildlife preserve. My gut tells me Velarde is up to his eyeballs in what's going down."

Alex grabbed his blazer. "Darlene, try to find a connection between Clum and Velarde. We're missing something. Something vital. Think you can help her with this, Detective?"

Kenoi nodded.

Pilar planted her hands on her hips. "What about me, Alex?"

"We need to talk to my grandmother again. See what else she can remember about that expedition and the Broncos."

"You don't believe the Broncos still exist, do you?" Pilar frowned. "You don't really think a rez legend is behind this?"

He shook his head. "I don't. But apparently, someone does."

19

THE FIRST STREAKS OF DAWN BRIGHTENED THE SKY BEFORE Alex and Pilar, pulling an all-nighter with the team, arrived back at the Torres ranch. Yet not a single light burned from the darkened hacienda. A strange quiver of fear stirred her heart. The Land Rover was gone.

She exited the SUV before Alex brought the car to a complete standstill. She ran inside. "Abuela?"

"What's wrong?" Hurrying after her, Alex's hand hovered over his gun. "Has there been an intruder?"

Pilar did a complete three-sixty in the high-ceiling foyer. "Manuel?" She dashed upstairs.

Alex took the steps two at a time. "Slow down. Tell me what's wrong."

"Manny!" She crisscrossed the hall flinging open doors. "Where are you?"

"No one's here." Alex reholstered his gun. "Nothing's out of place. What makes you think something's happened?"

She balled her fist. "I feel it. He's not here. Something's wrong."

Alex turned on lamps as he followed her from room to room. "I know a lot has been happening—bad things—but there's no need to assume the worst. Abuela probably took him to Saguaro Gulch for breakfast."

"I know when he's in danger. I know."

Alex furrowed his brow. "Wherever he is, he's with Abuela, Pilar."

"I don't like not knowing where he is."

She strode toward Abuela's bedroom at the end of the hall.

"Uh, Pia?" Alex backpedaled. "Abuela's room has always been off limits."

"Nothing's off limits until I find out what she's done with Manny."

Alex flicked the light switch, and Pilar took inventory of Abuela's sanctuary.

Elaborate brocade curtains and a canopied bed. A Torres heirloom, Pilar supposed. On the bedspread, the FBI file from the table downstairs. Its contents strewn across the fabric, a copy of Talitha Clum's driver's license rested on top.

At the end of the bed sat a brass-studded trunk. Pilar fingered the butter-soft leather of a fringed, child-size garment spread across the lid. Something rattled underneath the deerskin and rolled to the rug.

Her breath hitched. A gourd, a child's plaything. A *nineteenth-century* Apache child's plaything.

Alex seized the gourd. "Where'd this come from?"

"It's Apache." She unfolded a wrinkled, yellowed paper from Abuela's nightstand. Scanning it, she sagged against the baroque-style bed. "Abuela, what've you done?"

She handed Alex the hand-drawn map where the Peloncillo Mountains etched the boundary between Arizona and New Mexico's bootheel before emptying into the Chihuahuan plain. Where the vast open barrens of the desert ran into the horseshoe-shaped Bavispe River. And beyond the river, an X marking a distant, remote spot somewhere in the soaring sky islands of the Sierra Madre.

The ancient Apache route Abuela had spoken of?

"I cannot believe," he fumed, "they've gone searching for Reyna on their own."

"That stubborn old woman." Pilar squeezed her eyes shut. "She's taken Manny straight into the clutches of the devil."

Pilar disintegrated before Alex's eyes.

"She's taken my boy to Mexico." Pilar groaned. "Oh, God, anywhere but there."

141

Pilar sank to the floor beside the high-poster bed, knees to her chin. Her eyes closed, a guttural keening rose from the depths of her being.

His skin prickled. The sound like a creature in unrelenting, mortal pain. Most times he forgot Pilar was any different from him. But sometimes the otherness—the Apache in her—scared him. He'd never seen her this unglued.

Except at the hospital in Tucson.

Alex dropped to one knee. "I'll call border patrol. Stop them at the crossing."

"He's not yours," she whispered. "You can't have him. I won't let you..."

A certain, sinking suspicion filtered through Alex's consciousness. Gutting him. Flaying his nerve endings.

"Pilar—" He grasped hold of her hand. "Talk to me, baby." His voice broke. "Please..." Her fingers felt like ice.

His heart hammered. "Manny's not Byron's son, is he, Pilar?"

The keening stopped.

She opened her eyes. "No." Her voice quivered. "He's not."

Her eyes bored into Alex. Sensing his turmoil? Gauging his reaction.

Forcing himself to breathe, he settled beside her. "Manny's your child."

She lifted her chin. "Yes."

"And the beast's?" Raw pain lashed through Alex. "The man who—"

She shrank from him.

Remorse smote Alex. He was failing her. Again.

Oh, God... Emptiness consumed him. *Not this...*

He scrubbed his hand over his face. "Why the pretense of being his auntie? In every sense of the word you're his mother. The boy loves you. Why did you keep it from him?"

"Would you tell a child something like that?"

The torment in her eyes eviscerated Alex. "The sins of the father visited upon his son? I refused to make Manny suffer for something so totally beyond his control. Like the mistakes of his parents."

She dropped her head. "Do you have any idea how cruel other children would've been, even well-meaning adults? I couldn't take the chance of anyone knowing."

"Does Abuela know?"

Pilar shook her head. "Byron and I were careful to keep our story straight." She seized Alex's arm. "Manny mustn't ever know."

Such knowledge might cripple Manny. Destroy the innocence. The joy. The goodness Alex loved in the young man he'd only known a few days.

His heart lacerated, Alex ached for the child who should've been his...

Pilar's eyes glistened with unshed tears. "Byron's superpower, remember, is his loyalty. I didn't discover I was pregnant until he and I flew to Bragg. He begged me to end the pregnancy."

She took a shuddering breath. "I-I couldn't do that, Alex. I thought about it. I really did. But for more than one reason, I just couldn't."

"Why?" His voice sounded strangled to his own ears. "Why didn't you take that pill after they did the rape kit? Why put yourself through birthing a rapist's child?"

She rounded on him. "Manny is *my* child." She turned away. "And I had my reasons."

A dull throbbing began in Alex's temples. "You Apaches keep your secrets well, but Manny suspects something. He doesn't understand why Byron's in North Carolina and he's here with you. Manny thinks his dad doesn't want him to be a part of his new life with his fiancée."

"Byron wanted him to come to Bragg." Her mouth trembled. "I should've loved Manny enough to let him go. If I had, Manny would be far, far away from this monster."

Alex slumped. "And if I'd loved you enough to let you go to Bragg instead of running away to Mexico, the monster would've never been able to get his hands on you."

"Despite how things ended between us, Alex, I'd never want to lose those days we shared. Never."

He longed to touch her, to hold Pilar in the circle of his arms. But he dared do neither. "Why did you come back here, Pilar? Why put either of you at risk?"

"I wanted to go home. I missed the wide, open spaces. The blue sky. I wanted Manny to know his heritage."

She quirked an eyebrow at the deerskin on the bed. "Kind of went overboard in hindsight with that, I guess."

Gripping the bedspread, she rose. "I should've known better than to come back, though. I should've realized what *he* once takes, he regards as his. And that would include Manny. I can't let him get his hands on Manny. Everyone he touches he destroys."

Alex stood. "He didn't take Manny. Abuela did. Though I'm not sure the why behind her reasoning."

"Isabel's gone to find Segundo."

Pilar rummaged through the contents of the trunk. "That's who she always seeks out when she or someone she loves is in trouble. And knowing my headstrong Manny, I expect he refused to be left behind."

"Like his mother?"

She straightened. "Exactly like his mother."

Alex held up an old Douglas newspaper clipping. "What's this?"

She peered at the faded ink. "Something about three Apache children taken captive by a Mexican posse looking for a missing woman. Why would Abuela have this stuff, Alex?"

He shrugged. "Maybe from her father's expedition."

She studied the wrinkled paper. "Look at the date, Alex. May 1951."

He examined the clipping. "Broncos in the 1950s?"

She jutted her chin. "I'm going to Mexico and bring Manny home."

"At the risk of being called a tagalong, not without me you're not." Alex folded his arms. "You and I are going to bring them home. Manny, Abuela, and Reyna."

"Or I'll die trying." Pilar's eyes flashed. "Because no matter what we find there, I won't let *him* take me. Not again."

20

Before

Pɪʟᴀʀ ᴅɪᴅɴ'ᴛ ᴍᴀʀʀʏ ʜɪᴍ ᴛʜᴀᴛ ᴅᴀʏ. Nᴏᴛ ʙᴇᴄᴀᴜsᴇ sʜᴇ ᴅɪᴅɴ'ᴛ want to. But because Alex said he needed to work through some logistics first.

With mounting desperation, they coordinated their plans. Pilar would travel to Tucson in Abuela's Land Rover on the pretext of a track meet. She and Alex would then travel to the Nogales border crossing in his Jeep.

"Send your birth certificate registered mail," he texted. "Bring your baptism certificate."

Pilar pushed aside the guilt for deceiving Abuela. She didn't like lying to Isabel, or by extension to Byron. Only an unforeseen training mission on Byron's end had delayed her departure for Bragg thus far.

There'd be no second reprieve. If she and Alex wanted to be together, it was now or never. She was old enough to know her own mind and heart.

And her heart had known since they were children that Alex was the only one she'd ever love.

They'd slip across the border and disappear for a few days. Giving them the time to do what couldn't be undone.

She pulled into the parking lot of Alex's apartment complex. Doubt ate at her stomach.

Had he changed his mind? She gripped the steering wheel. What if he *hadn't* changed his mind? Would Abuela and Byron ever forgive her?

A tap on the window jolted Pilar. Alex grinned at her with his even, white teeth from the other side of the glass. And she shoved her misgivings into her gut.

This was Alex. *Her* Alex. And in a few days time, her heart thudded, they'd belong to each other forever.

She rolled down the window.

He leaned in and planted a swift kiss on her lips. "Ready for the adventure of a lifetime, Mia Pia?"

After getting in the Jeep, he handed her a brand new photo ID.

"What's this?"

"Used a few contacts from my former street life. Got you a new driver's license."

With a birthdate that made Pilar eighteen.

"Had to figure a way around the consent thing. The Civil Registry will require it."

Pilar's eyebrows rose. "We're getting married in a government office?" Somehow not all she'd hoped for.

He ran his finger along the length of her jawline. "Civil ceremonies are the only legal ceremony in Mexico. But I promise you, for Abuela's sake, we'll find a priest, too."

The purpose of the baptismal certificates.

She pressed her lips into his warm palm. And was pleased to see his Adam's apple bob.

He blew out a breath. "We'll do a big party when we return home."

"Think either of them will ever let us come home after this?"

Alex fondled the Apache tear on the chain he wore underneath his shirt. "I'd rather ask for forgiveness than permission. Once it's done, what can they do?"

He shrugged. "I'll grovel. I'll beg. I'll smile. Abuela always forgives me."

Pilar cut her eyes at him. "That self-confidence of yours may be your downfall yet. She may not forgive you or me this time. One day your so-called charm may not be enough. Some things may not be forgivable."

"So-called?"

Pilar play-punched him in his bicep.

"Ow!" He rubbed his shoulder.

"Don't you ever take anything seriously?"

He gazed forward through the windshield. "I take you and me very seriously, Pia." His hands flexed around the wheel. "It's going to be all right. I promise you. I'll make it right."

Alex drove south on Interstate 19. Her stomach muscles clenched as less than an hour later they exited at the International Border. He turned into the inspection line behind the other vehicles.

One of the busiest crossings in the world, streams of Mexicans flowed past the checkpoints between Nogales, Sonora, and Nogales, Arizona. Women sauntered through on foot with their babies and empty shopping baskets. Day workers entered through turnstiles. Produce trucks headed for American markets.

But she tensed as they crept closer. "They may not let us through. Our adventure may be over before it's begun."

"Faith, Pia. Trust me. I got this. 'Sides leaving the States is easy." He wiggled his eyebrows at her. "It's the getting back in that's harder."

"Why doesn't that comfort me?"

Although not the militant armed guards she'd been expecting, the Border Patrol agents were thorough in their examination of vehicles heading north. Heading south?

She held her breath as they neared the barricade. Mounted cameras recorded their license plate.

Flashing his trademark Alex Torres smile, he showed the agent the documents he'd secured. Agents examined Alex's ID, then hers.

Returning their papers, the agent motioned to the vehicle behind them. "Enjoy your trip."

Alex laughed as they passed over the border. "Told you. We're through, baby."

She released the breath she'd been holding as they emerged on the other side. Into another world. Into her new life with Alex.

In Nogales, the narrow, winding streets were crowded with pedestrians. Colorful fabrics, sombreros, and tourist kitsch hung from market stalls. Street vendors hawked their wares, selling everything from tortillas to *lemonada*.

He edged out of the congested traffic and pulled into a clinic on the other end of the boulevard. "Blood tests first."

She groaned.

Afterward, eager to leave Nogales and the American border as far behind them as they could, Alex left the city. They stopped at a small provincial village several hours farther south. In the distance, the lavender blue peaks of the Sierra Madre—ancestral stronghold of her people—rose like the bruised knuckles of a clenched fist above the desert.

Midafternoon, the town square appeared deserted, except for a few shifty-eyed patrons of the local *taberna* hanging about on the sidewalk. Wrought-iron balconies were strung with crepe paper streamers of every hue. Alex parked in a space outside the registrar's office.

"Looks like we've arrived at the beginning of a *novenario*." He pointed to the poster tacked to the office door. "Usually a nine-day celebration of some minor saint."

She smiled. "Leave it to you to time our wedding with a party."

Thirty minutes later, they found themselves once again on the sidewalk in front of the government office. Civil ceremony done.

Her head spun. She frowned at her knee through the hole in her jeans. That was it?

So not what she'd dreamed this day would be.

Alex clutched the marriage certificate in his hand, the same bemused expression on his face she imagined as her own. But the important thing was they were married. And there was nothing Byron nor Abuela could do to change that.

"Let's go find a priest." Alex's eyes glinted. "In the eyes of the law, we may be married. But let's do it right in the eyes of God."

Her heart lifted.

The square was beginning to awaken to life. Workers strung strands of light from tree to tree. Shop owners set out displays of their merchandise on the sidewalk. Matrons and young girls decorated the bandstand with bright, colorful poppies. A mariachi band tuned.

Swarthy men, in jeans and the white straw hats preferred south of the border, climbed out of the back of a fully loaded Ram truck. Music blared from the radio. Bling dangled from the mirror.

The village women wrapped the ends of their shawls closer around their bodies and grabbed hold of their young daughters.

Pilar felt the leering stares of the rough-faced men.

Alex stepped between her and the men across the square.

The pack shifted toward the *taberna*, breaking the sudden tension. The previous, bleary-eyed patrons dissipated like fog before the onslaught of the sun.

"Who are they?" she whispered.

Alex took her hand. "They farm the crop that pays."

She looked at him.

"That's what they call it around here."

"Drug—"

He silenced her, his finger against her lips. "Don't say it." His head swiveled. "Not a great time to be this close to the Sierra Madre. Harvest time. They've probably come to town because of the fiesta. We need to stay out of their way."

She nodded.

He led her to the entrance of a shop. "I'm going to inquire about a priest at the church over there. Stay here until I come back."

An old woman greeted her as she strolled inside. Pilar's heart pinged thinking of Abuela. Guilt smothered her chest. By now, her carefully timed e-mail had arrived in Isabel's inbox.

Pilar fingered the embroidered neckline of a white, peasant blouse. Pretty. She wished she'd thought to bring more proper bridal attire with her. Not that she owned anything this girly. Her wardrobe consisted solely of jeans and boots.

She smoothed her hand over a ruffled skirt, the banded ribbon tiers matching the peasant blouse. What she wouldn't give to be able to wow Alex today when she walked down the church aisle.

"It is pretty, no?"

She smiled at the old woman behind the counter. "Yes, it is."

The old woman placed a hand over her heart. "I sew."

"You do beautiful work."

The old woman ventured from behind the register. "You like? I can—"

"Oh, I'm sorry. It's lovely, but I can't afford—"

Sounds of a scuffle broke out on the sidewalk. A child cried out. The old woman and Pilar rushed outside.

A little girl cowered against the exterior wall of the shop. Alex landed a blow on a "farmer's" chin and sent the man reeling into the street.

The old woman shouted and waved her arms at the bully. He staggered to his feet, but the old woman seized a broom. He snarled.

Alex coiled his fist. Pilar hefted a dustpan, shoulder-to-shoulder with him and the woman.

"You disgusting, dirty pig!" The old woman jabbed the broom at the man. "Do not touch my granddaughter."

The man whipped out a knife from his pocket.

Pilar inhaled sharply. Alex's face hardened, but he didn't retreat.

"*Venga!*" A voice barked from the shadows of the *taberna*.

The florid man stiffened.

"*Ven aquí.* Here. *Pronto.*"

At the commanding authority in the other man's voice, the attacker let loose a stream of curses but complied. Backpedaling, he never took his eyes off them until he reached his fellow ruffians.

The old woman slackened her grip on the broom. "Nita." Her cacao bean eyes darted toward her granddaughter huddling against the wall. "Let us go inside." She motioned for Alex and Pilar.

"I did not realize the *narcotraficantes* had arrived. Or I wouldn't have sent Nita on an errand. Please," she gestured toward the shop. "Allow me to properly express my thanks for saving her."

Pilar helped the little girl to her feet. The child trembled beneath Pilar's touch. The old woman marched inside, broom held high as her head.

"Every fiesta they drive into town. Drink, fight, take our girls."

Alex closed the shop door behind them.

The woman's gaze flitted to Pilar. "Better not to linger during the *novenario*." She sighed. "It was not always this way. But they come with their wads of cash, and they take what they cannot buy."

Alex scowled. "Why don't the *policia* do something?"

The old woman gave a shrug. "Most of them are paid to ignore the antics of these foot soldiers. They are afraid of *el jefe*."

"The boss?"

"*Sí.* They are armed and they take whomever they desire. Once they are married—"

"Married?" Pilar's nose wrinkled. "They force themselves on these girls and then they—"

"*Rapto.* Old custom. You cannot be prosecuted once the girl is your wife. She is therefore," the old woman struggled for the right word. "Yours. Yours to have taken in the eyes of the law."

Pilar's skin crawled. The bright-eyed little girl, not yet in her teens, hid her face in her grandmother's embrace.

The old woman stroked the girl's hair. "But today the *americano* and *americana* saved you, Nita. *Gloria a Dios.*" She extended her blue-veined hand. "I am Señora Martinez, and I thank you for what you did."

Alex stuffed his hands into his pockets. "It was nothing. Anyone would've—"

"No one else did." Señora Martinez offered the beautiful ribboned skirt to Pilar. "You like? I give to you."

Pilar shook her head. "No, Mrs. Martinez. I couldn't. We're not starting married life beholden to anyone."

Her eyes shot to Pilar's bare hand. "You are married?"

Pilar hid her hand in the pocket of her jeans. "We were just married at the Civil Registry."

Alex flushed. Their carefully calculated finances hadn't stretched to buying a proper ring. "We were hoping to have a priest conduct the religious ceremony today also. But..." He sighed. "Father Miguel refused. Too short notice, he said, on the heels of the festival."

Señora Martinez nudged the skirt at Pilar. "Father Miguel." She sniffed. "Young still. He doesn't yet understand our heart. The old *padre*, however, Father Emmanuel..."

A speculative look crisscrossed her features. She snapped her fingers.

Pilar and Nita jumped.

"A church wedding you want? A church wedding you will get. I owe you a debt of honor and never let it be said that I, Rosa Maria Emilia Martinez y Diaz, do not pay my debts."

Pilar found herself in the dressing room trying on the skirt, the blouse, and handcrafted white leather slippers. She emerged to find Alex gone and a matronly lady conferring with Mrs. Martinez. The woman held a plaited garland of flowers.

At Pilar's searching look, Mrs. Martinez patted her arm. "Your *esposo* left with my son, Joaquin. Leave everything to us. It will be *perfecto.*"

Pilar soon lost her bearings as they wound through a maze of side streets and entered the rear entrance to the Spanish-style church that fronted the square. Inside, soaring wood rafters. Scarred but gleaming wood pews. And, on a gilded high altar, candles blazed.

"Come. *Rápido.* Before *tu esposo* see."

Her husband. Pilar's heart fluttered. The church setting made everything more real.

In an anteroom, Señora Martinez braided Pilar's hair into a low chignon at the nape of her neck. As a final touch, she laid the plaited garland atop Pilar's head. The women smiled, their eyes moist.

"*Excelente.*"

"*Muy bueno.*"

A knock sounded. Mrs. Martinez shooed Pilar out of sight. The old woman opened the door a sliver. Minutes later, Mrs. Martinez returned with a stack of folded lace in her arms.

Her face wreathed into a smile. "*Tu esposo.* He think of everything." She unfolded the mantilla, edged in delicate lace. "Proper to cover head in *la iglesia.*" She draped the elbow-length headdress over Pilar.

Another knock.

Señora Martinez threw out her hands, but a smile quirked at her lips. She returned with a bouquet of roses. "We go before he thinks of something else."

Taking the flowers, Pilar inhaled their loveliness. She felt lovely, thanks to the señora and Alex's determination to make this a perfect day. The other lady slipped from the room.

Señora Martinez steered Pilar toward the vestibule. "*Es el tiempo.* It is time."

Pilar's heart lurched. Her eyes locked onto Alex at the end of the long aisle.

He stood, hands folded in front of him, beside a bearded gentleman she assumed to be the Martinez son. An old priest leaned upon a lectern on the step above.

And her Alex? So handsome. The señora hadn't neglected his attire, either. The baggy white peasant shirt and white linen trousers reflected well against his dark skin.

But the thing Pilar vowed she'd never forget? His eyes. Full of promise and hope. Forever.

She glided toward Alex. Toward her truest love. Toward her future.

Behind Nita and the petals she'd strewn in her path, Pilar's doubts fell away. And only love remained. Her love for Alex. His love for her.

At the base of the altar, Alex reached for her hand.

They angled to face the old priest. The scent of candle wax filled her nostrils as the flames of the tapers on the altar gleamed behind the *padre*. Father Emmanuel read from the holy book on the lectern and for the first time, she noticed the forearm crutches cupping his arms below each elbow.

Her eyes lifted to the high, sharp bones of his face as he paused to hold the book toward Alex. Alex let go of her hands to place a gleaming silver band upon the open pages.

Intoning a prayer, the priest closed his eyes. She and Alex did likewise. "*Repita después de mí.*"

She opened her eyes. Alex removed the ring from the Bible. Uncharacteristically shy, he dropped his eyes as he slid the ring onto her finger.

"I, Alejandro Roberto Torres, take you, Maria Caterina Pilar To-Clanny, to be my lawfully wedded wife."

She swallowed. His eyes gazed into hers, as serious as she'd ever seen him. He clasped her hands in his. The priest said something in *español*. Alex nodded.

"To have and to hold from this day forward," Alex translated for Pilar. "For better. For worse. Richer," he gave her a lopsided grin. "Or poorer. To love, honor, and cherish until death us do part." Moisture welled in his eyes.

Her heart swelled with love.

Father Emmanuel resumed speaking.

Alex took a deep breath. "Forsaking all others, I promise to cleave only unto you as long as we both shall live."

Moments later, she repeated her vows before God, this priest, and these generous villagers deep in the foothills of the Sierra Madre.

Señora Martinez and the lady encircled their shoulders with a figure-eight lasso of beads. Señor Martinez produced a small wooden box of thirteen golden coins, *las arras*—another wedding tradition, Alex explained. Father Emmanuel made the sign of the cross above their bowed heads and pronounced them husband and wife.

"What God has joined together, let no one put asunder," Alex translated.

She slipped her arm through the crook of his elbow.

"*Permítanme que les presente, al señor y señora Alejandro Roberto Torres.*"

Wild clapping from Nita. Happy sobs from the señora into her lace handkerchief. Señor Martinez pounded Alex's back.

Alex grinned. "Maria Caterina Pilar Torres y To-Clanny. Mia Pia, we did it."

"Not quite."

He cocked his head.

She wrapped her arms around his neck. On tiptoe, her lips grazed his. Tightening his hold, he kissed her much more thoroughly.

Her heels drifted to earth. Alex drew her down the aisle to where Señor Martinez threw open the double doors. They emerged into the dusk of evening to a party in progress. Word had spread of their nuptials, and the kindhearted women of the village had prepared places of honor at a table.

Applause greeted their entrance onto the wide stone steps in front of the church. Alex kissed her again, and she found herself swept toward the table on the bandstand. Only the blaring gangster rap from the black Ram truck roaring down the street disrupted the joy of the occasion.

In fiesta merriment, dark-eyed children dressed in their traditional best performed dances, which predated the Conquistadors. Alex pulled her out onto the planked dais for a first dance. Slow and tender, he held her in his arms as they swayed from side-to-side to a Mexican love song.

As the beat intensified, he broke away and swung her into a fast cha-cha-cha. Her skirt swirling, she danced and laughed. And knew she'd never be as happy as she was this night. She gave herself to the revelry of the villagers. To the surreal quality of her wedding feast under a thousand pinpoints of light in the blue velvet of the Mexican night.

Much later, her feet sore and her heart full, Alex extracted Pilar from the crowded dance floor to where Señor Martinez beckoned. Señor Joaquin Martinez, she discovered, Nita's widowed father, owned an inn.

They followed him arm-in-arm to the señor's graceful two-story home. Past the vestiges that remained of Spanish colonial splendor, up the ornate curving stairs to a bedchamber overlooking the square. Candlelight flickered.

"*Buenas noches,*" Martinez called as he shut the door behind him.

Pilar blushed. She knew little of the love between a man and a woman. And Alex knew much.

She wrung her hands in the folds of her skirt, unsure what to do next. Her eyes darted toward the canopied bed. To the window. To the carved mahogany dresser.

Anywhere except toward the stranger she suddenly didn't know. Her husband? She bit her lip. She feared she'd disappoint Alex. Not be enough for him.

"Pia." He caught the end of her belted sash. "Don't be afraid. I love you. I am your Alex. And you are mine."

He tugged her nearer, hand over hand on the sash at her waist, until she was close enough to feel his breath upon her face. "Trust me," he whispered. "Trust us." A pulse ticked in his cheek.

She tucked a tendril of hair behind her ear.

Alex's gaze traveled with her hand. "You will let your hair down for your husband, Pia?" His eyes went opaque. "*Por favor.*"

Her eyes flickered to his face at the uneven tone of his voice. Was Alex as nervous as she?

Never taking her gaze off his, she reached behind her head and removed the pins. She shook her hair loose from the confines of the bun. Her hair cascaded over her shoulders.

He rubbed a strand of her hair between his thumb and forefinger. With great tenderness, he billowed the lock over her shoulder. "And will you always wear your hair this way for me, Señora Torres?" He moistened his lips.

She leaned closer and placed her hands flat upon his chest. "For you, *mi esposo?*"

Alex's heartbeat thundered against her palms.

Her lips parted. "Always."

21

Alex's mouth hardened. "Not an acceptable risk, Pilar."

"You've been ordered to stay out of Mexico, Alex. You can't cross the border without destroying your career."

He strode down the hall.

She dogged his heels. "Not to mention there are cartel lowlifes who might recognize you and decide to end your sorry life."

He yanked open the dresser drawers. "You get Manny, and I get what I deserve." He stuffed a few articles of clothing into a backpack. "Sounds like a win-win from your perspective, Pilar."

She scowled. "Not funny. And I'm perfectly capable of bringing Manny home without your help. I'm not one of your brainless blondes, Alex."

Alex slung the backpack over his shoulder. "Brainless comes in all hair colors, Pilar. Like going into a foreign country—a violent, drug-infested country—where you don't even speak the language."

He brushed past her toward the stairs. "You need me."

She followed him downstairs. "I don't need you. I don't need anybody but Manny. And whatever it takes, I'll get him back."

Alex grabbed several bottles of water out of the fridge. "You need more than a thirst for vengeance if you want to get your boy out of Salazar's kingdom alive."

He took a box of protein bars from the pantry. "You need a plan. You need someone who not only speaks Spanish but knows cartelese, too."

"Are you stupid or am I speaking a language *you* don't comprehend?" She clenched her fists. "I. Don't. Want. You."

He swung around. "Oh, you've made your feelings perfectly clear. But do you honestly hate me enough to gamble Manny's life on your distaste for me? Like it or not, I'm the best chance you've got."

Alex plopped the bag on the table. "You forget, Abuela's life is at stake, too. I'm going with or without you."

She ground her teeth.

"I suggest instead of arguing with me—something at which you excel—you pack your own bag while I gather supplies for the journey."

"Like my Glock."

"Not like your Glock." He reached for the bowl of fruit. "Try and smuggle a weapon across the border and you'll find yourself in a Mexican lockup with no hope of ever locating Manny."

He grimaced. "We can purchase whatever firepower we need, unfortunately, on most street corners on the other side."

"What about your team?"

He paused mid-step. "I may be willing to sacrifice my job, but I can't ask them to commit career suicide. Ignorance in this case is better than charges of obstruction of justice. Oh, and don't forget your passport." He headed toward the hall. "I'll meet you out front in ten minutes."

Just as he suspected, however, five minutes later he watched Pilar—out of uniform in casual attire—exit the hacienda with a furtive look before striding toward the Jeep. Rounding the vehicle, she stopped at the sight of him in the driver's seat.

"Get out of my car, Alex."

"A Jeep's the best vehicle for the terrain we'll be crossing. Not too new or flashy." He ran a hand across its battered, dust-coated dashboard. "Not something that'll draw attention."

She made a rude gesture. "How 'bout you get out or slide over? 'Cause it's my car and I'm driving."

He leaned across the seat and threw open the passenger side door. "Either get in or stay home. We're wasting time."

She glared at him. Ignoring her, he cranked the engine. With an explosion of released air, she threw her duffel into the floorboard and hopped inside the Jeep. She slammed the door shut, rocking the vehicle.

157

He shifted into drive. "Better buckle up, Pia. It's going to be a bumpy ride."

"When has any ride with you proven to be anything but bumpy?"

He surged forward. She caught the dashboard with one hand and with the other fumbled for the seatbelt. Alex laughed. "I warned you."

She clicked the belt into place. "I'm warning you, Torres. I won't let you slow me down. I'll do whatever I have to do to ensure Manny gets home."

He touched his hand to his forehead in a two-fingered salute. "Consider me forewarned. But as I told you before, you won't find it so easy to get rid of me this time."

Interstate 19 ended at the southern terminus of the international border crossing.

With a weird sense of deja vu, Pilar's heart quickened as the Jeep drew near Nogales. The wall separating the North American neighbors dissected the city into two halves. The fence ambulated across the landscape like the spiny ridges of an iguana. Two faces of the same coin—modernity and, on the other side, desperation.

Kind of like her.

"You're sure this is where she and Manny crossed?"

"I checked with one of my Border Patrol contacts. My grandmother's license plate was scanned through the Nogales terminal. We're about twelve hours behind them."

She grunted. "Soon as we clear, how about letting me drive?"

"How about taking a breath and letting me handle this, Pia? Unlike you, this actually isn't my second crossing. I've done this a few hundred times over the years when I worked undercover."

"What makes you think this is only my second crossing? Keeping track of me, Torres?"

"Maybe for the same reason you've kept tabs on me, too."

"I haven't…" She flushed. "And if I had, probably not for the same reason as you."

He faced forward and gripped the wheel. "I wouldn't be too quick to assume what you know about me, Pia. It's been a long time. Things change. So do people."

Not long enough apparently. She looked away. Though some things did appear to remain the same, no matter how long the passage of time.

Women with babies in strollers still waited to cross north on foot. Produce trucks idled in line, waiting for border patrol agents to clear their northbound run. With expensive Nikons begging to be robbed, Americans headed south for a day of fun, shopping, and tequila, not necessarily in that order.

She glanced over to find his dark eyes examining her face. The corner of his lips curved. "Just like old times, eh, Pia?"

Pilar cocked her head. "Old times brought nothing but trouble, Alex."

He tapped his fingers against the wheel. "Not everything was bad."

She held her breath as they neared the traffic light. Red for stop. She crossed her fingers. Green to go.

Green. She breathed a sigh of relief. At Kilometer 21, he turned into the parking lot of the immigration building.

Flashing his trademark Alex Torres smile, he paid the fees and secured the required visas and permits. Agents examined his passport, then hers.

She held her breath again. Had a Quantico watchdog put either of their names on a no-entry list? Handing over their documents, the agent motioned to the people behind them. "Next?"

Back on the road, Alex inched the Jeep forward in the long line of cars snaking south. "And once again, exiting doesn't seem to be a problem."

"Just the returning." She cut her eyes at him. "A thought that still fails to reassure me. But then, you're the expert, aren't you, on exiting?"

A muscle tightened in his jaw. "It's going to be okay, Pia. I promise." They emerged on the other side to Mexican Highway 15.

"Spare me, Alex." She angled. "Always so quick to promise what you can't deliver. I'm not buying what you're selling this time. Give it up."

"I won't give up, Pia. I'm not returning without them."

"Where do we begin to search for them, Alex?" She gestured at the passing scenery. "Where're we headed?"

159

He veered off the four-lane highway lined with gas stations and convenience stores onto a more desolate two-lane road. "Xoacatyl." He kept his eyes on the road. "Where once upon a time, your nightmare probably began."

"Dreams, too," she whispered more to herself than him. But his profile relaxed and he blinked rapidly.

Angry for revealing so much, she clenched her teeth. "Why Xoacatyl?"

"Only town labeled on Abuela's map." He nudged the drawing lying across the console. "See for yourself."

"Abuela knew about us there?"

He shrugged. "The ink is brown. Faded. Predates our wedding."

She hunched. "Strange coincidence. I don't believe in coincidences."

He fixed his eyes on the rearview mirror. "Me neither. But I do believe in acts of God."

Pilar's eyebrows rose.

He pressed the accelerator. She grabbed the luggage strap. His eyes darted to the mirror again.

"Why do you keep looking—?"

"Don't want to scare you or anything, Pia, but looks like together you and I produce more than just a storm of controversy. Late in the season for one of these. But as a lifelong desert rat, you know as well as me, we can't outrun it."

His knuckles whitened on the wheel. His boot pressed to the floor. The speedometer rose to fifty. Passed fifty-five. Hovered at sixty. The Jeep rocketed across the desert basin.

"What're you talking about?" She clutched the seatbelt. "You need to slow down."

"If I can find a more sheltered location instead of being caught out here in the open..." He clamped his lips together.

Her eyes flew to the side mirror where the world behind them had been engulfed into a sky-high cloud of dust. Barreling toward them, the dust storm consumed and obliterated everything in its path. A hurricane of flying debris—uprooted trees, pieces of siding, roofing, manmade everything—churned.

"Aleeeeex..."

"We've got to go off-road out of the way of traffic. Few years ago, there was a fiery five-car pileup in New Mexico during one of these things."

He gunned the engine and swerved to the shoulder of the road. "Hang on."

Pilar's teeth vibrated as did her bones. She kept her eyes peeled on the roaring monstrous cloud at their back. "Faster, Alex. It's gaining on us." She leaned forward as far as the seatbelt allowed. "Go. Go. Go."

"This is the best we can do." He slammed the brakes. The Jeep shuddered to a stop. "We've got minutes before it overtakes us."

Alex threw the car into park and cut the engine. Unleashing his seat belt, he put his knee in the seat. "Got any blankets, Pia?" He scrabbled in the space behind them.

"Hand me the emergency kit." She closed the vents on the dashboard. "There's bottles of water. Beef jerky. And a blanket."

Alex gave a low whistle and hoisted the bag over the seat. "I'm impressed. You're better prepared than most Girl Scouts, Pia."

She made sure he saw her roll her eyes. She rummaged in the side pocket and retrieved a gray roll of duct tape. She held it aloft. "Save the accolades. Help me tape the vents and doors."

He peeled off a length and cut it with his teeth. He fastened the tape around the frame of his door. The roar, like a runaway locomotive, increased. The Jeep rocked in the accelerating wind.

She sawed off another length with the knife she kept in her boot and plastered it over the dashboard vents. "Hurry."

He scrambled into the back, insulating the cracks and crevices with the tape. "Grab the blanket." Something thudded against the side of the Jeep. His eyes widened. "Cover yourself, Pia."

Draping the blanket over her body, she frowned. "What about you?" Drawing her feet, she anchored a portion of the blanket with her knees.

He favored her with a grin. "Not sure how you'll take this, but care to share your blanket with me?" He inserted a corner of the fabric around her body. The darkness outside their cocoon deepened.

"Better be careful what you say. To an Apache, that's tantamount to a marriage proposal."

"I know." He gathered the blanket around their bodies. "But if the blanket fits…"

She closed her lips, not trusting herself to speak. The nearness of him did funny things to her heart. Once upon a time, their marriage blanket had fit oh so well. She reminded herself Alex shouldn't be trusted. He was still capable of wreaking untold damage upon what remained of her heart.

"Oh, I forgot about...I'm sorry, Pia." He edged away. "I shouldn't have crowded—"

"Where're you going?"

He lifted the blanket. Sand and grit filtered inside. He coughed.

"What're you talking about, Alex?" She sneezed.

"I don't want to trigger a flashback. I'll just—"

"Wait." She folded the blanket around his body. "I'm okay under here with you. Only thing you trigger in me is annoyance." Which so wasn't true.

He laughed in the semidarkness. "Good to know some things never change."

She pried the cell phone from her cargo pants. Turning it on, she laid the cell on her thigh. "As your God once said, 'Let there be light.'"

"Good to know your time on Abuela's church pew wasn't wasted, Pia."

"Yep, I rock on Jeopardy's Bible Knowledge category." She tucked a strand of hair behind her ear. "How long you think we'll be stuck?"

"Hard to say. A few minutes? Sometimes these storms last a couple of hours."

A gust of wind sandblasted the vehicle. She gasped. Reacting instinctively, she wrapped her arms around his shoulders.

Pilar buried her nose in the laundered scent of his shirt. His arms reached around her waist. Beneath her cheek, she felt his heartbeat speed up.

She realized then she'd held on a second too long. But one moment more, her heart urged. To be with him like this, just a moment more.

Pilar stiffened. What was she thinking? She was still so pathetic when it came to Alex.

One moment more would only lead to a desire for another minute more. It'd be too easy to become addicted to Alex Torres again. To want all of him. One step further toward asking—begging—for more than he was capable of giving. Embarrassing them both. Humiliating herself.

She dropped her arms. "Sorry."

He didn't let go. "Don't be."

She gazed at the lean, chiseled features of his face. The phone cast a faint blue glow on his skin. And his eyes—she used to get so lost in them. She knotted her fingers in her lap.

"Do you want me to let go of you, Pia?"

The treacherous Pilar—the Cater-Pilar she'd never been able to quell—shook her head. "No."

"Okay..." He pulled her closer into the circle of his arms. He released a breath, as if he'd been holding it. "I don't want to frighten you." He averted his face. "To disgust you."

"I'm not fine china." She drew back an inch. "And for the record, I've never found Alex Torres disgusting."

She gave a derogatory laugh. "Besides, you can't hurt something already broken."

His thumb and forefinger caught her chin. He tugged her gaze toward his. "To me, you'll always be fine china. And I'm a living testament there's nothing so broken God can't heal."

She rested her forehead on his skin above the open collar of his shirt. "Glued together or not, I'm still cracked."

"Cracked, huh? You and me both." He brushed his lips against her hair. She squeezed her eyes shut. "But I'm learning the light shines better between the cracks. If we let it."

"Surrender doesn't come easy for me. I'm Apache, remember?"

He smiled into her hair. "Surrender doesn't come easy for human-kind, not just Apaches. But once we do.... When we let Him, His light banishes the darkness inside us."

She took a ragged breath. "I wish I could believe like you and Byron and Abuela. But I've seen things...experienced..." She shivered.

"I live with that every day." He closed his eyes. "That it was my fault. My fault the monster took you."

She straightened. "I've blamed you for a lot, Alex. But you weren't responsible for that. My own ill-advised choices put me in his clutches."

"I took you to Xoacatyl. I've always believed it was the man from the *taberna*. Some cartel thug who followed us and kidnapped you. It's my fault, Pia." His voice choked. "I would rather have died than what happened to you."

163

She caught his face between her palms. "I would not have rather you died."

"Even more than you hate me, I hate myself."

"I've never hated you enough to want you dead. The monster yes. You, never."

Alex stared at her. The blue light of the cell pulsed on her face. "If I could go back and change everything…"

She tilted her head. "You'd do away with those days in Xoacatyl?"

The vulnerability in her eyes reminded him of the little girl outside the high school locker room.

"No, Pia. God help me, I'd never want to lose those days with you."

Something softened in her face. "Me neither," she whispered. "Even knowing what was to follow. I called for you, you know."

He flinched.

"Whether out loud or only in my mind." She sighed. "And later, at the hospital. Why didn't you come then, Alex?"

"I did come, Pia. I was there almost as soon as they brought you into Emergency. I wanted to see you…" His voice broke. "I needed to see you, but Byron said you cursed me. That after a Mexican had done those things to you, you'd never want to lay eyes on me again."

"Byron told you that? It wasn't true." Her breath hitched. "He told me you weren't there. That you didn't want to see me. Why would he lie to me?"

"We lied to him first, Pia." Alex swallowed. "He was angry we deceived him."

"Apache vengeance."

He slumped. "I never knew you called for me. I would've done anything to be with you, to be there for you."

She bristled. "I believed of all the people in the world he'd never lie to me, never let me down."

"Don't hate Byron, Pia. He's suffered, too." Alex touched her sleeve. "Hate only opens the door to more darkness."

"I don't do forgiveness, Alex. You ought to know that by now."

"Neither did Byron, Pia. Until the drinking nearly consumed him. Almost entombed him in the darkness."

"How do you know about Byron's struggles over the last decade?"

"Byron telephoned me a month ago. First time I'd heard from him in sixteen years. He told me he'd made a lot of mistakes. Told me how he'd found God. And how finding Fiona—who loved him broken as he was—caused him to reexamine everything he believed. He regretted how he'd handled things in Arizona. That if he had to do it over again, he'd make different choices."

"Why did he bother to contact you after so long?"

Alex moistened his dry lips. "In dealing with the wreckage in his life, he'd unearthed something he'd forgotten, left undone in his decade-long alcoholic daze. When I told him about my faith walk, Byron said it was the confirmation he needed for something that had to be made right."

She frowned. "I don't understand."

"The annulment papers, Pia. Byron never filed them."

Alex held his breath and waited for her reaction.

Her eyes grew large. "What does that mean, Alex?"

Now for the tough part.

"It means you and me, Pia." Alex braced himself. "We're still married."

22

P<small>ILAR RUBBED AT HER EYES, GRITTY WITH THE BLOWING DUST</small> filtering through the blanket. But it was her hearing that needed checking. Had Alex just said what she thought he'd said?

She and Alex were still married.

An irrational joy fluttered in her chest. Then, the crashing pain of reality. All the years she'd been alone with the hurt, the fear, and the sadness.

Her lips trembled. How different her life and Manny's would've been if only...

But perhaps not. Alex hadn't said he still cared. Only they were still married.

Was this Mexican mission to retrieve Manny and Reyna fueled by his guilt?

And Byron's deceit rocked her world. She'd have bet her life— she *had* bet her life and Manny's—Byron would never betray her.

The Jeep swayed as sand buffeted the windshield. She winced as clods of dirt peppered the roof. Alex handed her a bottle of water.

"Here. The sand sucks the moisture out of the air."

Taking it, she closed her eyes and took a deep swallow. The water relieved her parched throat. If only it could relieve her raw emotions.

She let her head fall against the seat cushion. "So what does that mean, Alex? That we're still married."

He settled beside her. "It means whatever you want it to mean, Pilar."

"Why come forward with the truth now?"

"I've been trying to find a way to tell you since last week. Trying to find time alone with you so I could—"

"There's a woman in your life, isn't there? Makes this whole issue more urgent. Who is she? Wait." Pilar held her hand like a stop sign. "Forget I asked. It's none of my business."

"You're my wife." He ground his teeth. "Everything about me is your business. But there's no one. There's never been anyone for me since you."

She cocked her head. "You expect me to believe the Alejandro Roberto Torres I've known my entire life has been celibate for over a decade and a half?"

"The Alex you knew is gone." He drew himself up. "I could never...Have you—?" He turned away. "Not my business."

"No, it's not, but I could never get past the physical..." She hugged herself.

"I'm sorry."

"What exactly are you apologizing for, Alex? What happened, I repeat, wasn't your doing. Or maybe you're sorry for shackling yourself to me in the first place."

Alex clenched his hands. "More than a piece of paper has always bound us together, and you know it. Don't trivialize what we shared, Pia."

"How about we both make one blanket apology to the universe"—she punched the blanket above their heads. Dust drifted through the fibers—"for everything we've ever done wrong in both our miserable lives, let Him kill us and get it over with?"

"I talk—I pray—to a personal Creator, Pia. Not a remote inaccessible force. Unlike the serial, my Savior's given me the ultimate respect—the ability to choose Him or not. Who—despite the wrong choices I've made—has faithfully been there to sift the consequences of my sin through his fingers of love."

"Some love," she growled. "I owe gratitude to some entity out there who allowed me to suffer at the hands of the Wicked One? Why should I acknowledge, much less bow, to a god like that?"

"How about instead of questioning why this happened to you, Pia, you focus on how God didn't abandon you but helped you survive? And has it all been miserable, Pia? Even with Manny?"

Not so miserable. There was indeed Manny. And she loved her son with a fierceness that took her breath. The fierceness that wouldn't allow Byron to adopt him out—out of sight, out of mind. Perhaps healing would've come quicker if she'd been willing to give him up.

She stole a look at Alex's shuttered face.

But she couldn't give Manny up. Just as she'd never been able to let go of Alex Torres, either. She'd kept part of Alex close, safe in the stronghold of her heart. As for the annulment?

Her chest ached. Once again, she'd be forced to give up Alex. Or would she?

He'd no right to challenge her like that. Alex had no real comprehension of what she'd gone through. He'd no right to demand anything of her—much less force her to reexamine the worst days of her life.

All he wanted—all he'd ever wanted—was to love her again. Hold her again. Be everything to her—correction, second to God—again. As she was to him. He wanted Pia to allow herself to love him again. Allow him to be her husband, the brand-new, redeemed version of her husband.

Impossible? The enormity of the obstacles between them overwhelmed Alex. *With God, all things . . . ? Help my unbelief, mi Padre.*

He cast his gaze toward the roof and noticed for the first time the utter stillness. The winds died as suddenly as they were born. The storm was over.

Inside his heart? A storm would forever rage unless—

He lifted the blanket. "It's over."

"What's over?" Her voice sharpened.

"The storm." He eased from underneath the blanket. "What did you think I meant?"

She poked her head out of their shelter.

A coating of fine sand powdered the dashboard. Jerking off the duct tape, he butted his shoulder against the Jeep door and heaved it open. Grabbing the water bottle, he unfolded from the vehicle.

She pushed against the passenger door and exited. "Are the wheels stuck?" Hand on her hip, she surveyed the altered landscape.

He poured a stream of water into his cupped hand and splashed the liquid on his face. Blinking, he tossed his head, slinging water droplets against the dust-coated Jeep.

Alex walked around the vehicle to examine the tires for damage. He pitched her the water bottle. She pulled a handkerchief out of the glove compartment, wet the cloth, and ran it over her face.

"Ugh…" She crinkled her nose. "I'd give a lot for a shower right now."

He grinned across the Jeep. "You could use one. You look like a cinnamon-powdered donut."

She made a face at him. "You don't exactly look like you're ready for the cover of *GQ*, either."

He rested his forearms on the roof. "Which means you think I normally look like a cover model?"

"Lucky you, I don't have my sidearm or I'd be forced to shoot your overinflated ego."

Alex laughed. "A little further till we reach Xoacatyl and then I promise you'll have your chance."

He pushed off from the Jeep. "You figure you'd rather be a widow than a divorcée, is that it?"

Pilar's eyes lost their merriment. "Whatever." She crawled into the Jeep.

He slid behind the wheel. "I'm thinking about what's best for you, Pia. No more selfish jerk Alex. Byron and Abuela are right. Long past time to help you move on with your life."

"You found time to discuss this with everyone but me?"

"Pia—"

"Just get this vehicle moving, Torres." She yanked the seatbelt taut. "The sooner we get to town, find your grandmother and Manny, the sooner we can get the annulment and make everybody happy."

He cranked the engine and raced the motor. "Don't presume you have any idea about what makes me happy." He thrust the gear into drive. The Jeep lurched.

She angled toward the window. "Fine."

"Great."

He palmed the wheel and steered the vehicle onto the asphalt.

The Bavispe River paralleled the road, a watery ribbon cutting through the arid landscape. At the horseshoe bend in the river, he drove across the small bridge fording the stream and took the upper fork. The Jeep chugged as they climbed higher.

He grabbed the gearshift and brushed her arm. "Sorry."

She slammed her hand on the seat. "Stop apologizing for touching me."

The blinding whitewashed adobe village and red-tiled roofs glimmered at the base of the Sierra Madre.

"We're here," he announced, breaking the awkward silence between them.

He drove into the village and around the square. He averted his eyes from the church. The village appeared deserted. It no longer possessed the vibrant air he remembered. Or perhaps the romance of their previous visit colored his memories.

"Señora Martinez…Her shop's boarded over. Everything's changed." Pilar cut her eyes at him. "Like us, too, I guess."

Hostile, black-eyed stares followed their progress past the derelict *taberna*. He concentrated on avoiding eye contact with the locals. He pulled into a space outside the once elegant Martinez inn where they'd spent such a brief but happy time.

She put her hand on the handle. "What's going on, Alex?"

He flung out his arm. "Wait."

Cradling double barrels, a cluster of men encircled the Jeep.

"Appears our welcoming committee isn't so welcoming this time, Pia."

23

Before

Alex awoke to the sound of his cell phone buzzing. He eased off the bed, careful not to disturb his sleeping bride. Five days since Pilar became his.

But his funds were at an all-time low. Time to go home and face the wrath of Abuela. He grimaced as he padded toward the cell vibrating on the mahogany dresser.

He checked the caller ID and suppressed a groan. Byron. He'd ignored Byron and Abuela's previous calls.

The phone buzzed again. Alex glanced at his sleeping bride. He owed it to Pilar to work out this problem between him and Byron.

Slipping into a pair of jeans, he grabbed the phone. He edged out to the balcony overlooking the square. Festivities continued to reign each evening as the sun disappeared behind the jagged peaks of the Sierras.

Barefoot, he shivered in the early morning dawn and hit On. "Hello, Byron."

Alex folded his arms against his bare chest and held the phone away from his ear. As he expected, Byron erupted into a volley of expletives about what he planned to do to parts of Alex's anatomy. Which Alex probably deserved.

When Byron and the volume eventually wound down, Alex gripped the phone and huddled against the cold, wrought iron railing. "We're married. We explained in the e-mail. There's nothing you can do to undo it. We'd like your blessing."

Byron pitched his voice low. "I'm going to give you a chance to do the right thing for my sister before I have you arrested."

Despite himself, the skin on Alex's forearm prickled. "Accept our marriage, please, Byron. It doesn't have to be this way between us."

"Yes," Byron growled. "It does. I warned you. For her sake, I won't slit your throat. And for Abuela's sake, I'm giving you a chance to avoid prison instead of calling the *policia*."

Alex blinked. "What're you talking about?"

"You've taken my underage sister across an international border and ravished her. *Rapto*, I believe they call it down there."

"That's not what happened," Alex hissed into the phone. "We were married at the Civil Registry and in a church before God. I did not dishonor your sister. It's legal."

Byron snorted. "Not so legal. You had neither Abuela's nor my consent as required by law. I checked with the tribal legal representative. If you got married, you forged our consent and broke Mexican law."

"We're married!" Alex yelled into the phone. But a hollow dread set his limbs aquiver.

"I don't think your too-handsome-to-live face would survive long in one of those Mexican hellholes, Torres. Fact is, I can also have you arrested the moment you cross the American border."

"For what?" Alex barked into the phone.

"For statutory rape."

Alex's eyes widened. "I never—what're you talking about?"

"I'm talking about how my sister isn't of legal age. I'm talking about how you turned twenty a month ago. Under Arizona law, that three-year age gap constitutes statutory rape."

"No..."

"You always think you're so much smarter than everyone else, Torres. But you outsmarted yourself this time. I happen to know about the trouble you got into in L.A. And how the probation extends until you reach the age of twenty-one. Which you are not."

Alex clutched the phone to his ear.

"One call to your probation officer and your get-out-of-jail-free card is null and void."

Alex squeezed his eyes shut. "No, Byron. Please. Don't do this."

"I won't," Byron grunted. "As long as you bring my sister over the border today."

Byron's tone turned nasty. "You will return her to the United States, and I don't care what story you concoct. You're so smart," he snarled. "I'm sure you can come up with something that'll ensure my sister never wants to see you again. By tomorrow, she better be on a plane for North Carolina. Because if I have to go AWOL and come after you—"

"We're married," Alex whispered.

"Not for long. I promise you it'll be annulled."

Alex clenched his jaw muscles until they ached. "And *I* promise *you* grounds for that no longer exist."

Byron's reply blistered Alex's ear. "You get her across the border by sundown, Torres, or you'll wish you'd never been born."

As Byron clicked off, Alex already wished he never had.

24

A GRIZZLED OLD MAN IN A WHITE STRAW HAT BANGED THE rifle stock against Pilar's side of the Jeep. She jolted.

"*Sal del coche! Manos arriba!*"

Pilar cut her eyes at Alex. "What's he saying? What does he want?"

In slow motion, Alex raised his hands shoulder level. "Take it easy."

She wasn't sure if he was talking to her or the men.

Alex made a show of opening his door. "They want us to get out of the car and keep our hands up. Let them see your hands. Don't make any sudden moves."

The ring tightened around the vehicle.

Alex stepped out, his hands in the air. "If it's money they want or your cell phone, give it to them without a fight."

Keeping the gun beaded on Alex, the old man wrenched open her door.

What she wouldn't give for her Glock about now.

"*Ponte de rodillas!*" A younger man shoved Alex to the ground with his rifle.

The old man waved his gun toward the hood of the Jeep next to Alex. "*Ponte de rodillas! Ponte de rodillas!*"

"Kneel, Pia," Alex hissed. "Get on your knees."

The old man yanked her to the ground. "*Ponga sus manos en la cabeza.*"

"He wants our hands on our heads." Alex locked his hands on the top of his head. "*Sí? Manos en la cabeza.*"

Pilar didn't move quick enough. The old man wrested Pilar's arm to her head. She gasped.

"Stop!" Alex took down his hands. "Leave her alone!"

Two men grabbed his arms and pinned him in place.

Struggling against their bonds, Alex let loose in machine-gun rapid fire *español.*

"*No se mueva o disparo.*" The old man pressed the barrel into her chest. "*No se mueva o disparo.*"

"What does he want with us, Alex?"

"He's telling you if you move he will shoot you."

She and Alex jerked at the gravelly, somewhat familiar, voice from the crowd. The villagers parted as Señor Joaquin Martinez strode forward.

The courtly innkeeper had changed so much in the last sixteen years that Pilar couldn't believe it was him. His tight, black curls were now dotted with gray. Trim as ever in denim jeans and a red plaid shirt, underneath his suede jacket he wore a gun holster in addition to the bandolier of ammunition slung across his chest.

And his eyes?

Two black holes where no light existed. The gentle man Pilar had known—the Señora's son and Nita's father—was gone. In his place, a hard-bitten version of the man who'd once shown her and Alex such kindness.

"Señor Martinez, *por favor.*" Alex started to lift his hands from his head, but a grunted threat from one of the younger men, changed his mind. He froze.

Martinez's eyes narrowed. "How do you know me? *Digame, americano.* Tell me."

Her eyes flitted to the rusting wrought-iron balcony. "Where is Señora Martinez? Where is Nita, señor?"

A pain so fleeting, Pilar almost believed she'd imagined it, criss-crossed the man's dark complexion. But after the momentary spasm, Martinez's features went rigid. His hand fell to his holster. "What do you know of my Nita, *gringa?*"

"Not *gringa.*" The old man spat a stream of tobacco just missing her boot by inches. "*Indeh.*"

She drew back, her shoulder grazing Alex.

Alex glared at the old man. "What did he call you, Pia?"

"He called me what we Apaches call ourselves. Indeh." She shivered. "It means 'the dead ones.'"

The old man let loose a volley of vitriolic Spanish.

Martinez raised his hand. "Enough." His gaze sharpened on her. "What do you know of my daughter?"

"N-nothing. I'm looking for an old woman. *Americana* like me, but Latina. Isabel Torres and my-my…" Pilar took a breath. "She traveled here, we believe, with my son, Manuel, looking for an"—she gave the old man a quick look—"Indeh girl also from the United States."

Martinez straightened. "Isabel?" He pronounced it with the typical Spanish sibilant hiss on the *s*. His eyes cut toward the church and then upward as had Pilar's toward the balcony.

"The old woman?" Martinez angled to Alex. "*Tu abuela?*"

"*Sí*, señor." Alex nudged his head toward Pilar. "She and I stayed here once as your guests. A long time ago."

"We were married here. In the church. The old señora…" Pilar swallowed.

"Ah. Torres." Martinez released his hold on his pistol and scrubbed his mouth with his hand. "I remember now." His eyes ping-ponged between them. "*Los recién casados.* The newlyweds."

Martinez pointed his finger at Pilar and Alex. "*Americano y americana.*" He made a downward motion with both hands.

The rifles lowered.

His eyes not leaving Martinez, Alex dropped his hands and rose. "You know of my grandmother? Did she come through the village? Is she here now?" He took hold of Pilar as she got to her feet.

She strained forward. "And my boy, Manuel. Have you seen him? Is he okay? Where—?"

"*Venga conmigo.*" Martinez made a sweeping motion toward the two-story Spanish Colonial. "Come with me. *Perdóname* for the reception you received. But things are no longer as they were. And your people are no longer in Xoacatyl."

She bit her lip.

"Night falls quickly here." Martinez cast a look at the mountains. The golden orb of the sun had descended. Its molten glow faded to indigo. "It is best not to be on the road in the darkness of night."

Alex surged between Martinez and Pilar. "If you'll tell us what you know, we'll be on our way and catch them."

"I will tell you what I know of their short time in Xoacatyl. But"—Martinez sighed—"I warned them of the foolhardiness of venturing into the high places."

Martinez drew himself up. "We can only pray that in the mercy of *el Dios* they have found a safe haven before night descends."

"Please." She touched his sleeve. "We need to find them. The sooner we—"

"No one leaves the village after dusk. It is our law. Salazar and his men own the Sierra Madre." Martinez's lip curled. "And the jaguar stalks his prey by the light of the moon. No one leaves until morning."

Alex bristled. "You can't keep us here against our will."

Martinez scowled. "You are the stranger here. You do not make the rules, *americano*."

Alex balled his fists.

"You are in a war zone. I will not risk my men's lives by having to rescue you," Martinez growled. "That foolish old woman and the priest would not listen. They took the boy with them into the mountains. Daylight is soon enough, I tell you, to throw your lives into the grave."

"Father Emmanuel?" Pilar inhaled. "Manny's with him?"

Martinez's eyes dampened. "No." He swiveled to Alex. "Father Miguel went against my orders and took the woman and your son to the old mission church where Father Emmanuel died."

Alex, she noted, didn't bother to correct Martinez about Manny. "At daybreak you'll let us drive out of here?"

Martinez shrugged. "*Sí.* If you are so desperate to meet your creator."

She grasped his sleeve. "I have to find Manny, Señor Martinez."

The Latino's eyes softened. "Of course, you must try. It's Pilar, is it not? We must do what we can for our children. There is no other choice. But I fear…" His gaze once again shot to the darkening ridge.

Martinez made an effort to compose himself. "To old friends such as yourselves from happier times, I am Joaquin." He ushered them into the spacious, once grand inn. "You must be hungry."

Clutching the rifle to his chest, the old man followed them inside. So close, the heavily whiskered old man's sour breath ruffled the loosened tendrils of Pilar's bun.

Joaquin led them past the ornate front rooms into an open-air courtyard at the heart of the former inn. As she remembered, the upper story ringed the four sides. Wrought-iron tables and chairs lay scattered across the tiled patio. A stone fountain with the face of a great cat gurgled.

"Sit, *por favor*," Joaquin motioned.

Pilar sank into a chair. Alex grabbed another, turned it backward, and straddled it. Wary, he kept one eye trained on the old man and the other on Martinez.

"Your grandmother and son arrived this morning. Went straight to the church. The old woman asked for Father Emmanuel." Joaquin crossed himself. "Instead, they found Father Miguel. They told the *padre* they searched for a girl."

"Her name's Reyna Bui." Pilar placed her hands on top of the cold, metallic table. "She's thirteen, and she was taken from the San Carlos rez."

The old man smirked. "As long as they take one of their own, they leave ours alone."

Joaquin rolled his eyes. "How often do I have to tell you, Luis, it is not the Wild Ones who prey on our people?"

The former innkeeper blew out a breath. "Luis grew up in a time when your people raided the farms and ranches on both sides of the border. Unfortunately, their reign of terror lasted much longer here at the base of their mountain stronghold, well into the twentieth century."

He eased into a chair. "Their last raid occurred in the 1940s. They burned the old Franciscan outpost at the base of the Sierra Azul."

Joaquin's mouth twisted. "During a Sunday morning mass with mostly women and *las niñas* trapped inside. The men of the village, of course, tracked the band who extinguished our families and retaliated in like manner upon their hidden *rancheria* of wickiups."

She swallowed hard.

"The hatred runs deep. 'Apache' doesn't mean the same thing to us as it does to *americanos*. The memories"—he gestured at the old man—"are for some, fresh as yesterday and as raw. Only a boy, Luis lost his *madre* and *sus hermanas* that day."

Martinez tapped a finger to his temple. *Loco*, he mouthed. "But"—Joaquin's tone shifted—"the old days are gone, Luis. We have a new enemy."

"Salazar…" Alex gritted his teeth.

Joaquin's eyebrow rose. "As intelligent and cunning as the Apache of old, but with infinitely more firepower and resources."

"Not a new enemy." Luis glared. "The same wickedness with a new face. But the jaguar does not change his spots."

Joaquin's jaw tightened. "The Flores cartel ran their supply routes from the golden triangle in Sinaloa to El Paso. Three years ago, their empire was brought down by your own *federales* in the *Estados Unidos*."

She knew to keep quiet. In the *machismo* world of Mexico, the men would only deal with Alex.

Alex nodded. "Then a jockeying among local drug lords for ultimate power."

"*Sí*. And Franco Salazar emerged the winner."

Joaquin looked beyond the adobe brick walls as if he peered into the past. "Everything changed. Flores had allowed us to live in peace. We did not interfere in his drug trafficking, he did not interfere with us. Live and let live. But then Salazar declared himself *El Señor de los Cielos*."

Alex translated, "Lord of the Skies."

"Salazar told the surrounding mountain villages, '*Soy la ley*.'"

Alex's lips flattened. "I am the law."

"He tells the ranchers he will buy their land from them. Or he will buy it from their widows."

Alex exchanged looks with Pilar.

"One rule—obey or die." Joaquin fingered his chin. "He is *muy malo*. Very bad. *Lunático*."

Alex propped his elbows on the back of his chair. "Salazar's a mystery to American law enforcement. His rise to power caught people on our side of the fence off guard. Have you ever seen him?"

Joaquin frowned. "He's like one of the Apache Ghost Warriors. Not flamboyant or reckless like Esteban Flores, the drug lord killed a few years ago. Salazar is encircled by security forces and has insinuated a cadre of secret informers among our own people. This land has become his kingdom."

"Why don't the villages band together and fight him?" She leaned forward. "How does he get away with it?"

Alex stirred. "He rules through a combination of bribery and intimidation."

"*Sí*. Plus a healthy dose of inbred suspicion against outsiders, and he feeds village rivalries. The *federales* haven't been successful infiltrating his headquarters yet. We are at his mercy."

"He could live in these mountains for a century and never be found," Alex agreed. "Despite the most sophisticated American technology in partnership with the Mexican authorities, holed up in his mountain eyrie, Salazar is as good as untouchable."

"I only know it is rumored Franco Salazar came to Rancho Onca as the illiterate son of a peasant woman when Don Geraldo Velarde ran things."

"The Onca ranch, you say? Like the big cat." Alex raised an eyebrow at Pilar. "Also home to Velarde's son, Umberto."

Joaquin made a face. "The Velardes are no better than Salazar. Don Geraldo demanded his *rapto* rights as long as he lived. But it is there your son wanted to go—to the Velarde ranch."

Manny...

"I warned them not to go. You must cross the Valley of the Mists past the old Franciscan ruins to reach the Valley of the Eagles. The roads that side of the range are hazardous. Many travelers are robbed where the magic beans grow. But against my wishes, your grandmother prevailed—"

"Sounds like *mi abuela*," Alex muttered.

"And without our militia, Father Miguel decided to take them only as far as he dared to the church ruins." Joaquin slumped. "Father Miguel has not returned. I fear the worst."

"You have a village militia?"

"After the last time they came, we do now," the old man snarled.

Her eyes shot to Joaquin. "What happened the last time?"

"We began to find our courage, thanks to Father Emmanuel. To fight back. To refuse to grow the crop that pays. Three years ago."

"I don't understand."

Luis's gaze fastened onto Pilar. "The Indeh took Joaquin's daughter, Nita."

Her breath caught.

"Salazar, old man. Not the Apaches." Joaquin pursed his thin, patrician lips. "We have spent the better part of three years searching the mountains for her. Tracking. Following them. But the captives move with Salazar. He rotates among ten isolated *ranchos* in these mountains."

"If you have the locations," Alex glanced at the men. "The *federales* could storm—"

"And kill my daughter in the process?" Joaquin shook his head. "No, we cannot risk it. We will find them our own way."

"Your way is too slow." Pilar half-rose. "Three years might as well be forever."

"Forever is better than dead, Señora Torres."

Señora.

Pilar supposed that's who she was, in name only. But three years in the hands of a man like Salazar...She gulped. Or Umberto Velarde for that matter...

She couldn't think of that now or she'd shut down and be of no use to anyone. "Could I talk with Señora Martinez?"

"After Nita was taken," Joaquin shuffled his boots. "My mother would not eat or rest. She died of the heart pain from missing Nita."

Pilar stole a look at Alex. She'd nearly willed herself to die after she escaped from the Wicked One, before she discovered Manny grew in her womb.

Adapt or die.

The cutting, a futile attempt to remove her inner pain. But after all she'd endured—*survived*—Pilar wouldn't be able to bear never seeing Manny again. Like Señora Martinez, death would be a release.

Luis's face scrunched. "I tell Martinez once his daughter has lived with them, she can never return to us. She has been defiled, polluted, corrupted."

Pilar knotted her hands. Like her. Her shame forever carved into her flesh.

"Shut up, Luis." Joaquin scraped back his chair. "I will bring food."

Joaquin withdrew a paper from his jacket. "This was nailed to a tree outside the village not long ago. A warning you'd do well to heed before you rush into matters of which you know nothing."

Alex read the note. He stared at it before laying it on the table for Pilar.

She pushed the paper at him. "I don't know Spanish."

He started to speak, but the old man interrupted.

"It says, 'I, Lord of the Skies, only allow you to live so you raise the crop that pays. And breed the girls I take as my women. They are mine.'"

25

Bᴏɴᴇ-ᴅᴇᴇᴘ ᴡᴇᴀʀɪɴᴇss ᴅᴏɢɢᴇᴅ Aʟᴇx ᴀs ʜᴇ ꜰᴏʟʟᴏᴡᴇᴅ Jᴏᴀǫᴜɪɴ and Pilar.

At the top of the stairs, Joaquin transferred fresh towels over to Pilar. "You must refresh yourselves after your long journey. I will have your bags brought from the car."

"Go ahead, Pia," Alex motioned toward the bathroom. "I'll wait."

She disappeared inside with a grateful smile.

Joaquin hesitated on the landing. "You still love your wife, Señor Torres?"

Alex braced against the cool adobe and propped the heel of one boot against the wall. "Yes, I do."

Joaquin opened his arms and lifted his hands. "Then do not take her up the mountain, I beg you. We will look for your boy and your abuela. The girl you seek is already lost." His eyes glimmered. "As, I fear, is my Nita. But your wife, she must stay here."

"Would that I could leave her here." Alex allowed his head to fall back onto the wall. "But she's determined to find Manny." He stared at the wood rafters overhead. "And slay the fears of her past."

"As you say, señor. As God wills."

"Indeed," Alex pursed his lips. "As God wills."

Later, Pilar emerged in a camisole top, her black overshirt tucked into jeans. Catching him watching her, she regathered the damp tendrils of her hair to his chagrin. "Your turn."

With an effort, he tore his gaze from her fingers, weaving a three-ply braid into her hair.

After showering, he donned a blue plaid shirt and jeans. He returned to the hallway to find Joaquin and Pilar waiting for him.

Joaquin set off toward the front side of the courtyard. "This way."

And outside the door where Joaquin stopped, Alex came to an abrupt halt.

Joaquin held the lantern aloft. A smile softened his harsh features. "To happier times, my old friends."

The only happy time . . . for Alex and Pilar.

His temples thudded. "I appreciate the thought, but—"

"We'd be honored to accept your kind hospitality once more." Her eyes glinted at him in the lantern light.

Joaquin threw open the door and handed Alex the lantern. "*Buenas noches*, Señor and Señora Torres."

She smiled and glided inside. "You heard him, Alex."

Alex entered with reluctance.

"Until the morrow, then." Joaquin closed the door and left them alone in the room that had been their bridal chamber.

Alex's heart pounded as sudden memories assailed him.

She fingered the frayed fringe of the canopied bed. "Not much has changed."

Alex moved to a safer distance to breathe. "Not much and yet everything."

He focused on the faded burgundy curtains ruffling in the evening breeze from the open door of the balcony. "No need for an inn once the *narcotraficantes* drove the tourists away."

"But do you remember, Alex? Those days when we—"

"It's best not to remember." He gripped the lantern.

She touched his hand. Jerking, he walked to the dresser and set the lantern down.

Her nostrils flared. "Perhaps, Alex, the better question is do *I* disgust *you*?"

"No, of course—"

"That's why you can't touch me, why you can hardly bear to look at me. Because every time you see me, you see *him*."

In one quick stride, he crossed the distance separating them. "That's not true, Pia."

"You see him. And me." She sank onto the mattress. "You see me defiled and polluted."

He grabbed her arm. "You aren't defiled and polluted." He yanked her upright. "You are beautiful to me and in the sight of God."

"Prove it then, Alex." She searched his face. "You say I'm still your wife."

He let go of her.

She cocked her head. "And until we file the annulment, why not give it another go and see how we click after all this time?"

He fell back a step. "Your idea and mine of what you call 'clicking,' Pilar, I suspect are highly different."

Drifting upward, her hands locked behind the nape of his neck. "I *am* still your wife." Her lips brushed across the exposed skin at the hollow of his throat above his shirt.

The flame of his passion for her reignited. "Don't, Pilar." He made a halfhearted attempt to pull away.

She trailed one hand across his shoulder. Touching his bicep, down the length of his forearm. Until she captured his hand, balled into a fist against his thigh. "Why not take advantage of this time for us?"

He closed his eyes.

She unlocked his grip and laced her fingers into his. "Perhaps once and for all get each other out of our systems..."

That was the trouble. She'd never been out of his system. And she never would be.

Pilar brought his hand to her mouth. "It's been so long, husband." She kissed his palm.

"Stop, Pia."

He held his breath against the yearning. Fighting to control the longing he'd never stopped feeling for her.

Fire lit her dark eyes. "Love me, Alex." Her lips moved against his palm.

He made a sound in the back of his throat.

"Once more before you cast me away forever."

He ran his hand over the silk of her hair. "I would never—"

"Show me, Alex..." She strained forward on tiptoe. "Always so much talk with you. So little act—"

He seized her face with both hands and rammed his mouth onto hers. He drank in her senses, the fragrance of desert wildflowers after a rainstorm. He savored her lips, too long denied him.

Warning bells of alarm clamored inside his head. Alex told himself he needed to stop. That after what she'd been through, he'd frighten her. But she didn't appear frightened.

She returned kiss for kiss, exploring his mouth, his jawline. With a soft sigh of pleasure, she inhaled him as he inhaled her. And he stopped thinking.

He wrapped his arms around her waist and crushed her against him. His hands lifted to her shoulder blades and kneaded her back. Relishing the feel of her once more in his arms where she'd always belonged.

Locking lips, she angled toward the bed and toppled them onto the mattress. He sank beneath her weight and his. She fumbled with the buttons of his shirt.

But she paused and leaned for another lingering kiss as if she couldn't bear the seconds without his mouth on hers. She reached behind her head and with great deliberation uncoiled her hair.

"Pia…"

She threw back her head, laughing. Heady with love for him. Alive and vibrant in the way he remembered her. Once again, the girl he'd so desperately loved. His Pia.

His shirt riding out of his jeans, he lunged, tasting the sweetness of her.

Pilar's lips found his earlobe. "My Alex…The old Alex—"

He stilled. That was just it. He wasn't the old Alex. Thank God, he wasn't the same old Alex.

Alex's pulse hammered. "I can't do this, Pia."

Her fingers bunched in his shirt, her chest heaved. "Why not? You want this. I know you, Alex. You want me."

Alex attempted to sit up. "You don't know me. Not the new me. I'd like you to know me, but not this way." He pried her hands off his shirt.

She stiffened.

Alex held her hands in his. "Despite what you believe, only a very small part of my desire for you was fueled by lust."

Gritting his teeth at the exercise of his will over his want, Alex pushed her off him. "The greater portion of my desire for you was always driven by my love for you."

He inched away, inserting space between their bodies. For the safety of his soul. And hers.

Pilar's breath came in ragged, short spurts. "There's no need to deny yourself. Or me."

As he raked a hand over his head, his hand shook. "Is this about me or proving something to yourself, Pilar?"

"What about what *I* want, Alex?" She pounded her chest. "What *I* need? *I* need you."

"You don't need me. I can't fill the empty hole inside you, Pia. I never could. I shouldn't have tried back then. But I didn't know any better in those days."

She jutted her chin. "What is it, Alex, you think you know?"

"I know we're not really married. Not in the sense God intends it to be between a man and a woman." He swallowed past the lump clogging his throat. "And until we choose to say those vows of commitment again, Pia, I will not cheapen what I feel for you with mere sex."

Pilar fell back upon the pillows. "Mere? Who are you trying to kid, Alex Torres? You like sex. And you seemed to be enjoying it like always before your new morality took over the rest of your anatomy."

"Sex is the least of what I want with you, Pia." He got off the bed. "I'll sleep on the settee tonight."

Her eyes darkened. "You've changed, Alex."

"It wasn't me who did the changing, Pia." He took a deep, cleansing breath. "It was God who did the changing of me. I was lost, captive to the darkness, until He found me and set me free from the chains of my pride and self-sufficiency."

At his words, a look of utter aloneness blanketed her features. "I'll sign the papers when we get back to Arizona and free you from the rest of your chains." She turned her face to the pillow.

It was all he could do not to break every vow he'd ever made to God and take her into his arms. There was so much he wanted to say to her. So much love he wanted her to know.

But it wasn't him who could fix the broken places in Pilar. Only God could do that. And only one love in the end she needed the most.

Teach Pia how much you love her, God . . . Please . . .

He tugged the comforter folded at the foot of the bed. "Get some sleep, Pia. We're going to need all our wits and strength if we aim to find them and rescue Reyna."

Pilar awoke to the sound of a rooster crowing. A faint light glimmered through the windows. She sat up abruptly as consciousness returned. Her gaze swept the empty room.

She flung off the coverlet. But they'd left the door to the balcony ajar. She shivered.

Once again last night, Alex had shown he didn't love her. Or, if Alex were to be believed, he loved his God more. Her cheeks burned with the memory of how she'd thrown herself at him. Practically begging him to make love to her.

Now, all that mattered was finding Manny and Reyna. And if Alex believed he could leave her in the village...leave her behind like before...

She swung her feet off the bed, knocking her hiking boots askew. She winced as her bare feet skimmed the cold, wooden planks of the floor.

A trickle of air moved the curtain. The floorboard creaked. A shadow loomed. Her eyes shot up.

"It's just me." Silhouetted against the dawn, Alex's bare feet poked from underneath his jeans. "It's barely daybreak. I brought your breakfast from downstairs."

He handed her a mug. "Your coffee. The way you like it."

She wrapped her chilled hands around the ceramic mug. Its warmth seeped into her fingers. She brought the cup to her lips and inhaled the robust aroma.

He turned toward the balcony. "Joaquin said to be ready to go in about thirty minutes. I hated to wake you. You were sleeping so peacefully."

Peaceful? How long since that had happened?

Since the last time she and Alex slept in this room.

Pilar took a scalding gulp and choked. His eyes flickered. She rose and set the mug on the dresser beside a plate of food. Tucking the tank top into her jeans, she straightened her overshirt between forkfuls of the salsa-laden breakfast tortilla filled with eggs, spicy chorizo sausage, and peppers.

She felt his nervousness as Alex jammed his hands into his pockets and peered out the window. Avoiding her gaze. Unsure after last night how things stood between them.

Pilar laced her boots taut. "You ate something, too, didn't you?"

Alex settled beside her. "Yeah. But what I wouldn't give for a slice of American bacon." He grunted. "At home they call me Mexican. Here, I'm an *americano*. I can't win."

She laughed. "When in fact, you're just a guy from L.A."

He looked at her out of the corner of his eye. A smile tugged at his features. "Something like that."

And the tension between them eased for the moment.

"Truce?"

She nodded. The unresolved issues would wait. Perhaps friends, not lovers, was all they were meant to be.

"Okay." She swiped her hand across her mouth. "I'm good. Let's saddle up."

They took the Jeep. She and Joaquin in the back. Alex drove, and the old man rode shotgun. Literally.

Luis kept the rifle locked and loaded. He rested the gun across his knees as the Jeep left the sleeping village behind in the early morning light. The old man's eyes darted from one side of the graveled road to the other as the Jeep climbed above the mist enveloping the valley.

Higher and higher they wound up the mountain. The rear tires slipping, pebbles sprayed the sides of the vehicle. They climbed for hours. Then the road just stopped.

Alex braked beside Abuela's Land Rover.

The old man pointed through the dense jungle cover. "There."

Squinting through a shaft of sunlight, she detected a faint footpath. She and Alex slung their backpacks over their shoulders. Joaquin withdrew a machete from a scabbard hanging on his back and gestured at the overgrown trail. "The ruins lie not far off the road."

For the first time since she'd found Abuela and Manny gone, Pilar felt the stirrings of hope. And when she got hold of that boy— if she didn't hug him to death—she just might throttle him.

"We're close, Pia." Alex threw her that knee-knocking smile before following Joaquin into the interior.

Pilar prayed one day her heart would be immune. Pray? Alex would've been thrilled to know his influence was getting to her.

She kept Alex's broad shoulders in her sights. Luis brought up the rear. Pushing through the tangled underbrush, they stumbled into an open clearing.

The ruins of a soaring stone edifice touched the sky. Broken pillars lay strewn about. A charred seven-foot cross leaned crookedly in the middle of what had been the sacristy. The blackened, stone foundations were a testament to the horror perpetrated here when Luis was a boy.

And yet life remained. Every cracked wall—the overturned stone altar itself—draped in a green mantle of vines.

The bushes rustled. She and the others spun around as an overweight, middle-aged priest staggered out of the brush. Leaves and bracken protruded from his clerical collar.

"Father Miguel." Joaquin caught the priest's arm. "Are you alright?"

Alex pushed forward. "Where's my grandmother?"

Pilar inserted herself. "What about my boy?"

"Water…" Father Miguel gasped.

Joaquin unclasped the canteen attached to his waist. Luis brought the gun to chest level and kept guard, his eyes studying the surrounding jungle. Joaquin brought the canteen to the priest's lips.

Father Miguel drank greedily. Putting a hand to his head, he winced. Drops of blood stained his fingertips.

"My grandmother?"

Father Miguel squeezed his eyes shut. "I should've listened to you, Joaquin. But when I told the old lady yesterday what had happened to Father Emmanuel, she begged to come see where he died."

Pilar wrapped her arms inside her jacket. "Father Emmanuel died here?"

Luis didn't bother turning around. "When they took Joaquin's daughter three years ago, they left Father Emmanuel as a warning to the rest of us."

"Did you know Emmanuel means 'God with us'?" Joaquin glanced at the charred cross and his shoulders slumped. "I pray God was with him when Salazar's men crucified him and burned him alive."

She shuddered. The old priest's kind face at their wedding…crippled and defenseless against such evil. She swayed.

"*Animales*," Luis's lips bulged.

"Why did my grandmother want to come here?" Alex steadied her. "Did you ever tell her about Father Emmanuel?"

"No." She shook her head. "I've never spoken of those days. Not with another soul."

Father Miguel collapsed onto one of the fallen pillars. "Doña Torres wept when she beheld the cross. And she insisted we wait."

"Wait for what?" Pilar crouched beside the priest. "And was Manny okay?"

"He was impatient to find the girl child. Señora Torres told him they would come when they were ready and to quiet himself."

Alex's eyes sharpened. "They who?"

"We never saw them coming. Calls from the jungle like the yowling of the big cat, the *onca*." The priest crossed himself. "The old lady reacted first. She dragged me to the altar and yelled for Manny as gunfire erupted."

Father Miguel frowned. "I began to pray and suddenly it seemed as if the shots came from more than one direction. As if we were caught in a cross fire."

She seized his arm. "Was Manny hurt? Abuela?"

Father Miguel shook his head. "In the confusion, the boy was taken. And then, an unnatural quiet. We never saw their faces."

Luis smirked. "No one ever sees them."

What she'd feared most had come to pass. *He* had Manny. She knew it in the raw place where fear lived inside her.

Alex's jaw tensed. "We'll find him. We won't give up until we bring Manny home." He angled toward the priest. "What happened to my grandmother?"

"She scanned the pinnacles to the west. She went still as if she turned off all her senses but one."

Alex shivered as if someone had walked over his grave.

Father Miguel's brow wrinkled. "Her eyes closed, she lifted her nose to the wind."

Luis sneered. "You can always smell them. Hiding. They're always watching us."

At the raucous cry of jungle birds, the rest of them jolted.

Joaquin withdrew his pistol from his gun belt. "Hush, Luis... Stop with your ghost stories."

Father Miguel's eyes clouded. "Your grandmother said *they'd* told her they'd kill her if she ever tried to come back, but she didn't care. She'd get them to help her find Manny and the girl. No matter what it cost her."

The priest lifted his face to Pilar. "What do you think she meant?" She looked at Alex.

He shook his head. "To the best of my knowledge, Abuela has never set foot in Xoacatyl or on this mountain before."

Pilar got hold of herself. "And what then, Father Miguel?"

"She made a strange noise. Like the sound of a bird." The priest moistened his dry lips. "And another bird answered her call."

Father Miguel dropped his head into his hands. "Then she picked up a rock and bashed my head."

"Abuela hit you?" Alex's eyes widened. "You're sure it was her? Why would she do such a thing?"

"I do not know, señor. I awoke to darkness, and she was gone. Someone positioned my body underneath a large bush and placed fronds over me as if to hide me."

The other four exchanged looks.

"She may have saved your life, *padre*." Joaquin's mouth tightened. "No one goes beyond the Valley of the Mists and returns. Not alive anyway."

The priest gripped his head in a sudden spasm of pain.

Joaquin patted Father Miguel's arm. "We must get you to the village. You need medical treatment." He threw a look at Alex. "We will return tomorrow."

"No." She surged to her feet. "We have to follow the tracks while they're fresh or we'll lose them for good."

"You don't find them, *americana*," Luis grunted. "They find you."

Alex went shoulder-to-shoulder with her. "You take Father Miguel and Luis, Joaquin. We'll go on ahead."

Joaquin glared at them. "To move forward without armed men at your side is suicide."

"This is our fight. We don't expect you to risk your lives for our people." Alex tilted his head. "But I'd feel better if I could borrow some of your firepower."

Joaquin's gaze ping-ponged between them. "Such foolishness will put your lives in grave danger."

She planted her hands on her hips. "Him and me—we're known for foolishness." She cut her eyes at Alex.

Alex grinned. That gosh-I'm-so-irresistible smile that did her in every time. "Aren't we, though?"

With a deep sigh, Joaquin handed Alex his Smith and Wesson. Ducking under the strap of the bandolier, Joaquin handed the ammunition belt and machete to her. She sagged under the weight.

Joaquin took hold of Father Miguel. "We will return with reinforcements. Luis?"

"They want the children." Luis squinted into the dappled sunshine. "We need to gather the children inside the village. That's what *mi madre* always said when I was a boy."

Joaquin and Father Miguel released a simultaneous sigh.

Father Miguel made the sign of the cross over her and Alex's heads. "Go with God, my children."

"Luis..." Joaquin urged.

The old man nudged his chin in the direction of the road. "I'm comin'."

Joaquin and the limping *padre* disappeared into the brush. Luis extracted the steely blade of a knife from his boot and thrust the handle at Alex.

"You must not fall into their wicked hands. Whatever happens, don't let them take you."

The old man's wrinkled face creased like the knobby ridges to the west. "But if they do, you must do the señora a favor. Take her life first."

Luis spat at the ground between their feet. "And then, señor, you must take your own."

193

26

ALEX HELD THE MACHETE ALOFT AND WITH A DOWNWARD ARC hacked an opening through the jungle cover.

"The farther we climb out of the valley," he swung his arm left then right, clearing a path for Pilar, "the sooner we leave this jungle behind."

She paused, both hands propped on her knees. "The map takes us there?" She pointed her lips in the Apache Way toward the cloud-shrouded peak.

A sky island. An enclave of Apache pine and Mexican blue-oak surrounded by the Chihuahuan desert.

He leaned upon the butt of the machete. Its steel tip sank into the earth. Most of these peaks, he estimated, hovered at seven thousand feet. At four thousand, the volcanic labyrinths disappeared into the clouds.

"No wonder no one ever found the Broncos." He gulped air. The oxygen grew thinner as the elevation rose. "Not the Conquistadors. Not the Mexican government. Even Pancho Villa managed to 'get lost' here."

She nodded. "Let's push on."

He took point again. The ascent to the impregnable cliff fortress was taking longer than he'd anticipated. The hike out of the canyon proved to be forbidding as they scaled the rock-ribbed former mountain sanctuary of the Wild Ones.

Later, emerging from the jungle into the open, his lungs felt as if they'd burst out of his chest. His leg muscles ached. He glanced at Pilar and grimaced.

She didn't look winded.

Pilar frowned. "Why are we stopping?"

Much as he loved her, he decided she could also be downright annoying.

"We're here. As here as it gets."

She took a deep breath. "It's beautiful."

He scanned the yawning chasm below. The almost perpendicular walls of the ridge. A spring formed by a snow-melted stream gushed from the face of the mountain.

"I guess it is." He struggled to even his breathing. "If you enjoy defying gravity."

"What're you complaining about?" She laughed. "It's not too steep." She shoulder-butted him and moved ahead on the trailhead. "If you're an Apache."

"The last refuge of the Apache." He seized a handhold on one of the enormous boulders and scaled the remaining feet to the pinnacle. "Snow. We've probably only got days before this entire area's inaccessible. Winter's coming."

"Something's coming." She motioned toward the roiling black clouds over the desert plains. "On a clear day, I bet you can see all the way to New Mexico."

He twisted open his canteen and held it to the cold, clear water pouring out of the basaltic cliff. "We're going to have to make camp soon."

"I see something." She shaded her hand over her eyes. "It doesn't look natural. Manmade." She squinted beyond the cleft in a rock.

He capped off the canteen. "Where?"

"There."

Square shapes not found in nature. Camouflaged with the accumulating bracken of decades. Almost invisible beneath a standing grove of autumn-yellow ash.

"You've got good eyes. Let's go see."

They inched down the other side to another mountaintop knuckle. He breathed the pine-scented air and smelled rain. They needed to hurry. Find a dry place to bunk for the night.

"Careful," she warned as his boot slipped. She reached for him. "Alex—"

He grabbed the rock for support. Swallowing, he peered over the edge to the plunging ravine. "Not all of us are part mountain goat like you."

"What can I say? Some of us are more gifted than others. A real Apache was said to be able to cover fifty miles in a day. Seventy-five on horseback."

He grunted. "Good to know. I also hear these 'real' Apaches of yours were taught the value of silence."

She laughed, but fell silent, allowing him to concentrate on taking each breath.

They crested the high shelf she'd spotted. On one side, the sheer cliff and on the other, the drop-off to the gorge. A stronghold breached only by the eagle.

He took a good look around.

Or an Apache.

Pilar's eyes widened. "It's one of the Apache camps, isn't it?"

He didn't like this haunted place. "Probably abandoned for decades."

She disappeared into one of the dilapidated structures.

"Pia..." He sighed. "There could be rattlesnakes. Or other unfriendlies calling this place home."

"Look what I've found." Her voice echoed from the interior.

This tough, little Apache woman put the fear of God into his heart. Knowing Pilar, she'd make a pet of whatever she found. Including something as unsavory as a Gila monster.

He clamped his teeth together and followed the sound of her voice. "For somebody who claims to not like dark, enclosed places..."

She flicked the lighter, and light danced along the broken walls of the long-gone Apache's dwelling. "Doesn't resemble the traditional wickiups on the rez."

Alex ran his hand along the smooth, curved wall. "More like an adaptation of the Mexican adobes around here."

Her boot sent an object scuttling across the hard-packed dirt floor. "Adapt or die."

She brushed aside the dust and retrieved the jagged shard of black pottery, its color and crude design amazingly fresh. "It's as if one day they just walked away."

Pilar glanced around. "As if any moment they could return." She shook herself. "Should we camp here for the night?"

"No."

She cut her eyes at him at his abrupt tone.

He rubbed his arms. "This place gives me the heebie-jeebies."

She dropped the shard into the soil from which it had rested for probably the last three-quarters of a century. She wiped the dust from her hands onto her pants. "I'll protect you, Alex. I won't let them eat you."

"You're funny." Moving outside, he'd never been so glad to feel the wind upon his face. "Funny as a heart attack."

Bending to clear the entrance, she rose to her full height and joined him. Her hair had come unclasped during their hike. It flowed free around her shoulders.

The way he'd always loved it.

She snagged his arm. Her fingers burrowed into his flesh. "Alex…"

He pivoted. "Wha—?" Something blue slithered behind a rocky outcropping.

She froze. Her eyes darted among the encroaching shadows. Then, he glimpsed cold steel between the boulders.

The suddenness of the attack—as if out of nowhere—stunned them both.

Something whizzed past his face. He flinched. She cried out. There was an explosion of sound as the bullet splintered the boulder two feet from his arm.

"Take cover." He jerked her behind the outcropping. "Are you hit?"

"No. Are you?" She crouched, her mouth set in a tight line. "Luis was right. *They* found *us*."

He reached for the gun he'd tucked in his waistband. "Which them?"

"You'd think either would've hit us if they meant to."

An arrow flecked with gray and white feathers sailed over their heads and thudded into the ground upon which they'd been standing seconds before.

He ducked. "Their aim's improving."

Pilar's eyes darkened. "Alex, you don't think—"

"I think it's time for us to get out of here."

A clap of thunder jarred them. Lightning crackled. Electricity sizzled the air.

"Go."

He shoved her down the overgrown path between the last of the caved-in dwellings toward the steep-sided canyon beyond.

And for once, following his command, she ran.

The rain began immediately. Quickly accelerating to a drowning deluge. Pouring out of the leaden sky. Drenching and soaking Pilar's clothing. Making the climb downhill even more hazardous.

Close on her heels, Alex put away the gun in favor of running. He was fast, speeded along by the sheer fear of what lay behind them. But he wasn't as fast as her.

Using both hands to balance her weight, Pilar scrambled down the impenetrable terrain. Not heeding where she headed. Not caring where. Driven by an inescapable dread. A burning need to distance herself from the evil stalking their back.

Her foot slipped.

She clawed at the earth in a desperate attempt to halt her sliding fall. Maybe—she bit her tongue and tasted blood—maybe fast wasn't as good as cautious. Her joints pulled at the sockets.

Throwing himself forward, he caught her underneath her arms and slowed her downward momentum. She dug into the rain-slick soil with her boots. Scooting the rest of the way on her butt, she reached the bottom of the gully first.

Releasing her, he rose and swung around in one smooth motion, gun extended. He stared down the barrel site. But it was hard to shoot at something—or someone—you couldn't see.

"Come on." He lowered his arm and sprinted toward the Bavispe tributary. Leaping, he bounded over some sagebrush.

She took off again through the marshlike swale following the rising stream, passing Alex like he stood still. She zigzagged around a cluster of mesquite. "They're still coming."

A hail of arrows—arrows?—punctuated her words. Her heart thumped. Hunching, she dodged scattered clumps of the thorny ocotillo.

"Wait," his breath came in spurts. "We've got to get to higher ground. A flash flood in this valley would sweep us away."

She splashed through the water. "Maybe on the other side of the river we can lose them." Her boots struggled for traction on the rapidly swelling riverbed.

"Keep heading for the trees," he shouted as the wind picked up speed.

He'd almost caught her now. Somewhere along the way, he'd dropped his encumbering pack. Somehow, she'd managed to hang on to hers.

Fear drove them. An itchlike urgency compelled Pilar to turn her head, to see if their enemy was gaining on them.

But she dared not. Those wasted seconds of energy would slow her, the possible difference between life and death. Seconds neither she nor Alex had to spare.

She concentrated on making each stride count. Straining, her head pushed forward, fear propelling her feet into motion. She lunged for the trees.

Pilar felt Alex at her back. Close. Protective. Shielding her. A few more—

More whistling signaled the whine of additional arrows.

He bit off a groan.

She glanced over her shoulder.

He stumbled. The stone tip of an arrow burrowed from his back into his shoulder and through to the front.

She skidded and snatched hold of a tree trunk to stop her headlong flight. "Alex…"

Crumpling, he went down on one knee.

She pivoted.

"No." His head shot up. "Don't stop. Go."

Pilar dropped to his side. "I'm not leaving you."

Something swished in the trees. She and Alex tensed. Something black with golden eyes.

The ground to the right of them shook. Another bullet sprayed the dirt. He threw his arms over her.

He blanched as the embedded arrow pierced deeper into his flesh. "Looks like they mean to finish the job this time."

Boots scudded on the embankment behind them. The rain hadn't slackened, only intensified. As had their pursuers.

She hauled Alex to his feet. "Good thing you're with me, then. Apaches don't do surrender, remember?"

He convulsed in pain at her sudden movement.

"Suck it up, Alejandro Torres," she hissed in his ear. "Don't you dare pass out on me."

As his head fell forward, his mouth grazed her cheek. "Wouldn't dream of it."

She veered toward the cover of the trees as his feet dragged. His good arm draped over her shoulder, she spun in a slow one-eighty. Assessing their odds of eluding the killers at their back. Searching for a place to hide. Frantic. Panicked.

God of Alex... Please... Help me help him.

She wrinkled her nose at her own foolishness. A stupid waste of breath. She slumped under his weight. She couldn't carry him much farther. Her arms ached.

But under the canopy of the trees, the rain lessened for the first time. And to the left, yards above them, hidden among the dangling overgrowth, she sighted a small indentation in the mountain.

"If that was you, God, thanks," she whispered into the howling wind.

Firming her grip around his waist, she towed Alex forward. On the lip of the carved-out enclosure, she breathed deeply and tried adjusting his body weight. Gathering her courage.

"I hate the dark," she muttered.

At the sound of her voice, he moved and nudged her off balance.

Teetering, her free arm flailed. She tumbled face forward through the vines into nothingness. She rotated, placing her body between his and the bottom.

Cushioning his fall, the impact of the stony ground rattled her teeth. His rock-hard chest landed on Pilar, forcing the breath from her lungs.

Her eyes adjusted gradually to the half-light cast through the opening of a small cave. Forgotten since the time of the Broncos.

God, how she hoped so.

She rolled out from under him and onto her knees. "This is getting to be a bad habit, Torres." She poked his belly with her finger to see if he still lived.

He grunted.

A shadow of his old Mr. Charming smile flitted at the corners of his lips. He took a breath. "Oh, I don't know, Pia. I kinda enjoy it."

"Being you, I guess you'd have to be about dead not to."

Stooping, he lugged himself across the dirt enclosure and rested against the rock wall. "It'll take more than this for you to get rid of me, Pia. Things were getting heated last night. We both needed space. But I'm not done talking with you. About a lot of things. Not by a long shot."

Pilar placed her finger against his lips. "Shush…"

Voices. She bellycrawled to the entrance.

Pressing her spine against the rocky surface, she inched sideways toward the opening. The voices were too low to make out what they were saying. But it wasn't English. She knew that much.

Nor Spanish, either.

She craned her neck around the opening and held her breath lest they hear. She blinked. Once. Twice.

Not believing what her eyes were seeing.

Through the tangle of vines, she beheld four pairs of legs encased in wide-legged Mexican style trousers. Calico shirts draped over sashed waistbands.

And high-topped Apache upturned moccasins covered their feet.

Pilar gasped. Outside, movement ceased. She put her hand over her mouth.

She must've hit her head sliding down the mountain. There was no other explanation. Either that, or she and Alex had truly fallen through more than just a rabbit hole.

They'd fallen back into the last, bloody century of the past.

27

Before

"Where were you, Alex? I woke up and you were gone."

Holding the sheet against her chest in the chilly Xoacatyl air, Pilar rubbed the sleep from her eyes.

Alex stuffed the cell into his jeans.

"Where's my morning kiss?" She opened her arms to him. "Is this any way to greet your wife, my husband?"

A pained expression flickered across his features. He looked suddenly older and somehow more worn. He palmed his keys off the bureau and shoved them into his pocket.

Pilar's arms dropped. Something was wrong. Badly wrong. "Alex?"

He avoided her eyes and plucked the shirt he'd flung over the settee the night before.

"Talk to me, Alex. What is it?"

From the bottom up, he concentrated on buttoning his shirt as if his life depended on it. His hands shook. Halfway, he stopped, the buttons mismatched. The silver chain holding the Apache tear glimmered against his chest.

Her breath hitched. "Look at me." And she imagined her life might depend on what Alex said or did in the next few minutes.

"Alex?" she whispered.

He lifted his head.

The look in his eyes...Her stomach cramped.

With a guttural groan, he crawled onto the bed and cradled her face in his hands. His mouth engulfed hers. Hungry, insatiably devouring. With a desperation that chilled Pilar to the marrow of her bones.

Alex wrenched free, gasping.

Her heart pounded. "What's wrong?" She caressed his arm.

Alex bolted off the bed. "I'm sorry, Pia." He closed his eyes. "So sorry."

Disentangling from the comforter, she swung her legs to the floor. "You're scaring me, Alex. What's happened?"

Alex resumed his futile attempt to button his shirt. "We're—you're going home. It's time to go back."

Her eyes flitted toward the balcony. "But the fiesta? It isn't over yet."

Alex swallowed. "It's over for us." He shoveled his clothes into his bag. "Get dressed. Get packed. We're leaving."

"But—"

"Must you argue about everything?" He kept his back to her. "Just do it, Pia."

A lump formed in her throat. Then, a thought. Their first fight.

They were having their first fight exactly like all married couples. And what generally followed first fights? Her lips curved.

She looked forward to the making up part.

Ten minutes later, Alex stood stiff and silent as she—for the both of them—expressed their undying gratitude for the Martinezes' hospitality. As they drove away, she blew exuberant kisses to shy Nita, hiding in the skirts of the señora.

Driving toward Nogales, Alex maintained a brooding silence. She tried to draw him out with questions. But she got nothing from him, except stony coldness. She fingered the corded tassels of her wedding blouse.

"Whatever I did, I'm sorry, Alex."

His eyes cut to her before flicking to the road.

"If you'll tell me what I did, I won't ever do it again. Then we can move on to making up." A smile in her voice, she stroked his hand on the gearshift.

He moved his hand to the steering wheel. She blinked against the sudden onslaught of tears.

What was wrong with him? What had she done? What had changed since last night when he loved her so well?

Her inexperience gnawed at her insides. "Alex..."

"Let's get across the border." His hands white-knuckled the wheel. "We can talk when we're on the other side."

Chin dropping, she focused on the Saturday traffic as they neared the international crossing. Alex tensed as he answered the border agent's questions and waited for the inspection process to be complete. His unease catching, she found herself holding her breath as the agent perused their documents. Finally, the agent waved them through. And they were on American soil.

Alex's icy demeanor continued on the road to Tucson. There, he pulled into an empty space adjacent to Abuela's Land Rover outside his apartment building. The only empty space.

Lawn chairs littered the grass. Open doors reflected big screen televisions recording the big game. College students wove through the parked cars, plastic drink cups clutched in their hands. Pac-12 Wildcat fervor at fever pitch, raucous cheers rang out when the football team scored.

He cut the engine. Gripping the wheel, he stared through the windshield and said nothing. She knotted her fingers in her jean skirt.

Long minutes passed as the engine ticked and cooled.

"I think it's time you returned to Abuela's where you belong. She has your plane ticket to Bragg." He spoke without looking at her.

Her heart hammered. "I don't understand. We did this," she fluttered her beringed finger, "just so I wouldn't have to go to Bragg. So we could stay together."

Still he wouldn't look at her.

"You want me to go to North Carolina? But we're married…" She touched his sleeve.

He flinched.

Like an old man, he angled slow and looked at her for the first time. "Thing is, we're not."

She gasped. "But the priest? The registry? Of course we are. What're you talking about?"

"It's not legal without parental consent. Not even in Mexico." He shrugged. "We had our little fling. Fulfilling what we both know was inevitable from the moment we met. Satisfying our curiosity."

A sick feeling welled in her gut. "What are you saying, Alex? We love each other."

Opening his hands, he lifted one shoulder and let it drop. "We had our fun."

He gave her the trademark Alex Torres grin. "You know me. I don't do love. I do pleasure. And it's time to get back to reality. Time for you to finish growing up. Time for me to return to class."

She shrank into the seat. "I don't believe you. You love me. I know you do. And we're married. We are."

Pilar felt herself slipping, as if on the edge of a dark, fathomless abyss. "Why are you saying these things? Doing this to me? To us?" She caught his arm.

Alex flung her off. "Can't you act like a grownup for one minute, Pia? We loved; we laughed. It's time to move on." His face tightened in anger. "Why do you make me spell it out for you and hurt you?"

He gestured at two passing coeds. "Why can't you be more like them?"

The blondes waved.

She sucked in a breath. She hadn't been enough for him. She'd failed him. Disappointed him.

"If you'd give me another chance, Alex. I promise I'll be a better wife. I'll..." Her stomach lurched.

A muscle ticking in his cheek, he jerked the key from the ignition. "For the love of God, Pilar. I thought you had more pride than to beg. It's over. Get it through your thick Apache head."

Ear-deafening, pulse-jumping roars erupted as the Wildcats scored another touchdown.

He beckoned the blondes. "'Cause I've found another party."

Anger, unlike any she'd ever known before, seized control of Pilar. She slapped Alex Torres across the face. His head ricocheted at the impact of her hand on his cheek.

"You used me. You charmed me into going with you. Into lying to Abuela and my brother. So you could—"

"Just so I could." His face hardened. "Just so I could do what I did. What we both did. And don't come off all self-righteous, Pilar."

Alex adjusted his jaw with his hand. "You wanted it, too. You threw yourself at me every chance you got. Don't lie to yourself. You enjoyed it, too."

Her cheeks burned. Her palm burned. And she wanted to hit him again and again.

Smash his drop-dead gorgeous face. Grind her fist into his throat. She ached to eradicate once and for all his self-satisfied, cocky charm.

Pilar wanted to erase the memory of his touch on her skin. The look in his eyes when he said her name. The last five years of her life.

"I hate you." She hated she couldn't stop the quavering in her voice. "I despise you."

She hated and despised herself. For her gullibility. For her naïveté.

"I loathe you," she whispered.

His chest heaved and he dropped his eyes. "Loathe? Good one, Pilar. Your word for the day?"

Alex fumbled with the seat belt. "Don't tell me you're going to cry. Really, Pilar? Apaches don't cry, remember?"

The tears springing to her eyes evaporated into nothingness. She balled her fist in her lap. "You tricked me. You're everything and more Byron ever warned me about you."

And she called him the filthiest name she knew.

Rigid, he leaned past her and flung open her door. "Get out. And go home, little girl. Maybe when you're more sophisticated as to how the world rolls, we can try this again sometime. For laughs."

Her eyes widened. Her breath came in short spurts. He was throwing her out like yesterday's garbage.

She rocketed out of the Jeep. She slammed the door, catching him off guard. Almost slamming the door on his hand. He jerked his hand back at the last minute.

Which was too bad.

"Thanks for showing me the ropes, Torres."

Pilar pulled the blouse down, leaving her shoulders exposed. "I'll show you how grown-up I am. Grown-up, thanks to you."

She charged up the hill toward the party spilling onto the lawn.

"Pilar, don't—" He scrambled out of the Jeep.

She managed to lose him amid the throngs in one of the apartment parties.

"Hey, where you'd come from, little lady?" Fair-haired and bleary-eyed, an Anglo college boy rolled on his feet and grasped onto her shoulder for support.

The Anglo's eyes enlarged and narrowed in an attempt to focus. "What? No drink?"

He threw out his hand toward the pass-through window in the kitchen. "A glass for the lovely one here."

The motion almost toppled him. She snatched hold of the hem of his Oxford shirt. He draped his arm around her. She resisted the urge to throw him off as his flesh brushed across the bare skin on her shoulder.

"Get off her, Frat Boy," Alex's voice growled from the doorway.

She noted, with a great deal of satisfaction, that sweat had broken out on Alex's forehead.

Frat Boy peered at Alex. "You know this dude, sweetheart? You with him?"

"Yes, she is."

"No, I'm not."

She wound both arms around Frat Boy's waist. "Didn't you say something about a drink?"

Alex advanced. "She's underage. You serve alcohol to a minor and you'll find your butt in jail."

Frat Boy wobbled. "You underage, honey bun?"

She batted her lashes. "Do I look underage?"

Frat Boy laughed, low in his throat. "Why no, sweet cheeks." His admiring gaze undressed her with his eyes. "No, you don't."

Alex tugged at of her arm. "Pia... These aren't little boys you're playing with."

Pilar yanked free. "Maybe I want a real man now." She snuggled into Frat Boy.

Seizing a drink from a Latino through the cutout kitchen window, Frat Boy thrust the cup into her hands and wrapped his arms tighter around her neck. "I'll show you a real man. And I know how to give you a real good time." He whispered his version of sweet nothings into her ear.

Pilar steeled herself against the stale beer smell on his breath and forced herself to smile. She took a few sips of beer to show Alex she could.

Alex reached for her again. "Stop it, Pilar. You're stirring a fire you won't know how to put out."

Frat Boy jerked out of Alex's reach, knocking Pilar's feet out from under her. The drink in her hand sloshed and wet her blouse.

"Whoa there, little flower." Another student steadied her. His Irish green eyes squinted at Alex. "This desert rat giving you a hard time, brown sugar?"

Both men tightened their grip on her.

Alex clenched his fists. "Who you white boys calling a desert rat? I'm from L.A."

"Back off, José," Frat Boy sneered. "She doesn't want you. She's into us now. Find your own *muchacha*."

"Yeah," she smirked, making her lips pouty. "I'm into them now." She twined kittenlike into Frat Boy.

"Oh, baby." Frat Boy nuzzled her neck.

Alex's hand shot out and thumped Frat Boy's chest. "Get off her, white bread."

Frat Boy stumbled.

The crowded room went into a sudden, dead quiet. She glanced around at the sea of faces. Anglos, except for the lone Latino in the kitchen.

All angry. All eager to let loose some testosterone. All more than halfway drunk.

Righting himself and breathing heavily, Frat Boy jutted his chin at Irish Eyes and the others. "You going to let this taco eater disrespect us or what?"

Five men—shirttails hanging over their khaki cargo shorts like a uniform she thought irrelevantly—stepped forward, shoulder to shoulder with Frat Boy and Irish Eyes.

She gulped another swallow from her cup. She grimaced at the taste.

Irish Eyes pulled on her arm. Alex grabbed her other arm, and the drink flew out of her hand, dousing and enraging the college student.

With a roar, Irish Eyes let go of her and charged Alex. Alex dropped her arm and dodged left. He followed with a swift uppercut to Irish's jaw that sent the Anglo reeling into his backup offensive line.

Ducking, she sidled toward the perimeter as the battlefront heated up. She headed for the door and wiped her sticky hands on her sodden jean skirt.

Alex hadn't meant what he said. Somebody—Byron or Abuela—had gotten to him. She remembered how he'd tucked his cell into his pocket as he emerged from the balcony this morning. She'd get this whole misunderstanding sorted out as soon as she got to the ranch.

In the meantime, she glanced over her shoulder as punches flew and the room descended into chaos. She hoped they beat the crap out of Alex. Not too much, just enough to rid him of whatever ailed him. She hastily stepped outside as the melee intensified.

She wasn't worried. She'd seen Alex in action before in schoolyard brawls. He could handle himself. Give worse than he got.

Dusk descended as she tramped down the hill toward the jammed but deserted parking lot. Curbside, she put a hand to her head. She shook off the weird feelings of dizziness.

She retrieved her purse from the backseat of the Jeep and dug out her keys to the Land Rover. Unaccountably woozy, she let the purse fall to the floor mat. Backing away, she fell against the adjacent Land Rover.

"You okay, señorita?"

Blinking rapidly, she stiffened. The Latino from the party. Had she seen him somewhere before today? She squeezed her eyes shut as her perception wavered in and out.

"O-k-kay…" She frowned, slurring the words. She tried to shake her head.

But her head rotated wildly on her shoulders, off balance. Like her. She leaned against the cool metal of the green Land Rover.

She'd only had a few sips. With her mother's history, she never drank. She wasn't used to…

Her vision blurred. She tried to focus on the Latino's haughty face. But the edges of his broad features melted, curling at the edges. What was wrong with her?

Pilar's pulse ratcheted. Her instincts heightened, she shrank back, but the Latino forced her against the car. His jean knee nudged between her legs. She placed her trembling hands against his hard, muscular chest and shoved.

"G-get of-f m-me."

Scooting free but unbalanced, she landed in a heap on the ground. Her short skirt riding high, she tried to tug it down, but her hand wouldn't cooperate. She was so tired. So sleepy. She could barely keep her eyes open.

Panic hammered her heart.

Her drink. He'd been in the kitchen. What had he done to her drink?

Towering over her, the man's eyes glinted, yet a smile wreathed his sharp features. "I think I will take what you so freely offered the others, señorita." In a swift lunge, he gathered the keys she'd let slip from her hand when she fell.

She opened her mouth to tell him no, but found she couldn't manage to get the words from between her lips. The rowdy shouts and music with safety only a few yards away echoed strangely in her head. As if she were in a tunnel.

"No," she thought she shouted. Instead, only a whimper emerged. He bent over her.

She tried to raise her hands to fend him off, but her arms were dead weight.

He scooped her into his arms. Her head lolled. Why couldn't she think? Why was it so hard to—

Alex. Where are you? Help me.

Inside her head, her mind screamed. Her lips emitted only a groan.

The man moistened his lips. "Fighting me will only heighten the pleasure."

He pressed her into the smoothness of his chest gaping through his shirt. Terror-stricken, her eyes darted. His hand stroked her head as he carried her around to the passenger side.

"I know a special place where we can pledge our love to each other forever." Holding her in a strong one-armed grip, he clicked the lock on her keychain and wrested open the door.

She had the sensation of floating above herself. Above the man and his plans. Above the car and the deserted lot. As high as heaven.

Or did she mean hell?

The man gave a deep-throated laugh as he tucked her gently into the passenger seat. "A secret place."

Alex…Alex…Why didn't he come?

"Tonight," he whispered into her ear. "You will be mine."

28

Somewhere, a big cat's roar split the night.

"What did you see out there?" Alex whispered.

Shoulder to shoulder, they leaned against the cavern wall. Unlike the usual never-say-die girl he loved, Pilar seemed rattled. She huddled against him, her knees drawn to her chin.

"They're gone." But she refused to look at him. "It's the twenty-first century."

"Good." He frowned. "What—?"

Forgetting, he jostled his arm. Waves of pain radiated through his body. He gritted his teeth.

"It's getting dark." She cast one final look at the opening. "If we go deeper I don't think anyone outside can spot a light. I need to examine your wound. Take out the arrow and treat it before an infection sets in."

He gave her a wary look. "Since when did you become medical?"

"Can you make it on your own? I can—"

"I'm not helpless, Pilar." He staggered to his feet.

Flicking the lighter she'd scrounged from a pocket, she rounded a bend in the wall. "Have it your way, Mr. Mexican Macho."

"I'm from L.A.," he growled.

Alex stumbled toward the light. After a few steps, he stopped to catch his breath. He was weaker than he'd imagined.

Her arm swept the expanse, not more than twelve by twelve and about as high. "It'll be cozy."

Lightheaded, he braced himself against the wall and scanned upward for the source of the air on his face. "There's must be an air hole in the ceiling. We'll be able to breathe, but it's going to be cold when the temps drop."

Her eyes narrowed, not missing his unsteadiness.

Pilar, he reflected not for the first time, never missed much. One of the things he loved most about her.

If they could only survive long enough to find their loved ones and somehow carve out a future together.

She rummaged through the backpack again and retrieved a small, battery-powered lantern. "This is why I love being a twenty-first century woman." She cranked the nozzle and LED light flooded the chamber, flushing out the darkness.

"We can't start a fire." She slung the backpack into a shadowed corner. "A fire would provide a smoke signal straight to our hideout." Realizing what she'd said, her lips twitched.

He laughed. "You'd be the cultural expert on smoke signals, I'll grant you that."

"Shut up and get over here so I can jerk the arrow out of your shoulder, Torres. You're bleeding all over the cave." She stooped to examine some objects piled near a crevice.

He hugged the wall. "Your bedside manner needs work, Pia."

She arched a look at him over her shoulder. "That's not the signal I was getting from you last night."

"Everybody's a comedian when I'm bleeding out." He lurched.

She caught him as his knees buckled. "Any excuse to be in a woman's arms, eh, Alex?"

"Only yours, Pia. Only yours. And a poor excuse, Abuela says," he clenched his jaw. "Is better than none."

She lowered him to the packed earth floor. Dropping to her knees, she helped him recline against a rock formation. Alex squeezed his eyelids shut and tried to block the pain. He breathed slow and deep through his nostrils.

Regaining a semblance of control, he moistened his lips. "And exactly how do you plan to remove this arrow from my bruised and battered but still fabulous body?"

She made a face. "Oh, I don't know, Alex. Haven't removed any arrows in the line of duty lately. Maybe I'll just dial up an ancestor of mine, what do you think?"

"Don't joke about stuff like that, Pia." His eyes darted around the cavern. "Not here."

Pilar cut her eyes toward the tunnel. A funny look crisscrossed her face. "You're right. I shouldn't."

She positioned the light closer and examined the entry and exit points of the arrow.

"I've never doubted the authenticity of your Apacheness, Pilar."

She took a hard look over her shoulder toward the opening. "Well, I'm starting to question a lot of things I believed."

"Welcome to the club."

She eased the torn fabric off his shoulder.

He winced.

"Not smart to be insulting someone who holds your threshold of pain in her hands, Torres."

"I trust you, Pia."

Her eyes probed the wound. "This is going to hurt you more than it's going to hurt me."

"I wouldn't want it any other way, I promise you."

Her gaze locked with his. "You and your promises, Alex Torres." She leaned him forward. "Holler if you want to. One. Two…"

He tensed for the expected wrench of pain.

She broke the shaft of the arrow.

"Yowwww." He jerked. "You didn't say three."

She handed him the broken arrow. "I never said I was counting to three. You assumed. Always a bad mistake to assume. Let that be a lesson to you."

Alex glared at her.

"Hawk feathers on the end." She ran her finger over the tip sticking out of the front of his shoulder. "Probably not poisoned or you'd be dead already."

He rolled his eyes. "Why doesn't that comfort me?"

"The arrowhead will be a piece of cake to rip out. I'll yank it, pack it with—"

"Could you please try not to use words like 'rip' and 'yank' when we're talking about my injuries?"

"Such a big baby…" She tugged.

He yelped.

She held the obsidian point to the light. "See? The worst's over. Time to take off your shirt."

He cocked his head. "You never give up, do you?"

She laughed as he meant her to. "Now I know you're feeling better if you can make jokes." Scooting behind him, she helped him shrug out of the ripped half of his shirt.

Pilar unscrewed her canteen. "This is going to be cold." She poured the water over his shoulder, letting it dribble over his open wounds.

He gulped in air.

"Now for a trick a certain Diné EMT taught me when we dated."

"Dated?" His mouth turned down. "Weren't the Navajo traditional enemies of the Apache?"

"Not Jake. He was *mucho guapo*, to use a language you're sure to understand. Drove a pimped-out Chevy. Knew how to treat a lady."

Alex frowned.

"Besides, red-skinned brothers and sisters, no matter the tribe, need to stick together."

She removed a plastic sandwich bag from the confines of the pack and opened it.

His nostrils quirked at the pungent aroma. "What's that?"

"Ground sage. I'm going to pack the wound. Old desert rat—Navajo, Apache, and Tohono O'odham—trick."

His eyebrows rose. "You're putting that inside my body?"

"Relax, Alex. It helps the blood to clot and stops the bleeding. An organic, all-natural bandage, Apache style. I always carry some with me. You'd be surprised at the scrapes Manny has gotten into over the years."

Her nimble fingers made short work of the unpleasant task. Alex breathed easier once she finished. She ripped two squares of duct tape with her teeth.

"What else you got in there, Pia? The kitchen sink?"

"Duct tape rules." She taped the patches over his wounds, holding in the sage. "But what I wouldn't give for cell coverage about now."

Backing away, she removed her black overshirt. "We'll have to spend the night. Hopefully, the coast will be clear in the morning, and we can follow Abuela's map from here."

He grimaced. "Only problem is the map ended at the Apache campsite, Pia."

"We'll figure something out. We always do." She tore a strip of cloth off the bottom of her shirt. "You need a sling."

Leaning forward, she tied both ends into a knot around his neck. He couldn't help but fixate on her lips, so close to his. Her breath brushed his cheek. A pulse beat a furious tempo at the hollow of her throat.

Figure something out...He'd spent the last month since Byron called pulling strings to get himself reassigned closer to the rez. Facing the truth. Praying for the courage to let her go.

And tonight...maybe his last, best chance to say what he needed to say. What he should've said sixteen years ago.

29

Pᴵʟᴀʀ ᴄᴏɴᴄᴇɴᴛʀᴀᴛᴇᴅ ᴏɴ ꜱʟɪᴅɪɴɢ Aʟᴇx's ᴀʀᴍ ᴛʜʀᴏᴜɢʜ ᴛʜᴇ loop of the sling. "There."

It was hard being this close to him. Touching him. Being just his friend.

Putting space between them, she examined the heap of broken potsherds she'd found. "This may be one of those forgotten places where the Broncos stored food and weapons when they were on the run, moving from mountain range to mountain range."

She glanced toward the cave entrance and shivered. Those men, whoever they were, acted as if they knew she and Alex were holed up inside. Their attack almost seemed as if they'd driven her and Alex to the cave.

"But then why didn't they come...?"

"Why didn't who come?"

She'd spoken her thoughts aloud. "Never mind."

Pilar sifted through the artifacts. A few rusty iron nails. The remnants of a woven basket. A moldy stretch of animal skin. One moccasin, child-sized. And a woman's scratched, nineteenth-century pocketwatch.

Apaches had no use for keeping time with a clock. It more than likely belonged to an Anglo woman first. Before they'd taken it from her.

"What did you find?"

She pivoted on her heels. The gold gleamed in the lantern light. Alex said nothing, but his eyes traveled from the watch in her hand to her face.

And his face?

Unreadable.

Her breath hitched at the images the timepiece evoked and the savagery the woman probably endured. Pilar dropped the battered watch into the dirt.

She could, though, predict the line Alex's thoughts would travel. Disgust. Pity. Revulsion.

The typical emotions of the men with whom she'd attempted a relationship in the intervening years. She told them early on about the attack because there was no need to waste her time or theirs in dragging things out to their inevitable conclusion once they knew.

No man wanted her after what she'd been through. A fact to which she'd reconciled herself. She'd always be alone.

Her shoulders sagged, and the strap of her camisole fell off her shoulder.

"The scars faded," Alex whispered.

She flinched and grabed for the strap. She'd never meant for him to see. She angled the ropy tissue away from Alex, not able to bear him seeing her ultimate shame.

"Not really."

The physical wounds were nothing compared to the emotional scars she bore. The raw, aching places in her soul.

Her hand trembled as she repositioned the strap over the ugliness of the letters the monster had carved. Where he'd claimed and marked her. Like one of Abuela's cattle.

And then Alex's words struck Pilar.

"How do you know they're faded?" Her mouth quivered. "You saw the scars at the hospital?"

Alex's face clouded.

She slid to the wall. But left a distance between them. A distance that could never be bridged.

"That's why you never came back." She sighed. "The scars repulse me, too."

"No." He jerked. "I left because the police suspected someone we'd probably met across the border. Byron said my presence would delay your healing. Because every time *you* saw *me*," Alex's voice roughened. "You'd see *him*."

She laced her fingers through his. "Byron was half out of his mind with pain and revenge. It wouldn't have been true, Alex. I've always seen only you."

"I need to show you something." He let go of her hand. "What the beast did marked me, too. Your scars were my scars. Not even close to the pain you endured, but this was the only way to express what I felt."

Grunting with the effort, he shrugged out of the remaining half of his shirt. Her eyes widened when his shirt fell open, exposing the undamaged side of his chest. She stared at the tattoo etched on the pectoral closest to his heart.

A single word.

Yours.

Her breath hitched. The 'o' shaped into a heart. A crossbar inserted into the 'Y'.

Alex caught hold of her hand. "My heart was always yours." He brought her hand to his chest.

His skin warm to her touch, his heart thumped beneath her palm.

"The cross I added later because I realized I must belong to Him foremost."

She traced the heart with her finger. And, the sign of the cross. Tears blurred her vision. "Oh, Alex…"

"There are things I wanted to say to you. Things I felt in my heart but didn't know how to express. When I found God, He gave me the words to speak. Only by then, we'd lost each other."

She leaned against the rock. The smell of decay filled her nostrils.

"Would you allow me to say them to you now, Pia? God has given me a second chance. I do not wish to waste it. I don't know what tomorrow will bring. But we have this moment. To forgive each other if we can. To heal each other as much as we can."

Her heart ached. Did she have the courage to listen to what he had to say? How much pain would his words exact?

"Our mistake wasn't in loving each other, Pia."

Her throat constricted.

"I'll never regret loving you. Part of God's favor, I've come to believe, that we found each other so young. Our mistake—my mistake—was how I responded to our love."

She shifted. "Not just you."

"I was older. I should've made better decisions. Instead, I acted with impatience. With an unwillingness to allow the will of God to come to fruition. I convinced you to tell lies, to deceive those who loved us best. Who wanted only the best for us."

"We were both too young."

Alex nodded. "But God has allowed us another chance to make things right. When I stumbled out of the hospital that night, I dropped out of school. And I joined the army with the intended purpose of offing myself." He grimaced. "Death by Taliban."

Her stomach knotted.

"I took the most hazardous of duties. I wanted to die for what my selfishness caused."

The thought of his body in a military cemetery somewhere cut through Pilar like a white-hot blade.

"But God wasn't done with Alejandro Torres." He glanced at the darkened ceiling of the cave. "As He was not—is not—done with you, Maria Caterina Pilar To-Clanny."

"You survived. I'm glad."

He placed her palm on his jeaned thigh. "I wasn't glad. So when that didn't work, I joined the Bureau. My language skills outweighed my juvenile trouble with the law. They sent me first to Mexico to infiltrate the Flores fiefdom. In Sinaloa, my cover got blown."

Alex took a breath. "*Narcotraficantes* gave me two impossible choices. I chose to run. They chased me to the edge of a cliff. I had about a second to repent of the wreckage I'd made of my life and yours, to beg for an eleventh-hour forgiveness. As I stepped off into nothingness, I gave my soul and life over to God."

She rubbed her cheek against his shoulder.

"I never expected to clear the rocks. Somehow I found myself floating down a rain-swollen river. Villagers fished me out, and I made my escape north."

"What changed that morning in Xoacatyl, Alex?"

"Byron called me in Xoacatyl. He threatened if I didn't bring you back and put you on a plane for North Carolina he'd have me arrested for statutory rape."

She gasped. "I was old enough to make my own choices."

"You and I . . . There was a three-year age gap. And three years according to Arizona law makes the difference. He also reminded me of my probationary status. How I'd left the country without permission. How an arrest would revoke my probation and I'd land in jail."

"Why didn't you tell me, Alex? I would've—"

"Because I thought I was so smart, Pia. Smarter than everyone. In my pride, I believed I could manipulate and control everything. I decided I'd put you on that plane, wait a few months until you were legal, and then we'd remarry."

"If I had only..." She slumped. "I should have...I shouldn't have—"

"Stop right there." He touched her chin with his finger and tipped her face to his. "It sounds as if you're blaming yourself for what happened."

Pilar averted her eyes.

"It's not true, Pilar. The rape wasn't your fault."

She winced at that word.

His mouth tightened. "The guilt lies with the man who raped you."

"I felt so powerless, Alex." She gulped. "The shock of what happened. It was so sudden. And the fear..."

He clasped her hands in his. "You've got to understand none of the shame belongs to you. That monster worked hard to ensure the advantages were his."

"I fought him, Alex." Her pulse quickened. "I want you to know I tried—"

"Pia, baby," his dark eyes flashed. "All that matters to me is you did whatever you had to and survived. I will always choose you alive over anything else. He stacked the deck against you. He possessed the element of surprise, the power of physical superiority. He went to enormous lengths to make sure this wasn't a fair fight. There was nothing you could have—should have—done that would've altered what happened."

She let his words soak into her soul. Alex didn't blame her?

"Nobody could've predicted it, Pia. This was out of your control."

"That's the problem. I hate feeling out of control."

He cupped her cheek. "The shame doesn't belong to you, baby. It belongs to him. You need to forgive yourself for whatever it is you think you did to deserve this. Because you didn't deserve this. Nobody does. He planned his attack upon you oh so carefully. He made sure it was never fair. He was and is a predator. It didn't happen because you were stupid or weak."

She blinked against the tears. The major reason why she'd become a cop. To acquire the skills so she'd never be that helpless again. And why she taught self-defense classes at the tribal center to ensure other women never found themselves as vulnerable.

"As long as you hold onto the shame, you perpetuate his lies. He planted this shame, this lie, into you, Pilar. That was part of what he gets off on—not only his power over you physically, but in the pleasure he derives from making you ashamed. No matter what he said to you, it's wrong. Nothing he ever said to you is true. Everything he said to you was a lie intended to serve his evil desires."

Alex's words resonated truth into the darkest places of her soul. Dark places she preferred not to examine too closely. Only Manny and her desire for revenge on all the monsters out there had gotten her out of bed every morning. But the bitterness twisted her inside.

He ran his thumb over her jawline. "I wasn't just assigned this case. I joined the Bureau to look for *him*. I read everything I could about surviving rape. I talked to those who'd experienced similar violations."

"Why?"

"Because..." He dropped his eyes. "Because it was the only way I could in a small measure share your pain."

She'd been wrong about Alex. He was different. And so, unfortunately, was she. Past redemption.

"I'll never be anything but broken, Alex, don't you see?"

"No, I don't see that," he growled. "Stop allowing him this power over you. When you reject the shame, you're fighting back. When you reject this unjustified blame, you take away his power and empower yourself."

She took a ragged breath. "I don't know how to stop being broken, Alex. I don't think even your God can fix me."

"That's not true, Pia." He extracted a folded index card from his pocket. "Here. It's something I carry with me. Reminding me how much God loves me."

She held the card with Alex's bold script to the light.

> But now, says the Lord—
> the one who created you, Jacob,

the one who formed you, Israel:
Don't fear, for I have redeemed you;
    I have called you by name; you are mine.
When you pass through the waters, I will be
        with you;
        when through the rivers, they won't sweep
            over you.
When you walk through the fire, you won't
        be scorched
    and flame won't burn you.
I am the Lord your God,
    the holy one of Israel, your savior.
. . . .
Because you are precious in my eyes,
    you are honored, and I love you.
    I give people in your place,
        and nations in exchange for your life.

God, how Pilar wished she could live in the now. How she wished she could believe in a God like that. She crinkled the paper in her fist.

"I don't know why God allowed this to happen to you, Pia. I'd give anything to have been the one hurt, not you. But I believe nothing happens without a reason."

She recoiled.

"That's a step of tremendous trust, I'll grant you. But I pray what was meant for evil, God will use for good in your life and in the lives of others."

He leaned forward. "I wish you could see beyond the unwarranted shame to how God sees you. To how I see you, too. Precious. So loved, God sacrificed His own Self for your sins, for your pain, for your hurts. He loves you. You must always remember what God calls you."

Moisture tracked down her cheeks.

"He has called you, Pia, by name. And 'you are Mine,' God says."

She closed her eyes. *Mia.* Mine. Yours.

"The ultimate lie that monster told you was that you belonged to him—mind, body, and soul. It isn't true. And though I've always called you my Pia, that isn't true, either. For from the moment He created you, you've belonged to God. You are His. Not mine. Not anyone else's."

Alex swallowed. "Strange as it sounds, I've found there are blessings in the brokenness if you will embrace it."

She wrapped her arms around herself.

"I love you, Pia. I've loved you since we were children, and I never stopped. And I will always, I suspect, love you. Until the day, I—not you—die. But even more than I love you, God loves you better."

She shut her eyes, but his voice filled the cavern. The words of the Scripture pleaded to take root in her heart.

"Only He can truly restore your soul. I had to surrender everything to God—my past, my present, my future. And in the surrender of my desires, I found a blessing far greater than I could've ever discovered apart from first experiencing the brokenness."

Alex's face transformed. "He alone made me whole as He took the pieces of my brokenness and reassembled me into someone better. More like Jesus. I'm learning to walk in the power of the name God calls me—His."

Nothing could break the stronghold of shame and self-loathing inside her. The chains were too strong. She knew, if Alex didn't, there was no way to return to who they'd been to each other before.

The unbearable pain spiraled. Gouging. Scorching.

She fumbled in her boot for the blade Luis had given them. She had to cut out the pain or die if she didn't release it.

His eyelids tensed. "Pia...Please. Don't. You are not wrong in thinking only blood can cleanse. But it has to be His blood that cleanses, don't you see? Not yours." His lips moved, silent, as if in prayer. "This isn't the way to heal."

It was her way. The only thing that made *it* better. At least, for a little while.

But she couldn't, not while he watched. She reinserted the knife into her left boot. Oblivion would be her only recourse tonight.

She edged away. "We should get some sleep. We'll need our wits and strength if we hope to rescue anybody." Almost a replay of his words to her last night at the inn.

Confusion and pain shadowed his face as he closed his eyes.

Perhaps he slept through the long, cold night. She didn't.

She jostled him when morning light streamed through the hole in the cavern ceiling. "Let's go."

They ate the last of the protein bars and fruit. Though wounded, he insisted on carrying the backpack.

Exasperated, she parted the curtain of vines and found herself yanked forward.

She lashed out and bloodied the nose of a narco in a silk cowboy shirt and ostrich boots.

Alex rushed out only to be knocked to the ground by a pair of *pistolero*-clad bandits. Fists flying, they disarmed Alex of his gun.

Pilar lunged at the men, clawing at their faces. Smelling of Mexican beer and stale cigarettes, one of them backhanded her. Alex got up swinging.

She went for the knife she always kept in her right boot. She stabbed the man with the heavy gold chain. He fell into a tree. She surged toward another.

"You will drop the knife, señorita."

An automatic rifle swung toward Alex. He froze.

"Or by the name of Jesús Malverde, patron saint of bandits, I will kill your man."

"No, Pia…" Blood dripped from Alex's busted lip. "Don't."

Her chest heaving, she raised her hands. The knife dropped to the earth with a thud.

30

With the black cloth wrenched off her head and her hands secured, Pilar struggled to adjust her eyes to the hot glare of the sunshine.

Her head swiveled as the *bandidos* snatched Alex out of the Dodge Ram. When they yanked her from the vehicle, she tripped and landed sideways. Scraping the rough gravel, her elbow took the worst of it. She bit off a cry.

Alex head-butted one of Salazar's thugs onto the hood of the Ram. "Leave her alone." Blood spurted from the goon's nostrils.

Two others left their post at the entrance of the sprawling hacienda. One of them drew his gun.

Panic gripped Pilar. "Alex, don't fight them. I'm okay."

The guard felled Alex with a cracking blow from the butt of his pistol.

She scrambled to her feet and strained to reach Alex, to stop the man from beating him. Her Mexican keeper grabbed a chunk of her hair and jerked. Yelling, she twisted, trying to ease the pressure.

Two cartel soldiers grabbed Alex's arms.

"Don't hurt her." Alex broke their hold only to be seized again. A fisted punch to the abdomen sent him reeling.

Her burly tormentor hauled Pilar by her hair to within inches of his foul-smelling breath. He drew back his other hand. "Shut up, you little—"

"Cut her loose. Now."

The Mexican swung both of them around. She cried out again as her hair pulled.

Clad casually in a loose, white linen shirt, Umberto Velarde leaned against the massive pine door. He crossed his taupe-colored slacks at the ankle, the picture of refinement. "Do not make me repeat myself."

"She stabbed Alberto, boss," the Mexican snarled. "Stuck him like a pig. He bled out all over the truck. She fought us like a crazy wildcat." He shook Pilar by the handful of her hair he clutched in his fist.

Pilar wrestled against his grip to relieve the tension on her scalp.

"Of course, she fought you. She is Apache. Like *el tigre*, I would expect no less. Cut her loose." Umberto's voice had grown quieter. Deadlier.

A fact the Mexican did not fail to notice. He removed a switch-blade from his pocket and flicked it open. Jerking her around, he stretched her hands away from her back, pulling her joints in an unnatural direction. She stifled a groan, unwilling to give the scum-bag the satisfaction.

With a quick, sliding thrust, the Mexican snapped the plastic tie holding her captive, and her arms fell to her sides. She folded her arms around herself, rubbing her shoulder sockets. She stiffened as the Mexican placed his thick, meaty hand underneath her hair around the nape of her neck and squeezed.

Umberto's eyes narrowed. "Let go of her, *muchacho*."

Grunting, the Mexican released his hold upon Pilar and shoved her away. She landed on her hands.

The narco jabbed the switchblade in the air. "*Chica es muy loca, el jefe.*"

"She is…special." And the timbre of Umberto's voice altered. Subtly but distinctly.

Pilar raised her eyes.

Umberto loomed over her and it was as if someone—something—else shone out of his dark eyes. Changing the anthropologist's handsome features into a coarser, harder version of himself. Even his stance shifted. He balanced forward on the balls of his feet as if on the prowl.

And in that personification, she recognized her abductor. The personification of evil.

One man. Two identities. No wonder Mexican and American law enforcement had been unable to trap the elusive drug lord. He'd been hiding in plain sight for years. As Dr. Umberto Velarde—part of Mexico's elite intelligentsia, a landowning aristocrat.

She rose, disliking his advantage over her. Reminiscent of the utter power he'd once wielded over her helplessness. "You're Franco Salazar."

He moistened his full, sensual lips. "And you, *cara*, never disappoint."

She fought a shiver of revulsion.

"Pilar...I didn't know your name until recently." He cocked his head. "I couldn't find you until the day I spotted you in the canyon."

"You watched me from the cave."

"And once I recognized the tribal uniform, it was easy to trace your identity." His gaze intensified. "So you remember the cave, *cara*?"

Don't react. He's pushing your buttons. Think of his weakness, not your own. Think like an Apache tribal cop. You're not completely at his mercy this time.

But she didn't know where to look. Into his eyes or somewhere else? Did you stare a predator in the face or did that provoke his aggression?

With sheer force of will, she tamped down the fear threatening to overwhelm her. This Mexican-Apache wannabe respected strength. Unarmed and outnumbered, his grudging respect might be the only weapon she possessed to keep them alive.

Her eyes flitted toward a second-story window as a curtain parted. Manny or Reyna? Abuela?

She risked a glance at Velarde's face. "Which do you prefer? Umberto or Franco?"

"Out there," he gestured in the general direction of the United States. "I am Umberto Velarde, respected conservationist. Here," his prominent cheekbones lifted. "I am Franco Salazar. Lord of the Skies." He gave her a courtly bow. "I am both."

His sleek, self-satisfied smile chilled her. And his preening arrogance in the unassailability of his mountain stronghold. Perhaps that, too, was a chink in his armor.

"After all," another menacing smile, "it was Franco you knew..." a deliberate double-edged entendre, "...first."

Salazar took hold of her arm.

His flesh made her skin crawl.

"I knew you were intelligent. A worthy consort for Umberto or Franco. That's why I searched for you so long. No one else would do."

The way he talked of himself—of both his selves—made her want to shrink inside. But she controlled her gut reaction. Harnessing her courage, she donned the stoic demeanor Apaches wore with outsiders. Once before, Salazar had controlled her because of fear. She wouldn't give him that power over her again.

Salazar drew her upright and forced her to meet his gaze.

There the dancing shadows of her nightmares crystallized. In his eyes when he looked at her—a devouring rapaciousness. A barely contained anticipation.

Clicking the switchblade closed, the Mexican toyed with a strand of her hair.

Salazar's mouth tightened.

"As your second in command, when you finish with her, *el jefe*, I will enjoy—"

Salazar sprang at the narco. "She is mine."

Pilar stumbled into the bougainvillea.

In a motion so fast and practiced she almost missed it, Salazar drew a gun from his waistband.

The sound of the gunshot registered in her ears at the same moment the top half of the Mexican's head calved like a glacier before her eyes. Shock etched on his pockmarked face, his lifeless body dropped to the pavement.

"I will not tolerate such disrespect to my wife."

Her head snapped up.

Salazar's eyes blazed at the remaining men frozen in disbelief. "No one touches her but me." He waved the gun to punctuate his words. "Do I make myself clear?"

The men bobbed their heads and lowered their eyes. "*Sí, el jefe. Sí.*" Salazar tucked the gun into his slacks.

"Pilar doesn't belong to you." Alex struggled to his knees. "She's not your—"

Salazar's face darkened. In one quick stride, he wrested Alex's head backward and locked eyes with him.

Pilar reached out her hand. "Don't—"

"And you think she belongs to you, Special Agent Torres?" Salazar sneered. "I know about your pathetic undercover operations against the Flores *familia*. And as for Pilar, what you discarded, I reclaimed."

"In what schizophrenic world do you think she's your wife?" Alex jerked free. "She's not a possession to be owned. And I never discarded—"

"Ah, but you did and she is *my* wife now. I claimed her long ago by the law of *rapto*, and what is mine remains mine. I never stopped loving—"

"You don't know the meaning of the word *love*, you sick, crazy—"

Salazar's fist connected with Alex's jaw, whipping Alex's head around. He collapsed against the stone.

Fixing his collar, Salazar straightened. "If he talks again, silence him."

The drug lord flicked his hand toward the house. "Bring the boy." One of the men hurried inside to obey his command.

Pilar tensed. "Manny's here?"

Salazar ran his index finger across one eyebrow and then the other as if self-soothing. Exchanging the brutal Franco like a mask for the sophisticated Umberto. "For such unpleasantness, I apologize, *cara*."

Pilar wasn't his beloved. Not then, now, or ever.

At the sound of the door, she gazed beyond Salazar as a narco hauled Manny onto the stone veranda. His hair had come unloosed from the braid.

She surged forward. "Manny."

The thug grabbed Manny around the neck as he strained to reach Pilar.

Salazar snapped his fingers. "Let him see his mother."

The narco released Manny. With a small cry, Manny flew into her outstretched arms. Engulfing her body, Manny buried his face into her shoulder.

"Manny...Honey..." She cradled his face between her hands and examined his features. "Did he hurt you? Are you okay?"

Purple shadows bruised the skin below his red-rimmed eyes. As if he'd been crying for a long time.

"Is it true, Auntie? Are you my mother?"

She'd done everything in her power to ensure this moment never happened. That Manny never learned the truth. The secrets she'd kept for Manny's protection now destroyed by this monstrous beast. Manny must despise her. But what she feared worst—he'd hate himself.

"Answer me, Auntie." Manny's mouth twisted. "Or should I call you...Mother?"

The hurt and betrayal in his eyes rocked her.

"I am your mother." She cupped his cheek, relieved when he didn't pull away. "And you may not believe this, but I love you. I've always loved you."

At that, Manny extricated himself from her arms. Pilar ached with an emptiness she'd not experienced since those first days after the attack before she discovered life grew in her womb.

Manny's eyes welled, tortured. "Velarde says he's my father."

"It's not true." Alex somehow managed to hoist himself upright again. "He's not your father."

Salazar growled.

"Look at me, Manny." Alex's eyes pleaded. "See the truth. I'd never lie to you. You and I know the truth in our hearts. He could never be your father. But I am."

Her heart skipped a beat.

Salazar lunged and toppled Alex. His loafers pummeled Alex's stomach with repeated kicks. "He. Is. My. Son."

Pilar clutched Salazar's arm. "Stop hurting him. Stop."

Manny grasped Salazar's other arm. "No. No."

The other men rushed forward, but they fell shy of touching her, she noticed. Salazar didn't employ fools. They'd taken note of what he'd done to the man who laid hands on her. One man pulled Manny from Salazar. But the rest hung on the fringe.

Pilar might yet make use of Salazar's unpredictability and their fear of his brutality.

Salazar flung Pilar off. "She is mine." He never paused in his punishing blows to Alex's ribcage. "The. Mother. Of. My. Son."

Defenseless with his arms bound behind his back, blood oozed from a cut along Alex's cheekbone. Salazar balled his fist and drew back his arm.

Manny broke free and inserted himself between Alex and the drug lord. "Leave him alone."

Salazar pushed Manny aside. Manny fell into her arms as Salazar rammed his fist into the arrow wound in Alex's shoulder.

Going rigid, Alex crumpled onto the concrete. With a sigh of satisfaction, Salazar smoothed his bunched shirt over his chest. "And that, my son, is how I will teach you to deal with our enemies."

Pilar wrapped one arm around Manny. She pressed his shoulders against hers, only just preventing Manny from hurling himself at Salazar.

Salazar reached for the boy. Manny recoiled. The drug lord frowned. Clenching and unclenching his hands, Manny bristled with suppressed rage.

"Be still," she hissed in Manny's ear.

Salazar fondled Manny's head. "When you walked into my office...I had not realized until that moment that your mother had given me a son. Such a gift." His eyes gleamed.

Manny shook off Salazar's hand.

"Do not provoke him," she whispered.

Salazar's scowl erupted into a laugh. She and Manny jolted. "It is good the boy has such spirit. It will serve him well to one day run the empire I have built for him." His gaze swung to Pilar. "Built for you, too. Come, I will show you."

Prying them apart, he urged them across the threshold.

"Bring him," Salazar ordered with a cutting glance at Alex's unconscious form. "I will show my enemy and my *familia* the kingdom I have carved from this savage land."

Inside beyond the lavish entryway, three flagstone steps led to a sunken living room. A television was mounted over the mantel of an enormous stone fireplace. On another wall hung an oil painting of an old man with a long, Conquistador nose, an ugly scar on his face, and cruel lips.

And beside the portrait, the gaping jaw skull of the apex predator of the Sierra Madre. The jaguar.

Like his psycho connection to the mythical Broncos, Salazar probably styled himself as the apex predator of the mountains. Perhaps yet another one of Salazar's fantasies she could use against him.

Salazar's henchmen dumped Alex's body at the base of the fireplace and disappeared into the shadows. She fought her natural inclination, her desperate need to go to his side. She must think smart for all of them.

Corridors emptied on either side of the room. A bank of windows bookended the fireplace, giving her a glimpse of the Sierra Azul on the horizon. And of the high, fortified concrete wall, which encircled Salazar's compound. Between the wall and the villa was a large clearing, corrals, and outbuildings. Closest to the house, cypress trees and French doors led to a patio.

With a large, empty iron cage.

Salazar caught her eye. "Ah, you see where I keep my pets."

Her heart quailed, but she steeled herself. "Animal or human, Salazar?"

"That, my dear *esposa*, is entirely up to them." His eyes twinkled with amusement. "And I must insist you call me Franco." He stroked her cheek.

Manny knocked his hand away.

Salazar backhanded Manny. He landed amidst the profusion of cushions on the mission-style sofa. She dropped beside him.

"Don't hurt him, please." She brushed Manny's hair off his forehead. "Manny, honey—"

Manny shook free of her hand and glared at Salazar.

"You have raised for us a fierce cub." Salazar gave Manny a glacial look. "But you must learn respect for *tu padre*, Manuel."

The drug lord's face softened. "But as typical with the female *onca*, you've been raised without a father's influence. I must allow you time to adjust."

His gaze traveled to the framed portrait. "Unlike my father, Don Geraldo." Salazar's mouth contorted, a living reflection of the old man on the wall.

There was some issue between Salazar and the dead don, she noted for future exploitation.

"But we must adapt or die, isn't that right?" Pilar ventured.

He pivoted at her voice, hoarse and barely recognizable to herself. She cleared her throat. "Franco."

Manny's brow furrowed.

Salazar smiled. "I knew eventually you'd see the wisdom of what I've done to reunite our *familia*."

"Tell me," she injected a husky note into her voice. "How did all this come to be yours?"

As she suspected, he could no more resist showing off his prowess than a jaguar in heat.

Salazar widened his stance. "The don taught me, as a Mexican, life offers two possibilities." He squared his shoulders. "To either learn to endure suffering. Or, become the one who inflicts it."

"Prey versus predator. Strong versus weak."

Salazar came across the flagstone floor. "*Sí, cara*. When the don brought my mother and me here, I watched her suffer and decided I would be like him. Not her."

The illiterate, peasant boy of whom Joaquin Martinez had spoken. Salazar learned *rapto* at Don Geraldo's knee. Classic Stockholm Syndrome in the brutalized world of the drug culture.

"How did you become the accomplished Umberto?"

Salazar stroked his finger over his eyebrow. "There was already an Umberto, Don Geraldo Velarde's natural son. He was weak, stupid." Salazar touched his fingers to his lips. "Did you know the bite force of the jaguar can crush a human skull?"

He slid his hand the length of her arm. She forced herself to remain immobile.

"When the don tired of my mother, I watched him feed her to his favorite cat by the light of an Apache moon." His gaze flickered to the jaguar skull on the wall. "A captive female. Like *mi madre*. Ironic. *Sí*?"

His trigger. She did not know what was worse—the images he invoked? Or his nonchalant tone in recounting his mother's horrific murder?

"Like the Wild Ones, I went on a vision quest as a youth, and the *onca* became my power. I learned the ways of the *onca*. Her mate roams these mountains to this day. I've seen him several times over the years."

Salazar's eyes brightened. "He is beautiful. Powerful. Unlike her, completely black. Held captive by no man."

"And the real Umberto?"

"Like your Apache code, one is not a man here until he has killed another. *Murdret*, we call it. I was Manuel's age." Salazar shrugged. "When the time came to assume my rightful place, I fed the don's son to the cat."

Pilar didn't trust herself to speak.

Salazar tugged her to his side. "In the eyes of the outside world, I became Umberto. I attended university and compiled the degrees. The public face of *Rancho Onca.*"

"While the don ran his secret drug empire."

"Until he grew old and weak. When his Flores overlords were brought down by the *americanos*, I knew my time had come to rule this valley, my way."

Hunting as prey everyone within his realm of terror.

"I provide an important service to the *americanos, cara.* One kilo of my Sierra-grown cocaine crosses the border every ten minutes."

Salazar tapped her chin with his forefinger. "I am *muy importante* in my own country. Without my profitable corporation and others like it, the Mexican economy collapses."

He laughed. "Here, I am *El Señor de Los Cielos.*"

Manny swallowed. "While it lasts."

"You will learn as did I, my son, it is far better to live as a lord in the high places for one year," Salazar lifted his finger. "Than to grovel in the dirt for a lifetime."

"Better to be king in hell…" Alex stirred.

"Ah," Salazar angled. "You, too, know Milton." He snapped his fingers at the shadows.

Materializing, his soldiers seized Alex. He struggled. A scuffle ensued before one of them cuffed him into acquiescence.

"There are two choices the cartels allow our captured enemies, Special Agent Torres." Salazar crossed his arms over his chest. "I, being generous, will give you three. Unfortunately for you, living is not one of them."

He raised his thumb in the Mexican way of counting. "First, there is *leña*, where I allow my men to beat you to death."

Manny cried out, his eyes flashing.

"*Dos*," Franco held up his index finger. "*Plomo.* This is the brave *machismo* choice I would make in your situation. In the clearing at the base of the Azul, I set you free."

Pilar put her hand to her throat.

Suspended between two men, Alex snarled, "So you can shoot me in the back when I run?"

"Not at all. My men will not shoot until you reach the wall. But know if you elude them, the big cat will yet stalk you." Salazar gave a fatalistic shrug. "Because when it is your time to die, you die."

Alex grimaced. "And my third 'choice'?"

"To be kept in the cage as my pet while I get to know my son." Salazar tilted his head. "A living death."

And Salazar ravaged Pilar with a look. "Where also you watch as she once more becomes mine."

31

Tossed onto a bed in a room off a darkened corridor, Alex's gut churned. He assessed his situation.

No longer manacled, but imprisoned nonetheless. The window barred, a naked lightbulb dangled from the ceiling.

He'd never hated anyone as much as he hated Franco Salazar. For what he'd done to Pilar. For what Salazar still intended to do.

The old Alex threatening to resurface, he'd seethed with rage when Salazar put his hands on her. And he writhed with helplessness and guilt for not being able to stop Salazar then or now.

Red dots swam before his eyes. He wanted—he needed—to pound his fist into Salazar's face. Maim and destroy him. Make Salazar hurt as he'd hurt Pilar.

Beaten within an inch of his life, Alex ached in parts of his body he'd not realized could ache. He fought the rising tide of blackness. A plunging abyss dragging him farther and farther from the light. But a whisper at the edge of his conscious mind called to him— *Vengeance is Mine.*

Mine...Mia...

At the vision of Pilar and Manny in Salazar's ruthless hands, Alex groaned. "Oh, God. I can't let him do that to her again. And he'll destroy Manny."

Not the way you've learned, Alex... Trust Me.

But his tortured mind agonized over what horrors Salazar even now perpetrated on those Alex loved. Darkness spiraled once more.

The chasm in his soul yawned and called its siren song of obligatory revenge.

He didn't want to be that Alex again. He gritted his teeth. He didn't have to ever be that Alex again. Unlike Salazar, he'd left the kingdom of everlasting darkness. His destiny was marvelous light.

But what also had Salazar done to his grandmother?

He shook his head to clear it. He couldn't think of that now. He had to gather his depleted strength. He had to come up with a way to outsmart the devil.

"Protect them wherever they are." Alex crumpled onto the thin mattress. "Salazar can kill me, Father. But help me first to save them."

Pilar almost came unglued when Salazar's goons dragged Alex down the hallway.

Then Manny grabbed her arm.

Jolted from her dire imaginings, she followed his pointed gaze to where Talitha Clum stood poised on the staircase. And beside her, doll-like in the traditional Apache three-tiered skirt and Mexican overblouse—Reyna.

The child swayed against the carved newel post. Talitha steadied her arm. And Pilar realized Reyna had been drugged.

Manny leaped off the sofa and jerked Reyna free of the old woman's clasp. Reyna's head lolled.

Salazar chuckled as Manny drew Reyna to the sofa, his arm draping her thin shoulders. "I believe, *cara*, you've met Talitha."

His eyes gleamed. "An unrehabilitated savage. When her kind stole the don's wife, he captured her as a young girl and brought her down the mountain."

The old woman remained motionless.

"A pet of my father's, Talitha served him well until my mother and I were brought here. Later, I set Talitha free across the border. She owes her life to me. And she taught me what the books couldn't about her people."

Manny brushed the hair off Reyna's forehead. "What've you done to her?"

Salazar lifted his hands to shoulder level. "I have done nothing to her. It's the drugs. They will wear off, my son."

"He used Reyna to draw us here, Manny."

Salazar gestured at the old woman. "Talitha informed me of Manuel's attachment. She tricked the girl into coming to the cave, and once she took the child over the border on the secret paths known to the Broncos, it was only a matter of time before my son would follow and you'd come after him."

"You said this one," Talitha jabbed a gnarled finger at Reyna, "would be the last. That I've earned my right to return. That you'd help me find them."

Them . . . Salazar and his obsessions. Talitha and her lunacy.

Pilar stiffened. "You fed those innocent girls to him?"

"Do not be jealous, my sweet." Salazar reddened beneath the collar of his shirt. "They were nothing to me, *cara*. A matter of killing time while I searched for you."

Killing time . . .

And jealous? Hardly. Nauseous, yes.

"What have you done with Isabel Torres?"

Talitha's eyes ping-ponged to Franco. "Who is this Isabel?"

Salazar flitted his hand. "She is of no concern to me. I only wanted my son." He curled his lip. "Unlike you, they wanted her."

"They took *her*?" Talitha's eyes enlarged. "It cannot be true." Globules of saliva flew out of her mouth. "I've looked for them for so long. I belong to them."

Salazar rolled his eyes. "Then go to them, old woman. I am done with you."

He motioned toward the French doors and the lavender-blue ridgeline. "If you make it past the jaguar's den, I promise, *they* will find *you*. Whether they are yet ready to receive you among themselves after what Don Geraldo told me you did . . . ?" Salazar turned his back on the hunched figure of the old woman.

Flinging curses to his offspring, the old woman shuffled out of the house.

The drug lord folded his arms. "Now, one final matter."

Shielding her, Manny crooned something into Reyna's ear. Something about rocks.

Pilar positioned herself between the children and Salazar. She'd never allow him to put hands on the children or herself ever again, not without a fight. "You will drug me, too?"

Salazar tilted his head. "You misunderstand me, *cara*. This time I want a proper wife. Someone who will fully give herself to being my wife. This time, if you want the children to live, you will come to me of your own free will."

"No," Manny grunted.

She could not believe what Salazar demanded of her. She wanted to retch. But if somehow she could fool him, lull Salazar long enough...

Pilar found her voice. "Then you will let Alex go?"

The goons would never overtake Alex once he cleared the wall. If only Alex weren't so weak. Somehow she had to figure a way to buy him more time. To buy all of them more time.

Salazar's eyes raked her, head to toe. Refusing to cower, she lifted her chin.

"When you come to me..." He broadened his chest. "If you please me..."

She glanced away from the unholy caress of his eyes.

"Then, *cara*, then I will let him go."

Pilar wasn't stupid enough to take Salazar's word for it. And she must consider Manny. Time to tip the scales more to their favor.

"You will allow us a chance to say good-bye to him?" She lowered her eyes. "A wedding gift from *mi esposo*?"

She had fooled him once. She'd fool him again. Nothing Salazar liked better than feeling superior and in control. Her gaze flitted to his face.

Exasperation shone in his eyes, but victory assured, Salazar threw out his hands and laughed. "Women, eh, Manuel? But what is a man to do?"

He signaled one of his soldiers. "Take them to the agent. Station yourselves outside the door."

Salazar moved toward the staircase. "Thirty minutes I will give you, *cara*, and no more. Your bridegroom grows impatient for his bride." He disappeared toward the upper story.

Pilar and Manny dragged Reyna along the corridor between their armed escort. Unlocking the door, the guards shoved them inside.

Her breath caught at the sight of Alex coiled into a fetal position on the small bed.

She shrank from the single chair in the center of the room, leather straps attached to the wooden armrests. The floor underneath sloped toward a drain for a purpose she refused to contemplate. She and Manny bypassed the macabre arrangement and headed toward the other end of the bed.

They rested Reyna against the iron bedrail. "Get some water from the sink." Checking for cameras or listening devices, she also surveyed the room for an avenue of escape. And a weapon to use against their captors.

Nothing.

"We've got to get Reyna and Alex awake. Ready them for their chance to escape."

Manny hurried over to the sink and filled a tin basin with water. "You sound as if you're confident of that happening."

She laid her hand across Alex's forehead. He stirred at the feel of her hand. His skin felt clammy. And he'd already been hurt so badly.

God, please don't let him go into shock. Give him strength to run and live.

Tearing off a chunk of his sleeve, Manny bathed Reyna's face. "Is Alex okay?" His voice wobbled.

She felt Alex's slow but steady breath on her hand. "I think as much as we can hope for right now." Propping his head, she scooped the water into her hand and held it to his mouth.

His lips parted and he drank, but he didn't open his eyes. She repeated the gesture until he moaned, and she settled him against the pillow.

She angled. "How's Reyna?"

"I think she's coming around." Manny's voice rose. "Hey, Tagalong." He jostled the girl's shoulder. "Wake up. You hear me?"

Reyna's eyes fluttered. "Hey, Manny." She gave him a sleepy smile. Her eyes refused to focus.

Manny planted his hands on his hips. "Hey, yourself, Lazybones. Are we going rock hunting or what?"

Her eyelids drooped shut. "I love you, Manny."

"I know, Reyna." A muscle ticked in her son's cheek. "I know."

Stubborn as his mother, in a generational stronghold of mistrust, somehow Reyna had breached Manny's defenses. Not that he'd admit it. No more than Pilar herself would.

But she resolved to do everything in her power to give Manny and Reyna the future they deserved.

"I can't believe I was ever fooled by Umberto's lies, Auntie." Manny frowned. "What should I call you now?"

"Salazar fooled a lot of people for a long time." Her throat tightened. "And you call me whatever you want to call me, Manny."

Her chest ached. She'd lost Manny in all the ways that counted, for good. "You must hate me."

"I've known something was up for a long time." Manny sank down beside her. "But I could never hate you." He sighed. "So Byron's my uncle, right?"

Her lips trembled. "I never wanted you to learn the truth. I never wanted you to find out. Not this way."

"Find out what?" Manny jutted his jaw. "That the only person who ever loved me—took care of me, fed me, read to me, rocked me—is in fact my real mother?" He took her hand in his.

She stared at his slender, nimble fingers. The hand that used to slip into hers for reassurance each morning on his way into kindergarten. And now, he comforted her. Somewhere along the way, her Manny had grown up.

Her heart quivered. "I'm so sorry, Manny."

"I should be thanking you." Tears trembled on the edge of his lashes. "I should be thanking you that after what you went through with Salazar, you chose to give me life when few would've condemned you for ending it."

A lone tear trailed down his cheek. "I don't understand why you didn't give me to someone else and then walk away. Every day, I must've been a living, breathing reminder of the most horrible thing that ever happened to you."

"No, honey." His face between her hands, she brought Manny closer until her forehead touched his. "You are the best thing that ever happened to me." She could feel the moisture of his face beneath her palms.

"But you might have gotten better—no nightmares—if I hadn't been around."

She peered into his eyes. "There would've been no healing at all without you. I love you, Manny."

"I love you, too." He swallowed. "Just give me a little time to adjust." His chocolate eyes bored into hers. "You're not the only one with a secret, you know."

"What do you mean?"

"In the quiet prayers Abuela taught me, I've called you 'Mom' for years." Kissing her cheek, Manny tucked his head in the curve of her neck.

She cradled her beloved child in her arms. Maybe Abuela and Byron and Alex were right. Maybe God was good. Despite everything, He'd given her Manny.

And, He'd given her Alex. Allowed him into her life once more for at least a brief time.

"I finally figured it out, too, Pia."

She and Manny broke apart at the wheezing sound of Alex's voice.

32

Before

Byron warned you... I'm two seconds away from calling the cops on you myself, Grandson."

Alex scrubbed a hand over his face. He'd left the party as soon as he could extract himself, but Pilar was gone.

He hated himself for the lies he told her. Her wounded eyes haunted him until he'd fallen into a restless sleep. He'd relished the pain the Anglos inflicted. Not as much as he'd deserved, though, for hurting her.

Sudden fear hit him square in his solar plexus. "Pilar should've arrived home before nightfall."

Abuela gasped. "I thought she was with you. That you decided to defy—where is she, Alex? What's happened to her?"

"I'm calling the police." He grabbed his keys. "And then I'm going to look for her car."

"A flat tire? Engine trouble?" Abuela infused her voice with hope. "I'll get the ranch hands to scour the road on our end. She's probably trying to scare us. Punish us. We'll find her."

"Call me, please, when you do." He dropped his head. "I'm sorry for the way things went down, Grandmother. For deceiving you. But I love her. I've always..." He gulped.

"We'll talk about this later," Abuela's tone resumed its customary briskness. "And I know you love her. We'll find her and sort this out."

But they didn't find her. Not that night. Nor the next.

Instead, he discovered her purse beneath the seat in his Jeep. And her duffel bag alongside his still in the trunk. Detectives interviewed him. He gave them a description of the Land Rover and the clothes she'd last been seen wearing. The Pima County Sheriff's Department issued a BOLO, but it went unanswered. The San Carlos tribal police also searched the rez.

But it was if she'd vanished off the face of the earth.

The Land Rover was found the next morning only twenty minutes from the Torres ranch. But no Pilar.

He thought he'd go crazy. No longer just a missing person case, the police now considered her disappearance a kidnapping. The FBI were called in for a joint task force as two days merged into three.

Byron flew home on compassionate leave. Abuela, schooled by the federal agents, monitored the phone. Exiled, Alex kept vigil in Tucson. When Alex begged to come home, Abuela told him that it was better for him and Byron not to meet under these trying circumstances.

Out of the loop, he waited with intensifying dread as ransom demands weren't made. It didn't take a rocket scientist to understand women were kidnapped for one of two reasons. Money didn't appear to be the motive.

That thought—and the images of what she might be enduring—tortured him. He couldn't sleep. He couldn't eat. Helpless, he paced back and forth in his apartment.

Waiting for word. Waiting for news of Pilar's rescue. Waiting for the call that never came.

Hell.

Or so he believed until the call from Abuela came late in the evening on day four.

He caught it on the first ring. His pulse raced. "Is she alive?"

Silence.

Then, Abuela's shuddering sigh. "Barely."

He squeezed his eyes shut and collapsed against the wall.

"You need to come."

"Where?" he whispered.

"Memorial. She escaped her captor somehow and a family driving past found her staggering on the highway. Bleeding and—"

Alex sank to his knees. "What did he do to her?" His voice hardened. "Who did this to her?"

"We don't know. She's not coherent. She's—"

"I'm on my way."

Later, he never recalled how he got from his apartment to the hospital. He only remembered walking into the florescent glare of the emergency room with its overpowering antiseptic smell.

His grandmother rose from a cluster of chairs in the waiting area. Abuela looked every bit of her sixty years.

Rage darkened Byron's face. "He has no right to be here."

Abuela straightened. "He has as much right—more—to be here as any of us."

Byron sprang at him. "After all I did to make sure this never happened to her. After all I sacrificed for her. You did this!" His fist connected with Alex's face.

Felled, Alex hit the floor, wiping out two chairs. People scrambled out of the way. Blood spurted from a cut on his cheek.

"Byron, this is not the way!" Abuela shouted.

Dazed, Alex swiped his hand across his cheekbone and smeared the blood. He scowled. Jumping to his feet, head lowered, he charged at Byron.

"No, Alex!" Abuela yelled. "Boys! Stop this!"

Alex tackled the stockier Apache. They careened into another row of chairs. "You made me hurt her—" Alex rammed his fist into Byron's stomach.

Byron throttled him in a chokehold. They rolled.

"Pastor! Segundo!"

Byron pummeled Alex's chest, head, face. Alex landed a punch to Byron's nose but found himself suddenly wrenched backward, a sinewy arm around his neck.

His grandmother's pastor wrested Byron in the opposite direction. Blood dripped from Byron's nose. Chest heaving, Byron lunged again. Pastor Hernandez cemented his grip.

All reason gone, with bloodlust in his eyes, Alex flailed, straining to reach Byron. A subtle pressure against his windpipe brought flashing stars before his eyes.

"*Calmaté.* Settle down." The man's hand around Alex's throat tightened a notch.

He slumped. "Okay. Okay."

The man's stranglehold relaxed. A nurse and a security guard hurried over. Flicking a look between Alex and Byron, Abuela moved to intercept them. *"Perdóname."*

In soothing tones, Isabel promised there'd be no more trouble. She pleaded not to be kicked out. Alex and Byron exchanged glances, and they moved to either side of the diminutive woman.

Byron held up his hands. "No more trouble."

"We promise."

Alex flashed a wobbly version of his award-winning Alex Torres smile. Not much. But enough to flush the cheeks of the nurse who pulled the guard toward the station.

Pastor Hernandez set about righting the trashed waiting area. Byron glared at Alex from across the room. And whoever strong-armed Alex had melted away like the morning mist in the Sierra.

He bit back a groan, unable to bear thinking of that perfect time and place. Just last week? Perfect happiness replaced by complete despair.

Sinking into a chair, he rested his elbows on his thighs and knotted his hands together. "Have you seen her yet, Abuela?"

"Yeah, we've seen her," Byron stormed. "Beaten almost to death."

Alex hunkered in the chair.

"Clothes tattered from where he…he"—Byron blinked—"violated her."

Alex shut his eyes and moaned.

His grandmother settled into the chair beside him and covered his hand with hers. Surprised, he glanced up. She pressed his hand and released it as a fifty-something man in scrubs entered the waiting area. The three of them and Pastor Hernandez stood.

Exhaustion smudging his eyes, the doctor dropped into a chair.

"How's our girl?" Abuela's voice trembled.

Alex held his breath.

"We've done what we needed to do for the rape kit."

Alex wanted to vomit.

"So it's confirmed? She was…" The old woman quivered.

The doctor nodded. "Repeatedly. I'm sorry. We've stabilized her for now. She lost a lot of blood from where he cut her."

God in heaven. No… Alex swallowed past the bile in his throat.

"She's dehydrated. We don't know how long she wandered in the desert before being found. She's suffering from exposure and in shock, physically and emotionally."

A man in a charcoal suit entered and flashed his badge. "Detective Riggins."

Byron clenched both fists. "How did this happen?"

The lantern-jawed detective caught Abuela's arm as she started a downward spiral toward the carpet. "Ma'am? Please sit down."

The doctor removed his stethoscope. "Mrs. Torres, you need to breathe. Is your chest hurting?"

Pastor Hernandez headed toward the corridor. "I'll get Isabel some water."

The detective speared Alex and Byron with a look. "There needs to be no more of what happened here a few moments ago."

Isabel's hand shook as she took the cup from Pastor Hernandez. "Please, Detective. Tell us what you know. Not knowing is worse."

Alex caught the flicker in the detective's eyes at his grandmother's words. And braced himself. Because Alex had a feeling the worst was, in the detective's opinion, still to come.

Detective Riggins's face resumed its professional detachment.

An occupational necessity?

"From the video footage at the apartment complex, we believe her attacker was male, aged approximately twenty to thirty. We only got a picture of his back."

Riggins passed around the grainy photo. "We think he slipped something into Pilar's drink while at the party Mr. Torres described to my colleagues, followed her out into the parking lot, and abducted her."

The doctor cleared his throat. "The lab ran a tox screen. Minute traces of rohypnol were detected. The date rape drug."

Alex's heart spasmed.

The doctor laid his hand over Abuela's. "He must've continued to dope her over the four-day period she was missing"—his jaw tightened—"to keep her controlled. Rohypnol typically disappears from the bloodstream after twelve hours."

"While he—" Face contorting, Byron gagged.

Pastor Hernandez thrust a trashcan in his direction. Hunching, Byron lost the contents of his stomach.

"There's indications of defensive wounds," the doctor interjected. "Maybe when the drug was wearing off she fought him. Fought him hard. Perhaps how she managed to escape. We bagged her hands until any trace evidence to identify her attacker could be recovered."

Abuela's eyes widened. "What?"

But Alex understood. Pilar wasn't just the victim. She was a crime scene, too.

"I'll let you know if the database finds a match." Detective Riggins rose. "She was hysterical until the doc sedated her. I wasn't able to get much out of her. And frankly," he heaved a breath. "Most victims never remember much. These drug cocktails tend to wipe the memory."

Abuela clasped her hands together. "But she would've been helpless? At his mercy?"

"Conscious most probably." The doctor bit his lip. "Unable to speak or cry out. Unable to stop him from…"

But able to realize what was happening—Alex finished what the doctor left unspoken—yet unable to prevent it.

Alex jutted his jaw. "You'll find the monster who did this?"

The detective studied him. "I'll try."

A growing anger built inside Alex. Layer upon layer until it choked him of breath. Blazing. White hot. Towering as tall as a pyre.

He clamped his lips tight. "Do more than try."

Byron wiped his mouth with the back of his hand. "Or we'll find him for you."

The detective's gaze shot between them. "Justice will be done. You two stay out of our way."

Byron thumped his chest. "Vengeance is my right."

Detective Riggins narrowed his eyes. "None of this Apache Way business. Let law enforcement handle this. Or you'll end up in jail right beside this rapist."

Isabel gave him the imperious look she'd perfected. "How often do you catch rapists, Detective Riggins?"

The detective shuffled his feet. "One in four."

"And of those, how many serve time?"

The detective stuffed his hands into his trouser pockets. "Three percent."

"And what percentage is the justice for an Indian girl like Pilar?"

Riggins averted his eyes.

Hours later, Pilar awoke screaming. Wild, thrashing, uncontrollable, she lashed out at the medical personnel. She shrieked like a caged creature.

The doctor sedated her again. Abuela stayed close by Pilar's bed, holding her hand.

When the sedation wore off, once more Pilar awoke screaming as if from a nightmare. Prompting Alex to step forward at the nurse's summons only to be blocked by Byron.

"Back off, Torres. Haven't you done enough? I'm not letting you near my sister."

Alex made the waiting room his new home over the next few days. He prayed for a chance to see her. To comfort her. And rid himself of the heavy mantle of grief.

Two days later, the screaming stopped. But maybe worse, Abuela informed Alex, gut-wrenching sobs racked Pilar's battered form.

His heart twisted. He longed—he ached—to be with her. To help her.

When he could stand it no longer, he sneaked past the nursing station and peered unseen through the glass window into her room.

Bruises purpled her face. Curled into a fetal position, tears dripped down her cheeks. Sobs competed with the beeping noises of the monitors.

"Pia..." he whispered, his lips pressed against the cold glass. What had that monster done to her? "Baby..."

Lines and needles tethered her to the machines. Her hospital gown gaped on one side, and the nurse removed a large white bandage from her right shoulder blade.

He gasped at the sight of the angry, red wounds crisscrossing her back. The word carved into her flesh seared into his memory forever. Shattered and devastated, he fell back.

In the waiting room, he regathered the threads of his emotions. "I want to see her. I need to see her."

Byron's lip curled. "She doesn't want to see you."

"Ask her," Alex fisted his hands. "Let her—"

"That's the thing," Byron snarled. "I'm telling you she doesn't ask for you. She doesn't want to see you ever again."

He jabbed a meaty finger into Alex's chest. "You remind her of the animal that did this to her."

Anguish decimated Alex's heart.

"The Mexican pig, like you, who did this to her."

At Alex's involuntary inhale, Byron propped his hands on his hips and laughed. A sound entirely devoid of mirth. "Yeah. Latest newsflash from the detective. Probably some cartel-connected Mexican national over the border looking for a good time. Maybe not a random attack. Maybe she was targeted and he followed her from that dump in the Sierras. Lay in wait for her. And when she managed to escape, he probably slipped back into the Mexican slime pit he crawled out of."

"No." Alex fought to breathe. "No."

The man he'd fought on the street in Xoacatyl? His temples thudded. Alex's fault. He'd destroyed her.

He lurched away from Byron. A haze of near madness blinding his eyes, he stumbled. Righted himself. Gripping the wall, he pushed down the corridor. He fell through a swinging door into a room. His head clanged against a bank of lockers.

God, oh God, what have I done? God, oh God, not my sweet Pilar... Why not me? Alex pounded his chest. *Me...*

Alex had gambled on buying time. To seemingly comply with Byron's demands. To get Byron and Abuela off his back until the spring when Pilar came of age.

He'd intended—by hook or crook—to make his way to North Carolina after shoring up his savings. To charm. To beg forgiveness. To wheedle his way—whatever it took—to win back Pilar's affection.

She loved him. She'd always loved him. She wouldn't—couldn't—spurn him for long. He knew it in his gut. By June, come hell, high water or Byron, they'd be married again.

Alex hadn't reckoned on her defiant recklessness at the party. He hadn't figured on human predators stalking prey. He hadn't—*God help him*—he hadn't been good enough to let her go as Abuela begged him weeks ago.

He'd been selfish. Stupid. Arrogant to imagine he could out-smart them all.

Byron was right. He'd done this to her.

He, Alejandro Roberto Torres. The one supposed to love her the most. And the guilt ate Alex alive.

She'd never forgive him for the cruelties perpetrated upon her. She'd never be able to look at him—Byron was right again—without seeing in Alex's Latino features her nightmarish attacker.

He slammed his boot against the locker.

She'd never be able to bear his touch.

He kicked the metal. Over and over.

Why? He cried to the ceiling. *Why did you punish her? Why didn't you punish me?*

Alex's foot dented the metal door.

He wouldn't be able to bear the fear his presence would evoke in her eyes. The repugnance. He'd nauseate her.

Alex had lost her. And in losing her, lost himself.

Despair cloaked his heart. In utter hopelessness, he staggered out of the hospital and into the bleak night.

33

I MAY BE SLOW, BUT EVENTUALLY I GET THERE."

Alex coughed and jackknifed, clutching his ribs.

Broken, maybe. Bruised, for sure. He flinched as he hauled himself upright on the bed.

"Slow?" Pilar tapped a finger to her temple. "I've been telling you that for years."

But her eyes lit, and he felt their warmth as her gaze traveled over his face. When she looked at him that way, he felt bathed in sunlight. The sunlight at the top of a high mesa.

With painful effort, he turned his head and caught sight of Reyna. "Is she okay? Was I out long? Did he hurt Manny or you?"

Manny hovered over a slumped Reyna. "Not long. We're okay."

Pilar fretted at the hem of her shirt. "He drugged Reyna, but so far he's not harmed her."

"Good on all counts."

An understatement if ever one. Because Alex was so ridiculously, deliriously relieved to see Pilar alive and well.

She scowled at him. But he wasn't fooled by the chip on her shoulder. He'd stormed the fortress she'd erected around her heart and completely demolished her emotional barricades.

Again.

Pilar had an image to maintain. Him too. Tough, little Apache Pia. And the always joking, incredibly handsome—if he did say so himself—Alex.

The both of them so irrevocably, head over heels in love with each other.

Some things would never change. *Thank you, God.*

Pilar fidgeted. "What is it you think you've figured out in that dumb-jock brain of yours, Torres?"

Forgetting his busted lip, he gave her a lopsided smile and winced. "Don't make me laugh, Pia. Or smile." He took a deep breath and moaned. "Or breathe."

She rolled her eyes.

He inched higher on the wall. "I love your mother, Manny. And she loves me though she can't yet bring herself to say the words."

She feathered his hair with her fingers. Her face gentled.

He took a careful breath. "You love me, Pia, and that's the real reason why you refused to get an abortion. Why you raised Manny yourself. Why you never told me the truth when you thought I'd abandoned you."

Manny eased onto the mattress. "I don't understand, Alex." The springs groaned.

Alex never took his gaze from Pilar. "You knew or suspected you were pregnant the day we left Xoacatyl after our whirlwind honeymoon, didn't you, Pia?"

She folded her hands in her lap.

"Is that true?" Manny's teeth pulled at his lower lip. "Is Alex my father?"

Alex's eyes misted at the poignant hope in his voice.

Manny angled from Pilar to Alex. "We could get a DNA test when we get out of here."

"I don't need a test to prove what I know in my heart to be true." He touched Manny's shoulder. "Your mother's brains. My undeniable good looks. Plus the incredible basketball talent you inherited from yours truly. You won the lottery with your parental gene pool, kid."

Manny's eyes bored into him. "You'd be okay if I was your son?"

Alex allowed the boy to search his features, to see the truth for himself. "I love you, Manny. You are my son. And I'll never leave you or your mother willingly again."

His son—the thought opened a wellspring of unexpected joy in Alex's heart. His son and Pia's. The best of both of them.

Their son straightened. "My-my cheekbones do kinda of look like his. Don't you think?" His eyes flickered to Pilar. "I thought it was from the Anglo mother, but—"

"More Mexican than Apache." She cut her eyes at Alex. "But you'll be much better looking than"—she swallowed—"your dad."

"Still here." Alex waved a hand in front of their faces and then regretted the motion as pain rocketed through him. "And I'm not Mexican—"

"He's from L.A.," Manny and Pilar finished for him.

She gave Alex the first smile he'd seen from her since they were captured by Salazar's men.

"That means I was there, too, when that monster—" Manny broke off.

Her smile faded.

Alex seized her hand and Manny's. "What it means is that even then you were protecting your mother. As I would have, had I been able."

Manny lifted his chin. "And I'll keep protecting her. No matter what."

Alex ran his thumb over the back of Pilar's hand. Her hands were ice cold. "You fought for his life and your own. You fought to return to me."

His heart lurched as the strangest expression crossed her face. An unnatural calmness. A resignation.

Pilar laid her hand upon Alex's bruised cheek. "Fighting is what I do."

She drew Manny into their embrace. "I'm fighting for both of your lives. And I always will."

Boots thudded on the other side of the door.

Alex's heart squeezed. Fighting for his life and Manny's.

But what about her own?

Pilar rose as the door crashed open into the wall.

"*El jefe* say time is up."

Alex got to his feet. "Time for what?"

She avoided Alex's gaze. "Time for me to fulfill the terms of your release."

"No, Pia. What have you promised that monster? I won't let you—" Alex lunged.

Salazar's man landed a blow to his temple, throwing Alex to the floor. His head ricocheted off the tiled surface. He went deathly still.

"Alex," she screamed.

The soldier grabbed her. He wasn't quick enough to stop Manny. Manny checked the pulse in Alex's neck. "He's alive."

"Boss say you come now. He no like waiting. *El jefe* give *americano* chance to run for his life."

The man tightened his grip around her arm. Two other narcos dragged Alex's limp body into the hall.

She held out her hand to Manny. "Do what the man says, Manny. Come."

Her son threw a glance at Reyna, curled like a kitten on the bed. For now, she'd been forgotten. Anger at his powerlessness—how well Pilar understood the feeling—darkened his broad face.

Manny pushed the goon's hand off her arm. "Salazar said not to touch my mother."

Eyes widening, the thug dropped his hand. "*Lo siento.* No harm." He ushered them down the hall, forgetting in his haste to lock the door.

Good…

She released a breath. "We must both play the game for now."

The men carried Alex outside through the French doors. Placing an iron collar around his neck, they thrust Alex into the metal cage.

One of Salazar's lieutenants returned to the sunken living room. "I bring *el jefe.*"

As he plodded upstairs, she scanned the corners of the room to make sure no one had been left to watch them. She and Manny were alone. Such was Salazar's arrogance. He considered her surrender a sure thing. A matter of time.

There might never be a better opportunity.

Reaching inside her boot, she palmed the stiletto Luis had given them in the jungle.

Manny's eyes narrowed. "Where did you get that?"

"No one's touched me since Alex and I were captured." She handed it to Manny. "Hide it."

Manny recoiled. "You keep it."

"No." She pressed the handle of the dagger at the boy. "There will be an opportunity—"

"What opportunity?"

"An opportunity to free yourself and Reyna. When they let Alex go, the men will be occupied. And after I go upstairs…" She steadied her resolve. "No matter what happens. No matter what you hear, get out of the compound. Keep the sun at your back and get over the mountain. Don't stop. Get yourselves far, far away."

"But what about you? I'm not leaving you here. I won't."

He gave her that stubborn look he donned when she tried to get him to take out the trash.

"I need you to do what I say, Manuel."

"Don't ask me to leave you with him." His lip quivered. "I can't lose you."

Her heart tore.

She took her child into her arms. "You heard Salazar's other plans for Alex. You're old enough to know what men like him will do to Reyna. I can't live with either of those scenarios, Manny. And, I can't live seeing you become like Salazar. I'd rather see you dead than turned into what Salazar will make of you."

Was she asking too much of him?

"I'll deal with Salazar. But I can't—" She glanced away. "I can't do what I need to do if you're still here. Please, you must take Reyna and escape."

Manny's arms tightened around her so hard that momentarily she had trouble regaining her breath. "I'll get Reyna to a safe place. But I will come back."

He blinked away the tears he'd consider unmanly. "I won't leave you here forever with the Wicked One, I promise."

An unfamiliar gratitude filled her heart. Gratitude to Alex's God—who'd allowed her and Manny this time of truth together. To be mother and son just once.

Thank you.

"You will have yourself a good life, you hear, my Manuel?"

He refused to look at her.

"You finish school. Never forget those prayers Abuela taught you. Love the woman God grants you and be happy." She grasped his chin between her thumb and forefinger. She forced his eyes to hers. "You listen to your mother. *Sí?*"

His lips curved. "You threw in the *sí* for Alex, didn't you, even though he's not Mexican?"

She laughed.

Manny was, in fact, very much like his father. She'd never known for sure. But oh, how she'd hoped.

Thank you...For them both.

"*Mi familia* together at last."

She and Manny swiveled to where Salazar perched on the stairs. She took a step forward and blocked his view of her son. Manny bent as if to tie his shoe secured the blade under his pant leg.

Time to adapt or die.

Pilar offered the drug lord her hand.

Salazar raised it to his lips. "There is a dress, *cara*...upstairs next to the room I have prepared for us."

Her skin crawling, she kept her face purposefully blank.

"Of course." She extracted her hand. "Shall we go?"

Manny sucked in a breath and shifted.

Terrified Manny would rouse Salazar's suspicions and endanger his and Reyna's only chance, she motioned him away, her hand concealed behind her back.

But with victory seemingly assured, Salazar had eyes only for her. "I am as anxious, *cara*, as you to renew our 'vows.'" His lips curved. "But alas, I have unfinished business to attend to first."

Salazar strutted toward the French doors. "I have promised my men a reward for their long labor after supervising the marijuana harvest. A hunt."

It was too soon. Alex was still so weak. She'd hoped to buy him more time to recover his strength.

Distract. Disarm. Delay.

She edged to Salazar's side and tugged at the coiled muscle of his arm. "Franco..."

"*Uno momento, cara.* First things first."

Extricating himself from her hold, Salazar strode outdoors to the patio. Anticipating blood sport, his henchmen gathered from the perimeter of the compound. She flung Manny a sharp look and pointed her lips toward the empty hallway and Reyna. His face conflicted, Manny nonetheless disappeared into the shadows.

Pilar had to do something. *Think, think.* She hurried after Salazar.

Settling into a lounge chair, Salazar snapped his fingers. "Awaken him."

A narco seized one of two buckets next to the cage. Filling the bucket with water, he unceremoniously dumped the contents through the bars onto Alex. Sputtering and thrashing, Alex jerked to his feet.

Salazar removed a fat cigar from a box on the table. "Get him out."

Fighting them, it took two men to wrest Alex from the cage. Another unclasped the chain from the metal bars and allowed the chain to play out.

Dripping wet on the stone terrace below Salazar, Alex hunched his shoulders. "I will not provide entertainment for your men."

Salazar chuckled. "Oh, but you will, Special Agent. In fact, you are the showcase."

The drug lord wafted his hand toward a gigantic grill where meat roasted. "The pigs have been gutted, and we've planned a mouth-watering fiesta." Salazar laughed. "Not that you'll be here to enjoy it."

She had to stop this. Her heartbeat accelerated. She draped herself around Salazar's shoulders. "Franco…"

Revulsion coated Alex's features. "Pia, don't."

She averted her eyes. She couldn't look at Alex and force herself to do what needed to be done.

"Can't you do this later, Franco?" She grazed her lips against the monster's neck. "Tomorrow? After we—"

"I won't leave you here, Pia." Alex struggled against the men restraining him.

Salazar extended the cigar for his man to light. "You run or your blood runs on the paving stones. Your choice." He snapped his fingers.

The men raised the AK-47s strapped across their bodies, barrels pointed at Alex.

He froze, hands in the air. "Pia…don't. Not for me."

Biting her lip at his stubbornness, she slung herself into Salazar's lap. "Franco…*por favor*…"

Alex growled.

Over Salazar's shoulder, she spotted Manny's silhouette through the French doors. She held her breath, but no one appeared. She prayed the guards at the front entrance had also abandoned their posts for the prospect of a hunt.

Pilar watched as Manny lugged Reyna toward the door, but then her son disappeared from sight at the foot of the stairs. What was he doing? What was taking him so long to clear the house?

Salazar brushed his fingers over her cheek. Her gaze returned to his. She had to fight her disgust.

"There will be time, *cara*. Enough time for you to carry in your body more of my sons."

Alex erupted, but the thug snapped the chain. The manacle around his throat yanked Alex into place.

Salazar took a deep puff of the cigar and smiled. "She has made the best choice for herself and my son. I suggest you do the same, Special Agent."

Pilar clenched her teeth. "Adapt or die, Alex. We must all adapt or die."

Salazar's eyes glinted. She tilted his face toward her lips. Salazar's pulse quickened beneath her hand.

"*Cara*..." His lips parted. "All is as I've dreamed."

Play the game, Alex, she willed as her mouth made contact with Salazar's salacious lips.

Salazar let out a throaty rumble.

Pilar risked a glance at Alex's set face. *Please*...She begged Alex with her eyes. *Please.*

This time Alex wouldn't look at her. Her eyes burned from the hot prickle of tears.

Alex's chest rose and fell. "I will wipe your existence from the earth, Salazar."

He sprang forward. The iron fetter throttled him. He choked and clawed at the manacle.

"I suggest you conserve your energy for running, *amigo*." Salazar flicked the ash from his cigar. "First, you must clear the wall. Beyond that?"

The Lord of the Skies shrugged. "Good luck getting past the *onca* who prowls the mountain."

Salazar waved his hand. "Remove the collar. And let the games begin."

Alex held himself taut as the goon removed the shackle from his throat. He glared at Salazar, perched like a king on his throne. And Pilar?

He ground his teeth. Although he understood the dangerous, gutsy game she played, it gutted him to see her twined around the Wicked One.

But Alex couldn't allow her to do this abominable thing. His life wasn't worth to him what it would cost her. Yet outgunned and outnumbered, his immediate options were limited.

From inside the house, he glimpsed the one thing that could force him to go along with her plan. His stomach convulsed. Manny and Reyna were in plain sight of Salazar's men on the terrace if Alex didn't do something.

Baring his teeth, he congratulated Salazar on his mother's "professional" qualities, which had brought him to such a position of power.

Rage engorged Salazar's features.

A henchman socked Alex in the gut. Groaning, he sank to his knees. But he'd accomplished what he'd intended.

With everyone's attention turned toward him, none but Alex witnessed Manny exit the villa and dart toward the wall. Nor Manny boosting Reyna to the top of the pillared gate and climbing over the other side.

Pilar would trade her life for their son's. She'd willingly give Salazar the power to destroy her again. And because of Manny, Alex knew he could do no less. For now at least.

Alex rubbed his hand over the abrasions the collar had left around his neck.

He and Pilar had to buy time for the children to escape. With Salazar and his soldiers engaged in hunting him, Manny stood a real chance of making it. And Alex bet Salazar would leave Pilar alone for now, unable to resist being present for the "kill."

Alex had to elude Salazar's men. He'd find a way to draw Salazar away from the protection of his bodyguards. Then he'd settle with Salazar before the beast harmed Pilar.

Spitting blood, Alex rose. "I'm ready, Salazar." He squared his shoulders. "Come get me, if you dare."

Eyes gleaming, Salazar stood, dumping Pilar off his lap.

Pilar bit her lip. "Franco..."

Salazar pointed to the remaining bucket. "And now a treat for my favorite cat."

Grabbing the bucket, his lieutenant threw the contents at Alex's head.

He gasped as the wave of putrefying tissue washed over him. His eyes reflexively shut as the red liquid streamed down his torso. Shuddering, he swiped his face with his hand.

Pig guts.

"What did you do to him?" She started for Alex, forgetting for an instant the role she must play.

Salazar caught her arm. "Added incentive for the special agent to run. Before my pet locates his scent."

The beast jerked his chin toward the horizon. "I'll give you until you clear the wall." Salazar ground the half-smoked cigar into the glass-topped table. "Or until I reach the count of five."

Her breath hitched. "Franco—"

Salazar raised his hand as if readying for the start of a stock car race. "Gentlemen."

Guns prodded Alex to the edge of the pavement.

"*Uno...*"

"What happened to *go*?" Alex balanced on the balls of his feet, prepared to run. "Should've known you were incapable of playing by the rules."

Salazar laughed outright. "Special Agent Torres, I make the rules." He pressed Pilar against his side. "And I suggest you run. *Dos...*"

"Alex," she hissed, "less talk, more action. Go."

"*Tres...*"

Like a shot, he ran. Making for the opposite direction from which Manny disappeared, Alex's feet pounded the ground.

"*Cuatro...*" Salazar called.

Alex focused on clearing the open terrain between him and the wall. His heart thundered. Panting, he strained forward. He'd have to make a running jump for the top of the cement block wall. Like slam dunking a basketball. He could do it—

"*Cinco...*"

The rat-a-tat of gunfire.

God... Por favor.

He leaped for the wall, arms raised, and caught hold of the surface. As the embedded broken glass sliced his skin, he dropped his hand. Slipping, but fighting the pain, he held on and dangled.

Another staccato burst. Chips of blasted cement pummeled his face. His boots scrabbled for traction, a foothold to leverage upward.

Wrenching his shoulder, he hung on and swung himself on top. Ignoring the glass tearing his skin and clothing, he dropped to the other side. Safe, but not for long.

From the other side, the shouts drew nearer.

Alex used the time it would take the shorter, burlier men to clear the wall to his advantage. He sprinted toward the treeline expecting, dreading, every moment to feel a slug burrow into his back. His leg muscles burned.

He fought against a cramping stitch in his side. He desperately needed a deep draught of air to replenish his oxygen-starved lungs.

Someone shouted.

One of them had topped the wall. Alex sped into the scant cover of the trees through the waist-high brush. Bullets whistled and ricocheted off a nearby trunk. He dodged and zigzagged to disrupt their aim. Branches whiplashed him in the face, stinging his cheeks as he ran.

Then, something more ominous than the men hunting him. Hidden somewhere across the width of the valley, a big cat roared. The image of the black jaguar they'd seen in the Canyon of the Caves flitted through his mind and chilled his blood.

If only he could find the river....He had to get the stench of blood off his body.

He miscalculated the fallen timber lying across the path. Bounding over the log, his feet sank into a hole on the other side. He went down, the air knocked from his lungs.

Rolling, sticks jabbing his torso, he jerked to his feet and kept going. Another screech. The big cat probably had eyes on Alex, stalking him. Waiting for the perfect moment to drop from some high, concealed perch onto his back.

Alex's mouth went dry as he realized the bullets were too perfectly misaimed. Salazar's men toyed with him. Like the apex predator toyed with his chosen prey. Like Salazar played his victims.

He was being herded toward the lair of the beast. Relentlessly driven toward the jaguar's den.

Alex spotted the silvery ribbon of the river through the dense undergrowth. Fighting his way through, he erupted onto the riverbank. Bullets pinged at his heels.

He surged toward the water. Plunging in waist-deep, he sank beneath the swelling river.

Underwater, he ripped his shirt open. Tore it off and let it drift downstream. Holding his breath, he plowed his hands through his hair and worked any traces of the blood off his body, scrubbing his scalp.

He came up for air and dashed the water out of his eyes. AK-47s jabbing the sky, his pursuers jeered from the shoreline. He'd have to cross the river or let it carry him downstream where they couldn't pursue. Put distance between them so he could double back and rescue Pilar.

But the noise of the men ceased as if shutting off a valve.

Dog-paddling, he swirled. Rifles pointed along the embankment to his left, the hardened cartel members backed toward the trees. Their faces grim, he felt their palpable fear.

On the periphery of his vision, something large and black, shoulders hunched, crept across the pebbled shore toward the water.

Gliding toward Alex.

The jaguar's muscles rippled. Even from the distance separating them, Alex almost lost himself in the golden, unblinking gleam of those menacing eyes. Death stared him in the face.

His heart stopped for a second in sheer primal fear.

The jaguar tensed, coiled and ready to spring.

Scissoring, Alex dove under the water.

34

Alone with the enormity of the decision she'd made, Pilar could no longer outrun the truth.

"I was raped."

Trapped in the dressing room outside Franco's bedroom, for the first time she said it out loud. Admitted what might yet unfold for her again.

She forced herself to remember. To face what she'd been unwilling or unable to face before. She staggered against the dressing room sink at the remembered flashes of horror. The suffocating darkness of the cave.

The terror had choked her. She sagged, recalling her helplessness. The knife he'd used on her...

Oh, God, the pain.

She closed her eyes at the memory of the weight of Salazar's limbs. And the acrid smell of his sweat mixed with the pungency of the peyote he smoked. She gripped the cold porcelain to keep from falling.

Leaning over, she vomited. Over and over. Until there was nothing left but dry heaves. Sorrow, grief, and loss overwhelmed her. Sobs racked her body.

I can't...

Pilar stared at her anguished reflection in the mirror.

She didn't have to do this. But she'd face anything—including allowing Salazar to touch her again—if it meant giving Alex, Manny, and Reyna a chance to escape.

This time—she gritted her teeth—this time it was about her choice. She didn't belong to Salazar.

No matter what he'd done to her—no matter what she'd done to survive—she'd never belonged to Salazar. Because she belonged to God.

Pilar wept for the lost years with Alex and Manny. The years she'd never get to live with either of them now. And for the lost years she'd not spent with the Christ Alex spoke of with such passion.

I want to be clean again. I want to be clean again. Oh, God, I just want to be clean again.

She took a deep breath and pushed off from the sink. "I want to be Yours, Creator God. Wash me. Cleanse me of my unbelief. Forgive me. Rescue me from myself..."

Pilar had measured her life by the Before and After. Before she'd been raped. After she'd been raped.

But now, she pressed past the pain. She gathered the heartbreak, the shame and despair and lay them at the foot of the cross of love. "Jesus..."

The only name powerful enough to break strongholds.

A gentle breeze billowed the curtain of her gilded cage. Blowing across her face. A whisper. A caress. And the chains harnessing her to Before fell away.

She soaked deeply of a peace such as she'd never known. And discovered the paradox of paradoxes. Especially to an Apache who didn't do surrender. She almost laughed at the irony.

For in surrender, she discovered lasting strength.

It was time to reclaim her power. Not the power the Old Ones spoke of. The power that could only come from the Ancient of Days.

She'd distracted Salazar before, lulled him into an arrogant assumption of her capitulation. She'd do it again—to give those she loved more than life, a fighting chance for survival.

You are Mine...

Her hand rubbed at the scars on her arms. *Yes. I am Yours...*

She understood at long last the kind of love for which you'd willingly die. The love that made Byron strong enough to sacrifice himself for her. And she understood why her betrayal of Byron prompted him to do what he'd done—lashing out in hurt at her and Alex.

"I forgive you, Brother," she whispered.

And in the sacrifice of Christ, for the first time she caught a glimpse of the depth of a love like none she'd ever known. The relentless love that compelled a savior to sacrifice Himself for her. So that a lost, throwaway stray like Maria Caterina Pilar could one day find her way home to Him.

She removed the white dress from its hanger. Her hands shook as she unbuttoned her shirt. Unbuckled and slid out of her jeans. She stepped into the filmy dress.

Pilar never wore sleeveless dresses like this, always trying to hide the scars she'd made on her arms. The hemline flared above her kneecaps. The neckline plunged, provocative and revealing. The soft spaghetti straps did little to cover where Salazar had marked his territory on her flesh. He'd want to see the evidence of his total domination of her.

She shivered. Would he mark her tonight? Once again, she'd be at his mercy, defenseless against his brutality.

God... she quaked.

But she moved toward the dresser, determined to do what must be done. Lifting the lid of the mahogany jewelry box, her eyes widened. Inside, the stiletto she'd given to Manny was duct-taped to the lid.

Pilar shook her head at her stubborn son. He'd wasted precious minutes hiding the blade to give her a chance.

Stubborn like his father... she bit the inside of her cheek. Okay, maybe he got that from both sides of his parentage. She secured the knife against her outer thigh underneath the dress with the tape Manny obligingly left.

Pilar clamped the antique pearl earring onto her earlobe. Where had the boy found duct tape? Resourceful... like his mother. She nearly smiled.

And if Salazar found the knife and disarmed her?

She swallowed. God willing, when Salazar discovered her treachery, he'd snap her neck and end her torment forever. She had to make him kill her.

Father Emmanuel flashed across her mind. Manuel's namesake. The name meant 'God with us,' Joaquin Martinez said.

And God would be with her, she prayed, until the end. The very end. She clipped the other earring in place.

God, she breathed, *set me free from this final stronghold.*

When death caught her, time to go not to oblivion but home. Her spirit would float free—*please, Jesus*—and fall into the sweet arms of God.

No one could run forever. She couldn't outrun death any more than she could outrun truth. Neither could she outdistance God's love. Stronger, God's love outlasted death.

And love waited, always waiting like God Himself, for her.

Taking a deep breath, she opened the door.

In the lair of the beast, Salazar's eyes devoured her, lit by the flames of his desire. "*Cara...*"

She allowed him to sweep her into his arms. One arm around her waist, he crushed her spine against his chest. He slid the strap off her shoulder.

He brushed his lips across the scars he'd left for her to remember him by. Inhaling, she squeezed her eyes shut and fought the nausea his touch evoked. *Jesus...*

Sunshine.

Pilar reached for the memory like a lifeline. She cleared her mind of everything, except the sunlight dappling Alex's dark hair as she wrapped her arms around him. That day on the mesa when Alex first kissed her.

The day they were drenched in the sunlight of their love.

A staccato burst of distant gunfire outside the wall wrested Pilar from her dream world.

Salazar laughed. "The special agent falls prey to the predator." He tugged at her dress.

But he stilled at the popping whine of automatic weapons firing. And closer, the revving of engines. The sounds of men in heavy hand-to-hand combat.

She flinched as the window shattered behind her. "Perhaps the prey becomes predator."

Cursing, Salazar thrust her aside and stalked toward the gaping window.

She watched as seasoned troops from Mexico's version of DEA clambered over the walls to storm the compound. The *soldados* destroyed another section of the wall with a rocket-propelled grenade. Brandishing his gun, Martinez and a group of village men poured through the smoking hole, seeking their own brand of justice.

In a hail of bullets, an armored truck burst through the scrolled iron gate. Its scattered fire raked the outbuildings. Caught outside the walls, Salazar's men didn't stand a chance. But they fought with fury. Neither giving any quarter nor expecting any. The screams and moans of dying narcos punctuated the air.

Salazar whirled. "What have you done?" He backhanded her.

Pilar fell to the carpet.

He towered over her, fists clenched. "You have brought them to my doorstep."

Salazar froze. "My son." He stepped over her, making for the door. "I must get my—"

With a guttural cry, she reached for the knife she'd hidden and sprang at Salazar. Ripping it free, she raised her arm, gripping the handle.

She brought the knife down in an arc. Salazar pivoted. The blade slashed his cheekbone to his ear. His eyes enlarged. Madness reddened his pupils.

Pilar reared to strike again. But he batted her arm, deflecting the blade and sent the knife flying across the room. She scrabbled to recapture it.

But he caught the tail of her dress and yanked. The fabric tearing, she struggled against his hold. She strained to crawl forward. Reaching.... Her fingers touched the blade.

He captured her leg. She back-kicked. The stiletto heel stabbed Salazar in the neck.

Roaring, he let go of her for an instant. Scrambling on her hands and knees, she seized the knife. He pounced.

Knocked backward, she clutched the knife against her side. He came at her, hands outstretched, and reached for her throat. She plunged the dagger into his underbelly.

Gasping, he collapsed on top of her. His fist closed around her neck, cutting off her oxygen. Tears streaked across her cheeks. His hand flexed around her windpipe.

She twisted the knife into his groin. Salazar convulsed. She brought the dagger up.

Yanking the knife sideways, she jerked the blade one final time for all he'd taken from her. His body arched, and he released her.

Shoving his limp body off hers, she staggered to her feet. She lurched toward the stairs. The heavy front door blew.

Pilar fell to her knees, knocked into the bannister by the force of the explosion. In stack formation, Mexican Special Forces breached the house. Joaquin Martinez and an officer entered as the smoke settled.

"Manos arriba! Manos arriba!"

She rose slowly, hands in the air, as a dozen M4s beaded on her.

"It's Señora Torres," Joaquin shouted. "Do not shoot her."

With a terse command from the captain, the rifles lowered. The captain waved his men forward to secure the ground floor.

She stumbled down the stairs. "Where are the children? Alex?"

"Your son and the girl flagged us halfway down the mountain. He gave us the details we lacked of Salazar's firepower and strength. Without him, the captain and I would've never been able to pinpoint Salazar's location and penetrate his stronghold. Where is my Nita?"

"I don't think she's here." Pilar gripped Joaquin's jacket. "Is Manny okay? Reyna, too?"

"*Sí*, señora."

God, thank you...

The captain shuttled her aside as more men filled the grand foyer. "My second took them to the village while we pushed on ahead."

"Capitán." A soldier rushed out from the corridor. "We found tunnels."

The captain swore.

Joaquin frowned. "The blood, señora?"

She followed his gaze. Blood stained the entire length of her dress. "Not mine."

Joaquin nodded. "It would appear you've everything under control then."

"Not quite." The captain cleared his throat. "We've not apprehended Salazar."

"Upstairs," she pointed with her lips.

"Ah." A smile came and went across Joaquin's hardened features. "His blood. Not yours."

Motioning the soldiers, the captain took the stairs two at a time.

Pilar stepped out of her shoes. In bare feet better for running, she headed for the door.

"Señora," Joaquin called. "Where do you go?"

Pilar gestured toward the ridgeline. "I've got to find Alex."

"Señora," Joaquin grabbed her hand. "He could be dead."

Pilar broke away from him. "I'd know if he were dead."

"I cannot allow you to venture into that wild place alone." Joaquin caught her on the porch. "You and I will find him together, señora."

He drew her past the cartel members, arms bound and on their knees. An assorted group of Xoacatyl villagers and professional soldiers loaded the prisoners onto transport. With a rapid-fire explanation, Joaquin requisitioned an undamaged cartel vehicle.

"Those men will never see the light of day again. Mexican prisons are not much like your jails north of the border, Señora." Joaquin hustled her into the passenger side. "No television or lattes."

Cranking the engine, Joaquin threw the truck into drive. "There's a road on this side of the mountain that climbs. We will drive as far as it allows. On the way, you will tell me what has become of my daughter, Nita."

His lungs bursting, Alex rocketed out of the water. Sucking in oxygen, he splashed around and scrutinized the riverbanks for any signs of life—animal or human.

Nothing.

He searched his brain for every scrap of remembered knowledge about the habits of the jaguar that he'd learned from Salazar's wildlife brochure.

One thing he recalled: jaguars loved the water. Alex prayed the current had carried him far out of the reach of the lethal cat.

Due to the recent rain, the river currents were swift and strong. How far had he drifted downstream? His strength to stay afloat ebbed. Hypothermia from the coldness of the water already hampered his movements. He had to get out of the water and get dry before night set in.

Another comforting thought? Jaguars preferred to prowl at dawn or dusk. And dusk wasn't far behind.

That put a little extra oomph in his stroke as his arms sliced through the water. He propelled himself to a nearby boulder jutting from the shore. He surveyed the stand of cottonwoods lining the bank. All clear as far as he could determine.

He heard the distant popping of automatic rifles. Rival *bandidos*? Or had the villagers taken matters into their own hands and stormed Salazar's walled fortress?

Let them be in time to protect Pia, please God...

Maybe the gunfire had also—he prayed—scared the jaguar into fading away into the security of his den.

Dragging himself out of the river, rivulets of water flowed down Alex's torso and pants. He shivered and folded his arms across his bare chest. Orientating himself, he headed upstream. Back into Salazar's stronghold. Back to Pilar.

Wet and cold, he slogged forward. Under the canopy of the trees, the muted light chilled him further. Shaking uncontrollably, he forced himself onward. One step at a time, he followed the sounds of the firefight.

Alex tripped and fell. He lurched to his feet. Pilar...he had to find her.

His mind sluggish, he concentrated on putting one foot in front of the next. At a sudden rustle from the underbrush, he spun.

The gargoylish face of Pilar's nightmares erupted from behind a boulder. His cheek sliced to his ear and blood oozing from his belly, Salazar pulled a gun from his waistband. "Once again, I defeat you, Torres. I save you for the last, best kill." He cocked the revolver.

Alex stilled. "You're a dead man walking, Salazar. And if you're waiting for me to beg you for my life, you're wasting your time."

"Dead or no, I am still the Lord of the Skies." Salazar held himself upright with visible effort. "And I decide when you die."

Alex prayed for the chance to get his hands around Salazar's throat one more time—with perhaps his dying breath—to prevent Salazar from hurting anyone else ever again.

The drug lord fired.

Alex expected to feel the burning pain of steel entering his flesh. But the bullet whizzed past Alex's ear. Wood splintered the tree behind his head.

It was now or never. He charged.

Head bent, he rammed the drug lord into the stony outcropping. The gun flew out of Salazar's hand and skittered across the ground. Alex lunged to retrieve the gun. Gripping the cold steel with both hands, he rose.

"Alas…" Salazar slid to the earth, his back pressed against the rock. "You have me now, Special Agent. Dead to rights." Yet he leered at Alex.

"You're under arrest, Salazar."

"Is this the best you can do, Special Agent?" The drug lord threw back his head and laughed. "If I were in your place, I think to myself I could kill you with my bare hands."

"That's just the thing. I'm not you." Alex tightened his finger on the trigger. "It's over, Salazar. Your reign of terror is finished."

Something fanatical—beyond sanity—gleamed from Salazar's eyes. "I say when it's over." The drug lord spat at the ground between them. "You think yourself so much better. But you are me, Special Agent. All men are me."

Alex kept the gun trained on the drug lord. "You are a monster. Not like other men. I am nothing like you."

Salazar stroked his eyebrow with his finger. "Ah, but you are wrong. Finally, here's your chance. An eye for an eye. A life for a life." He sneered. "In my case, many lives. At the end, the boy in the canyon, he cried out for his mother."

His smile chilled Alex.

Images of the murdered Apache teenagers swam before Alex's eyes. "It's about justice." But his aim faltered.

Using the boulder for support, Salazar staggered to his feet. "You think to give me mercy? Mercy is merely another excuse for weakness."

Alex's resolve wavered. Salazar deserved to suffer. Why not let him die a slow and agonizing death? Alex recalled the scars, both mental and physical, this monster had inflicted upon his beautiful Pilar. The pain that still tortured her, from which she might never overcome.

"Is that what you really want to do, Special Agent? Your choice is to let me live?" The drug lord bared his teeth. "And so I win. Again."

His choice? Had Salazar given those children or Pilar a choice?

"*Venganza* is what you want. *Venganza* is what you crave. I even depart my bridal chamber early to finish with you, Torres."

Salazar had already hurt her… *Oh, God*… Alex was too late. His heart eviscerated, he surged forward. "No…"

"Yes…" Another throaty laugh. "Right before I took everything from her again and this time her life also."

Dead? Not his Pia. Salazar lied. It couldn't be true. Alex would know. Surely he'd feel it in his gut if she were gone from this earth?

A primal, killing rage erupted in Alex. His arm with the gun flew upward. "I will kill you..." This Wicked One who'd destroyed Pilar's life.

"Do you not yet understand, Special Agent?" Salazar lifted his chin. "There is no mercy. There is no goodness. There is only power."

Then, an eternal whisper so faint, Alex could easily ignore it if he chose. *But... You are Mine.*

He shook his head. *What about when Pilar begged for this monster's mercy, God?*

And what of My mercy?

The same divine mercy that rescued Alex from himself. Giving him a second chance with the son he never knew he had. His son... Alex's heart ached. An utter stillness pervaded the glade.

Was this how Alex wanted to go into a future with Manny? Alex squeezed his eyes shut. When he opened them, he saw that triumph, not fear, shone from Salazar's face. And at last, Alex did understand. If he pulled the trigger, Salazar would indeed win. Because he would have driven Alex to choose to become like him.

Exactly like him.

Alex threw down the gun. "You are wrong about me, Salazar. Wrong about everything. Mercy is the only real strength." Salazar's features sagged.

Nearby an engine groaned and shifted gears. Tires churned gravel. Alex angled toward the trees. But dropping to his knees, Salazar scrambled for the gun lying in the dirt.

Alex whirled, but not soon enough.

Fatalism glinted in Salazar's dark eyes. He pressed the barrel against the side of his temple. "As you say, better to be king in hell—"

A gunshot rang out. The retort echoed in the canyon wilderness.

Footsteps crackled in the bracken. Alex's heart went into overdrive. The henchmen.

Two figures ran through the trees. The stocky Joaquin Martinez, fully armed. And Pilar.

Alex's knees buckled. *Thank you. Thank you. Thank you.*

Pilar surged ahead of the innkeeper. "Alex!"

"You're alive." He caught her in his arms. "Salazar said he—"

Unwilling to complete the thought, Alex ran his gaze from the top of her head to the dried blood staining the front of her dress.

She flung herself at him. "I'm okay. He didn't..."

Alex examined her face. "Salazar said he killed you." His voice shook.

She wrapped her arms around his neck and averted her gaze from Salazar's body. "He lies. He's always lied." She shuddered in Alex's arms. "Thank you for ending this."

He swallowed. Would she hate him for not choosing the Apache Way? Would she understand why he chose mercy over vengeance?

"I was going to let him live. At least as long as his wounds allowed. But the coward ended himself." He sighed. "On his own terms."

She raised her head. "But you couldn't truly be His, if you chose any other way." She gazed into his eyes. "And I'm learning God's way of love is far harder. And better."

"I never stopped loving you, Pilar."

Reaching on tiptoe, she leaned into him. "Alex—"

From deep within the forest, a blood-curdling screech raised the hair on the nape of Alex's neck. The air was thick with the scent of blood. Salazar's blood.

"*Señor y señora*, perhaps declarations of love can wait for a more opportune time?" Gripping the rifle, Joaquin backed away. "We're not safe till we put *mucho* distance between the true king of the Azul and ourselves."

Alex caught Pilar's hand. They ran with Joaquin on their heels. Breathless, they reached a gravel road and a vehicle.

She slumped against the door. "It's over."

"Get in." Joaquin threw himself into the truck. "We go now. Fast."

But Alex couldn't shake the feeling they were being watched. Someone had eyes on them. "We need to get off this mountain. Something's not right. I feel it."

"Your instincts serve you well, Alejandro."

The three of them jolted. A lieutenant in the Mexican forces stepped out of the thicket, gun cocked. Joaquin gasped.

Alex placed his body between Pilar and this new, unknown threat.

Not unknown. He'd seen this man before. Where?

Sixteen years ago...in a Tucson hospital.

35

Wait, Alex." Pilar grabbed his arm. "It's Segundo."

"You know this man?" Alex frowned. "He was at the hospital after..." He swallowed.

"It's okay to say it." She ran her hand down his arm. "I was raped."

Alex didn't lower the rifle. "He's Special Forces. The *Los Zetas* broke off from the army commandos and formed their own drug cartel."

"I am not *Los Zetas*," Segundo hissed.

"Segundo, it was you who found me in the desert when I escaped Salazar, wasn't it? You carried me to the highway." She blinked at another sudden memory. "On a horse with hooves covered in buckskin?"

At that, Alex lowered the weapon. "You saved Pia? And you're Abuela's...?"

"Her friend," Segundo rasped. "From a long time past."

Alex jutted his chin at the insignia on the man's combat fatigues. "And an officer in the *Fuerzas Especiales*."

She studied the man's face, mapped like the scarred chasms of the Sierra canyonlands. "I thought you were a *vaquero*."

"I am what I need to be. We've been trying to topple Salazar since he assumed control from Velarde three years ago. He took one of our girl children."

Pilar flashed to the child who'd leapt off the roof at the Nogales Detention Center.

Alex stiffened. "What about my grandmother? Where is she?"

"This is not yet over." Segundo's slightly skewed right eye gave him a sinister appearance. "One more threat remains. She who has betrayed the children is a rabid dog. And the only thing to do with a rabid dog is to put them down. Your abuela sent me to find you. I know a shortcut to the high place."

Alex angled. "What's he talking about?"

Pilar moved forward. "Talitha Clum."

Alex caught her arm. "I don't trust this guy."

"He's saved my life more than once, Alex." She stepped around him. "And Segundo may be the only one who can help Abuela now."

Joaquin emerged from the truck. "I only want my daughter returned."

"Not him." Segundo pointed with his lips. "He does not go where we must."

Joaquin growled.

Segundo cocked the gun. "I go no further with him."

"Please, Joaquin." She touched his sleeve. "I will find out more about Nita. But we must do as he says. Abuela's life is at stake, too."

"Go then. I will return to the village and wait for you." Joaquin clenched the keys in his hand. "I must find my daughter, señora. Is she safe? Is she hurt? Dead or alive, I must know."

Pilar nodded. "I understand, Joaquin."

"Why do I get the feeling we could be walking into another ambush?" Alex hefted the rifle to his shoulder. "I'll take this with me, if it's okay by you, Martinez."

"Go with God." Joaquin cast his eyes toward the sky. "And if God so wills, you will return with Nita. Here." He wrestled out of his coat and tossed the jacket to Alex.

Bruised and wincing, Alex slipped his arms into the coat. Taller and broader than the innkeeper, the jacket hugged Alex's shoulders and gaped open. But for now, she adjusted the collar, it was the best they could do.

Segundo disappeared among the trees. She and Alex hurried to overtake him.

Fording the river at a narrow spot, she leapfrogged from rock to rock, helping Alex find his balance. His exhaustion was catching up to him. The icy water and the cold stones chilled her feet.

Segundo made no allowance for Alex's injuries. Nor would Alex have wanted him to. She shot a glance at Alex's set features, determined to match Segundo's pace no matter what it cost him physically.

"We must hurry," Segundo beckoned. "We must not allow the old woman to escape this time."

She clambered up the jagged hillside behind the wiry, never-tiring Segundo.

"We're almost there." Segundo propped his leg on a large rock and granted them the chance to catch their breath. "We have the female Coyote trapped."

Alex's eyebrows rose. "We?"

Towering piñon pines clung to either side of the range. In the bowels of the slotted canyon pockmarked with caverns, the shadows swallowed them whole. Only a sliver of sky shone above the *cordillera* ridgeline.

Segundo strode ahead.

Pilar eyed the unforgiving terrain. "I don't like this place."

Alex dropped to an outcropping and offered his hand. "Your instincts serve you well," he whispered, imitating Segundo's gravelly tone.

She smiled as he'd meant her to. "I do have good instincts." She clasped his hand and allowed him to guide her footing down the steep slope.

A slow, rakish grin lifted the haggard look from his face. "Of course you do. You love me." His smile faltered. "Don't you?"

"I do." She kissed the corner of his mouth. "I love you, Alex. I always have. I never stopped. I will always love you."

Searching her face, a muscle beat furiously in his jaw.

He swallowed and glanced away. "That is enough." He squeezed her hand. "For now."

They rounded an overhang to find Abuela in riding pants and a jean jacket sitting regally in front of the haunting cave where they'd been captured by Salazar's men this morning. An eternity, considering the tumultuous events of the past hours.

Abuela rose at Segundo's approach. "Old friend."

Her smile widened at the sight of Alex and Pilar.

Alex rushed into her open arms. "Are you all right?"

She patted his cheek and drew Pilar into their embrace. "Heart of *mi nieto's* heart, it is well with you?"

277

Pilar's lips trembled. "God is good."

Isabel stroked Pilar's cheek. "Yes, He is. And my great-grandson?"

Pilar and Alex looked at each other.

Alex rocked on his heels. "You knew, didn't you?"

"Not much gets past me." Isabel gave an elaborate shrug. "I prayed all would be as God wills."

"We go," grunted Segundo. "I brought them according to your wishes. But to you belongs the right of *venganza*, vengeance."

"I recognized Ih-tedda even after all these years from the driver's license in the file." Isabel crossed her arms. "She has suffered much. We must get her the help she needed sixty years ago."

Segundo's mouth twisted. "Forgiveness is not our way. The word does not exist in our tongue. You saw what she did to the boy child."

"The boy child forgave her," Isabel countered. "Papa Torres rescued Emmanuel and me. Her—he could not save. Papa's cousins left with us, and then Velarde's immutable grief turned into a terrible hatred."

Abuela's eyes welled. "Which he vented upon Ih-tedda."

"If you're talking about Talitha Clum," Alex grasped her arm. "You saw in the photos what happened to those children. She fed them to Velarde."

"You do not know what that *diablo* don did to Ih-tedda after she was taken." Isabel wrenched free of his hand. "Segundo said the don tethered her by a rope to a tree like an animal."

Segundo's mouth hardened. "Ih-tedda was taught not to be taken. She locked herself in a prison of hate. A prison of her own making."

Isabel whirled. "I surrendered, too, Segundo." She balled her fist and thumped her chest. "When Emmanuel fell—"

"—when Ih-tedda threw the boy child to the Nakayé—"

"I climbed down to him. I gave myself up."

Segundo shook his head. "Ih-tedda sacrificed him to save herself. You sacrificed yourself for another. Like that Jesus the boy-become-priest talked about."

Tiny, diminutive Abuela tilted her chin. "Love's a stronger Power than hate or fear."

"Father Emmanuel?" Alex straightened. "You knew him, Abuela?"

"Xoacatyl's priest." Segundo shifted. "He'd come to the ruins in the jungle. For days he'd read aloud the Power words from the black book of his god."

Segundo raised his shoulders and let them drop. "Like the eagle, the wind carried his words along the high places. Into the strongholds. He called the Name as Salazar burned him alive."

Isabel pursed her lips. "A name stronger than death."

"We were too late to save him." Segundo glowered. "But we saved the girl from Salazar."

"Nita Martinez?" Pilar leaned forward. "You know where she is?"

"She is alive. She is well. She saw what they did to her priest, and her memory was wiped clean. She is content where she is now."

"Her father desperately longs for her." Pilar turned toward Isabel. "Like me, she may be suffering from post-traumatic stress. We can help her."

Isabel refused to look at her. "If she is with them, Pilar, we must not interfere."

"The law of *rapto*?" Pilar's eyes widened. "Abuela, after what happened to me—"

"She is not as you were." Segundo went rigid. "She is happy and loved. She bears the child of my grandson in her body."

"It is a law older than *rapto*." Isabel bit her lip. "What they take is theirs. It has always been so here."

Segundo tucked the pistol in his waistband. "Her father's dead to her now. She must become dead to him."

"This is what I'm supposed to tell her grieving father?" Pilar squared her shoulders. "He'll never stop looking for her."

Segundo's eyes went as cold as a winter's day. "Then he will die."

Pilar opened her mouth, but Alex shook his head at her.

Segundo glanced from Isabel to the cave. "You did not go inside?"

"No," Isabel sighed. "It was as you told me that long ago day in Arizona when my Papa Torres died. I do not belong here anymore."

She squinted into the blue haze of the mountains. "Perhaps if we'd made it to the cave the day the Nakayé came, our lives would've been different."

Isabel gave Segundo that autocratic look that had cowed more than one ranch hand—Anglo, Latino, and Apache. "You will allow me the chance to try and reach her. To find the girl I once knew."

Segundo scowled. "The girl you once knew would've killed you both to save herself. That girl grew to be a woman who traded your great-grandson to Salazar to use for his own purposes."

Isabel arched her aristocratic eyebrow. "You know of my great-grandson?"

Forging up the path, Segundo smirked. "I, too, do not allow much to get past me, Haozinne."

An interesting blush mounted from beneath the collar of Isabel's crisp riding shirt. The doña charged up the slope after Segundo.

"Do you get the feeling these two are a lot tougher than either of us, Alex?"

He grimaced as he forgot his injuries and took too robust a breath. "I *know* they're tougher than either of us."

Scrambling around the boulders, Pilar found herself once more in the abandoned Apache *rancheria* that time had forgotten. They hiked past the collapsed dwellings toward the cliff face. There, Talitha Clum hunched like a cornered animal at the edge of the dropping-off point.

Pilar and Alex halted at the foot of the incline. "Why doesn't she come down, Alex?"

Alex's eyes scanned left to right. "Perhaps someone has her treed there."

Pilar jerked around. "Someone?"

She blinked as shadows like long sinewy fingers flickered across the cliff wall. Swaying, the shadows parted, allowing Segundo and Isabel through. But not her and Alex. Alex snagged her arm as the shadows coalesced, then separated. And merged once more.

A misty barrier of dark energy between Abuela and them.

"I'm not sure what part we have to play in what's happening here." Alex gripped Joaquin's rifle. "Maybe only to bring Abuela off the mountain when it's finished. Stay close, *mi corazón*."

His heart. And Alex, a blessing out of the brokenness as he'd promised, was hers.

Pilar leaned into his strength as the wind whipped the dress around her legs.

Segundo assisted Isabel to a sandstone shelf.

"Ih-tedda," Isabel called.

The shrunken, old woman hissed. Her hands clawed. "It is you, the Other."

Isabel nodded. "The other girl. Old now like you. But the both of us, we survived that terrible day, did we not? For that we can be grateful."

"*Pues me agradacio nada.*" Talitha Clum bared her teeth. "I feel gratitude for nothing."

"Let me help you. It doesn't have to end this way. Please..." Isabel extended her hand.

Talitha recoiled. "You've become Nakayé. The ones who killed our families. Who destroyed our world in the high places." She teetered. The heels of her boots hung over the abyss.

Isabel moved closer. "Ih-tedda, no!"

"Nana was right. I should've chosen death over surrender."

At the raucous cry of an eagle, Talitha's eyes jerked skyward. Wings outstretched, the eagle floated on the wind and soared high above the Apache stronghold.

Talitha beat her fist upon her bosom. "My one desire was to put the knife between the ribs of all who violated my people." Her face smoldered with a burning, unquenchable hatred.

"Come down." Isabel crept forward, inch by slow inch, as if not to startle a wild creature. "Let me—"

"No." Talitha whipped a knife from the sash around her skirt. "But I die content with killing you." She pounced.

Isabel gasped.

Segundo flattened Isabel to the ground, covering her with his body as Pilar and Alex—realizing a second too late Talitha's intentions—jumped forward.

A gunshot split the air.

Talitha's eyes enlarged as a bright red circle dotted the middle of her torso. She dropped the knife. As her body sailed off the precipice, she flung her arms wide. Her bestial scream echoed across the undulating mountains. Like a vapor dissipating the farther it traveled into nothingness.

Clutching the rifle, Alex swung around.

Luis, the old man from Xoacatyl, rose from his hiding place. On his wizened features, a malevolence resembling the woman he'd executed. Hatred formed its own scar tissue. Made its own stronghold.

And Pilar knew an immense gratitude she'd been set free from her own arid place.

Luis jabbed the sky with his rifle. "Now it is done."

The eagle's shrill cry rent the air. Pilar jolted, her eyes drawn upward. And when she lowered her eyes, the shadows were gone.

As if they'd never been.

The old man creeped Alex out. As he and Segundo helped Isabel to her feet, Alex wasn't sorry to see Luis disappear into the trees. The old man whistled as he headed down the mountain.

His abuela halted on the path, worn by generations of Bronco Apache feet long ago.

Alex surveyed the deserted *rancheria*. Maybe not so long ago as he supposed. He kept his grip on Joaquin's rifle.

His grandmother's boot sent a shard of pottery skittering. Retrieving it, she held it in her palm. Her dark eyes probed the ruined dwellings.

She went still. Closed her eyes and lifted her nostrils to the wind. That sixth-sense thing she did. Accessing, listening, turning off all senses but one.

Remembering?

"You live as does your woman, Torres, only because of my great affection for your grandmother."

Alex bristled at Segundo's tone.

"But my advice to you, Nakayé? Return your grandmother to her home. Do not return to these mountains ever. Not if you wish to enjoy a long life."

Pilar wrapped her arms around his indomitable grandmother. "Abuela, we must go to Manny and Reyna. They wait for us."

His abuela's eyes flew open. She dropped the piece of black pottery, and using the toe of her boot, covered it with dirt. "I will not come here again, Segundo, will I?"

"No, Haozinne. You will not."

His grandmother took one more sweeping look. "It's good for me to go home." She caught hold of Segundo's sleeve. "But will I see you again?"

A softness breached the hawklike eyes. "In your waking dreams, as always, I will call to you."

"Until then, my old friend." Isabel Torres took a deep breath and released it. "Until then."

Somewhere between the stronghold and the charred ruins of the mission church, Segundo faded into the dense forest.

Pilar believed she knew the exact moment only because Isabel momentarily faltered. But the old woman never took her eyes off following Alex. She never looked back.

At Xoacatyl, Manny ran out of the inn and enveloped Pilar in his arms. "My mother," he whispered into her hair.

In Manny-speak, she knew he acknowledged the pain of the secrets she'd endured for his sake. And that he loved her. Would always love her.

She tightened her hold around Manny.

"Mom..." He coughed. "You're choking me."

She let go. He laughed and squeezed her hand. Reyna peeked from behind one of the columns in Joaquin's coutyard.

Pilar opened her arms. "Reyna, honey."

Reyna fell into her embrace.

"Manny." Alex stood apart, his hands jammed into his pockets. Unsure of his place in their lives?

Not quite grown into the lanky bones he'd inherited from his father, Manny shuffled his feet. Awkward, unsure of what place his father wanted in his life.

The two men—plus Byron—she loved most in the world.

"I'm thinking of helping Abuela on the ranch for a while when we return to the States." Alex scrubbed his neck with his hand. "Until I figure things out in my life."

Manny's eyes shot to Alex's face. "Things"—his nostrils flared— "that include my mom and me?"

Her tough, not-so-little Apache child.

Alex gazed at him. "I love you, Manny. And from now on there's nothing in my life that doesn't include your mother and you, son."

She held her breath. And watched the all-too-familiar struggle battle across Manny's face. To trust. To believe. To hope.

"You're near-grown, Manny, but I want to be as much of a father as you'll allow me to be."

"I'd like to be a starter on the basketball team next winter." Manny tossed his braid over his shoulder. "I reckon I could use a coach. Even an old guy like you."

Alex bit the inside of his cheek. "I could do that, Manny. Share what I know."

Reyna hip-bumped Manny. He fell into Alex. "Stop being stupid, Manny. Hug it out, guys."

Pilar and Alex laughed.

"Maybe some dad stuff, too." With a mock-glare for Reyna, Manny slung his arm around Alex's shoulders. "They start this bossy business young, don't they?"

Alex gave Manny a one-armed hug and cut his eyes at Pilar. "From the womb, I tell you, son. From the womb."

"This isn't what I meant by hugging it out." Reyna rolled her eyes. "Guys…next thing they'll be patting each other's butts."

"Chest bumps, Reyna." Manny shook his head. "Athletes don't pat butts."

Pilar laughed as the two teens took charge of bandaging Alex's cuts.

Help me, Alex mouthed as they hustled him inside to find Abuela.

"Señora Torres?"

At the pleading note in Joaquin's voice, Pilar told him what she'd learned. And despite the warning, an implacable resolve once again darkened his face.

"Do you think the Broncos have Nita, Joaquin?"

"No." His face contorted. "*Los Zetas.*"

The boogeymen of modern Mexico.

She had a bad feeling she'd just signed Joaquin's death warrant by telling him the truth.

"What do you think happened to the Broncos?"

The innkeeper curled his lip. "Mexican folklore says those who remained alive fled north over the border and integrated into the reservation tribes. Even today their descendants remain hidden in plain sight."

"And those who couldn't assimilate?"

He cocked his head. "A Mexican myth says they exist in secret enclaves deep in the heart of the Sierra Madre, speaking the old language and wearing traditional clothes."

Joaquin laughed. "An urban legend. Others say they've concealed their identities for over a hundred and twenty years among farm villagers."

She shivered. "Is it true?"

Joaquin fingered the bandolier slung across his chest. "There were rumors their descendants, armed with AK-47s, now work for the cartels." He snorted. "That I might be willing to believe."

Yet she knew what she'd seen outside the cave. Segundo was real, though she had no proof he was one of them. But always there—as if Segundo watched just beyond the periphery of her vision—whenever she or Abuela needed him.

The vast area south of Xoacatyl remained wild. No roads. Populated by the Tarahumara and the mountain Pimas. The Pima homeland had been the legendary escape hatch for Apaches on the run.

Was it so hard to believe some Apaches might've survived the bounty wars of the 1930s and 1940s? Or just wishful thinking? But if these Mexican Apaches still existed, she did not doubt they preferred to stay lost.

And perhaps lost was better for them all.

On a nearby bench, Luis stared at the blue mountains. "They're still up there," he whispered to himself as much as to Pilar. "They rest and wait."

"Wait for what, Luis?"

He shrugged. "Who can say? A more fortuitous time?" He propped the shotgun across his shoulder. "But come they will, Señora."

Luis rose. "And when they come," he caressed the wooden stock of the gun as if soothing a fractious child. "I will be ready."

36

Arizona—Now

ALEX LAID THE CELL PHONE ON THE TABLE.

Pilar brought the coffee mug to her lips. "Well?"

"The Bureau accepted my belated resignation." He grimaced. "Suggesting with my career over, I find other options."

"I'm sorry, Alex."

"I'm not, Pia."

He gazed around the kitchen, the heart of the ranch. At Abuela, as she stirred spices into the stew on the stovetop. At his son...Alex's chest ached with a love he'd never imagined possible.

At Reyna hunched over the checkerboard, outwitting and outplaying Manny with every move. With her mother in rehab, Reyna lived at the ranch now, the little stray Manny had practically adopted. Alex smiled, thinking of his son.

Some apples didn't fall far from their maternal trees.

He cut his eyes at Pilar. She gave him a knowing smile. She'd caught him taking stock of his happiness.

Filling another mug, Abuela sank into a chair.

He took a quick sip of coffee. "Talitha Clum, Father Emmanuel, and you were taken by the Mexicans as children. The last Apache captives."

His grandmother pursed her lips. "The last ever recorded."

Manny paused, the red checker between his fingers. "What was it like, Abuela? Being a Bronco?"

"I was probably only about seven years old when the Nakayé came to our camp seeking revenge." His grandmother studied her great-grandson. "I do not remember much of that time Before. I do remember always being hungry and afraid."

Some of the fascination dimmed in Manny's eyes. "I hadn't thought of it that way."

"We lived in a wickiup with an old woman. She must've been my grandmother."

Abuela's eyes took on a faraway look. As if she once again stood on the ramparts of the Bronco village, high in the Sierra Madre.

"What I remember is the sound of the mice crawling in the boughs of the wickiup. It scared me. But it made the old woman angry when I showed fear. So, I didn't." His grandmother stared out the picture window toward the mesa. "Because most of all, I was afraid of her."

Alex kept silent, questions burning on his tongue, afraid to interrupt her musings. He'd always considered himself Latino. This Apache aspect of his lineage was new. Surprising. And to be honest, discomforting.

"In the evening and at sunrise," Abuela continued, "the Old One took us children to face the sun, and she said prayers to something."

Abuela shrugged. "I never understood to what or whom she prayed. Perhaps if I'd lived there longer, I would, of course, have been taught. I would've known more."

"Were there other children?" Reyna, too, had become engrossed in Abuela's reminiscences.

She flicked a fond look at the girl. "I think there were other women. Other children. Life was hard. The older girls, like Ih-tedda, were trained to take their place as, one by one, the warriors died. We separated into different encampments. So the Nakayé wouldn't find us in one place and destroy The People forever. Nana made sure we knew the hiding places."

Pilar exchanged glances with Alex. "Like in the Canyon of the Caves."

"Where the ancestors dwelled. If we were overrun, Nana told us to find our way there and wait for others who escaped."

Manny flipped the checker between his fingers. "The Apache Way. Split and regroup in a predesignated location."

Abuela's face darkened. "When the Nakayé came, Nana told us to run. The little boy's hand felt so small in mine."

His grandmother swallowed. "Only three or four, he couldn't run as fast as Ih-tedda—the girl, that's what Nana called her—and me." Abuela tilted her head. "Ih-tedda was maybe twelve."

Alex flinched and thought of what could've happened to thirteen-year-old Reyna in Salazar's hands.

Doña Isabel Torres closed her eyes as if reliving that awful day. "I remember the shouts, the curses, the screams of the women. And the boy sobbing."

At Reyna's quiet inhalation, his grandmother opened her eyes. "I think he was my half-brother. I shushed him, but he'd managed to hold onto this gourd rattle and it made a sound."

Manny got out of his chair. "That's how you were discovered."

Pilar covered the old woman's blue-veined hand. "What did Talitha do that turned the Broncos against her?"

"Ih-tedda paused so we could catch her. I remember thinking we were going to make it. But instead, she picked up the boy and threw him upon the rocks." His grandmother's voice broke.

Manny touched her shoulder.

Reyna crept to the table. "Why did she do that to him, Abuela?" Seeing her ashen face, Pilar hugged Reyna closer.

His grandmother clasped her hands together on top of the table. "She thought only to delay and distract those who pursued us and save herself. Even then, I believe there was something twisted inside Ih-tedda. Something irretrievably bent as if she'd already given herself over to the darkness. Or perhaps, that was the moment she did."

"What did you do?"

"I-I…" His grandmother moistened her lips. "I couldn't leave him so I climbed to where his body lay mangled among the rocks."

Abuela shuddered. "I remember the rearing horses. The foul stink of the Nakayé in the air. But one of the ranchers climbed from his horse. He pried me off the boy, handed me kicking and screaming to another on horseback."

"'Do not harm her,' he said. The other rancher told him, 'She's nothing but a feral cat, Don Torres.'"

His grandmother smiled. "And Don Torres said, 'But even wild cats can be tamed.' He looked into my eyes then. And he saw, he told me later, the soul of a frightened child locked inside a savage."

Abuela squeezed Pilar's hand. "And God told him it'd be his mission to set me free."

Manny's brow puckered. "What happened to the boy, Abuela?"

"Don Torres brought us down the mountain. At Xoacatyl, Don Torres turned the care of the boy over to the priests at the church. Don Torres took me home." She motioned at the kitchen. "But from time to time, Papa Torres inquired on his visits south of the border about the boy whose legs were forever useless but whose mind and spirit were strong."

Pilar's eyes watered. "Father Emmanuel."

Alex slipped his hand into hers.

His grandmother noticed his gesture and smiled. "Truly God was with him and with me. We never saw each other again. Papa advised me to forget what I'd known before. I threw myself into becoming Isabel Torres. I loved Papa. It wasn't hard to forget the Before."

Pilar looked at Alex with a softening that hadn't been there when their paths crossed mere weeks ago. Alex laced his fingers in hers.

His grandmother settled into the chair. "When Papa died, there was talk Fernando would marry a neighboring rancher's daughter so the properties might conjoin. But atop the high mesa behind the Torres ranch as I wept one day, a man appeared, the likes of which I'd only seen in fragments of dreams barely remembered. A man about my age from Before."

"Segundo," Pilar whispered.

Abuela inclined her head. "I'm not sure I ever knew his real name, but he knew me."

"He called you Haozinne."

She nodded. "A name I didn't remember. He said he'd kept watch throughout the years to see I came to no harm among the *americanos*."

Reyna smiled. "Perhaps betrothed to you as children in the old Apache Way."

His grandmother blushed. "I told him I was no longer under the protection of Papa Torres, and it was time to go home. But Segundo gazed across the mountains and told me there was no going back. I'd been among *them* too long. And my Power had decided the path my life would take. That it was here."

Reyna's gaze ping-ponged from Alex to his grandmother. "You married Fernando, right? Or Alex wouldn't be here."

"*Sí*," Abuela patted her hand. "Segundo pointed with his lips to a lone rider coming up the mesa trail. 'This man,' Segundo told me, 'he searches for you. Go to him. You must now live the life you've been given.'"

"And Segundo?"

"I turned for the slightest of seconds to watch as Fernando's horse crossed the distance between us. And when I turned back, Segundo was gone."

"Segundo helped Byron and me when my stepfather…" Pilar faltered.

Abuela waved her hand as if waving away a pesky fly. "From time to time after I married, always when I found myself alone, something in the air would change. And I'd know." She shook her head. "I just know when they are near."

"They?" Alex raised his eyebrows.

Abuela's eyes went inscrutable. "I misspoke. Him."

Manny leaned forward. "What do you think happened to those other Bronco bands?"

"Death before surrender. Extinction through bloodshed or starvation." She shrugged. "That was in the Before time. We must live in the Now."

His abuela stood. Her joints creaked. "Meals don't prepare themselves."

Alex rose, too, steadying Abuela's balance. He kissed her soft, paper-thin cheek, and she ambled toward the stovetop. How he loved her.

How grateful he was to God for Abuela's faithful influence in shaping the man he'd become. Byron, Pilar, and Manny, too. He also had the feeling she'd said all she ever would about her past.

Because true Apaches, like Doña Isabel Torres, knew how to keep their secrets well.

Manny slouched over to the kitchen island. He snitched a piece of chicken waiting to go into the cookpot. "Maybe Tagalong and I can shoot hoops before lunch?"

Pilar started to wince for the girl, but something about the way Manny said it now…

Reyna looked at Manny as solemn as the day she'd first laid eyes on him as an adoring toddler. "Do you want me to come, Manny?"

Manny straightened. "That's what I said, wasn't it?"

Reyna crossed her arms, one eyebrow arched.

Pilar smiled. *Don't make it too easy for him.*

Manny's brow furrowed, but he reached for her hand. "I do want you to come."

Reyna's eyes cut sideways and up at Manny. "How about you tag-along with me and go look for rocks instead?"

Pilar knew better than to laugh.

Manny blew out a breath. "I guess..." His shoulders rose and fell. "Whatever."

"I'm looking to add a special piece of obsidian to my collection."

Manny frowned. "A what?"

"An Apache teardrop." Her dark eyes sparkled. "If you help me, I'll give it to you to keep."

Reyna stuck out her still-to-develop chest. "I'm going to be a famous geologist and work for the tribe to safeguard our natural treasures. Maybe I'll let you be my assistant when you grow up."

Manny's mouth dropped.

"After you retire from your professional basketball career, of course." Reyna headed toward the front hall. "I gotta get my *Rock Hunters Guide to Arizona.*"

Manny closed his mouth with a snap. "Her assistant, huh?" His mulish expression eased. "Though the pro ball part sounds pretty sweet."

He scowled. "I think Reyna likes those ole rocks better than me."

Pilar went ahead and laughed.

"And she thinks I need to grow up?" Manny rolled his eyes. "She's the one taking her own sweet time about growing up."

With a meaningful look at Pilar, Alex grimaced. "Trust me, bud, I know the feeling."

Pilar's turn to blush.

Alex seized her hand. "But I have a feeling she'll be worth the wait."

Manny gave them a funny smile, a most grown-up look. "Yeah, I know she will."

So many changes in her life. Manny would be off to college long before Pilar was ready. Her mother's heart pinged.

But then, the I'd-rather-play-ball-than-eat look returned to Manny's face.

LISA CARTER

"Come on, Reyna." Manny cupped his hands around his mouth and yelled. "I ain't got all week."

Reyna reappeared with her backpack. "Hey, Manny. Ready to go?"

"Hey yourself, Reyna." Manny looked at her silhouetted in the window against the mountain. "And yeah, I'm as ready as I'll ever be."

Reyna waved. "We'll be back for lunch, I promise."

"Best not to allow the rez's true natural treasures"—Manny winked at them as Reyna pulled him out the door—"to wander too far."

Alex pulled Pilar into his arms. "I have a feeling the next few years are going to get interesting with those two."

She mock-groaned. "The highs and lows of young love."

"Young love," he nuzzled his cheek against hers. "Old love." His breath feathered her neck.

As his lips found the sweet spot above the V in her throat, her arms turned into goosebumps. The things Alejandro Roberto Torres did to her insides...

His mouth blazed a trail across her jawline.

There ought to be warning labels...

Abuela cleared her throat.

They sprang apart and flushed like guilty teenagers.

"Seems to me there's important details that need working out before you two jump to that again." Abuela pointed the wooden spoon at them. "But then again what do I know? I'm just an old woman."

Alex made a face. "She's right. We need to talk."

Pilar's stomach clenched. Despite what Alex promised Manny, did his future plans include her?

"I've done enough running in the Sierra Madre to last me a while." He held out his hand. "But how about we take a walk?"

She took his hand, not trusting herself to speak. After a couple of emotional phone calls earlier in the week, Byron and Fiona were coming home for a visit.

God had, indeed, brought her and Alex together as children. She'd also come to realize God didn't abandon her to Salazar. And God, despite the mistakes they'd made, in His infinite mercy brought her and Alex together again.

She had no idea what the future held. The past was gone. Now was all any of them possessed. Now might be all Alex wanted. As friends.

In her distraction, she followed Alex past the barns and corral. He let go of her hand somewhere along the trail on the mesa behind the ranch. Her heart sank further.

At the top, he leaned against an outcropping, winded. "Ever get a hankering to live at sea level, Pia?"

She bit her lip. Her hankering then and now had been to live wherever Alex Torres lived.

When she didn't answer, his gaze swept across the rock-studded plateau. "What are your plans now, Pia?"

"This will sound crazy..."

"Pia, I long ago stopped being surprised by anything you decide to do." His eyes teased.

She didn't know how what she was about to say would fit in with his vision of the future. But this had been on her heart since they returned from Mexico. And Alex, she cautioned herself, might not have any plans for a future for them together anyway.

"I'm ready to visit the rape counselor at the tribal clinic. And talk to Abuela's pastor. Someday I want to be a rape victim advocacy specialist."

She took a deep breath. "There are so many like me in Native communities where sexual violence has been a generational norm. Nobody will talk about it, but I'd like to do what I can to stop the cycle and help others heal." She darted a look at him. "Crazy, huh?"

Alex tilted his head. "More like another blessing out of brokenness."

He brushed a strand of hair off her forehead. "Would you give me a second chance to love you, Pia? Would you marry me again?"

"I-I'm not the same seventeen-year-old girl you married before, Alex."

"No, you're not." His eyes bored into hers. "You're better. I'm not that selfish twenty-year-old boy, either. We're both better. And I don't want to live another day without you."

In his gaze, she finally beheld herself and her future. Full of a steadfast love that adversity had only deepened. And in his eyes, the pure passion of a bridegroom for his beloved bride.

The ever-present, tangible awareness quivered between them.

She stepped into the solid buttress of his arms. Enjoying the play of sunlight on his dark hair, her arms drifted around him. He cupped her face in the cradle of his hands. His eyes beckoned.

At the warmth of his palms upon her skin, she held her breath. Waiting. Anticipating. Yearning. His essence tugged at her heart. Filled her senses.

His lips brushed across hers, featherlight. She inhaled. He drew back a few inches. His dark eyes blazed. Yet his body trembled beneath her hands.

Unclasping the chain, he removed the Apache tear necklace she'd given him so long ago. "Will you wear this symbol of my true love, Pia? Until I can put a ring on your finger and we declare our love before God?"

She nodded.

Alex draped the chain around her neck. Her eyes welling, she put her hands over her mouth.

His lips grazed her ear. "Maria Caterina Pilar, my heart has always been yours."

She turned in his arms, cupping his face with her hand. "And you, Alejandro Roberto Torres, will always be mine."

Drenched in the sunlight of their love on a high mesa, he kissed her again. Pledging his love. Sealing his commitment. Burning away the pain of the lost years as if they'd never been with the promise of a sweet forever.

The love in his face when he looked at her took Pilar's breath.

"You will let your hair down when I become your husband once more, Pia?" His eyes went opaque. "*Por favor.*"

Never taking her eyes off his, she reached behind her head and unwound her braid. She shook her hair loose. Her hair cascaded over her shoulders.

He rubbed a strand of her hair between his thumb and forefinger. "And will you always wear your hair this way for me?" He moistened his lips.

She leaned closer and placed her hands flat upon his chest. "For you?"

Alex's heartbeat thundered against her palms.

Her lips parted. "Always."

Author's Note

Readers—This wasn't an easy story to tell. In the writing of this book, I wrestled with my own strongholds. My prayer is that, if you are struggling, you will find in God the relentless love for which you've longed. It is because of this love for you that He willingly died—a sacrifice of Himself—for all our sins, pain, and wounds. He alone can restore the broken soul. I pray that you would find the only One whose love, power, and name can break any stronghold. He sets free all those who are captive. His love is indeed stronger than death.

May you fully know and bask in the sunlight of His love. God longs to know and be known by you. I pray that each of you would grasp the name by which God calls you—Mine. For from the moment He created you, you belonged to Him. And never forget that no matter what has been done to you, no matter what you've done, you are precious to Him.

I hope those who've suffered much will see in Jesus' eyes the pure passion of a bridegroom for His beloved bride. And that in His love the lost years might be burned away as if they'd never been. May you, even today, catch a glimpse of the sweet forever He's promised to all who believe in Him.

Group Discussion Questions

1. Why is the symbolism of Apache tears so poignant in light of Pilar's life?

2. Pilar struggled to believe in God's goodness. Why? With what do you wrestle?

3. What surprised you in *The Stronghold*? What made you laugh? What made you cry?

4. What is the difference between guilt and shame? Have you ever experienced either of these? How did you handle it?

5. How is God the God of second chances in this book?

6. The physical journey to find their loved ones is a metaphor for the spiritual journey both Pilar and Alex must undertake toward wholeness. What stages and truths do you see in their quest?

7. Has anything like what happened to Pilar ever happened to you or someone you know? What could you do to help someone suffering in this way?

8. Who was your favorite character? Why?

9. By what mantra have you lived your life?

10. How did each character's "superpower" turn out to be both a strength and a weakness? What would others say is your superpower?

11. What barricades had Pilar built around her heart? How did these walls become strongholds in her life? What did she have to do to be free of them? What barricades have you erected to protect yourself? What walls need to be torn down in your life?

12. Pilar cut herself in an attempt to expunge the pain inside. What other ways do people attempt to deal with inner hurts? How do you deal with your pain and hurt?

13. Alex said his source of power and strength was the One True God. What is yours? How did Pilar learn this the hard way?

14. How would you write Manny and Reyna's future love story?

15. How did "it'll take an Apache to catch an Apache" play out in this story?

16. How were Pilar and Reyna's lives similar and different?

17. Has there been an Abuela in your life who first pointed you toward God?

18. *To-Clanny* means "lots of water." What ultimately did Pilar discover is the only water that truly cleanses?

19. Do you agree that not choosing God is the first step toward evil? How would you explain real love to someone as seen through God's love?

20. What are the cracks in your jar of clay? Does your life depict light shining all the better through your broken jar? Or not?

21. What blessings out of brokenness have you experienced?

22. What was your favorite scene? Why?

23. Who is the true Lord of the Skies?

24. What empty holes are in your life? How have you tried to fill them?

25. How did Alex and Pilar illustrate the changing power of God in their lives?

26. What, like Alex and Pilar, do you need the courage to let go of? Do you struggle with living in the past? How might you learn to live in the Now?

27. Are there people too broken for redemption?

28. Has there ever been a defining moment in your life of Before and After?

29. How have you experienced God's way being the harder way? The better way?

Want to learn more about Lisa Carter
and check out other great fiction from
Abingdon Press?

Check out our website at
www.AbingdonPress.com
to read interviews with your favorite authors,
find tips for starting a reading group,
and stay posted on what new titles are on the horizon.

Be sure to visit Lisa online!

www.lisacarter.com

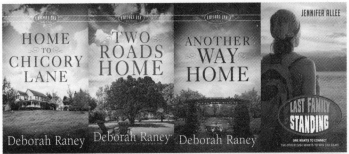